Nicole Helm grew up ~~with the~~ ~~dream of one day be~~ ~~Luckily, after~~ a few failed career choices, she gets to follow that dream—writing down-to-earth contemporary romance and romantic suspense. From farmers to cowboys, Midwest to the West, Nicole writes stories about people finding themselves and finding love in the process. She lives in Missouri with her husband and two sons and dreams of someday owning a barn.

Cindi Myers is the author of more than fifty novels. When she's not crafting new romance plots, she enjoys skiing, gardening, cooking, crafting and daydreaming. A lover of small-town life, she lives with her husband and two spoiled dogs in the Colorado mountains.

Also by Nicole Helm

South Dakota Showdown
Covert Complication
Backcountry Escape
Isolated Threat
Badlands Beware
Wyoming Cowboy Marine
Wyoming Cowboy Sniper
Wyoming Cowboy Ranger
Wyoming Cowboy Bodyguard
Wyoming Cowboy Justice

Also by Cindi Myers

Ice Cold Killer
Snowbound Suspicion
Cold Conspiracy
Snowblind Justice
Saved by the Sheriff
Avalanche of Trouble
Deputy Defender
Danger on Dakota Ridge
Murder in Black Canyon
Undercover Husband

Discover more at millsandboon.co.uk

CLOSE RANGE CHRISTMAS

NICOLE HELM

INVESTIGATION IN BLACK CANYON

CINDI MYERS

MILLS & BOON

First Published in Great Britain 2020
by Mills & Boon, an imprint of HarperCollins*Publishers*
1 London Bridge Street, London, SE1 9GF

Close Range Christmas © 2020 Nicole Helm
Investigation in Black Canyon © 2020 Cynthia Myers

ISBN: 978-0-263-28054-8

1120

MIX
Paper from
responsible sources
FSC™ C007454

This book is produced from independently certified FSC™ paper to ensure responsible forest management.

For more information visit: www.harpercollins.co.uk/green

Printed and bound in Spain
by CPI, Barcelona

CLOSE RANGE
CHRISTMAS

NICOLE HELM

I have to dedicate my fiftieth published work to computers, because after watching the recent *Little Women* movie, I know I couldn't have done it by pen.

Prologue

"You're avoiding me."

Dev Wyatt looked up from the beer in his hand to the woman he was indeed avoiding at all costs. He didn't know if she meant tonight at his brother's and her foster sister's wedding or in general, because both were true.

But he was *especially* avoiding her tonight because she was wearing a dress that made what he had been trying to ignore for years all too clear. Sarah Knight was hot and he had no business noticing the generous curves all too invitingly showcased in some silky siren-red fabric.

Worse, he had no business considering her…proposition. Even though it had been lodged in his head for the entire month she'd been hounding him over it. She was his neighbor, adopted daughter of the man he looked up most to in the world, a good eight years younger than him, *and* a business partner of sorts. With neighboring ranches, and their siblings losing their minds and all marrying each other, they helped each other quite a bit.

He took a swig of beer then scowled at her. "Of course I'm avoiding you, Sarah. You've lost your mind and I'm tired of you trying to drag me into it."

He didn't have to look at her to know she would have raised her chin at that.

"It isn't losing my mind to go after what I want," she said stubbornly. And worse, resolutely. Even his hard head had nothing on Sarah's resolute.

She wanted a baby. Dev couldn't figure out why. She was only twenty-five. She wasn't exactly running out of time for the whole husband and kids thing.

When he'd brought that up, she'd scoffed.

I'm never going to find someone. I don't leave my ranch, and I don't want to. But I do want to be a mother. I've given it a lot of thought and you are the best option for father.

He'd given her every argument he could think of.

Sperm bank? Too expensive. Adoption? She herself was adopted and wanted someone in her life to be genetically related to her. Stranger at a bar? Similar reasons to the adoption and worse, what if the stranger wanted to be involved?

He'd tried them all, and she had rational, reasonable responses to every excuse he put up. Not that having sex with him to get a baby was in any way rational or reasonable to begin with.

"You're young," Dev insisted. "You might change your mind." He nodded out to where his brother Brady was dancing with his new wife, Cecilia. He never would have predicted that. Things and people changed. "You might want all that in a few years."

Sarah looked at Cecilia and Brady smiling at each other. She seemed to give that some thought, but he should have known better. She turned her big blue eyes on him.

"Are you going to change your mind about not wanting a family? Are you going to change your mind about running Reaves Ranch?"

He could lie and say a person never knew what might change, but no. Those were the two tenets of his life—keeping everyone at arm's length and running his grandmother's ranch, which had been in his family for generations. Something *good* his blood had done with this earth.

Sarah knew it just as well as he did, so he said nothing.

But she nodded as if he'd agreed with her. "And I'm not going to change my mind about wanting to be a mother, and not really wanting a partner to do it. You're the only guy I know who doesn't want a family and isn't going to change his mind, but who I know well enough to...you know. So I'm not letting this go. Might as well give in."

The worst part was knowing that when Sarah got an idea in her head, she did *not* let it go. He'd have to keep fending her off for...forever.

She touched his arm so he had to look down at her. Sarah was usually all sharp edges and sharper words, but her expression was open and vulnerable here. Which was *horrifying*.

"You're the only one who can help me, Dev. Please."

Dev couldn't remember Sarah ever saying please to him, or worse, asking him for anything. No one asked him for anything anymore. Ever since he'd barely survived his father's attack on him over a decade ago, leaving him permanently damaged—body and spirit—the best he could hope for was ranching. For being considered the grumpy Wyatt brother, whose only use was keeping an eye on Grandma Pauline. Not that she needed any tending.

Sarah wanted to get pregnant and raise a baby on her own, with no one knowing he was the father. Which didn't bother him because he didn't want to be a father or a husband. He had plans to be alone for the rest of his life.

Still, she was asking him to...sleep with her. Maybe the reasons were biological. The act was *personal*, though.

It was wrong, but she was looking up at him, blue eyes sincere rather than piercing daggers like usual. Her touch was light instead of the random punches she usually aimed at him if she was going to touch him.

Because Sarah was the only one in his life who rarely treated him like he was fragile. Enough that she was asking him for this. She thought he could do it. Give her this thing she so desperately wanted that she'd been bugging him about it for weeks. Hounding him and refusing to find another alternative. Because she wanted it this way.

And she needed him.

No one should need him, and he shouldn't fool himself into thinking he could help. Not anymore.

He tried to fight the overwhelming need to give in. Maybe Sarah knew what she wanted, but she didn't know what she was *asking*. She couldn't want help from him. No one could.

"Dev. Just once." She slid her hand up his arm, and of all the ways she'd touched him in the twenty-some years he'd lived with his grandmother at Reaves Ranch with Sarah next door at Knight Ranch, she'd never once touched him like *that*. "If it doesn't work," she continued, leaning in so that her painted mouth was all too close to his, "I'll let it go. Promise."

He'd be stupid to believe her. She'd never let it go. And just once would be...well, something like a catastrophe.

Aren't you intimately acquainted with catastrophe?

He downed his beer. He couldn't do it. He couldn't.

But he had a very bad feeling he was going to end up doing it, one way or another.

"Better drink up," he muttered, heading for the bar.

SARAH WOKE UP the next morning with a pounding headache, and only fuzzy memories of Dev in her hotel room. Much as it had been her idea, and she'd relentlessly hounded Dev until he'd given in, she'd still been more than a little nervous to have sex with someone she'd known her whole life. With the sole purpose of getting pregnant. So getting *really* drunk had been an excellent plan.

She even applauded herself for it as weeks passed. That's what she'd wanted. The act that led to a baby, not the act that *meant* something. She tried not to think of the night that was just fuzzy memories of a few kisses and touches and laughing a little *too* hard at Dev Wyatt kissing her.

When she did think about it, she was glad for the lack of memory. She couldn't remember what Dev looked like naked, which was good considering how closely they worked together on their neighboring ranches. Sometimes she wasn't even sure they'd actually *done* anything, considering how Dev didn't treat her any differently as the weeks piled up. Maybe he'd just let her think they had.

Or maybe her plan had worked.

From that morning after, she'd counted down the days until the earliest moment she could take a pregnancy test. Now she just had to pray that one drunk hookup with one of her best friends in the world had yielded what she'd always wanted.

A baby.

She inhaled sharply. Today was the day. She'd driven two towns over to buy the pregnancy test. In the Walmart bathroom, she'd discovered that her insane plan had indeed worked.

She was pregnant. The test in her hand said so.

It didn't feel real. She'd expected to be magically transformed. Her plan had worked. There were still a hell of a lot more steps to go: a doctor's appointment, lying to her family that she'd hooked up with a random stranger, and then actually preparing for a baby. But she'd expected to feel settled and ready once she'd seen the positive result.

She was thrilled. Ecstatic. But…was there *really* a baby in there? She hadn't had any noticeable symptoms. She'd overanalyzed every cramp, every moment of tiredness, and determined that nothing was all that different.

Maybe the test was wrong. She went through the whole process over again, with the same result. She threw everything away, washed her hands and then headed out of the store to her truck.

She was going to believe she'd succeeded. She was pregnant. Maybe she didn't feel different yet, but she would. As she went through everything she had to do, she'd have more and more belief, until there was a little baby in her arms.

Her own baby. Someone who shared her blood. Someone she'd be able to look at and maybe see her own eyes or nose. A mix of her and…

Dev.

She couldn't tell anyone else yet, but she could tell him. She drove back home, deciding she'd stop by the Reaves ranch.

She wanted a baby for herself. Someone to belong to her. Her sisters were all off married or living with their Wyatt boyfriends. The Knight house was quiet with just

her and Dad. Much as Sarah loved her adopted father—
the only father she could remember—she wanted more
than just…the two of them.

She wanted to be a mother. She wanted a child. The
plan had been a little far-fetched but it had given her exactly what she wanted—what she needed.

It was all about her. She convinced herself of that over
and over again. Until she parked her car next to the barn
on the Reaves Ranch.

She walked inside. Dev was brushing down his horse,
that permanent scowl affixed to his face. He said it was
just his expression, but Sarah knew it was pain. After a
long day of riding, his leg hurt him.

She stood in the doorway of the barn and admitted that
as much as she'd done this for her own self, she'd also
harbored a tiny hope that the reality of a baby might…
reach Dev. He was a good man—as good as his brothers.
The problem was, since his injuries had kept him from
returning to law enforcement, he considered himself less
than those brothers.

He wasn't, but he'd have to come to that conclusion
on his own.

So if a baby woke him up out of the dark cloud he kept
himself in, that would be icing on the cake. She wouldn't
expect it, but she could *hope* for it.

"Help you?" he demanded when she thought she'd
been staring unnoticed.

Still, she didn't startle. She was too used to his grumpy
preternatural observations. So she stepped forward.
The faint light of the barn highlighted him, and his face
looked…hard. There was something edgy and dangerous about him in this light.

It gave her an odd shiver of foreboding, but she pushed

that away. She came up to stand next to him. "Well, it worked. The whole baby thing."

He looked down at her, expression guarded. "Congratulations," he said, with absolutely no inflection on the word.

"Thank you. It's early yet, and I'll have to go to the doctor, but…" She felt teary, surprisingly emotional over telling him. But it was big. Huge. "Thank you, Dev. I don't think I could ever tell you how much it means to me that—"

"Don't mention it. Ever. Really."

He didn't ask her anything else, but he gave her a brush and they worked in companionable silence. It felt… right. He'd given her what she'd always wanted, and now things would go back to normal.

Until she had to tell her family. Until she started to show. Until she had a baby.

She laughed and shook her head. Life was about to get flipped on its head, and that was fine. That was what she wanted. But there was more to this than what she wanted. Something she hadn't predicted. "If you ever want to—"

"I don't," he said, and there was more emotion in those two words than everything he'd said so far.

"Okay, I'm only saying it because you're alone, Dev. Not because I need you to be involved. You're just the only one who…" She trailed off. It seemed cruel to point out all their siblings were building lives, she was having a baby and Dev was still…in a black cloud of his own making.

"I'm exactly where I have to be," Dev replied. He took the brush from her and tossed it in a pail. "I'm heading inside for dinner. I'm sure Grandma Pauline made enough." Then he walked away with that kind-of invitation hanging there.

Sarah could only frown after him, mulling over what he'd said. Because *have* to be wasn't the same as *want* to be.

Chapter One

In June, Sarah had broken the news to her family. She'd refused to name the father no matter how they'd prodded. From there, she'd begun to adjust to her new normal. It wasn't all that different than her old one.

If she lived with the tiny hope Dev might slowly come around, she didn't let on to that expectation to him or anyone else. She kept it buried deep.

In August, she'd found out she was having a boy. While her sisters all had girls, *she* was going to have a boy. Much as she would have been happy with any healthy child, a boy was a relief. Sarah wouldn't know what to do with a girl. She barely knew what to do with herself when it came to all the girly things her sisters seemed so natural at.

Now, as November rolled on toward Christmas, she was having to come to grips with the reality of being a very pregnant woman on an isolated ranch during a severe, unpredictable winter.

She would say Dev didn't act any differently toward her—they still argued and bickered. He was annoyingly high-handed about decisions that affected both ranches. But he sneakily kept her from overtaxing herself, especially in these later months, and he had a way of watching her that made goose bumps pop up on her arms and had her casting back for any dim memory of that night.

She reminded herself, almost daily, that she had gotten exactly what she'd wanted, and any lingering weirdness she sensed was both a figment of her imagination and something that would disappear once the baby was born.

Baby boy Knight was due on Christmas Day, and Sarah liked the idea of it. He'd always have a birthday full of family, no matter how far-flung they may all be.

She still hadn't figured out a name. She could name him Evan after her late adopted mother, Eva. Evan Knight. It might work.

There was always DJ. She couldn't help but laughing at the image of telling Dev she was going to name the baby Devin Junior. His horror would be epic. But it could also be an homage to her father. Duke Knight.

There were so many options. She pulled her scarf up over her mouth as she walked from her truck to the barn where she knew Dev would be mucking out the stalls. It was a frigid cold winter already, and every day seemed to dig deeper into the subzero temperatures. Inside, Sarah was an overheated mess of giant pregnant belly, so the cold felt good.

She walked into the stables, knowing Dev would kick her right back out. She'd needed the walk, the fresh air. A few moments alone, and then spending some time with someone who wouldn't fuss.

He'd tell her to go away, or to sit down, but he wouldn't flutter about like her father and sisters did. She stepped into the building, immediately smiling at the smell of hay and manure. Home.

"You aren't supposed to be here," Dev said without turning around.

"Why not?"

"No mucking. No overexerting yourself. Isn't that what your doctor said after your last checkup?"

Sarah wrinkled her nose. Her blood pressure had been a little high and she'd been having some mild on-and-off contractions. She was supposed to "take it easy" and it was driving her insane.

"I'm bored to death. Women on the prairie—"

"Spare me a lecture about women on the prairie and sit your butt down," Dev muttered irritably, never breaking his mucking stride. "There's plenty of paperwork to do."

"God help me."

Still, she sat down. Because the baby had begun to kick. She could feel the press of either his heel or knee against her belly. She loved feeling the shape of him through her stomach, the roll and kicks. Even the hiccups.

She looked up to find Dev watching her. He did that more and more as her body bloomed. She hadn't pressed him on becoming more involved. That wouldn't work with Dev. She just held on to that hope.

She pushed herself back up to her feet and waved him over. "Come here."

"Why?" he asked suspiciously.

"Because I'm fat and miserable. Come over here."

Reluctantly, he moved to her. She grabbed his hand and placed it over her stomach, under her coat but over her sweater.

He made a pained face, like she was forcing him to pet a snake. But what he could hide on his face, he couldn't hide in his voice. "That feels like a foot," he said, full of awe.

"Doesn't it?" She kept pressing his hand right there, following the rolling movement of the foot across her side. "He can kick like the devil, right up here in my ribs. He's going to be a hell of a rider. I can tell."

Dev shook his head. "You can't tell," he muttered, but he didn't take his hand away.

She let the moment stretch out, and even knowing what his reaction could be, she felt like she had to offer it again. "Dev… Just so you know. If you ever want—"

"I don't."

Well, she supposed that was that.

"Let's go get some breakfast."

She forced a smile. "It's almost like you knew I came over here to have Grandma Pauline ply me with biscuits and gravy."

He made a noncommittal noise as he limped for the door. Winter made his limp worse, which meant his pain was worse. Sarah wished there was some way to help him. Usually she took over chores this time of year— snuck in before he could get to them. One week last December she'd had to get up at three in the morning every day to beat him, but she'd done it.

None of that this winter, only sympathy and a weird twist of guilt that was totally out of place.

She followed him outside and toward the house. Dev's truck was parked in front of it, at an odd angle.

"You lose a tire?"

Dev stopped short, studied his truck and shook his head at the way it listed to one side. "Not that I knew of."

She followed him closer to the truck, but her heart started beating hard in her ears as she realized the cause of the flat tire.

A knife was sticking out of the rubber, a note attached. *It's Not Over* was written in big thick black letters. Underneath were two letters. AW. Ace Wyatt.

Sarah could scarcely catch her breath. It couldn't be. Ace Wyatt was dead. It had to be a mistake. She looked to Dev for some kind of reassurance, but he stood so preternaturally still, there was no comfort to be found.

DEV STARED AT the words. The letters. He'd forgotten Sarah behind him. Forgotten the world around him entirely. For a few awful seconds he was back in the Badlands with his father.

It'll never be over, Devin.

"It can't be Ace." Sarah's voice was shrill behind him. "He's dead. You all made sure. He's dead."

Dev came back to the present, to the reality. "We identified his body," he said, his voice an awful rasp even to his own ears.

"And Jamison had those tests done. He made sure it was Ace."

Dev sucked in a breath. Sarah was right. Even though he'd seen Ace's lifeless body in the morgue himself, it was so easy to believe he was some kind of…evil spirit. But Sarah's reminder grounded him to reality. They'd seen him. They'd tested the body to make sure.

Ace was dead. The father who'd tortured them as children in his dangerous biker gang, then made their adulthoods as much hell as he could, was gone.

But there was an AW from his past who wasn't.

"You have to—"

Before Sarah could tell him what he had to do, the sound of an engine interrupted the quiet of the morning. Faint at first, but growing louder until Jamison's truck appeared on the rise.

Sarah let out an audible whoosh of breath, but Dev didn't match her relief. She was happy Jamison was here to take care of things, but if Jamison was here this early, it could only mean he'd gotten a similar threat.

When Dev realized Cody was in the passenger seat,

his dread dug even deeper. The secret he'd kept, no matter how guilty it had made him feel for a decade now, was showing up on his doorstep in the worst possible way.

A threat to his brothers.

They got out of the truck—his oldest and youngest brothers, respectively. Both lived out in Bonesteel with their wives and children. For Jamison that meant his wife, Liza, and her young half sister, Gigi. For Cody that meant his high-school sweetheart, Nina, eight-year-old daughter, Brianna, and a baby on the way.

Just like you.

Except he did everything in his power not to think about Sarah's baby as anything close to his. Because Sarah's baby wasn't his. It was a favor he'd done her at only a slight cost to himself. Mainly, his sanity. There couldn't even be that cost now. That secret was even more paramount than the one he'd carried since his father had injured him irrevocably.

Jamison and Cody wore matching grim expressions as they walked toward him and Sarah.

"I see you got the same message we did," Cody said, nodding toward the tire.

Dev pointed at Jamison's truck. "Quick fix."

Jamison shook his head. "Mine was on the door to my office at city hall. Along with a machete."

"Mine was wrapped around a brick that went through my storefront window," Cody said with an even tone, though fury was stamped across his features.

"Gage had an arrow through his patrol car window, Brady had a dead animal on the porch with the note, and Tucker's was on his porch as well—sticking out of a charred, headless doll," Jamison continued, using that emotionless cop voice that usually grated on Dev's nerves.

This morning he found it oddly reassuring.

"The notes all said the same thing," Cody continued, as if the image of a charred, headless doll didn't bother him.

"It can't be Ace," Sarah said, her voice an octave too high. Dev had forgotten about her there.

"You need to get inside," he said gruffly. It was cold and she was supposed to be taking it easy, not panicking in the frigid temperatures. He thought of the feeling of the baby's foot pushing against her stomach. A real, living, thriving human being.

He couldn't think about any of that.

"You will not order me inside, Dev Wyatt," she fumed.

"We'll all go inside," Jamison offered in a conciliatory tone, gesturing Sarah toward the house. "And you're right, it can't be Ace," he agreed as they all trudged toward the door of Grandma Pauline's house. Except for Cody, who was collecting the note and knife in evidence bags.

"We were too careful to doubt he's dead," Jamison was saying to Sarah as he held the door open for her.

"What else isn't over that has to do with all six of you, though?" Sarah asked.

Jamison and Sarah moved into the warmth of Grandma Pauline's kitchen, but warmth seemed all wrong. So Dev could only hesitate on the threshold, even as Cody came in behind him.

Grandma stood at the stove. She had a wooden spoon in one hand and her white hair was pulled back in a bun. Dev noticed the flash of worry in her gaze before she schooled it away into her usual take-no-prisoners demeanor.

"Well, what are the cavalry doing here?" she demanded.

Jamison and Cody gave her weak smiles. When

Grandma saw Sarah she immediately grabbed her and had her in a chair with a plate of food in front of her before Dev could even move.

"You rest and eat," Grandma ordered Sarah. "You three can discuss your business elsewhere."

"No," Sarah argued through a mouth full of biscuit. "I have to hear this too. I think we all do."

"Tucker, Brady and Gage will all be here when they can. We want to compare notes," Cody said. "We all got threatening notes this morning." He held up the bag to Grandma Pauline, and she squinted to read.

Her mouth firmed, but she went back to stirring her gravy without another word.

"I talked to my friend at North Star on the way over," Cody said, referring to the secretive group he'd worked for to help take down their father's gang. "The Sons of the Badlands are weak, mostly disbanded, but that doesn't mean they're all gone or in jail. Any one of them could still harbor a grudge."

"Wouldn't they just hold that grudge against North Star?" Sarah asked.

"Not just. I think they'd hold a grudge against anyone they could. And North Star is a group of highly trained operatives. Hard to find, harder to pin down. We're a much easier target. We're the reason Ace was in jail when he was killed."

"But you're not the reason he's dead," Sarah argued.

"Depends on how in touch with reality you are. Ace's cronies often weren't. We'd be easy to blame. He doesn't get stabbed in jail if he's not there," Jamison said.

"But that wasn't all six of you," Sarah insisted. "You and Cody were the ones instrumental in getting him in jail."

"But Felicity and Gage were instrumental in the trial,"

Cody returned, speaking of their brother Gage and his wife, Felicity. "Which was what prompted Ace to be moved to the prison where he died. Brady too, for that matter."

"What about Dev? He hasn't done anything."

That might have felt like a stab if it were true. Unfortunately, it wasn't true at all. He'd done something no one was ever going to forgive him for.

He thought of the list Cody had gone through outside. All the different ways this message had been given to his brothers. All the ways they were now in danger. Maybe it wasn't because of him, but it didn't matter now. He had to tell them the truth.

And it would change everything.

"There's something I've never told you. Any of you." Dev heard nothing but a buzzing in his own ears. He didn't want to say the words. Didn't want to do any of this, but that AW was impossible to ignore.

And his brothers' lives were at stake...their families' lives. "Ace had another son. His name is Anth Wyatt. AW."

Chapter Two

Dev waited. For the questions, the demands, the accusations. He should have known better. All of those things he expected he could have met with cool detachment.

"Why didn't you tell us?" Jamison asked, his voice rough and…wrecked. Dev had never heard that tone from his brother no matter what had happened in their lives. And boy, had they survived some wreckage.

Dev swallowed down the emotion coating his throat. He fell back into the black void of detachment that had gotten him through those first months after he'd come out of the coma his father had beaten him into. "Anth is the only reason Ace didn't kill me back then," he managed to say, sounding flat and unaffected even though he was anything but. "In return, I made a promise. Which I'm now breaking by telling you he exists."

"You think it's him?" Cody asked. He'd recovered his voice more than Jamison.

"I don't know why, after all this time. But AW isn't some coincidence. You don't sign a note to us with AW and not expect it to be Ace or someone connected to him." Ace was dead. They'd made sure of that.

But the effects of Ace would live on. Why had he been stupid enough to think they wouldn't?

Silence swallowed the kitchen whole. Dev wasn't sure

he'd ever heard such a silence in this kitchen. There had been months of danger and fears last year, but someone had always had something to say.

Dev couldn't help but glance at Sarah. She sat at the table, eyes wide, mouth open, still holding onto a forkful of food that had never made it up to her mouth. Her belly was big and round and all he could think about was his hand on her belly—feeling the outline of that foot inside of her.

A foot they'd made together during a night that played over and over again in his mind when he didn't want it to.

Especially now.

He'd failed her. He'd believed it was over and let himself be stupid enough to think he could give someone something.

"I guess you should tell us everything you know about this Anth Wyatt," Cody said, finally breaking the heavy, choking silence. "Starting with…" Cody trailed off. That stoic demeanor he'd been trying to hold on to slipped, and he raked his hands through his hair. "I don't understand, Dev."

His brothers looked at him like he'd killed something in front of them. And he supposed he had. Their trust. So, what was there to understand? He was no upstanding Wyatt. He wouldn't say he was like his father—he wasn't an evil madman. He was like their mother—weak-willed enough to care more about self-preservation than any of his loved ones. The ones he should have protected.

Sarah got up from her seat and came to stand between him and his brothers. She laid her hand on his arm—gently like she had at Brady's wedding. Like Sarah had some well of *gentleness* she'd always hidden.

"I'm sure if we all sit down, Dev can tell us the whole story," Sarah said authoritatively, reminding him of Grandma Pauline. Until she tried to force a smile at him. "There's an explanation, of course."

"Not the one you're hoping for," he replied bleakly.

She swallowed at that, but she didn't drop her hand or flinch. She pointed him to the table, and Dev didn't know what else to do but sit.

His brothers did too, on the opposite side of the table from him and Sarah. Grandma Pauline piled plates with food and set them in front of each of her grandsons. She still hadn't said anything.

When had Grandma Pauline ever not said anything?

Dev could only stare at his plate, words tumbling around in his brain, but none of them making it to his mouth.

Sarah reached beneath the table and took his hand. He didn't know what to do with her faith in him, because God knew he was about to destroy it. But wasn't that what he needed to do? Just blow it all up, lay it all out there.

Because someone thought it wasn't over, and he knew who.

"It goes back to when Dad and I had our little stand-off," Dev managed to say. He didn't sound so devoid of emotion now. The emotions all but strangled the words and they sounded like just that.

He wasn't sure he could do this with Sarah holding his hand. He wasn't sure he could do it without.

"You've never told us much about that," Cody said, with enough detachment Dev could only be jealous.

"What was there to tell? I thought I had him. I thought in a one-on-one fight I could take him down and arrest him. I didn't. He beat me within an inch of my life and then let me go." Dev tried to tug his hand away from Sarah's, but she held firm under the table. It was a curse and a relief. "The only part I left out was that someone else was there."

"This…other son?" Jamison supplied.

"I didn't know that at first, though he looked like Ace. More like Ace than we do, except he had blue eyes." Dev could remember all too well. He'd been cocky and stupid and had tried to take down his father on his own.

Then there'd been another Ace. Same face. Same build. Same sneer, but blue eyes instead of hazel.

"He stopped Ace. I was in and out. I don't remember much." He didn't tell his brothers the pain had been so bad he'd half wished to die. At least then it would be over. He'd been twenty-two and stupid. So damn stupid. "He gave Ace some song and dance about how killing your own son, even one as shameful as me, was a distraction from what Ace was meant to do. That it might even ruin his karmic reward or whatever Ace was always going on about. I'm not sure Ace was swayed so much as he paused to think."

Think about the ways he could torture his son so much better if he were alive—alive and unable to continue in law enforcement. Alive and the weakest link in the Wyatt brothers.

But that wasn't what they were talking about.

"Anth came over and told me his name. Told me we were brothers. He said if I wanted to live, if I wanted my family to live, I had to promise to never mention his existence to anyone. If I agreed, I'd survive. If I didn't, we'd all be dead."

The worst part in telling his brothers was he knew what they would have done. They would have accepted death. Better to die a noble one than lie for Ace.

"I promised," Dev managed to say, though it felt like

being back in the Badlands, broken and bloody. Failing. "Next thing I knew I woke up in the hospital."

"Why didn't you tell us when Ace died? That there might still be someone out there who wanted to hurt us?"

"Anth didn't hurt me. He saved my life, what was left of it. I thought it was over. Whatever or whoever he was."

"But it's not," Jamison said flatly.

Dev thought of the notes they'd all gotten. No, the worst part wasn't knowing his brothers would have handled it differently. The worst part was knowing he wouldn't change a second of it if he could go back. Even knowing it'd come back to bite him. "No. No, it isn't over."

No ONE HAD EATEN. Even Sarah hadn't been able to stomach more than a few bites. Despite everything that had happened last year as the Wyatts had navigated Ace and the Sons' constant attempts to hurt them, she had never seen everyone look so…wrecked.

No one was going to speak, and even though Sarah had no right, she couldn't stand this. "Well, I'm sure we're all glad you made the choice that kept you alive, Dev," she said, maybe a little too loudly and a little too pointedly at Jamison and Cody.

She was gratified to see Cody wince and Jamison close his eyes as if physically pained.

"She's right, Dev," Jamison said, opening his eyes and looking right at him. "You did what you had to do to survive. We understand that. It's… The notes are concerning, but we'd never blame you for doing what you had to."

Dev didn't say anything, just tried to tug his hand away from hers under the table again, but she wouldn't let him. She held on tight.

"Besides," Cody offered. "Now we know. Which

means once Brady, Gage and Tucker get here, we can figure out a way to protect ourselves from this Anth Wyatt."

Dev looked down at his plate. Then, in a sudden move that finally freed his hand from hers, he scraped back from the table. "Got chores," he muttered. He stalked outside before anyone could stop him.

Sarah thought about letting him go. He needed some time to work through this, and Dev best worked through things alone. But he would convince himself he was in the wrong, and she couldn't let him do that.

She got to her feet, ready to follow, but both Jamison and Cody hurried to block the door. "This isn't about you, Sarah," Cody said.

She wanted to smack him, but instead she fixed him with her most imperious scowl—one she'd learned from watching Grandma Pauline for years. "You're right, this is about Dev. Believing he failed you somehow."

Jamison and Cody exchanged a glance as though that's exactly what Dev had done. Her fingers curled into fists, though she kept them at her sides.

"He did what he had to do to keep himself alive. If you blame him for that, for even a second, you're nothing but egotistical, self-centered blowhards who don't love your brother the way you should."

"I said we didn't blame him. Right here at this table. You heard me."

"Yeah, you said it. Now, why don't you work on believing it." She pushed between them and out into the mudroom, pulled her coat on, and then braved the outside.

Sarah knew there were only two reasons they'd let her leave without following. One, she was pregnant and they were all treating her with kid gloves, and two, because Grandma Pauline likely stepped in and stopped them.

She headed right for the stables and wasn't surprised

to find Dev saddling up his horse. He didn't turn around, though she could tell he knew she was there by the slight pause in his movements.

"You want to yell at me, fine, but it'll have to wait until I've done the morning rounds."

"Yell at you?" Sarah could only stand in confusion as he cinched the saddle and started moving Roscoe toward the door.

"In fact, don't bother," he continued, as if she hadn't voiced any confusion. "I'm sorry. No amount of yelling is going to make me feel more sorry."

"Why would you feel sorry?"

For the first time he stopped moving. He held Roscoe's reins in his hand and looked at her like she was the one who wasn't making any sense. "If you'd known I'm sure you wouldn't have involved me in the whole..." He waved at her stomach with his free hand.

Sarah settled her hands over her bump. "You gave me exactly what I asked for. I don't know why you'd be sorry about that. And I really don't know why this would have changed my mind."

"Ace— "

"—is dead," Sarah said firmly, cutting him off. She stepped toward him and took his hand just as she had inside. She needed that anchor as much as she suspected he did. Because the thought of him so close to death... It had been bad enough those ten years ago when she'd been an emotional teenager and visited him in the hospital. Worse now knowing how...he'd survived it. All alone. "You said you had to do it."

"No," Dev said in that voice she remembered from that awful time. He'd spent weeks in the hospital after he'd finally woken up from the coma, but when he'd gotten home it hadn't been...good. Dev had been like a void.

No emotions. No…personality. He'd been a shell. It had taken him years to come back to himself. He still wasn't all the way there, but this made it all worse again.

It about broke her heart.

"I said he saved my life on a condition. It's not the same as *having* to do it."

"It is to me," Sarah said quietly, afraid if she spoke any louder her voice and composure might break.

He shook his head. "Jamison never would have agreed to that deal. That I know for sure."

"And Jamison would be dead. That *I* know for sure. And if he'd died then, Liza and Gigi would probably be dead, too, since Jamison was the reason they escaped the Sons. Heck, maybe all of you would be dead after last year's troubles. So if this whole thing with Ace and his other son had to happen, then I'm damn glad it happened to you, who'd had the sense to make a deal."

He tugged his hand out of hers and she couldn't hold on to his grasp though she tried.

"A deal with the devil?"

"With the outcome that let you live." Since she couldn't hold on to his hand, she reached up and touched his face. She wasn't prone to physical acts of affection, but the thought of life and death had her feeling weepy and desperate. Or maybe that was pregnancy hormones. She'd happily blame it on that. "You being alive is the most important thing to me."

He covered her hand as if to pull it off his face, but she had a flash of a kiss, a murmur. The feelings of their bodies moving together. Something…otherworldly.

She blinked as he removed her hand and dropped it. Memory or fantasy, hard to tell. And pointless either way.

"Stop being nice to me," he muttered. "It's weird."

"It isn't weird when you're the—"

He cut her off with a look. Because she wasn't supposed to think of him as the father of her baby. Her baby didn't have a father in *that* sense, and she'd been okay with that. Grandma Pauline had raised those six grandsons of hers on her own. Turned them into amazing, wonderful men after terrible childhoods stuck in their father's gang. She'd wanted to do that, too.

Sometimes she just had a hard time remembering that. Which irritated her, though she wasn't even sure why or who she was irritated with. Him or herself.

"It's Christmastime," Sarah said loftily. "Peace on earth and goodwill toward men. I'm good-willing you. Get used to it." She winced as pain tightened her belly. Stupid early contractions.

Dev was immediately dropping his horse's reins and propelling her back and onto the rickety bench. "Damn it, Sarah."

"It's nothing," she said, breathing like the doctor had told her to. "The doctor said so."

"No, the doctor said you had to take it easy. Not that it was *nothing.*"

"I *am* taking it easy." The pain eased, slowly, but it eased. She managed a smile up at him. "See? All gone. The doctor said the contractions should come and go for *weeks* without any progress. That is why I have an appointment every week until the due date. It's fine. I promise."

"Sarah." The stark way he said her name had the smile dying on her face as he kneeled before her.

"This is bad. It's danger all over again, and one we have less experience with. It's even more imperative that no one ever suspect…" There was a twist of pain on his face as he looked at her belly—a kind of pain she'd never seen him allow to show on his face like that. This time it was him grabbing her hands. "You need to stay away," he said resolutely. "Stay on your property. I'll keep helping out at your ranch for you, but you need to stay away. Stay in bed. Rest, like the doctor said. Please. I'm begging you."

She swallowed the lump in her throat. She didn't know how to do what he was asking, but she also didn't know how to say no to him when he was like this. Emotional and very close to desperate.

No, she couldn't argue with him. "I'll…try," she promised.

Chapter Three

Sarah spent the morning away from Dev and the Reaves ranch. She took some time off her feet until the contractions were completely gone. People might think she pushed herself too hard, but she was careful.

Besides, she was only two weeks away from her due date. What would be the harm in the baby coming now? She'd happily bake him a little longer, but labor wouldn't be the worst thing at this point. Especially on a day when there was no snow in the forecast.

Once she'd felt better and eaten some lunch, she'd bundled up and headed outside. Dev's dogs, which he'd insisted on having live at the Knight Ranch since the trouble last year, pranced ahead of her.

Staying inside made her too antsy and anxious and today, it made her replay Dev's emotional plea over and over in her head.

I'm begging you.

She couldn't...sit with that. She needed a chore to do, even if it wasn't labor intensive. She needed the cold winter air and something to do with her hands. She needed the ranch. It had always been her solace, her heart. No one could stop her from seeking that out just because she was going to have a baby soon.

She smoothed her hands over her belly—even bulkier

with the heavy coat on over it. She'd give her baby the space to like and love whatever he wanted, but that didn't mean she couldn't fantasize about him feeling the same way about the Knight Ranch as she did.

What about Reaves Ranch?

She looked to the west. Dev was the only Wyatt brother who'd shown an actual interest in Grandma Pauline's ranch. If he didn't have any kids, what would happen to it? Would the Reaves Ranch be sold off to a stranger?

She shook her head as if to shake the thoughts away. There would be many, many years of Dev and Grandma Pauline inhabiting this earth before she had to worry about that. Maybe her baby was technically a Wyatt, but right now Dev didn't want to acknowledge that.

Not just for his own reasons anymore, but for safety. Because Anth Wyatt apparently existed and was threatening all six brothers.

It made her want to cry. This was supposed to be over—the shadow of Ace Wyatt on their lives gone. Instead, just as they'd settled into this new normal…here was another facet of Ace haunting them.

Would that always be the case?

She knew that was bothering Dev, likely his brothers too. That horrible feeling they'd never be free of Ace even in death. And it wasn't just them—they'd all married or were in the process of marrying her sisters. Making families of their own.

Wyatts and her sisters pairing up wasn't a great thing to dwell on with her hands on her stomach, where Dev's child grew. She marched forward. Maybe she couldn't muck stalls, ride a horse or even go around breaking up ice in the troughs, but she could tidy the tools or do a little light sweeping or *something*.

But before she could make it to the stables, Duke pulled up next to her in his truck. She knew he'd been out checking fence lines to make sure they were strong enough to survive any winter storm that blew through.

He put the truck into Park and got out. "What do you think you're doing wandering around in this cold?"

She smiled at her father. He was a good man, even if he'd kept his share of secrets from them. He did what was right, and he was fiercely protective of his daughters—biological, adopted or fostered.

"I'm just antsy. I'm being careful. Promise."

He made a noise that was neither belief nor acceptance. Simple acknowledgment she'd spoken and he'd heard it. "Where were you this morning?"

Sarah wouldn't let herself fidget even though it felt a bit like an accusation. "Let Grandma Pauline feed me."

Duke studied her, clearly not believing that was the only reason she'd gone over there. Instead of lecturing her more, he reached out and squeezed her shoulder.

"Sarah, I hope you know what a joy you've been to me. Not just because you love the ranch like I do, but because you're a fine young woman with a good head on her shoulders."

Sarah blinked. Duke was the best dad in the world as far as she was concerned, but he wasn't big on emotional heart-to-hearts. Thank God. She didn't know what to do with…this. "Well, thanks."

"I may not be thrilled about the circumstances, but I'll support you and my grandchild any way I can."

"I… I know." She'd always known that, even if him saying it had a lump forming in her throat.

"Which is why I feel like it's pretty important to tell you something, and usually when I tell you something you get that hard head on and do the opposite. So I need you to promise me you'll listen."

Sarah wrinkled her nose. "You fight dirty."

"You're darn right," he said, smiling at her, his big hand still on her shoulder. Because he was always there.

"I don't know that I can promise outright, but I can promise to try not to be contrary for the sake of it."

Duke chuckled softly. "Well, I suppose that's about all I can ask." Then he sighed, almost sadly, as if the words weighed him down and were far more serious than she wanted to deal with when she was worried about Dev and this new danger.

Which she should probably tell Dad about.

Dad grabbed her other shoulder, gave her a gentle squeeze and met her gaze with his steady one. "Sarah, you can't save that boy. He has to save himself."

That simple statement hit its mark—a mark she hadn't realized she had. She wasn't trying to save Dev... She was just trying to...to... "I'm not trying to save anyone," she insisted, though of course she couldn't believe it now that she'd felt the weight of how right Duke was.

Duke gave her a pointed look. "Baby girl, you have been poking that boy back into the living since the day he got home from the hospital. And you've done a good job. He wouldn't be where he is without you. But the rest of that journey is his to make."

She thought about Dev's blankness in the kitchen when he'd recounted Anth Wyatt to his brothers. How could emotional healing be his to do when he could simply shut down like that?

"I haven't heard the details yet, but if everyone's descending on Grandma Pauline's tonight, sounds like more trouble is brewing," Duke continued. "I don't want you involved. You've got to take it easy for that baby. I want you to stay away from the Wyatts for a while. Including tonight's dinner."

The knee-jerk emotions that had plagued her this entire pregnancy sprung to life, and she had to fight to keep the tears out of her eyes. "They're my family. And yours."

"Of course they are. I'm not saying it's their fault they've got trouble again. I'm not saying we should all hide and run away. I'm saying *you* need to stay away from it in your condition."

Dev had said the same thing, of course. She understood why, but that didn't mean she needed to be hidden away. "If there's trouble, I doubt me staying home by myself is—"

"Liza will come here with the girls. You two will babysit."

Sarah scowled. "While the menfolk have their grown-up conversation."

Duke sighed. "With four out of your five sisters. Come on now, girl. You have a baby to care about."

She put her hands protectively over her belly. "Caring about this baby doesn't mean I don't care about the safety of everyone I love. If some long-lost half brother is after them, it's not just them. It's *my* sisters too and—"

Duke's hands tightened on her shoulders.

"What did you say?" he demanded, suddenly fierce.

Sarah blinked at the sudden change in his demeanor. Had he not thought the dinner was as serious as that? "They got notes. All the brothers. From one of Ace's sons they didn't know about." She didn't add the part about Dev knowing. Didn't need to get into—

"I have to go." Duke released her abruptly and was immediately striding for his truck.

"Wha—"

"Liza will be over in a bit. You stay put, now." He

got in the truck, pointed at her like she was a little girl again. "I mean it." The dogs sat on their butts as if he'd been talking to them.

Then he drove off, and Sarah stood in the stark winter afternoon wondering what on earth had gotten into everyone.

IT WASN'T ANY easier telling the truth to the rest of his brothers. Jamison was the oldest, the one who'd saved them all from the Sons, the one Dev had idolized before he'd ended up broken—so Dev had assumed that would be the worst. Letting down the person you most wanted to make proud.

The others were younger than him. They hadn't spent as much time in the Sons as he and Jamison had. They didn't fully...

But of course they did. Ace had kept Cody's wife on the run, resulting in his daughter being a secret from him for seven years. Ace had almost killed Gage last summer and had been instrumental in Felicity's own biological father hurting her. Ace had been in the periphery of Tucker and Brady's troubles this summer—but he'd been there. The reason. Always.

"It didn't occur to you to tell us once Ace was dead?" Brady said, his expression cop-blank and his voice grim.

"No. I thought it was over. Just like you."

"Clearly it's not."

"Clearly," Dev echoed.

"I'm still not following," Gage said. Usually the most easygoing brother, or at least the one more likely to tell a joke, there was nothing remotely light about Gage right now. "This Anth guy saved you?"

"He said he would make sure I didn't die if I promised to never tell anyone about his existence. I figured it was some kind of…conscience or whatever. We all have one. Why wouldn't this… Wyatt?" Which of course had an easy answer. Ace was always the why.

"And you don't have any idea who his mother is?"

Dev shook his head. "We didn't have much time for a heart-to-heart."

"After. You didn't even think to tell us?"

"I was a little busy, you know, recovering from a coma and learning how to walk again." Dev knew it was wrong to snap at his brothers. Their questions were valid, necessary even. "In the moment, I would have agreed to just about anything. After… Well, he'd held up his end of the bargain. Clearly he knew who I was, if not all of us. If he wanted to be a part of us, he could have been."

"Clearly he didn't want to be."

"Regardless, I'm alive, aren't I? I certainly don't know how. Ace wanted to kill me that day. None of this 'you're my progeny' stuff like he had with Jamison and Gage. He wanted me to be the lesson to all of you. So, whatever Anth did—I'm alive because of it. At the time, telling you guaranteed that I'd be bringing Ace back to our doorstep."

"He could have been behind any of what happened last year," Jamison said. "Framing Felicity for murder, everything that went down in the Badlands with Brady and Cecilia."

Dev was still struggling to deal with how utterly *destroyed* Jamison sounded. As if it was a personal betrayal he'd never get over. Because Jamison couldn't imagine it. Dev knew Jamison was good through and through, and he would have rather died than make a deal.

Just like then, Dev couldn't live up to Jamison's perfect example. "He wasn't behind any of it though, was he?"

"That we know of," Jamison said softly.

No matter how soft, the truth of that was like a knife to the heart. Obviously he'd considered Anth might have something to do with all the danger that had befallen them last year. How could he not consider it? But there'd never been any evidence pointing to someone other than Ace or one of his Sons of the Badlands cronies.

But you didn't have to be the perpetrator of something to be involved. Ace had escaped connection with who knew how many crimes.

Duke burst into the kitchen, looking a little wild as all the brothers turned to him.

"What is it? Is something wrong?" Dev demanded, thoughts immediately going to Sarah and those contractions this morning.

"Tell me what's going on," Duke said, a little out of breath. "You were threatened."

"Duke, I can't tell you not to worry when there's a threat against us and your girls are involved, but it's being taken care of," Jamison said calmly, none of that hurt in his tone like it was when he spoke to Dev.

"Don't take that high-handed tone with me. Not only are all my daughters in the crosshairs here, but... Tell me about this son of Ace's."

All Dev's brothers turned to him. Because Anth Wyatt was his cross to bear. "I don't know much about him. Anth Wyatt spared my life back when Ace wanted to kill me. I don't have the slightest clue why he'd be threatening the six of us now, but I think it's him."

"He could have others," Tucker offered—speaking for the first time. "If Ace had one son with another woman, there could be more than one."

Duke scraped his hands over his face. "Could be, it's true, but this one...this Anth..." Duke trailed off on a pained breath.

"You know something about him?" Jamison asked.

"Not exactly. But I know who his mother is."

"How?"

Duke's expression was so grim, and the eye contact he made was with Dev and Dev alone. "Sarah's mother. Biological mother. She'd had a son with Ace, which was why Sarah's father asked Eva and me to take her. They were scared for her safety. Not because of Ace. Because of the son. Anth Wyatt."

Chapter Four

"I don't need babysitting."

Liza cooed at their niece, Felicity and Gage's sweet little Claire who was quickly creeping toward her first birthday. It would have been a nice moment. Hanging out with just Liza and the girls. Liza had six-year-old Gigi, technically her half sister, but Liza and Jamison were her guardians with her parents dead. Cody and Nina's eldest daughter Brianna and Gigi were good friends and were occupying each other upstairs.

"You can't be alone this close to your due date. Besides, Jamison already filled me in on what they're covering over at the ranch."

"What about *me*?"

"Your job is baby-growing and, soon enough, baby-pushing into the world. That's the big stuff, Sarah." Liza smiled reassuringly, but there was something all wrong about everything. The way Duke had taken off, the way Liza refused to talk about Anth Wyatt.

"Nina's pregnant," Sarah pointed out petulantly.

"She's five months pregnant and not having contractions on and off," Liza returned equitably.

"What's going on over there? I know about the mysterious brother, but…" She couldn't put her finger on the *wrong* feeling that kept crawling up her spine. Ever since Duke had taken off.

When Liza turned her back to Sarah, making a big fuss over putting Claire in her travel crib, Sarah's dread sank deeper.

"Liza, what is going on?"

Liza took a deep breath and let it out. She came back to Sarah, kneeling in front of where Sarah sat on what was usually Duke's recliner but she'd commandeered during this last month of her pregnancy.

"We all want you to take care of yourself," Liza said, patting Sarah's knee. "Contractions are nothing to mess around with."

"I wasn't even dilated. The doctor told me what to do and I have an appointment every week. Baby is pretty much all baked in there. The worry is over the top, unless there is something bigger at work here."

Liza started to shake her head, but Sarah pressed.

"Explain to me how knowing there's danger, but no one will tell me exactly what, is supposed to give me a calm, relaxing last few weeks of pregnancy?"

Brianna thundered down the stairs from where she and Gigi had been playing dolls. She slid into the living room in her usual boisterous fashion. "Aunt Sarah, can I feel your baby?" Brianna asked. Eight year old Brianna had been fascinated with Sarah's pregnancy ever since finding out her own mom was pregnant.

Sarah nodded and motioned her over. She took Brianna's hands and placed them on her stomach. "He's not moving around much right now, but you never know when he'll start kicking up a storm."

Gigi had followed and was peering down into Claire's crib, making funny faces at the baby who squealed in appreciative laughter.

Sarah wished she could enjoy it. Her nieces, her sister. Liza had only lived with the Knights a couple years after she'd escaped the Sons of the Badlands with Jamison when she'd been a teenager. Then she'd run away to go back into the gang and keep her sister safe. But Sarah had always looked up to her. She'd missed her when she'd left, been so angry at her for disappearing, but the past year and a half had done a lot to heal those hurts.

Liza was still that oldest sister who seemed to know how to hold everything together. After the girls got tired of baby watch, they moved to TV, and Claire dozed in her crib. Liza forced Sarah to eat dinner on the chair, fussing over her as if she was an invalid.

If it had been any other night, Sarah might have been able to relax and enjoy it, but worry kept her tense and frustrated.

Liza returned from the kitchen with a brownie, and Sarah took it eagerly as Liza perched on the arm of the chair and ate her own.

"Are you ever going to tell us who the father is?" Liza asked, quiet enough that the girls wouldn't hear as they watched their show.

Sarah shifted uncomfortably—both emotionally and physically. "It doesn't matter. Wouldn't you have rather lived a life without your father? Gigi's okay now, but wouldn't she have been better off if her mother had been able to get her away from your father?"

Liza pressed her lips together. "You're not doing this alone, because you have all us, but there is something to be said for a partner. I know you can do this, but I don't want you to close yourself off to possibilities."

Brownie finished, Sarah placed her hands firmly on her belly. "The only possibility I want is holding my son and raising him here. I'm not closing myself off to a partnership. I just know that everything I want is right here."

"Here. On this ranch with Duke. Getting a whole heck of a lot of help from Dev."

"We're neighbors. That's what ranching neighbors do. Help each other out. Especially when we're practically family what with the way you lot have off and married Wyatts."

"You two have an interesting relationship."

Sarah scooted down in the armchair. She had a bad feeling she knew where Liza was going, but she wasn't going to play along. "Interesting. Antagonistic. Potato potahto."

"You're a unit. You have been for quite some time. You work together. You have your own weird language. Dev's a tough nut to crack, but you seem to have cracked it on occasion."

Sarah snorted. "I wouldn't go that far."

"I know you, Sarah. You get plans and you go about enacting them without letting anyone know what you're doing. You have ideas that you keep to yourself but make happen through sheer force of will. I'm not saying I wouldn't bet on you if it came to it, but betting on Dev is…well, people are complicated."

Sarah fidgeted, her belly felt too weighted and her back was aching. Which was totally about pregnancy and not how Liza's words seemed to hit their mark. "I'm not betting on Dev."

Liza shrugged. "I don't believe you."

Before Sarah could get bent out of shape about that, Jamison came to collect Liza and Gigi, then Cody and Nina to pick up Brianna. They took Claire with them to drop back off at the Reaves Ranch since Felicity and Gage were staying with Grandma Pauline.

When Duke came in, he wasn't alone, and that scared Sarah to her bones. Dev was with him and they both looked at *her* with a grimness that could never be good.

DEV KNEW HE shouldn't have come. He should have let Duke handle this aspect of things. Duke would take care of his own. They'd all take care of each other. He didn't need to be smack dab in the middle of anything that involved Sarah.

But he'd found himself trailing after Duke anyway, and when Duke hadn't offered any objections, they'd driven over to the Knight house together.

Sarah eyed them both with mounting suspicion, her hands coming over her belly in a protective gesture. Something he refused to acknowledge twisted in Dev's gut.

"What is it?" she asked, her voice coming out strong even if the worry showed in her eyes.

"We're just going to move you over to Grandma Pauline's. Aside from Jamison and Cody's families in Bonesteel, everyone's going to be staying there, much as they can. Strength in numbers."

"What about you?" Sarah demanded, as Dev had known she would. Before Duke could give his lame excuses, Sarah continued. "If we're all going to be there, you should be, too."

"We've been trying to tell him that," Dev muttered, earning a glare from Duke.

"It's not necessary."

"Why not?" Sarah insisted.

"I'm not a part of this."

"Then neither am I," Sarah replied. "Not married to a Wyatt, and if working together on both ranches doesn't count for you, it doesn't count for me either. And if this is about me being pregnant—"

"It isn't," Dev said firmly. Again he got a glare from Duke. Maybe this was why he'd come though, because he knew she wouldn't get the unvarnished truth from anyone else. They'd try to dance around the problem—the danger.

He understood why. She was supposed to be relaxing and avoiding stress—but she had a connection to the man threatening them and it could not be ignored.

"Duke, you have to tell her. No amount of moving her and installing people around her is going to keep her safe if she doesn't know."

"Knew I shouldn't have let you come," Duke muttered.

"If someone doesn't tell me what I don't know right this second I am liable to go straight into labor. Spit it out."

Dev wished it was a much less scary a situation so he could find some enjoyment in how quickly Duke jumped to explain himself after that.

"I know a little about Anth Wyatt."

Sarah's eyebrows drew together. "More secrets?"

Dev winced at the hurt in her tone. Because this whole disaster was the unraveling of more secrets than he'd ever expected.

"I won't apologize for this secret. When your parents—"

"My parents!" she screeched, trying to push herself out of the chair, but Dev was quicker and was gently pressing his hand into her shoulder to keep her put.

"Let him finish," Dev ordered.

Sarah whipped a killing look up at him, but he nodded toward Duke.

"Your father was friends with Eva. From way back.

We were friendly with your parents. They knew we had fostered girls. At that point we thought we couldn't have any children of our own." Duke rubbed a hand over his graying hair. "They came to us, a few weeks before you were born. Your mother had had a child from a previous relationship. They were afraid of both the man and the child. He'd been threatening your mother. They were worried about your safety. They wanted someone to take you until they could be sure they were safe."

"What does this have to do with the Wyatts?" Sarah asked. Her voice was flat and emotionless, but her hand had come up to grip Dev's on her shoulder.

"Your mother had been involved with Ace Wyatt."

The hand that had been clutching his fell off and into her lap. She didn't say anything, so Duke continued. But Dev knew what those little gestures meant. She didn't want any kind of link with a Wyatt.

Even him.

Still, he couldn't bring himself to pull his hand off her shoulder and leave her sitting there absorbing all that information without some kind of understanding. Connections to monsters he knew all too well.

"Ace and your mother had a son before she managed to leave," Duke continued. "She met your father, started a new life. Or thought she had."

"Anth Wyatt is the son," Sarah said, her voice even flatter. She slid her hands over her belly, that protective gesture.

It wasn't about him, but it still made Dev feel like slime. He'd known Anth was out there and hadn't used that as a reason to keep her at arm's length when it came to the whole helping her have a baby thing.

"Yes. They knew Eva and I would take good care of

their child, and they knew that being close to Pauline Reaves wouldn't hurt any."

Sarah swallowed loudly, though absolutely no emotion showed on her face. "My...parents. Are they..."

"They both died, sweetheart. I'm sorry." Duke sighed heavily. "Eva and I had agreed that if Ace wasn't a threat anymore, we'd tell you. Once he finally wasn't, it didn't seem any good to stir up a hornet's nest."

Sarah was quiet for a long time, and Dev and Duke stood in silence, letting her decide what to say next.

"But right now the threat is against you." She looked up at Dev. Her blue eyes weren't accusing, but Dev wasn't accustomed to the cold light in them.

"My brothers and I got notes, yes."

"I didn't get one. The threat wasn't against me. If everything you're saying is true, he doesn't even know—"

"We don't know what he knows, Sarah. Which means we need to take all the precautions we can." Dev tried to say what needed to be said gently, but his words came out harsh.

It shouldn't be so hard to protect someone. Sarah always made it far more difficult than it had to be. This pregnancy was no exception, and because he was already tired of worrying over her on that score, he was not going to tiptoe around this.

"We don't know what Anth is capable of. We don't know what ways Ace warped him. In the moment, I thought him helping me was charity or a conscience. Now..."

"Now what?"

"I think it was just like Ace. To let me think I'd survived. To think I was free and clear, only to have a note show up that things aren't over. I think it was a plan—

whether between the two of them or Anth alone—so that when it would hurt even more, he could come after me."

He kneeled in front of Sarah, because she had to get it through her thick skull that protecting her was the only thing that mattered. "Maybe he doesn't know about you, Sarah, but it wouldn't take much digging for him to figure it out. We won't know when or if he does, and our baby is going to be here sooner rather than later. I know you'd do everything in your power to protect him, so let us do everything in our power to protect you."

Sarah opened her mouth, but whatever she was going to say was lost in Duke's booming voice.

In an instant Duke squared off with Dev and demanded, "You better explain that, because it sure as hell sounded like you just said *our* baby."

Chapter Five

Sarah's heart leaped into her throat. Dev had said *our* baby.

In front of Dad, yes, which was less than ideal. Less than less ideal, if she was being honest. But he'd… In the midst of all his awfulness he'd talked about protecting *our* baby. As if he held some ownership in this child. The way she'd desperately wanted him to.

She blinked at the silly tears and swallowed down the laugh that wanted to bubble over at the utter *horror* in Dev's eyes as Duke waited furiously for an explanation. Clearly Dev had not meant to say *our*, but that made it all the more special—it meant he felt it, even if he didn't want to admit it.

Though she was moved by the admission, hoped it was the starting point for Dev to see he had this little life to truly live for, she tried to smooth things over. "Dev just meant the royal *our*. You know. This baby is all of ours," Sarah said, her voice squeaky. It was with emotion, but she was a little afraid Duke would read it as nerves.

"Bull," Duke spat. "Explain this, Wyatt."

Sarah winced. Dad using a last name was *never* good. Dev slowly stood from his kneeling position at her chair. His expression was hard and that blank look that had her heart pinching in her chest.

She was desperate to get rid of that default reaction in him. She tried to scoot off the chair, but it was an ungainly struggle and she gave up on a huff as Dev and Duke stared at each other in a silent standoff. "Don't we have more important things to—"

"Are you the father?" Duke demanded, wholly unconcerned with *her* at the moment.

Which had her temper bubbling up over the giddy hope she'd been feeling. She managed to get to her feet this time and stepped in between Dev's motionless, emotionless form and Duke's furious one.

"Dad! I got pregnant because I wanted to have a baby."

Duke's gaze finally left Dev's and met hers. "With him?"

She met his fury with her own. "I wanted a baby, and I didn't want a baby daddy. So Dev did me a favor and supplied the…necessary components."

She heard Dev groan behind her and Duke winced a little bit at that himself. Well, good, if she could make both men uncomfortable, maybe they'd stop being angry or defensive or *whatever.*

"It was my choice and I begged him to do it. Trust me, he didn't want to. He did me a favor."

"I…can't pretend to understand any of this," Duke said, shaking his head.

"You don't need to. Anth Wyatt is threatening six of us." The mention of the real reason they were here sobered both men. "I'll move into Pauline's as long as you do too, Dad. I think it's good for as many of us as possible to be under the same roof. That way we can always pair up to do the chores. Someone can always be with me. It makes sense. You staying here alone does not make sense."

"You're changing the subject," Duke said, crossing his arms over his chest.

"For the time being. Because protecting ourselves is a little more important than you acting like you have a say in the matter—" she pointed at her large stomach "—when we're already here."

Duke's gaze moved back to Dev behind her. Narrowed and angry. Sarah didn't have to look at Dev to know what the expression on his face would be. Blank. Maybe with the ghost of self-loathing.

"I'd say both are pretty important," Duke said at length.

"I'd say it's not between you and Dev to work out. It's between you and me," Sarah argued. "And I'm not speaking another word about it until we're all together at Grandma Pauline's." With that, she turned on a heel and marched—or, more accurately, waddled—out of the room.

She had to use the banister for support to help get her up the stairs. She didn't feel any contractions but she felt *heavy* as she huffed and puffed up to her room.

"I'm mostly ready to get you out of there, little man, but you're probably safer inside and, oh yeah, I'm terrified of pushing you out of me." She rubbed her stomach, comforted by the little conversation with her baby. Maybe he was just hearing garbled nonsense in there, but it was *her* garbled nonsense.

She wasn't afraid of being a mother. She'd watched Felicity and Gage deal with the demands of pregnancy and a newborn. Sarah knew it would be hard and exhausting, but she also knew she'd have help and love to get through it.

But no matter how she told herself she'd watched horses and cattle birth their young—and if they could do it out there with no intervention, she could certainly do it in a hospital with an epidural—the worry and fear of actual labor were overwhelming at times.

Now she didn't have to just fear labor, she had to fear Anth Wyatt. Not just Dev's half brother, but her own.

She couldn't wrap her head around it. Her mother had conceived a child with Ace Wyatt. This biological mother she'd never known—but Duke had.

She stood in her room trying to work out how she felt about it, but there were too many realities assaulting her to get too wrapped up in the past at the moment. She was so pregnant she didn't even want to sit down for fear of not wanting to get back up. The Wyatts were being threatened, which left her sisters all in a dangerous position. Duke knew Dev was the father of her baby and she'd left them downstairs to squabble pointlessly.

How could she stand here and try to understand the mother and father she'd never known, who were dead anyway?

She had to focus on the task at hand, which was packing some things so she could spend the next few days at Grandma Pauline's with the rest of her family. Grandma Pauline's house was big, with all sorts of hodgepodge rooms added on over the years, but it'd still be a tight fit even if Jamison's and Cody's families stayed in Bonesteel.

She found a duffel bag and packed all of her oversize sweats that managed to fit over her pregnant belly. She tossed in her pregnancy book and set her body pillow next to the bag on the bed. If she forgot something, she could always come back and get it. The houses weren't that far apart, and just because they were in danger didn't mean the ranch work got to stop. They'd have to keep going back and forth for the time being.

She heard footsteps on the stairs down the hall. She knew it wasn't Duke. He didn't take the steps that fast or with that much…the word *menace* floated through her mind. But what was menacing about Dev? That he was grumpy? She'd handled that forever.

Or is the thing you can't handle the fact he said our baby like it matters?

Well.

When he appeared at her doorway, he stayed right there. "Duke's packing. You shouldn't be carrying anything you need, so I will when you're done."

He stood there looking grumpy, which was his norm, but there was a way he held himself—hands deep in his pockets, gaze refusing to meet hers—that told her he was also very uncomfortable. Not just because he'd never been in her bedroom before, but she was sure because he'd spilled the beans.

He'd said *our baby*.

She couldn't fight away the tide of emotion. The want she kept trying to convince herself she didn't have. Duke knew he was the father because… "You said *our* baby," she managed on a whisper.

"It doesn't matter." His voice was flat. So were his eyes.

She could be devastated by that, but she'd never been any good at letting other people dictate how she felt or what she should think. "It matters to me."

"This isn't a fairy tale, Sarah. You don't want it to be. Let's just—"

"Do you want it to be?"

Some of his composure cracked and he raked his hands through his dark hair. "No," he said emphatically, but there was something wild in his expression—far closer to fear than denial.

"So, it's not a fairy tale. That doesn't mean it can't be something… It doesn't mean you have to close yourself off from him. He's ours."

"Nothing is mine."

He just cracked her heart in two. She moved to him and touched his face, couldn't seem to *stop* touching him lately when she'd always been the perfect paragon of restraint. She wasn't a touchy-feely person and the random want to touch Dev was always shoved ruthlessly away.

But this baby, and this danger, it changed things… whether she'd planned on it or not. Then there was this old Dev she thought he'd moved past.

"Please don't go back there," she said.

"Back where?"

"To that awful shell you were after you came home from the hospital. I know this is hard, and I know you've got your guilt complex, and this weird idea you're somehow less than your brothers, but for ten years you have slowly stepped out of that and into the land of the living. It would break my heart if you lost all that."

He looked at her like she'd lanced him straight through—which didn't bother her because it was emotion, not blankness. And he *looked* at her—met her gaze and didn't turn away.

There was too much emotion swirling inside of her, too many of the feelings she usually convinced herself were silly fantasies. It was hard here in her room, touching him, her belly between them. Especially when he didn't move away from her hand, just stood there looking down at her.

And she wanted to kiss him. It wasn't all that unheard of a feeling. Throughout her teenage years she'd convinced herself she found him *repulsive*. And obnoxious. He was still obnoxious, but when she'd made any attempts to date outside the ranch, she compared every guy to Dev.

And they all were lacking. Still, even after she'd accepted that—that he was, for whatever reason, the only man she was ever going to truly be able to give her heart to—she'd been completely and utterly determined to just keep her heart to herself.

She didn't touch him. She didn't flirt with him. She *had* asked him for a baby, but she'd been determined to leave it at that.

For the first time in her life, something had blown up in her face. Even without remembering all of it, she knew he was it for her. And he was looking at her. She was touching him. Danger was encroaching.

Why not go for broke?

She rose to her toes and pressed her mouth to his. He didn't exactly kiss her back, but he didn't push her away or dart off. He let her move her mouth softly against his, igniting a memory of the night they'd conceived their child.

He'd told her not to kiss him and that they should just get it over with. So she'd kissed him right then and there in the hotel hallway because he did *not* get to tell her what to do—drunk or sober.

Except all those months ago he'd kissed her back, with a passion that had surprised her then and now as she remembered it. Could that have really been Dev? Kissing her? Was her memory just some overactive imagination... when she'd never had one of those before?

She couldn't hold herself up on her tiptoes any longer, so she had to pull away, back to her normal height.

DEV GENTLY PUSHED Sarah back a full step. Then he took his own steps backwards and away from *her*.

Why had she kissed him? Why had he let her? Everything was messed up and he could not let that continue.

"I'm sure that was pregnancy hormones or something," he muttered, offering her *any* excuse to let this go.

But fury leaped into her eyes and her hand balled into a fist. "No, this is pregnancy hormones or something." And before he realized what she was doing, she landed a jab right in his gut. He bent over with an *oof,* the air whooshing out of his lungs.

He straightened his shoulders, sucked in a breath and glared at her. "Pack your bag, Sarah."

"It's packed, *Devin.* I have to grab my toiletries." With that she sailed out of the room like some queen on high, belly and all.

Dev huffed. *Women.* He grabbed the duffel off the bed and slung it over his shoulder, stuffing the pillow under his arm. It *was* pregnancy hormones. And fear. Because Sarah had never been so gentle with him. She'd never given him stark honesty about the state he'd been in after his injuries…or the way he'd slowly crawled out of the dark space.

Not that he'd crawled into a *light* space. He wasn't an optimistic guy, and he *wasn't* as good as his brothers—that much was certain in a million different ways. He didn't want the families they were building, but he also wanted to, well, live. Take care of the ranch and Grandma. It had taken him a few years of being in a bad place to get there, but he had gotten there.

Would he go back? Just because a truth he'd hidden had come back to bite him in the butt? Would he fight off that feeling just because Sarah had said it would break her heart if he didn't?

He grumbled to himself all the way down the stairs.

Duke was already ready, standing in the kitchen. When Dev entered, he glowered.

Dev sighed. "She's getting her toiletries."

Duke huffed. "Good. I have more to say to you. Whatever she thinks, I *do* have a say in all this. I'm her father and it's my job to protect her. I don't know what the hell you were thinking, but—"

He'd been thinking he could give Sarah something, no strings attached. He'd been thinking he could feel like some kind of help for once. Of course, he'd never actually felt any of those things, even before this moment, but *that's* what he'd been thinking.

"—you will do right by her."

Dev shook his head. He wasn't going to explain himself to Duke. Or anyone, for that matter. "Hate me if you want, Duke, but this is between..." Except it wasn't between anybody. It was up to him. He'd done what Sarah had asked of him, and now they had to keep it a secret at all costs. "I get to decide what's right, and it clearly isn't whatever you think is."

Duke's brow furrowed and he studied Dev with a sincerity and perception that made Dev shift uncomfortably on his feet.

"You *want* me to hate you," Duke said after a while, as if it was some dawning realization.

Dev snorted, perhaps a little too loud. He didn't want anyone to hate him. He just wanted everyone to understand things were better when he was on the periphery. Didn't this whole thing with Anth *prove* that? "I don't want you to—"

"You do. You want to feel guilty. You want everyone to hate you so you can mope around this ranch feeling sorry for yourself. So you can keep yourself separate and consider it noble. You might have gotten away with

that for too long, but time's up. You've got people to protect, and a baby to be a father to—whether that's Sarah's
plan or not."

Panic bloomed in his chest, but something bigger than
that. Fear. A blinding, terrifying fear. At the word *father.* At Sarah depending on him to protect her, when he
knew he wasn't any good at that. "It's not her plan." His
voice was too rusty, but he couldn't let Duke think any
of what he wanted was ever going to come to fruition.
"She doesn't want a partner in this. She—"

"Bull. She wants *you* as a partner, boy. God knows
why."

Dev thought of that kiss, but refused to accept what
Duke was saying. Sarah was…churned up. Maybe she
didn't want to call it hormones, but she wasn't herself.
She'd have the kid and go back to being… Sarah. Real
Sarah who didn't touch him or cut him open with a few
words, showing just how well she saw through him. "I
can't… Don't you see the danger that puts her in?"

"I've got five of my daughters married to or living
with your brothers. I tried to warn every last one of them
off, because trouble is in the Wyatt name and in the Wyatt
blood. Boy, I know. I was like you once upon a time. But
they all chose love and life over fear. You might not have
that in you, Dev, but Sarah sure does."

With that, he took the duffel out of Dev's hands and
headed for the door. Leaving Dev alone, holding a body
pillow, with far too many revelations, and way worse, far
too many emotions.

Chapter Six

Sarah woke up in a strange bed. For all the hubbub, and the giant stomach impeding any comfortable movement, she had slept pretty well. At least imminent danger couldn't disrupt her sleep schedule like a baby was inevitably going to.

She ran her hands over her stomach in her morning ritual. She whispered a few greeting words to the baby, tried out names like she did every morning, and then finally forced herself to get out of bed.

She'd help Grandma Pauline wash up after breakfast. Then maybe she could talk to Duke about her parents.

Her chest got too tight. Her parents were dead, and they'd given her away to protect her. For so long Sarah had done everything she could not to think about them, to convince herself she was better off without them and vice versa—she didn't want to know if they were good or bad people because both options were awful.

Now, both options were pointless because they were dead.

And her mother had been impregnated by Ace Wyatt. So she did have something in common with her mother, one way or another.

There was one big difference, of course. Dev wasn't Ace. He might be grumpy and have a guilt complex the size of the Badlands, but he was a good man. He watched over his grandmother, took care of the ranch—and helped with hers and Duke's when they were needing it. He was grumbly and contentious, but it hid a kindness he couldn't fight no matter how much he seemed to want to.

"You'll never have to wonder if your father is a good man," she promised her boy.

Except, how could she keep that promise if Dev was determined to be nothing more than sperm donor?

Our baby.

All this time she'd held onto a hope that *our* would mean something. Shouldn't she just keep holding on to that hope until this danger with Anth passed? What was more important: feelings or surviving a lunatic making threats against some of the most important people in her life?

She heaved herself out of bed. Too much thinking for one morning. Besides, a giant baby kicking her bladder wasn't exactly the stuff relaxation was made of. She waddled across the hall and took care of the morning unpleasantry, then waddled right back to the room and threw on a few layers.

Even with pregnancy hormones and overheating, it was dang cold this morning. Of course by the time she'd managed to pull on socks she was breathing heavily.

No, she wouldn't miss pregnancy in the practical sense. Once dressed more warmly, she headed for downstairs. She knew Grandma Pauline had given her the room that best suited her needs—close to the bathroom, sandwiched between Grandma Pauline and the room Felicity and Gage were staying in so she had quick access to help if she needed any, but boy were the stairs something she dreaded.

Still, she could hardly kick Dev out of his room downstairs when he had an actual physical injury—one that pained him, especially in the winter and especially since he'd been doing extra ranch duty for months now.

It was very hard to be appreciative when she'd always prided herself on being so self-sufficient. She often had to remind herself it was for the baby, not her, before she snapped at some well-meaning family member or Wyatt brother.

As if thinking of one conjured one up, as she gripped the railing to help her down the stairs, Dev appeared below.

His nose was red with cold, and she had no doubt his leg was paining him, but more than that he looked tired, exhausted really. Dark shadows under his eyes, and slumped shoulders she'd learned meant he hadn't had a good night's sleep. "Looks like you had a rough night."

Dev grunted. "You look like a snowman."

She scowled at him. "It's cold. And I'm *pregnant*."

His mouth twitched a little, bordering on a smile. She wanted to really make him smile. Or laugh. Before the whole baby thing she'd been on a personal mission to get him to do both more, but then Brady and Cecilia's wedding plans and Rachel moving in with Tucker had made her feel a melancholy that could only be filled with achieving the next goal.

Motherhood.

Now she was here and it felt less like a goal to accomplish. She wasn't sure what it felt like instead, but nothing so cut and dried as a goal or an achievement. It was too big for that. Too all encompassing. Oddly like the danger they were in. She didn't know what lay ahead, or how to plan it out so things would go the way she wanted.

To an extent she was used to that with ranch life.

Weather turned, cows died, years were bad. But the ranch and the land remained. People didn't necessarily.

"Grandma wanted me to come check on you. Having some problems with the heater."

Sarah forced herself to smile, still gripping the railing tightly. "I'll survive. I have all this extra insulation now."

He nodded, but he didn't move out of the stairway. He stared at her as if puzzling out some unsolved mystery.

Since she was familiar with that look, and that Dev might stand there and puzzle for a good few minutes before he got around to telling her what it was all about, she waited. She'd learned to have patience with Dev. Not that he'd ever see it that way. She still moved too fast and too decisively for him.

They balanced each other out rather nicely all in all.

"You kissed me," he finally said, eyebrows drawn together and voice equal parts lecturing and confused.

She crossed her arms over her chest, which meant resting them on her belly. "Yeah. So?"

Dev's gaze drifted there for a second and then back up to her face. "Duke's acting like…like you want more from me."

She wanted to curse her father, but instead she focused on the irritating man in front of her. "More than what?"

He scowled. "You know damn well what."

She didn't know why it hurt her feelings that he'd ask that. He had every right to speculate over her reasons for wanting him to be the father of her child. Which meant she'd have to give him a truth she wasn't too keen on laying at anyone's feet.

"I didn't get pregnant to trap you into having feelings for me if that's what you're asking. At the time, I wasn't too keen on having a Wyatt brother stomp my heart to bits, even if I did want his sperm."

Dev winced at the word *sperm* as she'd hoped he might. Honestly, men were so overly squeamish about some things. But his expression quickly sobered.

"What does 'at the time' mean?"

Sarah sighed. How could she explain how things had changed? How *she* had changed. How she wanted something from him, but didn't expect something from him. Hoped maybe, but not *expected*.

In the end, like so many things lately, it all boiled down to their baby. She unfolded her arms and placed her palms on either side of the round lump. "I love this baby and I don't even know him yet. I can't imagine what it'll feel like when he's real and in my arms and I'm in charge of keeping him alive. I've had to come to terms with being that vulnerable, and I imagine I've got a ways to go, but I'm not so afraid of it anymore."

"Of what?"

"Love."

Any confusion or effort to understand disappeared from his face. Emotion shuttered away to blankness. It made her want to cry, but she blinked back the tears.

For a moment, he'd wanted to know. Maybe he didn't like her answers, but he'd wanted to understand.

"Grandma will be wanting to feed you now that you're up," he grumbled, then turned on a heel and disappeared down the stairs.

Sarah stayed where she was for a few moments. It was hard to let him walk away, because she was better suited to be a bulldozer. Still, she'd learned a thing or two. Dev needed a good hard push sometimes, but more often than not he needed time to work out a problem to his own satisfaction. He was an internal kind of guy.

It was just a shame so often he came to the *wrong* conclusion, that she'd have to talk him out of.

DEV FELT AS IF someone had shoved a cattle prod into his chest. There was a disquieting, painful buzzing lodged there and no matter how much distance he put between him and Sarah, it remained.

What the hell was she talking about *love* for?

He paused outside the kitchen. Too many of his family members were in there and would read something in his expression, in his demeanor. He needed a moment to bury it.

He took a deep breath and listened to the voices in the kitchen.

"I think town is the safer option when she's *that* pregnant."

Dev closed his eyes. Oh, they couldn't be so stupid as to think they could make a decision about Sarah without her in the room. She would not handle that well *at all*.

He glanced back at the stairs. She'd waited to follow him, but not long. She took the last step and moved toward him, her expression oddly…blank.

He wasn't sure he'd ever seen that kind of expression on her face before. She was a woman who was not afraid to show how she felt. Well, that wasn't true. She didn't care to show off sad or sweet, but pregnancy had brought down some of those walls.

God help him.

She came to stand next to him and cocked her head.

"We need to convince her it's her own idea. She'll never agree if we tell her to do it. We'll have to be careful about how we approach her…"

Dev closed his yes. Oh, no. No, no, no. This was not going to go well. When he reopened them and glanced down at Sarah he saw just what he'd expected.

Wild, untethered fury.

"Sarah, why don't you calm down before—"

She shook her head and brought her fingers to her lips.

"I'm not going to stand here and eavesdrop," he whispered to her, though he supposed the whispering kind of undercut his grand stand against listening in.

"We'll just pretend it's random," Cecilia was saying from inside the kitchen. "Sarah, Dev, and Rach and Tucker. That's four in town. Four in Bonesteel, and leaves us five here. It's not such a bad split."

Dev felt his own anger begin to simmer. That wasn't just *random*. He and Rachel both had physical limitations, what with Rachel being legally blind. It wasn't just *coincidence* they thought it was a good idea to ship him into town.

When he had a ranch to run *and* was the whole reason danger was at their doorstep in the first place.

Sarah raised an eyebrow at him and gave him a smirk, as if to say *see, I'm not overreacting*.

Dev grunted and charged in, though Sarah was right at his heels. The conversation came to a clear stop as they entered. Felicity and Cecilia were standing in the kitchen area, likely helping Grandma Pauline with kitchen duties. Gage was sitting at the table, helping feed his daughter breakfast.

Dev knew Brady, Tucker, Duke and Rachel were out doing chores at both ranches, but would likely be in soon. He hoped they would be here soon enough to get an earful.

"So, you have to be careful huh?" Sarah demanded of her sisters, hands on her hips.

Felicity and Cecilia shared a look, while Grandma Pauline kept cleaning and Gage kept feeding.

Felicity sighed. "Now, Sarah. We're only trying to look out for you. You should be close to the hospital. That's just common sense," Felicity insisted.

"How come up to this point it was common sense to keep us all together?"

"We're not saying you should stay in town alone, Sarah," Cecilia replied.

"No, you want to ship the guy with the limp off with her," Dev added. "Like some sort of weakest link eradication."

Cecilia frowned at him. "You're both being overly sensitive. We're working out best options to keep *everyone* safe, including and most especially the children." She gestured at Sarah's stomach.

"Why on earth would she be safe with me? I think we're well aware I'm a big part of the target here. I got a note just like the rest of my brothers. I'm the one who actually *knows* Anth. Why don't you women take her off to town? No one's threatening you."

"Oh, Dev," Gage said sadly.

Dev didn't even have time to ask Gage what he meant before all four women in the kitchen were glaring daggers at him. Even one-year-old Claire seemed to give him a dirty look.

The door to the mudroom opened and Tucker and Brady came in, though they both stopped short at the tension in the room.

"Abort. Save yourselves," Gage muttered, earning him a light slap on the shoulder from his wife before Felicity swooped in and picked up Claire.

"I'll just go change her and you all can have the knock-out drag-out fight you're so desperate to have." She stopped in front of Sarah, expression going sad. "I hope you know we're all just looking out for you."

If Sarah was mollified, she didn't show it. She turned her anger toward Brady and Tucker at the door. "So, which scenario do you two agree with?"

"Uh," Tucker said. "What were the options again?"

"What happens if you're stuck out here in labor while there's danger?" Cecilia demanded of Sarah, ignoring Tucker's question.

"What happens if I'm off in town in labor while there's danger? Not much different, to my way of thinking."

"A lot quicker to get you to the hospital though. Brady agrees with me," Cecilia said resolutely. "Everyone agrees because it's the most sensible, reasonable option."

Sarah took exception to that. Brady tried to smooth things over, which only got *his* wife angry at him. Gage cracked a joke which made *everyone* mad until the voices all rose over each other and the entire kitchen was just an unholy din that made Dev's temples pound.

The clanging bell echoed through the kitchen, making everyone wince, but also bringing the arguing and shouting to a dead silence. No one dared break it until Grandma Pauline said her piece.

"How did we weather last year?" she demanded. "Going off in different directions? A few of you did, and what happened? I'll tell you what happened. You got your butts kicked—every time—except when you got it through your thick skulls to ask for help. Now you." Grandma Pauline turned and pointed at Sarah.

Sarah blinked, even kind of leaned toward Dev as if she could hide behind him and avoid Grandma's lecture.

"You're nine months pregnant in the dead of winter and acting like a stubborn mule. And you!" She moved the pointed finger to him. "Are acting like an egotistical teenager who can't get it through his head that not *everything* is about him." She huffed out a breath. "And the rest of you are shouting out orders without asking anyone how they feel about them—which is not how a family does things. Now, we're going to start over, and we're going to act like a family—*not* a military institution, *not* a high school cafeteria, and most especially *not* like one of those god-awful reality TV programs."

"That you love to watch," Gage muttered, ever attempting to lighten a moment.

Sarah sighed heavily, massaging her stomach like she did when it was paining her but not a contraction. "Grandma's right. We need to talk. Really talk. And I think most of all, we need to stick together." She looked up at Dev, something unreadable in her expression. "How can one man beat us if we all stick together?"

Dev didn't know how to answer that question. The truth was, Ace had always seemed to win—even escaping the Sons of the Badlands, even being raised by Grandma Pauline, it hadn't saved them from everything. Not the first terrible years of their childhood. Not their mother's death. It certainly hadn't solved any of the rage inside of him that he'd forever be cursed by who and what his father was.

Even now, Ace was dead, but they were still in danger. Still trying to figure out how to fight bad with good—almost as if good could never permanently win.

But Sarah rubbed her stomach and something shifted in his chest. There was a baby in there—one that would be making his appearance very soon. That baby didn't deserve to be born into a world of fear and gravity. He didn't deserve what Dev had been forced to endure as a child.

Maybe Dev had a hard time believing good could win—maybe he'd even given up on truly winning—but there was a child that needed more from him than giving up.

"He won't beat us," Dev managed. Maybe he'd failed everything up to this point, and maybe he'd never be a

father to that child, but the baby *was* his. Part of him.
Part of Sarah.

No matter the consequences, he'd fight to give that
baby something better.

Chapter Seven

Trying to find consensus amidst the varying opinions of fourteen people was, to Sarah's way of thinking, impossible.

She'd managed to talk almost everyone out of the whole ship-her-off-to-town plan—at least for another few days. Everyone wanted to "reevaluate" after her doctor's appointment on Tuesday.

Eventually she'd given up. She'd tried to help Grandma Pauline with kitchen chores but had been shooed away. She'd tried to help Felicity with Claire, but Claire had been taking a nap and, well, it sounded like a fine idea to Sarah.

She was tired and uncomfortable and grumpy, and a good sleep in a quiet room was just what she needed. Especially since no one would let her *do* anything.

But it would require the endless trek up the stairs. Sarah looked up the staircase. Never in her life had it looked so gigantic. May as well have been Mount Everest.

She could go doze on the recliner in the living room, but with so many people coming and going it wouldn't be very restful. It also wasn't the image she wanted to present right now. She didn't want people to see her tired or worn out—they'd worry about the drive time to the hospital and anything else.

No, better to do the resting in her own room.

Still, she stood at the bottom of the stairs, grimacing, and wishing there was any other option.

She heard footsteps behind her, turned to see Dev step into the hallway. He still had his coat on, though it was unzipped, plus a stocking hat and gloves.

"You okay?"

Sarah let out a hefty sigh. "I want to take a nap. My bed is very far away."

He seemed to consider this, then started walking toward her. "Come on," he grumbled. He made a move like he was going to take her arm, but in the end he just kept walking, passed her and then went into the short hallway that led to his room.

Growing up it had been a laundry room, but after Dev's accident he hadn't been able to use the stairs for quite some time so his brothers had renovated the room into a bedroom.

She imagined he could move upstairs now, but he hadn't.

He pointed at his bed—which was made. An odd detail to notice, but she never made her bed. Then again Duke hadn't been a stickler for household cleanliness like Grandma Pauline was.

"Knock yourself out."

"You're going to let me sleep in your bed?"

"Yeah. Why not?"

An excellent question. It wasn't a big deal or anything all that amazing—but the idea of crawling into his bed had her thinking about an intimacy she didn't have with him.

You've slept together.

But not in one of their beds. Not even in one of their

houses. It had been in a hotel room and she barely remembered it.

He won't be in bed with you now. Get a grip.

Right. "Well, what are you going to do?"

He pulled a drawer open and grabbed a pair of thick socks. "Told Tuck I'd let him borrow a pair since he's a moron who stepped in a giant puddle. Just getting these to take back out to him. Lots of chores to do."

So he was doing chores with Tuck. Which was good. No one was going off on their own.

And it was weird standing in his room with him. "Well, thanks for the bed."

He shrugged. "No problem. Door doesn't lock but I'll let everyone know so they don't bother you."

"Oh, don't do that. I don't want them thinking I need a nap."

"But you do need a nap."

"I don't *need* one. I want one because nobody will let me do anything. But if they're worried I'm too tired or whatever it starts the move-me-to-town discussion all over again."

"It isn't such a terrible idea."

She frowned up at him. "See?"

"It's a good thirty miles to the hospital from here. If the roads are bad when you're in labor…"

"I've discussed that with my doctor, Dev. She wasn't concerned. First-time labor is rarely fast, and so far my contractions are sporadic at worst."

"Well, we'll see what she says next week, won't we?" His expression changed as she massaged her side. She wasn't feeling any contractions, just a general ache of her stomach being stretched to capacity.

His expression now was like the expression he'd gotten on his face when he'd started saying Anth wouldn't beat them. A determination and fire she couldn't remember seeing in him since he'd been a teenager. It made her heart do wild windmills in her chest.

"I could come with," he said after a long while.

"To my doctor's appointment?"

"Yeah."

The cartwheeling died because it was no kind offer. It wasn't about wanting to be a part of it. "You just want to make sure I don't lie about what the doctor says."

He held her gaze, so serious and…direct. "No."

"Then why?" Sarah demanded. She wasn't falling for it. She knew him well enough to know this was all about having his way. Not about…what she wanted it to be about.

"Listen. If we settle things with Anth—"

"When we beat him, you mean."

"Sure, whatever. I'm just saying, if there's no danger and everything is settled—"

"Everything will be settled. No *if*s about it."

Dev scrubbed his hands over his face. "Why do you have to be so infuriating?"

"It's only infuriating because I'm right. Maybe you should just defer to me more often."

He snorted. "Like you'd want that. You live for an argument."

"I wouldn't go that far."

"I would."

"Seems to me that you're the one arg—"

"Would you shut up and let me say my piece before I change my mind?"

Sarah was surprised into silence if only because for as often as Dev got annoyed with her, argued and bickered with her, he rarely ever snapped in this way. A loss of temper. As if he was actually letting himself *care*.

"All right," she said, some odd mixture of anxiety and hope twining around her heart like a vise.

"You weren't totally off base about the guilt complex things and the less-than-my-brothers thing. I know I'm not as good as my brothers. I figure that's just fact, and you can close your big mouth and not argue with me for once so I can finish what I'm trying to say."

She snapped her mouth shut, though it took some willpower not to defend him to himself. Still, he was addressing a thing she'd said—a real, emotional, important thing. And that was some kind of amazing progress.

"But I'm not my father. I don't want to hurt anyone, and… Grandma was right. I've been thinking about my role in this whole thing selfishly. Who I am and what I am, but what Cecilia said about…protecting the children. The kid is part of me, even if I don't take any role as father. Maybe I'm not as noble or righteous as my brothers, but I… I had a bad father. The worst kind. I know what that's like, and I know how terrible the world can be, and no child deserves that."

"Our son would never…" She stopped herself from finishing the sentence when he glared at her.

He was trying to say…something. She might not understand where he was going, but it was important. He was actually showing her some of his feelings and emotions and she wanted to encourage that. Always.

"As long as Anth is dealt with, I want…" He blew out a long, tortuous breath. "I want to be part of it. Not passively like I was planning. But a father. A real father. The kind who protects his kid and gives him or her the best life he can."

Sarah couldn't remember a time she'd ever been fully speechless, but she couldn't think of a word to say. Not one word. All she could do was stand there, tears welling in her eyes and emotion clogging her throat.

His scowl deepened. "You said I could. You said you wanted me to."

Sarah nodded, trying to control her emotions that wanted to overflow. "I mean it," she managed to croak.

He shoved his hands into his pockets and scowled. "Well, good then. Anth has to be taken care of first, but… Once he is… Well. Yeah."

Sarah forced herself to take a deep breath. He wanted to be a father to their baby. It was what she'd hoped for, what she'd been certain *eventually* she'd be able to convince him to want as well. But this wasn't… As much as she'd believed he would, she hadn't ever considered how he'd tell her, or when, or what she'd want to say in response.

She should thank him. Or hug him. Or say it was good and take her nap, but Sarah had never been any good at not trying for the mile when an inch was given. "And what about us?"

Dev blinked then, looking a bit like he'd been stricken. "What do you mean?"

She knew full well he understood what she meant, but if he needed to hear it, so be it. "If you're going to be a dad, what does that make us?"

He took a step away from her, hands so deep in his pockets it was a wonder they didn't break through the fabric. "W-what we've always been. Friends."

"I don't think—"

Jamison appeared in the doorway, which had the words drying up in her mouth. Jamison was supposed to be in Bonesteel. Not standing in Dev's bedroom doorway, grave and imposing.

"Dev. Sarah. Sorry to interrupt, but we need you in the kitchen."

Dev was glad for the interruption, or so he thought until he walked into the kitchen and all his brothers were there and worse, so much worse, Liza—tear-stained and not doing anything to cover that up.

Liza who never cried. Who was so strong and tough and thumbed her nose at danger and threats.

"What is it?" Sarah asked.

Jamison sighed and gestured to the table. "This was nailed to my door this morning. At home."

Dev leaned forward with Sarah. A piece of paper lay on the table. It wasn't like the handwritten It's Not Over note. This had been typed and had a lot more text.

"It looks like a court document," Dev muttered.

"Not exactly."

Dev skimmed the writing on the paper, then went back to the beginning and read it word for word, his body getting colder and heart getting heavier.

Jamison Wyatt
Crimes:
   The subject has been the perpetrator of a wide variety of crimes since childhood. A history of lying, stealing, and the repeated, malicious torture and killing of his own kin.
Sentencing:
   For these acts of violence, treason and destruction, I do hereby sentence Jamison Wyatt to death. This will be meted out at the judge's discretion through the method J. Wyatt deemed acceptable through his own actions against his own brethren, for personal gain.
—AW

"I don't understand," Sarah whispered. "I don't understand."

"Kin and brethren. He means the Sons." Dev shook his head because he didn't understand either. "We didn't know he existed. How could Anth have anything to do with the Sons?"

"He was there, though, when Ace tried to kill you," Brady pointed out. "So at some point after we were out of the fold, he was brought in."

"I was in the fold," Liza said, her voice scratchy. "There were only a few years between when Jamison and I escaped and I went back to try and save my sister. He was never mentioned. I never once heard about some secret son of Ace's. I know they didn't trust me or anything, but I'm pretty sure I would have known about that."

"I take it no one else got one of these," Jamison said flatly.

Dev exchanged looks with his brothers. They all were just as bewildered as he was.

"It says one of six," Sarah said, her voice still little more than a whisper.

"What?" Jamison demanded.

Sarah leaned forward and pointed at the right-hand corner of the paper. In smaller text, there was a 1/6.

"I just figured it was the number of pages printed out," Liza said, frowning down at the paper.

"Six is no coincidence. He's not singling you out," Dev muttered. "He's taking us one by one."

Liza buried her face in her hands. "This is supposed to be over."

She was right. It was supposed to be over. For all of them. He should have told this secret last year—if he had, maybe it would be over.

But he couldn't rewind and fix things then—so he

had to fix them now. He looked back at the paper. "Look. He's given us this document. It's some kind of warning. He could have just taken us all out, one by one, last year. He's had all this time. Instead he's doing some elaborate Ace-like plan. Which means we've got the time to shore up our protections. Maybe there are even clues in this thing. Maybe it gives us the opportunity to work through it before he can do anything."

"And if we can't?" Liza demanded. She glared up at Dev, but tears were tracking down her cheeks.

"Liza…" Jamison said, sounding wounded.

"We stick together," Brady said firmly. "We protect each other. It got us through last year. It'll get us through this."

"If there are clues here, and we can figure them out, we can be ready for him. Not just keep Jamison safe, but take Anth down. He's giving us the opportunity to win. He's giving us a fair fight."

"None of this is fair," Liza said, pushing away from the table. "I need some air," she muttered, then slammed out of the kitchen.

Jamison closed his eyes, then rubbed his hands over his face. Sarah gave him a pat on the shoulder.

"I'll go sit with her."

He nodded grimly. Once both women were gone, Jamison slowly turned back to them. For a few seconds, all six of them stood in the kitchen in utter silence.

Dev had promised himself he'd fight for his child, but now his brother had been specifically singled out. He didn't need any realizations to know what to do now.

"It's one of six. Which means we have six chances—six chances not just to fight Anth, but to take him down. He's taking us one by one. And warning us. There's something to this…performance. Some code or something—like Ace had."

"Good. Another Ace to fight," Brady said disgustedly.

"Who knows if he's the only one?" Tucker added.

"He's the only one," Dev replied. "There's no way Ace could have kept multiple children a secret. He certainly wouldn't have time to warp all of them."

"You hope," Brady said.

"This is it. I'm sure of it. Our last ghost to fight."

"How can you be sure of it?" Jamison asked, his gaze still on the door Liza had gone out of.

"Nothing else adds up," Dev said. "Maybe Ace was crazy. Maybe the Sons are evil. But the numbers always add up. Anth is our last hurdle. The North Star group has mostly disbanded the Sons. All those federal raids left them with next to no resources, loyalty or power. If there was anyone else to come after us, Anth would have recruited them. We would have heard Sons rumblings. But no, they've been thrown in jail or they ran. All that's left is Anth, and us. So we just have to figure out what he's trying to tell us and beat him at his own game."

"If we can stay alive," Jamison muttered.

"The Sons haven't beaten us yet, Jamison. I don't intend for that to change, do you?" Dev demanded.

Gage chuckled. "He sounded just like you, J." Gage gave a mock shiver. "Downright creepy."

Jamison frowned at Gage, but his expression had changed. The hurt and worry over Liza were still there, but that battle light was back. He looked down at the paper. "What kind of clues could there be?"

"Let's read it again—line by line—and go from there." Dev took an empty seat and waited for Jamison to take the other one. He looked at each of his brothers, sitting

around Grandma Pauline's table. They'd been here before—too many times to count.

This would be the last time. Dev was determined.
"We'll beat him. We have to." There were too many lives
at stake not to.

Chapter Eight

Sarah wasn't sure she'd ever seen Liza so visibly distraught, and Liza had not had an easy life. She'd been in danger for most of it. So it was beyond concerning she'd been so visibly upset—even if she had every right to be.

She was sitting on the back step. Cash sitting in front of her, wagging his tail as if waiting for a game of fetch. It was only then Sarah realized there was a mangy ball at Liza's feet.

Sarah moved to sit next to Liza on the back porch step, but it was a narrow step and would have been a tight fit even if she didn't have a giant belly impeding her way.

"For heaven's sake, don't sit here," Liza said, wiping her face with her sleeve. She popped to her feet. "You don't need to cheer me up."

"I'm not here to cheer you up. I'm just here to hold your hand. Also to throw that poor dog a ball since you won't."

Liza rolled her eyes, but she bent down and picked up the ball. She heaved it with impressive power, and Cash took off like a bullet.

She turned to face Sarah, eyes puffy and face blotchy.

Sarah's heart twisted. She'd never seen Liza like this. "This isn't like you, Liza. You're usually more angry than…"

"A whiny, crying mess?"

"Well, I wasn't going to use those words."

Liza smirked, but it died quickly. She looked out over the horizon. It was cold, but there wasn't much of a wind today, so it was bearable in her heavy sweaters. Especially standing here in the midday sun.

Cash brought back the ball and Liza hurled it again.

"We really thought it was over, you know? That's the part I just can't… Our fathers are dead. The Sons are rubble. I shouldn't still have to be afraid."

"Does the fear ever really go away? Jamison is a sheriff's deputy. We both know that an illness can come in and take someone away. I think fear is just a part of loving."

Liza seemed to mull that over, but then she shook her head. "I don't think normal people have to fear the way we do."

"Maybe not, but I can't… We survived last year. Threat after threat and we worked together and survived and kept everyone safe. We weren't unscathed, but we're all together. I can't believe we won't be able to do that again."

Liza sighed heavily. "It's not that I don't think we can survive. It's not even the fear exactly. I…" She kicked at the short railing. "We'd started the whole process to adopt."

"Oh, Liza."

"But we can hardly bring kids home with death threats nailed to the door." She shook her head, staring hard at the horizon. Cash hadn't reappeared with the ball. He'd bark occasionally, so Sarah assumed he was off chasing a squirrel or maybe Duke or Rachel coming in from the fields.

"We'd be really good parents to more than just Gigi.

It isn't fair we can't give some kids what Duke and Eva gave us." Sarah was the only child Duke and Eva had adopted, but they'd fostered Sarah's four other sisters, and then had Rachel biologically. And Liza was right, they'd always given the girls—biological, adopted or fostered, a loving home. Even after Eva had died.

Sarah placed her hands on her own belly. So much of why she wanted to be a mother was because of Duke and Eva. She'd wanted to be like them—give like them, love like them.

Briefly she thought of Dev saying he actually wanted to be a father, and how much that gave Sarah the hope she could *really* be like Duke and Eva—a partnership raising kids together.

But Jamison being specifically targeted was a much bigger issue at hand. "We're going to survive this. All of us intact. When we do, you'll have your chance to adopt. I know it's an awful thing to have to put it off, but—"

"But what if this is the time we don't win, Sarah? Even if we do, how many times are we going to think it's over when it's not?" Liza's eyes were getting shiny again.

Cash's barking was growing incessant, but Sarah focused on Liza. "As many times as it takes, because... Well, you love Jamison. You always have."

"Of course I do."

"So, you can be mad at the circumstance. You can think it's unfair, because it is, but it's Jamison. So we'll all suck it up and keep him safe, whether we should have to or not. You can be mad as hell about that, Liza. No one's stopping you."

"You're trying to stop me with all this wisdom."

"It's not wisdom. It's just common sense. You can feel what you feel and still suck it up and do what you have to."

"Sarah sense. Life's a crapshoot so suck it up and do what you can."

Sarah lifted her hands. "Hard to argue with that kind of sense, isn't it?"

Liza stepped forward and pulled Sarah into a hug—which was notable since neither of them were particularly touchy-feely. Still, Sarah could tell Liza needed some kind of comfort. Jamison would comfort her too, but Liza would convince herself it was only to make her feel better—not because he actually believed that they could beat the threats against him.

"I do think they're right. The letter is a warning," Sarah said, hoping to soothe Liza more. "For whatever reason, this Anth wants us to know he's coming. Which gives us a much better chance to win."

"A man who can wait like this one has isn't stupid. If he's giving us a warning…" Liza shook her head. "That could be just to mess with our heads. After all, he accuses Jamison of killing his own kin and we know he hasn't and never would. I was with him all those years in the Sons, so I know. He didn't kill anyone."

"He's been responsible for the death of Sons members since leaving, though," Sarah pointed out, pulling away from Liza's arms. "Jailed some too, which may have led to their deaths, including Ace. If we look at it from their perspective, maybe Anth really does believe Jamison is responsible for killing his brethren. Maybe Ace made sure he believed it."

Liza grimaced. "I don't know how any of them could think the Sons were ever Jamison's kin, even when he was stuck in there. Even Ace."

"But you said it yourself. Another son of Ace's was never mentioned. No one named Anth was around when you were stuck in there. Maybe this guy only knows what Ace has told him about the Sons and the Wyatt brothers."

"Maybe. The horrible part is it's all possible. We at least *knew* Ace was our enemy before. Even knowing he was a dangerous psychopath gave us something to go on. We don't know anything about Anth Wyatt."

Sarah thought about the fact that she did. She knew that she shared blood with the man. That her mother had been afraid enough of her own son to ask someone else to take her brand-new baby with another man.

Technically, she herself was Anth's kin and brethren too. Did he know that? Did he consider the Wyatt brothers his kin? And why had he used those two words? Repeatedly?

Cash's barking had stopped, but he hadn't run back with the ball. A little flutter of panic started in her chest, but Sarah pushed it away. There were a million things Cash could be out there chasing.

Including bad men.

Sarah whistled for him, called his name, but he didn't reappear.

Dread skittered up her spine. Wouldn't Anth expect Jamison to come right here after that letter—to his *real* brethren? Wouldn't he be able to plan some kind of ambush?

Sarah grabbed Liza's arm. "We have to get inside."

Liza's eyes widened, but she didn't argue. Clearly she understood Sarah's train of thought. She reached for the storm door, pulling it open. An explosion sounded and the glass shattered as they hurried through it. Sarah dropped to her knees. She tried to wriggle away from Liza, who was using her body to shield Sarah from the falling glass.

"You're going to get hurt," Sarah said, giving another ineffective push on Liza's body.

"That's the point. Better me than you and your baby. Can you crawl forward? Get to the main door?"

There was another gunshot, but no shattering glass this time.

"That came from inside," Liza said, pushing Sarah toward the door that led into the kitchen. "They're shooting back."

Sarah crawled over the concrete floor of the mudroom. It was awkward and painful in her current state, and the panicking beat of her heart didn't exactly help her arms stay steady as she tried to crawl without cutting herself on the glass.

She reached up to grab the knob, but another shot rang out, splintering into the house somewhere too close to Sarah for comfort. She snatched her hand back and huddled lower.

Liza scooted up next to her, but before she could pound on the door, it opened. Then, before Sarah had a chance to crawl forward, she was being pulled inside and immediately out of the doorway.

Despite her extra girth, Dev had moved her quite easily, Liza scurrying in behind her. Dev practically had Sarah in his lap by the time she looked around the room. Liza was sitting on the floor and leaning against the wall, breathing heavily. Jamison and Tucker were at the window above the kitchen sink, guns pointed out the opening. With no words spoken, Gage took the gun from Jamison and replaced him at the window. Jamison fell to his knees next to Liza.

"I'm okay," she said before Jamison could say or do anything. She reached out and cupped his cheek. "Might have a few cuts from the glass, but nothing serious. Would have been worse, but Sarah figured things out."

"I'm not sure I figured them out so much as Cash…

He was barking. Then he stopped." Sarah tried not to think the worst. After all, no gunshot had gone off before Cash's barking stopped. He couldn't have been killed. *Please.* Sarah looked up at Dev, who was smoothing down her hair. "He's out there."

"That's okay. He's a smart dog. He'll be all right," Dev said roughly.

Then another, more horrifying thought pierced Sarah's mind. She whipped her head toward Liza. "Is Gigi with Nina and Brianna?"

"And Cody. We told them about the note before coming here, so they're being careful," Liza said, but she had paled, and she looked to Jamison as if seeking reassurance.

No one mentioned that someone had snuck past all the security defenses Cody had set up around the property—and if someone could do that here, surely they could do it at Cody's house in Bonesteel.

"He didn't kill anyone, and he could have," Dev said. "Maybe this is just another warning."

But it was a warning with bullets, and Sarah knew that meant things were escalating. Danger was well and truly here, and they somehow had to find the strength to fight it again.

WHOEVER WAS OUT there stopped returning fire after Sarah and Liza were safely inside.

After minutes of endless waiting, there'd been a heated argument about how they would go about determining if the gunman had left, had been injured in return fire or was waiting them out.

Tucker had called Duke and Rachel immediately, having them take shelter at the Knight house since that's where they'd been closest to while dealing with the cattle feeding. He'd kept them on speakerphone, so if anything changed on their end, they'd know about it right away and could send help. Brady had Cody on speakerphone for the same reason.

Grandma Pauline was upstairs with Felicity and Claire, and Cecilia was still at work at the reservation. They'd texted her to stay put for the time being.

"It's been long enough. If we don't go out soon, we're going to lose daylight," Jamison said, pacing the length of the kitchen.

"Maybe that's what he's counting on," Liza insisted.

"Maybe, but how will we know if some of us don't look?" Dev asked. He was doing his best to remain still, to remain calm. Not to let his brain go back to when that gunshot had gone off and they hadn't known if Liza and Sarah were okay.

It had been a brief second before Tucker had looked out the window and been able to see them crawl inside. But it had been a terrible, bleak second.

"Any luck on those cameras, Cody?" Brady said into his phone.

"No. Whatever he did, he cut my mainframe. I don't have any video feed—or anything recorded."

"How would he do that?" Dev asked.

"Not a clue." Cody didn't have to be in the same physical space as Dev for him to be able to read Cody's frustration.

"We have to do a sweep," Jamison demanded. "Nobody goes alone, and we don't do anything stupid. But we have to look."

"He's right," Gage added. "We can't just sit in here and twiddle our thumbs. Especially when we know he's cut the video. Who knows what other security measures Cody put up have been tampered with?"

"Why don't two of you search the main area around the house. Have Duke and Rachel drive over, keeping an eye out on that end. I'll pack up the girls here and drive for you guys—which will give me a look around the highway side of the property. There's no way we can reach everything, but we can scope out a lot."

"He's right," Dev agreed. "If we do a quick sweep and don't find anything, we'll need all hands on deck to keep a lookout through the night."

Liza scowled, but she didn't pose an argument.

"Rachel and I are on our way," Duke said from Tucker's speakerphone.

"Nina and I will be on our way with the girls in a few," Cody said from Brady's speakerphone.

"We'll go out," Dev said to Jamison. "Search around the house and the stables."

"Why you?" Sarah demanded at the same time Liza did.

"I know where everything should be better than anyone," Dev said to Sarah. "And Jamison is the best shot," he said to Liza.

"Well, now, I wouldn't go *that* far," Gage muttered.

"He is and we all know it. So, he'll have my back and I can see if anything is off."

"Don't you think we should all agree and not just listen to orders from you?" Sarah said. She looked terribly uncomfortable, fidgeting in the kitchen chair like she couldn't find a position that didn't hurt her back. They'd tried to convince her to lie down or at least go relax in the recliner in the living room, but she'd refused.

"We'll never get anything done if we wait for consensus," Jamison said gently. He was holding Liza's hand. Even though she looked furious, she wasn't arguing anymore. He gave Dev a nod.

Dev followed Jamison to the door, shrugging on his coat as he went. He looked back once at Sarah. Her face was a storm of fury, but she didn't say a word, so Dev followed Jamison into the mudroom. There were two bullet holes in the siding of the house. One had come through the window of the storm door before Liza and Sarah had a chance to close it. The second had sliced through the bottom aluminum portion of the storm door and into the wall of the mudroom.

Dev tried not to think too deeply about how close Liza and Sarah had been to those bullet holes—and how there'd been nothing to do to get them inside any quicker except shoot back in the general direction of where the original shots had come from.

"Head for where the shots came from first?"

"Surely he's moved on from there," Jamison said. He had his gun in his hand, gaze sweeping the vast landscape in front of them. The rolling hills of the ranch were brown this time of year, dotted with patches of snow from the last accumulation they'd had.

"Unless we hit him." Dev hoped to God they had. Let this be over. Now.

Jamison grunted, which wasn't an argument, so they headed for the stables. Dev looked around for anything off. Shells, debris of any kind. A footprint in the patches of snow. Anything that shouldn't fit the normal day-to-day of the ranch.

Nothing out of the ordinary…except a sound. He and Jamison stopped, ears straining.

"It sounds like…scratching," Dev said. Then he broke out in a run, though it jarred his bad leg. He made it to the back of the stables, and then there was a bark. It was coming from the old chicken coop that hadn't been used in years.

"How the hell did Cash get in there?" Jamison muttered, jogging with Jamison to the old coop. Someone had used an old pipe to latch the door closed. Dev supposed he should be relieved whoever had been out here hadn't hurt Cash.

Dev pulled the pipe out so the door swung open. Cash flew out, snarling and barking. He darted off due north and Jamison and Dev exchanged a glance.

"I guess we follow."

Dev nodded, pointed at the shells littering the ground on this side of the stables. "This was his shooting point. Then he ran away?"

Cash darted back, then ran off again, the barking becoming more frenzied. The darting becoming more insistent. Quietly, gun tight in hand, Dev followed. They wouldn't sneak up on anyone with Cash losing it like this, but they didn't have a choice.

Dev and Jamison stopped on a dime at the top of a small rise of land. The grazing pasture stretched out before them, but not far off was a body. A very still, face-down-in-the-dirt body.

Dev started forward, but Jamison grabbed his arm and stopped him. "Could be a trap."

Dev gestured around. "We can pretty much see everything. Cody will check out the trees over there when he drives in, but that's too far away to get any good shot off on us—even with a high-powered weapon."

Jamison frowned, but he let go of Dev's arm and together they started forward. They took careful steps, guns at the ready, eyes trained around them until they reached the lifeless body. There was a gun still in the man's hand, but there was also a piece of paper pinned to the back of his shirt.

"It's set up just like my note," Jamison said, crouching to get a better look. Dev kicked the gun out of the lifeless man's hands.

"'Mike Christopher,'" Jamison read aloud. "'Crimes: armed robbery, battery, second-degree murder, but most of all—failure. Sentencing: death by firing squad.' Signed AW."

"Hardly a firing squad," Dev muttered. There was one bullet hole and it was clear the shot had been close range.

"Anth thinks he's judge, jury and executioner," Jamison said, looking away from the body and around them as if he could see something that would make any of this make sense.

"Then why did he send someone else to kill you?" Dev crouched too and studied the paper. It was typed like Jamison's, and set up exactly the same. Sort of like a court document, but more informal.

"Kill my family, you mean. That gunshot was meant for Liza."

But the more Dev thought about it, the more he wondered. Idly he petted Cash, who'd finally come to sit next to them now that he'd led them where he wanted them to be. "I'm not so sure it was meant for anyone. Maybe it was just to scare us. To scatter us like this." Jamison looked around them. No sign of another soul. "He sure didn't give this guy much of a chance. He got off two shots—then got murdered for his trouble."

"I think that means he didn't hit his target, Dev." Jamison stood, pulling his phone out of his pocket. "I'll call County. They'll want to do their own investigation, and get the ME to take the body."

"Sure," Dev agreed. Something about this was off to Dev, but that didn't mean more eyes trying to figure it out was a bad thing. "Good boy," Dev murmured, giving Cash a scratch behind the ears. "I bet we can even convince Grandma Pauline to let you sleep inside to-night." They'd need the extra lookout, because one thing was for sure.

This wasn't over. It was only the beginning.

Chapter Nine

The house was even more crowded now, though Sarah had to admit it helped her nerves feel less…frayed, she supposed. She was still nervous and scared. She kept thinking every little unexpected noise was a gunshot, but there was always someone to talk to or a kid or dog to play with.

The local police came and Jamison and Dev headed outside with them to show them all they'd found. Liza, Nina and Gage went upstairs to put their girls to bed. Once the police had finished their investigation and the removal of the body of the man who'd shot at them, Brady and Tucker drove out to the reservation to pick up Cecilia.

There was no more arguing, and no one tried to go off on their own. The aftermath was subdued.

Sarah was dead on her feet, and she knew she should go upstairs and sleep while she could. But she couldn't make herself leave the kitchen when Dev and Jamison hadn't come inside yet.

"They'll be in soon enough," Duke said gruffly from where he sat next to Grandma Pauline, working on a puzzle. They both had their reading glasses on and Sarah wanted to be amused, to feel cozily, Christmasy happy.

Instead she was jittery and anxious and…

She heard the outer door creak open, followed by the

sound of stomping feet. When Dev and Jamison stepped inside, they'd shed their coats, but snowflakes still clung to their hair and Dev's beard.

Dev frowned at her. "I sure hope you're planning on cooking that baby a while longer. Roads are going to be a mess tonight."

"That is the plan."

"If Brady doesn't get back, you're full out of luck on the emergency medical personnel."

"I wasn't really planning on your brother delivering my baby, EMT training or no. And if you're trying to make some point about me staying in town—"

"I'm not trying to make any points. I'm just saying," he grumbled.

The kitchen descended into an uncomfortable silence. All eyes were on them and Sarah felt suddenly…see-through. Which was silly. They were always bickering. There was nothing weird about this to garner *looks*.

"I'm going to run through the shower," Dev muttered, moving into the hallway back to his room. Sarah watched him go until Jamison cleared his throat.

"Police took everything they could find. They'll be investigating. We've got an unmarked car on the road watching, but that's all they could spare. I know him though. We'll still want to have lookouts all night. A lot of ways to get on the ranch without using the road."

"Felicity came up with a schedule, but I don't think anyone will be sleeping until Brady, Cecilia and Tucker are back. Except this one here." Grandma Pauline pointed to Sarah.

"Go to bed, Sarah. Get some sleep," Jamison said gently. "We've got plenty of lookouts."

She should. She was *exhausted*. These were the last few days of having the luxury of just going to sleep when she wanted. "All right," she said, even though her easy agreement clearly shocked everyone in the kitchen. She gave Duke a hug and Grandma Pauline a shoulder squeeze and left the kitchen.

Much like earlier in the day, when she got to the stairs, she stood at the bottom and dreaded the uncomfortable climb. She could hear the shuffle of feet upstairs, the hushed murmurs of parents hoping their children were asleep.

She looked down the hall. She was going to be that parent soon enough. Whether the danger was over or it kept going for weeks. She was still going to be mom. And Dev wanted to be a father.

It was a huge step. One she should be happy about—satisfied with. But Sarah didn't know how to sit back and *accept* when there was so much more to have.

So, why stop now? Danger or no, life didn't stop. Maybe it had to pause for horrible threatening notes and gunshots, but she didn't have to let that stop her completely. Besides, what if something terrible *did* happen and she hadn't gone after everything?

She marched down the hall. She could hear the sound of the shower running in the tiny closet of a bathroom closest to Dev's room. She passed that door then stepped into Dev's bedroom.

It was also tiny. Sparse.

Grandma Pauline had groused about giving the dog special treatment, but she'd relented…and even let Brownie join Cash inside. Brownie was probably up in the girls' room being petted into oblivion. But Cash had settled onto Dev's bed and thumped his tail happily as Sarah walked in.

Sarah settled herself on the bed in the most comfortable sitting position she could manage. Cash put his head in her lap and she stroked his ears. It was calming, to the point she found herself nodding off. Every time her head drooped, she jerked back awake.

After who knew how many times of that, she jerked awake and Dev was standing in the doorway in sweatpants and a T-shirt. His feet were bare and his hair was wet and he was still holding a towel. He was staring at her with his perpetual scowl.

Her heart stumbled in her chest the way it always did when he caught her off guard.

"What are you doing?" he demanded gruffly.

Sarah stifled a yawn and sat up straighter. "Waiting for you."

He scrubbed the towel against his wet hair. "Why?"

"We didn't finish our conversation earlier."

There was a slight pause before he stepped fully into the room. "We did finish it. I told you I'd be involved with the baby. The end." He stalked over to his dresser and jerked open a drawer.

"That's one part of it."

He pulled out a sweatshirt. "It's all parts of it."

"What I'll never understand about you, Dev, is you thinking I'm ever going to sit back and agree with your gruff declarations when I feel differently. You know I'm going to sit right here and poke at you until you have the conversation I want to have."

He stood completely still and didn't say anything, his back to her. She supposed because he knew she was right. She was who she was, and that wasn't a pushover or someone afraid to speak her mind.

If he didn't like that about her he was just going to have to come out and tell her point blank.

He dropped the towel in a laundry basket and pulled the sweatshirt over his head in quick, jerky movements.

"I don't know what you're trying to get at. You wanted me to be involved, with the baby or…didn't care if I was or whatever—"

"I wanted you to be," Sarah said, all those emotions crashing around inside of her making her voice crack. "I want you to be involved."

"Okay, fine, great. So, you got your way. And we're friends. What more do you want?"

She frowned. If she thought he was being deliberately obtuse she would have been really mad, but he seemed actually baffled. "I want… I just think there could be more."

"We're friends," Dev said firmly.

"We had to be more than friends to make this baby."

"No. We had to be really drunk to make this baby. And you had to be really, really persistent."

"Dev." She slid off the bed. Her heart hammered in her chest. She could poke at him, and usually get her way, but this was more than getting her way. It was being honest. It was laying herself out for rejection.

Because truth be told, all the things she felt for him, she wasn't certain he reciprocated. Why had she avoided it all this time? Because she didn't know if Dev could ever look at her and see something other than an annoying neighbor who was slightly helpful with the whole ranching situation.

But that meant she didn't know if he *could* feel something for her. Or did. The only way to know was to put herself out there.

She considered getting up and going upstairs and leaving it at that. It would keep everything the way she was comfortable with, and wasn't that important when there was a madman threatening them and shooting at them?

But she found herself stepping forward, even as Dev

stilled and looked down at her with that unreadable expression. She swallowed at her dry throat and lifted her hand to his cheek. He kept staring at her and nothing changed.

But he didn't step away. He didn't take her hand off his face. She wanted to do more. Press her mouth to his like she had back home. Hug him until something made sense and the fear melted away.

For so long she hadn't let herself feel this. She'd pushed it away. Prodded at him when what she'd always wanted to do was…this. Be there for him. Help him. *Love* him.

"I think there could be an us," she said, though her voice sounded strangled and her heart was beating so hard in her ears she could scarcely hear herself.

"Why the hell would you want there to be an us?" he asked, his voice ragged with pain. Then he stepped away from her hand and locked it all down. "We argue all the time. I'm old and grumpy and my leg doesn't work right," he said, his voice flat, his reasons just as flat.

The only way she'd ever figured to get through that shield of his was to be infuriating. "So?"

He curled his fingers in his hair like he was tempted to pull it out. "Go to bed, Sarah."

"Give me one good reason. All those things you listed? They're things I know about you. Have worked beside and cared about for most of my life. Your grumpy doesn't scare me. I don't care how many years older you are, and your reasoning is pretty bad if you're using your leg as an excuse."

"I am the son of Ace Wyatt, damn it."

He said it as if that was supposed to shock her. Or change her mind. When it was just another fact in a long line of them she'd always known. "Well, I'm the half sister of Anth Wyatt, apparently. I don't know what that has to do with anything."

"Why do you have to be such a steamroller?"

"It's the only way to get what you want."

"You don't know what you want."

"*You* apparently want me to punch you again." This time when she moved to touch him, it wasn't gently. She grabbed his forearms—to keep him there, to keep him still, to keep him connected. "If I was worried about the Wyatt blood, I wouldn't have badgered you into doing this for me. If I was worried about that... I can't even imagine. I never knew anything about my parents before this week. Not one thing. I told myself I didn't want to. Because it doesn't matter. They weren't in my life. I wish they'd had a chance to be, but... I had Duke and Eva. You had Grandma Pauline and your brothers. *That's* what matters."

"You always had Duke and Eva. I had the Sons. For years."

"So, I suppose Jamison is bad news. After all, he spent eighteen years with the Sons. And this baby? Tainted. Your blood's in there, Ace's too. Doesn't stand a chance, does he?"

"That isn't what I'm saying," Dev said, his teeth gritted.

"Then what *are* you saying?" She had to swallow at the lump in her throat. If he said he didn't feel that way—if he came out and truly rejected her—she would have to accept it. She would have to accept it and still allow his help raising the baby because she wanted him to be a father. He was still her partner in ranching. If he rejected her, she didn't get to run away or cut him out. He was always going to be here, and she'd have to suck it up and deal.

This was why you kept your stupid feelings to yourself.

But she remembered that he'd kissed her. Even if the aftermath was fuzzy. In that hotel hallway he'd kissed her. They'd made a baby together. When she touched him, he didn't bolt.

He settled.

There was something here. But it was Dev, so the only way to get to it was to fight for it. "You want to prove there's nothing here or it wouldn't work or whatever it is you're looking to prove—fine. Prove it. Kiss me."

SHE'D NEVER KNOW how for a split second Dev had been all too tempted to do just that—to shut her up, to stop this obnoxious, circular conversation, but most of all to have his arms around her.

She'd been shot at. Pregnant with his child and shot at because of her connection to him—more or less. He wanted to hold her and he wanted…

So many things he couldn't want. "Sarah." The problem was coming up with the words to get it through to her that this couldn't happen. *She* didn't want it to happen. Not really. Not for the right reasons.

"It's simple," she said, her voice maddeningly calm and her expression heartbreakingly vulnerable. Like she was laying her heart in his hands. "Kiss me. Prove there's no chemistry. We're just friends. Kiss me and prove there's *nothing* there."

He wished he could, but he remembered their night together all too well. There were all *sorts* of things there. But she was… She was Sarah, and he was him. Which was not good enough. Plain and simple. It had nothing to do with Ace and everything to do with him.

He wasn't noble. He wasn't brave. He was a failure at

all the things Jamison had tried to teach him to be when the Sons had been their lives.

Sarah slid her hands up his arms and linked her arms around his neck.

His body was a traitor, because it took all the will-power in all the world not to wrap his arms around her in return. A world of grit not to sink into what she wanted to prove. But he had to be stronger. For the both of them. For the *three* of them.

Eventually she'd realize she'd made a mistake. Maybe she would with him and the father thing too, but... A kid deserved a father who'd fight for him, even if he wasn't the best guy around. But Sarah...

She deserved the world. So he had to be a jerk. "I can be your friend and think you're hot and not have it mean anything."

She smirked up at him, arms still tight around his neck. "If you think I'm hot and it doesn't mean anything, then you can kiss me and it won't mean anything."

She wouldn't let this go. Didn't he know her? She didn't let anything go.

So, he'd have to somehow steel himself against it. Prove what he wanted to prove out of sheer force of will. Give her a bad, nothing kiss so she'd walk away understanding there was *nothing* here.

But of course the minute his mouth touched hers, he couldn't remember what he was supposed to be proving. He couldn't think past *her*. He was no saint. There was no nobility in him. One touch and he wanted more. One kiss and he wanted it all.

She opened up for him, just like she'd done at the hotel after the wedding. She wasn't drunk now, but she reacted all the same. As if this feeling had always been there, waiting underneath the surface.

He kissed her deeply, holding her tight against him. The evidence of their one night there between them, but that only made him want more. Want it all over again.

She'd said she didn't remember, but he remembered every minute, and it had tortured him for approximately nine months. To know everything could be that good, that hot, that *right* with someone who was supposed to be his friend, his business partner. The *girl* next door.

Not all this.

She slid her hands underneath his shirt, spreading her palms across his chest. He wanted to do the same, but…

He pulled his mouth from hers, though his arms stayed locked around her. "We have to stop." Had to. This was insanity on three hundred different levels.

"Why?" Sarah murmured, her fingers trailing down to the waistband of his pants.

He grabbed her wrists before she managed to get there. Thank *God*. "My grandmother and your father are in the next room. Also my dog is watching."

She looked down at Cash and then back up at him. "Well, I'll give you the family in the next room excuse." Her smile widened. "I don't think you proved your point just now."

"So there's chemistry," he grumbled, somehow both irritated and aroused by her smugness.

"Excellent chemistry."

"There is a madman out there who wants to hurt me and my brothers. You were almost in the crossfire today." Before she could open her mouth to go on and on and on, he kept talking. Focusing on reality rather than the desperate *want* raging through him. "Sarah, if Anth knows you're connected to him, it's bad enough. If he knows you mean something to me—Liza was the target there today. Don't you think?"

She frowned, her shoulders slumping. "Well, yes."

"I can't have you be a target. Not now." He lifted his hands to rest on her belly. Felt the odd rippling movement of baby inside. "This has to wait."

She studied his face, blue eyes sharp and assessing. He'd always felt like she'd seen him better than anyone. She always seemed to know what to do or say…except when she set out to irritate him. He was beginning to realize they were all purposeful. The understanding and the irritation.

Often just what he needed even if he didn't particularly *want* whatever she was pushing him toward.

"You know waiting is just going to give me more opportunity to strengthen my steamroller."

He chuckled in spite of himself. "Yeah, I'm well aware."

She let out a gusty sigh. "All right. I'll be good."

He wanted his mouth on her, so he shoved his hands in his pockets. He didn't trust her fake innocent look at all. "My butt you will."

She grinned. "Goodish?"

He grunted.

She bit her lip and he blew out a ragged breath. He couldn't convince her he was the wrong guy. Yet. There was still time. Once the danger was over, yeah, she'd come at him even harder, but she'd have a baby. Surely that would open her eyes. Surely having a real-life baby to take care of would make her realize he wasn't up to the task.

If the thought broke his heart a bit, well, good. It would get him ready for the inevitable. "Go on now. Get some sleep. We don't know when more danger is coming. Better get it while you can."

She nodded, studying his face as if she could read all

his thoughts. Still, she didn't say anything and eventually moved slowly to the door, but she stopped there before opening it. "Dev?"

"What?"

She paused, that awful vulnerability and openness crossing over her face. "I know exactly what and who you are. I've always known. It's never changed how I felt about you, or what I thought you were capable of. I thought maybe I couldn't reach that part of you—not that it wasn't there." Then she left.

I thought maybe I couldn't reach that part of you—not that it wasn't there.

Not always so confident and sure of herself. Not always a steamroller going after what she wanted. He rubbed at the pain in his chest, knowing that realization would haunt him.

Even when the present danger was taken care of, he'd have a whole lot more to tackle with Sarah. And his heart.

Chapter Ten

The sound of crashing glass had Sarah's eyes flying open. There'd been a scream, she was sure of it. She whipped the covers off her and struggled to get out of bed quickly. It had come from somewhere upstairs, but not here in her room.

Once she got up, she ran for the door. By the time she made it to the hallway, everyone upstairs was crowded around the door to Cody and Nina's room.

Liza pushed through. She gave Sarah's arm a quick squeeze. "Everything's okay but I'm going to check on the girls."

"What happened?" But Liza had already moved down the hall to where the girls were sleeping.

Sarah grabbed the nearest person since she couldn't get close to Nina and Cody's door.

"A brick. Through the window. No one's hurt," Jamison said grimly.

A brick.

"Now, now. We aren't going to solve anything standing here with no room. Let's go downstairs and talk this through," Grandma Pauline ordered. She started shooing people down the hall.

Sarah backed up into her bedroom doorway as everyone who'd been upstairs started to file down the hall and to the stairs, including the dogs. Sarah moved to obey, but Dev crested the stairs. He patted Grandma Pauline's shoulder and headed for Cody and Nina's room.

Sarah followed him. He'd had his boots on, which Sarah realized was purposeful when he walked through the glass. Nina was still in bed, and Cody was standing next to it.

Dev carefully picked up the brick. He pulled a rubber band off of it, shook out the piece of paper wrapped around it, then handed it to Cody.

Cody's expression got even more grim. "I guess I've got my sentencing," Cody said.

Nina made a noise and Sarah thought about moving to offer some support, but there was window glass all over the floor and her feet were bare.

"Grab us some shoes out of the closet?"

Dev nodded and went to the closet. He pulled out pairs of shoes for Cody and then Nina and handed them over. Cody and Nina slid the shoes on in silence.

"We'll need to clean this up, but let's all go downstairs and talk things through first, yeah?"

Nina nodded, and she and Cody slid their arms around each other. Sarah moved out of the doorway again as Cody and Nina exited.

As Dev came out, he rubbed his hand over his beard before looking down at her. "You could go back to bed," he said, gently enough she didn't bristle. "It's the middle of the night. Nothing changes if you go back to bed."

"He knows what rooms we're sleeping in, Dev."

Dev expression went lax. He looked stricken, as though that hadn't occurred to him yet.

"The brick went through Cody's window and the paper was for Cody. None of us are safe in our rooms."

He swallowed and then slid his arm around her shoulders and started leading her to the stairs. "Okay, you're right."

It was the first time he'd admitted she was right and she couldn't take any pleasure in it. When they got downstairs everyone was in the kitchen, and the dogs were settled under the table, making Sarah think no one was still outside. Grandma was already reheating leftovers even though the clock said it was three.

"We didn't see anything," Cecilia said. She was sitting at the table, frowning at her hands.

Brady put his hand over hers. "None of the security lights went off. We were awake and paying attention. I didn't hear anything. I didn't… There was no warning."

"He's probably cut those too," Cody replied, his voice eerily calm as he encouraged Nina to sit down. "If he got the cameras, why not the motion sensors? I keep trying to rewire, add new passwords, but he cuts through all the tech. I hate to admit it, but I'm out of my league here."

Nina reached up and put her hand over Cody's on her shoulder. "We can't think of everything. It's impossible in a situation like this."

Dev nudged Sarah into an empty chair, then stood behind it. Grandma Pauline put a mug of hot tea in front of her. Duke paced the kitchen, and Jamison stood by the kitchen sink, looking out the window, as if he could see anything in the dark.

Liza was still upstairs with the kids, but everyone else was sitting around the table.

"Well, what does it say?" Duke demanded. "Just like Jamison's?"

Cody looked down at the paper. "Same setup. Slightly different wording."

Cody Wyatt
Crimes:

The subject has been the perpetrator of a wide variety of crimes since childhood, but the most egregious of these is his involvement with the terrorist North Star Group. Murder, kidnapping, treason, terrorism.

Sentencing:

For these acts, I do hereby sentence Cody Wyatt to death. This will be meted out at the judge's discretion through the method C. Wyatt deemed acceptable through his own connection to the terrorist group.

—AW

"Terrorist group," Cody muttered. "What a bunch of bull."

"It makes sense though," Sarah offered. "If you look at it from his standpoint. North Star's mission was to take down the Sons. That's terrorism. To them."

"I don't understand where an affiliation with the Sons would come from if he was never *in* the Sons," Dev said, not dismissively but thoughtfully as though he were trying to work it out.

"But he was involved with Ace. Which means there could have been areas of the Sons he was involved in. We just don't know enough to make that assumption. But if he's blaming Cody for his work with North Star, and North Star's work was taking down the Sons, there has to be *some* connection."

"We only arrested Ace because of Cody and North Star's help," Jamison said. "It connects to Ace, even if it doesn't connect to the Sons. He's not going in age order with these letters. Or escape order. He's going in order of our involvement with Ace as adults. How did Ace going to jail start? With me helping Liza get Gigi out of the Sons. Which led us to the trafficking ring. Cody's North Star group was taking out their main guys, and the two of us coming together on that is what sent Ace to jail."

"I could have killed him," Cody said flatly. "I didn't."

"We have to remember we don't know what Ace told Anth," Sarah said. "We can only operate on what we know, but Ace could have told Anth *anything*. Truth or lie or a combination of both."

"But if he let Dev go all those years ago, helped Dev escape being killed by Ace, why would he… Why?" Liza said.

"Helping me escape doesn't have to mean he's good. I think the past twenty-four hours proves he's not. We know the games Ace liked to play. This is another game. I think it also proves it isn't sudden. Anth has been planning this out for a while. Maybe since Ace died."

It was a terrible thought. If he'd had that long to plan, how could they win?

IT WAS A long night. It took a while for the girls to settle back down, and a while to clean up the mess of the glass. No one was too keen to go back to sleep in their rooms, but Dev convinced Sarah to lie down in his since there was no window. Felicity, Liza and Nina were all in the girls' room though he doubted with the cramped quarters and worried minds anyone was getting any sleep.

His brothers certainly weren't. They had someone at every entrance point on the lower level. Dev couldn't help but think the brick had been meant to scare them more than anything—a reminder AW could reach them whenever and however.

"How would he know which rooms we're sleeping

in?" Dev wondered aloud. Dawn was beginning to break outside the large living room window he was guarding. Cody was leaning against the front door, eyes trained out the small sidelight window.

He looked exhausted. They probably all did. Another thing Anth likely wanted.

"No idea."

"It's weird though. Not just your average weird. With all of us here, we're not following any normal plan. Duke and Sarah never spend the night here, so there's no protocol to follow. Only the kids are in the room they're usually in, and he didn't go after them."

"Thank God," Cody muttered. "He touches my daughter, I won't be responsible for my actions."

"So, how? How did he know which room you and Nina were going to be in? How did he know to throw the brick in that window?"

"Could be a coincidence."

"Doubt it."

"I do too." Cody sighed. "There'd be no floor plan on file. The ranch isn't ever empty enough for a break-in, and like you said, we're not using our normal rooms anyway. I guess he could have planted a bug? But it's not like we talked about what rooms we're going to be in."

"No, and I don't think he can hear us. If he could... I feel like there'd be...more. He's cutting through your tech, but maybe that's because he's had time to figure it all out."

Cody nodded. "I can put up new stuff, but it'll take time. All the tech we've got involves the outdoors. The cameras, the lights—they're outside. He can't get in, or hasn't tried to, but he's messed with what's outside. He can't *hear* us in here, but what if he can see us?"

"What? Like X-ray vision?"

"No. No." Cody clapped his hands together. "Like my cameras. Not just taken out but rewired. Repurposed."

"That's possible?"

"It's *possible*. Especially if he's had so much time to plan." Cody stepped away from the door. "It's getting light out. Watch my back while I—"

"You can't go out there. You're a specific target."

"I'm just going to check the cameras on the porch here."

"No, you're going to sit tight." Dev gave one last scan of the front yard he could see from the window, then strode for the kitchen. Gage was at the back door and Tucker was looking out through the window over the sink. "Cody thinks he might be getting our locations from the cameras and wants to go out and check."

"I don't think anyone should go out now that it's light," Tucker said.

"But if we can figure out how he knows what rooms we're in, isn't it worth the risk?" Gage replied. He stomped on the floor three times, a sign for Jamison to come up from the basement.

After a few seconds, Jamison stuck his out of the doorway into the basement. "See anything?"

"Cody thinks Anth might have tampered with the cameras and that's how he's getting an idea of where we are. He wants to go check it out."

"Not alone," Jamison said resolutely.

"We're trying to figure out how."

Jamison nodded. "All right. We'll have to assess. Together. Block all the doors except the one Cody wants to go out."

"What about windows?" Tucker asked.

"Close the curtains for now. If it's going to take too long we'll put lookouts back in place." They all moved to use the kitchen chairs as door barricades, then went to the front, where Cody was still looking out the door's sidelight, both dogs whining at his feet.

"I don't need to be out long. I'll just pull the camera off and bring it inside and see if I can find any evidence of tampering."

Dev didn't like it and knew none of his brothers did either. "I should do it."

"You don't know anything about cameras. No offense, but none of you do. I installed it. I can uninstall it quicker than any one of you."

"He could be hoping to draw you out of the house with that letter, Cody," Jamison replied.

"If he's sending letters to you then me, he's going to eventually send them to all of us. We're all targets. We're all in danger. I want to end that as soon as possible. I'm going to go out there and pull the camera off. It'll take me two, three minutes tops."

"Plenty of time to get shot," Gage muttered.

"I'll shield him," Dev said.

"Damn it, Dev."

"You can't be watching your back while you're uninstalling. You need at least one other person out there to be the eyes while you get it off the porch."

Cody couldn't argue with that, though Dev could tell he wanted to. "I could take the dogs."

Dev looked at Cash and Brownie. They were good ranch dogs, but... "They can't fight. They could easily be picked off. In fact, I think it'd be best if we get them off the ranch for the time being. Them going in and out for bathroom breaks is a liability."

"I agree," Tucker said. "But one thing at a time. Dev will watch north and east, I'll watch south and west. You guys will watch from in here. If we've got five sets of eyes on the situation, we'll be able to abort or defend ourselves."

All the brothers paused and looked at Jamison. It didn't seem to matter how old they all got, or how many times they'd saved people or themselves on their own, Jamison was their leader. He'd gotten them out of the Sons, and even now they'd seek his approval.

He gave a slight nod. So Dev immediately got to work. They switched weapons, giving Dev and Gage shotguns and Jamison and Brady the rifles.

"You move quick and quiet. The second you've got that camera off, you're back inside with Dev and Gage right behind. Jamison, hold the dogs."

They all nodded in affirmation. Dev went out first, watching the north and east side of the property they could see, immediately followed by Gage. Cody brought up the rear, keeping his eyes and focus on the camera.

Dev hadn't been a police officer for over a decade now, and it wasn't often that he missed it. He'd only gone into law enforcement to be like Jamison, and maybe to prove there was some goodness in him. Rancher was a better fit, though. He could understand and admit that now.

Today there was something bittersweet about being the protector, working side by side with his brothers to defend.

Dev didn't see anything, and based on the silence around him, Gage didn't either.

"Got it," Cody said after a while, and they all moved back inside as one unit.

Jamison pulled the door closed behind them and they huddled around Cody and the black box that housed the camera. He examined the wires, popped the back wall off and looked inside. He shook his head.

"It hasn't been tampered with," Cody said in disgust.

"There weren't even any lines cut. Whatever blocking he did… I can't figure it out."

"Maybe it's not this camera," Dev said. "You have how many? And where are they?"

"There was the one on the front. I've got one on the stable that scans the entranceway. Then I've got three on the fence line. One at the gate, one on the west side of the house, and one on the south side of the property."

"West side of the house. Which way is that one facing?" Tucker asked.

"Toward the Knight property." Cody swiped his hand over his mouth. "But if it were moved, it could look into the west windows of the house."

"The only window on the west side is…" Jamison trailed off and they all rushed for the stairs. The only window was a long, narrow one at the end of the hall. Daylight was growing brighter, though everything was still dim. Still, Dev could see the small black box that would denote it was one of Cody's cameras.

"That where it's supposed to be?" Dev asked.

Cody's expression was barely banked fury. "Yes, but it isn't facing the Knight Ranch. It's facing us."

Dev caught a glimpse of something glinting in the rising sun. Even before he fully realized what it was, he was dropping to the floor and pulling as many brothers as he could with him. "Down!" Dev shouted.

They all hit the floor as the glass shattered above them.

Chapter Eleven

Sarah woke once again to the sound of a bang and shattering glass. At first she thought it had been a nightmare, just a replay of what had happened hours earlier. After all, they'd covered the bedroom windows where people were sleeping. She was in Dev's room, so there was no window here.

Surely it had been a nightmare.

But the dogs were barking like crazy and there were footsteps rushing above. Then her door opened and Dev moved inside. Before he even spoke she knew it wasn't a nightmare.

"Stay where you are."

"What? What's happened?"

"Another shot fired at the house. The six of us were together when it happened. Then we split up to tell everyone to stay put."

"More shooting at the house?" Her brain was sluggish and she tried to remember everything that had happened in the middle of the night. Too much, and this wasn't good. "Is everyone okay?"

"We're all fine. Jamison called the guy who was on patrol and he's on his way, but I don't think he's going to find anything."

"What are we going to do?"

"I just need you to stay put for the time being. Once Jamison gets the all clear, we're going to go out ourselves and see if we can find a clue."

"You shouldn't go out." She flung the covers off her with the thought to jump out of bed and grab him, but he stalked over to the bed and pulled the covers right back over her.

"Stay put like I said," he ordered.

"You guys can't go out there. We are being *shot* at. You have to stay inside and…"

"And what? We have a ranch to run. You have a doctor's appointment today. We can't stay shut up inside hoping he goes away."

Sarah felt like crying. Of course the cattle couldn't be ignored. It wasn't smart to skip the doctor's appointment when she was this close to her due date. But didn't the people she loved outweigh all that?

He sighed and sat on the very edge of the bed. After a minute of clear internal debate, he took her hand and gave it a squeeze. "No one's been hurt. There are threats, and obviously this is scary, especially with you pregnant and the girls here, but we're handling it as best we can."

"We are sitting ducks."

He held her hand between his much bigger ones. There was some comfort in that, but not enough to soothe any of the fears. Twice they'd been shot at, and maybe the fact no one had been hurt meant something, but bullets flying around weren't ever a good thing.

"He'll make a mistake. He can't keep lurking around and not get caught."

"Why not? We live in the middle of *nowhere*. He's taken out almost all of Cody's security measures. He could lurk all day and all night and we'll never be able to do anything about it."

"I think at some point the five law enforcement officers living under the same roof means something."

She wished that comforted her any. It should. The Wyatt brothers were smart. Tucker was a detective so he was used to putting together clues and cases like this.

But so far, Anth was winning. He had the upper hand.

"What if you go out there to take care of the cattle and he ambushes you? What if all these scare tactics are to keep us inside so he has us all in one spot to—"

Jamison knocked on the door frame, peeking his head in. "Cops are finished. Found the gun. Why don't you all come out to the kitchen so we can talk about our next steps?"

"We'll be out in just a second," Dev said.

Jamison disappeared and Dev let go of her hand. Next steps. What could they possibly do next except hunker down?

"Sarah. You want to panic, that's just fine."

"I don't want to panic. I'm not panicking!"

She caught the way he pressed his lips together, as though he was trying not to laugh or point out she sounded a heck of a lot like someone panicking.

"Oh, shut up," she muttered. She let him help her out of the bed and they walked into the kitchen where, once again, everyone was huddled around the table. Except Grandma Pauline and Liza, who Sarah assumed were upstairs with the girls.

"I called the officer who was out in the car at the entrance. He did a quick search and found the gun that shot at us," Jamison said. "It was lying in the snow. There are footprints. He's called in some backup and they'll take the gun to see if they can lift a print. They're following the footprints too, best they can, though I suspect the wind will erase the trail before they get anything out of it. With all of us out of commission while we're under threat, they're stretched thin as it is." Four of the six Wyatt brothers worked for Valiant County, and though it was a big county with a big department, losing four officers from active duty probably was pretty stressful.

"I should help."

Sarah opened her mouth to argue, to demand everyone stay put, but Dev gave a dismissive wave her way.

"I'll be back in time to go with you to your appointment."

The smart aleck response died before she could say it as she realized there were questioning looks around the room. Confusion. Except from Duke.

In all the craziness, Sarah hadn't fully thought about the fact Dev wanting to be a father to the baby would mean telling everyone. No one knew yet and it would be a whole…thing, in the midst of this other thing.

"I think you should go see your doctor too," Cody said to Nina, dragging people's attention away from Sarah and Dev. "It's just a little bit earlier than your normal appointment time. I don't see the harm in getting checked out. You can take Brianna and—"

"Separating us isn't going to do any good. If he wants me to get to you, then I'm a target too."

Sarah shook her head. There was a pattern, and maybe Anth could deviate from it, but why would he have a pattern if he wasn't using it for some reason? "Gage would be next," she said. "Anth sent a note to Jamison, then shot at Liza. Or had someone shoot at Liza. Then there was a note to Cody, and he shot at you guys. That's a pattern, and it means the next thing to happen would be for Gage to get a note, since he was the next one to have a run-in with Ace."

"Lucky me," Gage muttered as Felicity wrapped her arm around his.

"This is a North Star gun," Cody said, placing his phone in the middle of the table. On the screen was a picture of a gun in the snow. "The gun he used—it's from North Star. Or at least it's the kind we were issued. He could get his hands on it easy enough without going through North Star, but doesn't that feel…"

"Pointed?" Sarah supplied. "It connects to your note. Just like shooting at Liza connected to all the uses of kin in Jamison's note."

"But neither attempt succeeded at killing their target," Dev said thoughtfully, staring down at the picture of the gun.

"Maybe he doesn't want to succeed. Maybe this is the game."

"The paper says we're sentenced to death. Why would he sentence us to death, then play a game?"

"I don't know, but why take a shot at Liza? That doesn't kill you. Metaphorically, maybe. But are we dealing in metaphors? Maybe the letters and the attempts to hurt us aren't connected in the way we're thinking," Sarah insisted. "First it was Jamison, then Cody. If they're going in involvement with Ace order, like I said, Gage would be next. Some kind of attempt that connects to the note. Then a note for Brady."

"What Cecilia and I dealt with was Elijah, not Ace," Brady said. But Sarah could tell even though they were voicing arguments, what they were really doing was thinking it through. Working out the angles.

"Elijah was a protégé of Ace," Sarah continued. "Besides, you were involved with saving Gage from Ace even before that. So, either way, you'd be after Gage." Sarah looked at Tucker. "Ace didn't have too much to do with your showdown with the Sons, but he died while you were fighting them."

"It doesn't make sense, though," Dev said gruffly. "If it was about Ace, I would have been first. It would have gone back to me. It doesn't make sense to leave me for last."

"Maybe it doesn't have to make sense to us," Nina said quietly. "It makes sense to him."

Sarah couldn't help but think there was something they were missing. Some piece of the puzzle that would allow them to make sense of things.

"I'm going to go help them follow the trail. I'll notice things they won't."

"Not alone," Jamison said sharply. "Under no circumstances are any of us going anywhere alone."

"I'll go," Duke said, standing. "May not be as young as you lot, but I know how to shoot a gun and follow a trail. It's my land too."

Dev nodded and they both headed for the mudroom to get bundled up. When she stood, Duke gave her a censoring look. "Stay put." Then they headed outside into the snowy, cold morning.

Sarah scowled after them. She was very tempted *not* to stay put, but she was nine months pregnant. She couldn't go waddling around trying to track a killer. But what she could do was try to get to the bottom of the pattern. "I want to see the letters again. We need to compare them."

DEV FOLLOWED THE trail of boot prints in the snow that led from where the county cops had parked their car, to the place they'd found the gun. It had since been processed and taken in as evidence with the hope of lifting a print.

Dev had his doubts. Why would Anth—or someone

Anth had hired—drop a weapon that might have finger-prints on it? Didn't make any sense.

Still, there could be something left behind. Some clue—either from the direction the trail went or something *accidentally* left behind. Something the cops might not know to look for.

"He isn't headed back to my house, and he isn't headed to the highway," Duke said from behind Dev. They were walking close together, eyes sweeping the wide-open spread of land between them.

"If the trail is headed to where he's going. Not sure he's that dumb."

"One way or another, we need this done before that baby comes along. You're running out of time."

Dev kept his sarcastic *no kidding* to himself. In an effort to not mess up the path the shooter had left, the police officers had ruined any secondary evidence Dev might have been able to pick up on. Necessary for them, but a shame for Dev.

He tried to focus on that. The footprints, what the path meant, and what he was looking for, but he could practi-cally *feel* Duke's disapproval waving over him.

He shouldn't care. Duke's approval didn't matter. Maybe it had once upon a time, but Dev had given up on seeking approval after he'd ended up in the hospital, his law enforcement career over, and knowing he was a failure.

Utterly, in every way that mattered.

He'd eventually pulled himself out of that dark, self-pitying place. Or maybe more accurately, Sarah had poked him out of that place.

On purpose, he realized with a start. He'd always thought she was just annoying, but no. She'd gone about dragging him back into the land of the living since he'd been able to walk again.

She'd never given up on him, and never tipped her hand. She'd always known exactly what she was doing, but she'd never let him know. Probably because she knew he'd balk at it.

His chest felt too tight and now was not the time for after-the-fact realizations or emotions he didn't want to analyze. But he owed Duke something, because through Sarah's badgering and Grandma Pauline's calm presence and his own stubbornness, he'd pulled himself out of that ugly place. He wasn't perfect or maybe any good, but he'd put some pride in this ranch and his hard work here.

He'd made progress. Not just in the years, but maybe even in the months of Sarah's pregnancy. "I'm not going to…shirk my responsibilities with her. Well, with the baby," he said, half hoping the words died in the wind.

"Please tell me you didn't say it like that when you told her," Duke replied. "Well, you don't have a black eye so you must have phrased it better."

"Yeah, I phrased it better," Dev muttered. "I said I'd be a father. That I wanted to be. I… Someone who'd protect my kid no matter what. I guess you don't have to be perfect to do that."

"No, son. You don't. But it isn't just about protecting. Being a parent is so much bigger than that."

Dev stopped and rubbed at his aching leg. The cold exacerbated the pain and Duke's words had a clutching, crushing sensation rocketing through his chest. *So much bigger. You really think you can handle that?*

Too late to rethink. He'd said he'd be a father to the baby, and he wouldn't go back on his word. Besides, there was no time to panic about the future when the present was just as ominous.

"Then there's being a partner to think about. You'll both have different ideas of how to raise the boy. Then there's your own relationship, which… Well, it's hard enough to make those decisions when you're settled and married. It's a balancing act. It's—"

"Is now really the time to lecture me on all the ways I'm going to screw it up?"

"No time like the present," Duke said. He almost sounded cheerful, but Dev supposed that's because he was distracting himself by trying to scare the bejesus out of Dev. "Besides, you'll both screw it up. That's the beauty of life if you think about it. Everybody makes mistakes, so it hardly makes yours the end of the world like you're so prone to do."

"I'm not prone to do that," Dev muttered. "Much." But before he could analyze how right Duke might be, his attention was drawn to a difference in the snow. There were still footprints here, but the snow was packed differently. He could see where the cops had gone on, following the prints.

But there was something off here, even if he couldn't figure out what. "Do you see this?"

Duke studied the snow too. "Something isn't right. Is it packed in?"

"Seems to be. But that's a heck of a lot of packing."

"Unless…" Duke trailed off, but he lifted a gloved hand and pointed a little ways off. After an area of packed snow, there were two indentations. Like snowmobile tracks.

"Let's be careful where we walk," Dev said, starting to head that way and trying to avoid marring any tracks. After just a few steps, he saw a dark stain of red between the indentations. It was a narrow trickle following the path of the mobile.

Dev looked at Duke, who already had his phone to his

ear. "Jamison. We found something. Don't know how far your deputy friends are ahead of us, but can you radio them back? They'll be able to see our trail and follow us."

Duke hung up and they kept walking.

"Better watch out for an ambush, boy."

Dev looked around. It was an open field. Though the land rolled a bit here and there, with the snow it would be almost impossible to hide.

The snowmobile tracks curved around a swell of land. Duke and Dev slowed in unison as they rounded the tiny hill. The red dribble of blood stopped behind the swell, where Dev could spot hair.

He held out an arm and stopped Duke, but Duke shook his head. "I don't think that's a live one."

Dev let out a breath and then they walked closer, the body coming more into view. He didn't recognize the man, though he was clearly dead. A giant arrow was coming out of his chest, and he didn't move. His unseeing eyes just stared at the bright sun above.

Attached to the body, via the arrow, was another piece of paper. Duke swore. Dev moved closer to read the note, being careful not to disrupt any more of the scene.

Craig Timothy
Crimes:
    Armed robbery, rape, first and second-degree murder, but most of all—failure.
Sentencing:
    Death by lethal injection.
—AW

"Seems to me a man with all these notes, who can disappear or send other people to do his dirty work, would choose people less likely to fail."

Dev would agree, but he thought about what Sarah had said. That this was just a game. Or maybe unrelated to the Wyatts. Maybe Anth simply wanted to get rid of these men for whatever reason, and this was the way to do it. Maybe he wanted to confuse them, or just scare them by showing them what he could do.

Too many options, but so much failure didn't make sense. It had to be planned. It had to be purposeful. Which put Dev even more on edge than he already was.

"Dev." Duke's voice was especially grave, and when Dev looked back at the man, Duke nodded toward the corpse's hand.

There was a folded up piece of paper, but clearly printed on the part Dev could see was his brother's name. Gage Wyatt. Just like Sarah had predicted.

"Let's go find the cops," Dev said grimly.

Chapter Twelve

By the time Dev and Duke returned to the house, Sarah had read and reread the notes left for Jamison and Cody. Now she had a third note to read. Gage, just as she'd predicted.

"Oh, allow me," Gage said when Dev said he was going to read it to everyone.

"It's just a picture. The cops took the original to see if they could lift some prints off it." Dev handed his phone to Gage. Felicity sat down, Claire squirming in her lap.

Sarah thought the way Claire was cheerfully babbling at Felicity helped ease some of Felicity's tension now that her husband received the specific threat.

"'Gage Wyatt. Crimes: The subject has been the perpetrator of a wide variety of crimes since childhood. Manslaughter. Battery. Treason. Escape from custody and sentencing. Attempted patricide.'" Gage smirked. "Hard to argue with that one."

"What's the sentencing?" Sarah encouraged him. They'd all followed the same lines, and the sentencing was always the clue to how they were going to be attacked.

"'Sentencing: For these acts, I do hereby sentence Gage Wyatt to death. This will be meted out at the judge's discretion through the method G. Wyatt saw fit to use on his own father.' Signed AW." Gage handed Dev his phone back. "Well, unless he plans on dragging me off to a cave somewhere, I think I'm safe."

"Don't say that," Felicity said. She'd gone more and more pale as Gage had read the note and his last little quip hadn't helped. But Felicity had been there when Ace had tied Gage up in a cave in the Badlands. She'd been the one to save Gage from Ace.

"It doesn't make sense anyway. I didn't try to kill him. *He* tried to kill *me*. Felicity is the one who shot him."

"We keep running into a lot of things not making sense," Dev said grimly. "I imagine we'll meet a few more before this is all over. We need to keep being diligent, but the current challenge is going to be getting Sarah to her doctor's appointment."

"The cops could take her. We could hide her, you know? Sneak her out to the cop car so no one who might be watching would even know."

"No," Dev said. "I'll be going."

The room went silent, those speculative glances they'd gotten earlier increasing with real interest. Sarah knew there was no way to avoid this. No matter the danger. Her family deserved to know and unless Anth Wyatt had planted some kind of listening device…

"You don't think we're being listened to, do you?" she asked Cody.

Cody shook his head. "I've swept this room in particular up and down and sideways. I can't find any evidence he can hear us. Him knowing which bedrooms we're in would have been easy enough to determine by watching through the camera he had pointed in the hallway window upstairs. I think if he could *hear* us, we would have been ambushed any of the times we've gone outside."

Sarah nodded, then shared a look with Dev. She didn't

have to say anything for him to incline his head. A silent *go ahead*. "I'm going with Sarah because I'm the father."

There was nothing but silence at first. Even Duke was silent though he already knew. Everyone looked down-right shocked, except maybe Grandma Pauline who'd always had an excellent poker face. Surely even *she* couldn't have predicted this news.

"As in…" Nina cleared her throat. "Like you're *actually* the father, or you're stepping in to play—"

"I'm *actually* the father."

Cecilia let out a gasping noise. "Oh my… You had sex at our wedding."

Sarah didn't consider herself someone who embar-rassed easily or almost ever, but heat stole over her cheeks and she got the feeling she was bright red.

"I don't think we need to go into the details," Dev said dryly. "Now. It shouldn't be just the two of us. Nina, did you want to go in and get checked out?"

Nina shook her head as if needing the physical move-ment to change topics. She cleared her throat again. "Right. Yes. Cody made an appointment for me, though it's later than yours." She shot her husband a disapprov-ing look, but she'd placed a protective hand over her still-flat stomach. "But Cody should come too."

"I agree," Sarah said before Cody or Dev could argue. "We're all in this house because we believe there's safety in numbers. We should go to town and back in more than just a duo or a trio. Four is good."

"And a police escort," Jamison said authoritatively. "I've already talked to the department. The weather is stretching them even thinner, but they've called in some road help from neighboring departments. They've agreed the best course of action was to have a marked police car following you guys."

There were a few more practicalities, but before Sarah could really study Gage's note to her liking, she was being ushered out the door to head to her doctor's appointment.

Cody was driving, and they'd decided to take Brady's truck since he'd yet to get a note with his name on it. Though it was only a matter of time, it seemed smarter to avoid a vehicle specifically owned by someone who'd already been "sentenced."

Once Cody drove out onto the highway, a cop car pulled behind them. Following them toward town.

Sarah sat in the back with Nina, who she could all but *feel* studying her. Sarah didn't know what to say, so she kept her mouth shut.

Until Nina broke the silence. "You really...slept together?"

Sarah gave Nina a doleful look. "That *is* how babies are made."

"Why didn't you tell anyone? For *nine* months?"

Dev's gaze met hers in the rearview mirror. She didn't know what to say. Sure, she could give the truth. He probably wanted her to. But it wasn't exactly the whole truth, no matter how she'd convinced herself it was.

Turned out, with the actual possibility of Dev as a father to her child, as a partner, she could admit to herself she'd convinced herself of the insane plan because she'd hoped for this. She just hadn't dared *plan* for it.

"It's complicated," Dev said before she could think of what to say. "And we have a few more complicated matters to focus on."

Nina frowned at the back of his head, but she didn't press the matter. They finished the drive in tense silence, all eyes on the world around them as they drove. Wondering if something would jump out and harm them.

It was a terrible way to live. Sarah wished she could be *doing* something, but instead she had to walk into the medical building and wait for what felt like eternity to be led back to one of the exam rooms. There was the weighing, the peeing in a cup and then more waiting.

Dev looked large and uncomfortable in the small chairs in the exam room. He kept adjusting his weight.

"Honestly, you'd think *you* were the one nine months pregnant in a paper gown."

He glanced at her in the paper gown, then looked up at the ceiling. "You're not exactly covered up very well."

"That's because she's going to shove her—"

A knock cut off what Sarah had been going to horrify Dev with. The doctor stepped in, then stopped short at the man in the chair. "Well, hello. I'm Dr. Marks."

"Dev. Dev Wyatt." He shook the doctor's hand. "I'm the father."

"Well, lovely. Let's get started then, shall we? Everything looks good with your weight and blood pressure and sample. We'll do the heartbeat, then do an internal."

Sarah had to bite back a laugh at the way Dev paled. Her humor faded, as it always did, when the doctor put the monitor on her stomach and the quick, mechanical *womp womp* filled the room.

"Heart rate is good," the doctor said.

Sarah hadn't noticed Dev had come to stand beside her, she'd been so focused on the heartbeat. His fingers intertwined with hers and she looked up at him. There was sheer *awe* on his face—she knew because she felt it every time. But it was bigger, more emotional with him here to share it.

She hadn't come to these appointments alone. She'd always had one of her sisters insist on coming with. She'd always known she wouldn't raise this baby alone, but knowing she—or this baby—had reached Dev and brought him here…where he could experience *life*. And wonder. And joy.

She wanted to cry, but she blinked the tears back.

"Now to check your cervix." Casually explaining what she was doing and why to Dev, the doctor went through the exam. When she was finished, she gave Sarah a sympathetic smile.

"No dilation. I think he's content to stay put for a while longer yet. We might even want to schedule an induction for after Christmas. We don't want him hanging out in there too long."

"Even with the contractions she's been having, you think he's going to stay put?"

The doctor smiled indulgently. "Anything is possible, Mr. Wyatt. She could have him tomorrow. But the likelihood of him coming early at this point is slim. First-time births are notoriously late and slow. She should have plenty of warning when he's coming."

"So, what you're saying is it's perfectly safe to stay out at the ranch through Christmas, even if the weather forecast is bad," Sarah said.

The doctor paused, looked from Dev's scowling face to Sarah. "Well. It'd be good to pay attention to the weather forecast. You wouldn't want to be caught too far away from a medical facility. But I think you're pretty safe as long as there aren't any more contractions. Considering how far you are from the hospital, I'd say you start getting regular contractions, even if they're pretty far apart, you'd want to make your way close. Especially if the weather is bad."

Sarah gave Dev a triumphant smile.

"If he's not here for Christmas, we'll see you back next week. I'm out of the office until the new year, but my nurse practitioner can check you out, and I'll be on call for any births. You both have a nice holiday. Take your time getting dressed."

Sarah thanked the doctor before she left. She needed Dev's help to get herself off the table. Getting undressed in front of him hadn't been that big of a deal because she'd had the paper gown to put over her before she'd shimmied out of her pants.

Now it was a little more awkward. Especially when he handed her her pants. Still, she felt more weird about asking him to turn around or close his eyes or something, so she twisted and turned to pull her pants back on while keeping the paper in place.

Of course, then she had to slide it off to put on her shirt, but that was… Well, her bra was no different than a swimsuit really.

Uncomfortable but unwilling to say so, she let the paper gown drop and took the sweatshirt Dev handed to her. But before she could pull it over her head, he placed his hands over her belly. His bare hands on her bare belly. "I can feel him kick you. I heard his heart beat. But he still doesn't feel…*real*."

No, none of any of this felt real, most especially Dev touching her like this. But it would. At least the baby would. "He will. When you hold him. When he's here. It'll feel more real than we can imagine."

"You're so sure?"

"I watched Gage and Felicity. Pretty intently, since I was starting to hatch my plan then. So, yeah, I'm sure. Something changes when he actually gets here. Something big."

He looked at her then—*her*—not her belly. The gaze was searching. Open. There was something in those hazel eyes that had her breath catching in her throat.

But then he only dropped his hands and stepped back. "We should get going. Don't want to be separated any more than we have to be."

Sarah could only nod, because her throat was too tight, and everything she'd dreamed of was too close. But instead of reaching for it, demanding it, she kept her mouth shut and followed Dev back out to the waiting room where Nina and Cody were.

Because there was still a madman torturing them, and no dreams were going to be realized in the midst of that.

DEV KEPT EXPECTING something to happen, but they were back at the ranch by suppertime safe and sound. Not even the hint that anyone had followed, nor had anything new happened at the ranch while they were gone.

After supper, Sarah went to bed early. They'd agreed on four people staying awake for four hours, then another four people for the next, to get them through the night. Dev was on the first shift tonight.

He stood in the kitchen while his brothers said goodnight to their kids and wives and people slowly settled into bed. He should be thinking about Anth. About the notes and sentences and the dead bodies.

But all he could think about was that doctor's office. He'd heard his child's heartbeat. An odd noise. Not really human. Not really...

It hadn't been magic. He didn't suddenly think he'd be some amazing father, or that Sarah didn't deserve better. Like he'd told her, it still didn't feel *real*. But it had touched something inside of him. Something he'd preferred to have left dead.

Life was easier that way. Easier without all this... this...

This.

But now that the Pandora's box was open, there was no shoving it back.

When Jamison, Cody and Gage all walked into the kitchen and instead of determining lookout posts, grabbed four beers from the fridge and handed him one, Dev blinked. "What's this?"

"The Dad crew," Gage said, clinking his bottle of beer to Dev's. "Welcome."

"I'm not a dad yet."

"Dad enough," Cody said with a grin. "The real terror is *just* beginning."

Dev shifted uncomfortably. "We've got actual terror to deal with first."

Gage laughed. "Buddy, you don't *know* real terror 'til that baby is crying at two in the morning and you ain't got a clue as to why."

"Or your eight-year-old looks up at you and says, 'Daddy, where do babies come from?'"

Gage snorted out a laugh at Cody's rendition of Brianna's high-pitched questions.

"We just wanted to congratulate you," Jamison said. "Whatever the circumstances that brought you here, being a father is… It's a big thing. It's a good thing."

Dev wanted to shrug away all that…emotion. Before his brush with death, he'd wanted to model himself after Jamison. Then he'd realized he was such a coward. He'd given up on that dream. So having any kind of Jamison's approval felt like a noose. "Maybe for the likes of you, but I'm pretty sure it's a terribly selfish thing for me."

"Selfish?"

"I wasn't going to be involved. Before you get that battle light in your eye, Jamison, Sarah didn't *want* me to be. Or at least, she said she didn't. But when all the danger started, I got to thinking about how we weren't protected when we were babies. We had each other, but we didn't have a parent who'd lay it all down to keep us safe and I just… I wanted to be that. Isn't that selfish?"

His brothers were silent and Dev wished he'd kept his big mouth shut.

"I think we can convince ourselves of a lot of things," Jamison said at length. "That we're the most selfish. Or the most noble. I think it's human nature to cast ourselves in some role—hero or villain. Maybe most especially when we grew up with nothing but villains."

That made a little too much sense to Dev, who'd often wanted to cast himself as the villain because… Well, he hadn't been as good as the heroes in his life. But he hadn't been as bad as the villains in his life, had he?

"Maybe it's part selfish to want to give someone what you didn't have, but being a father isn't a selfish act. Giving isn't… It can be for selfish reasons, but it'll change you. Having that kid. It changed me and I didn't meet Brianna until she was seven."

"Gigi isn't mine in the biological sense of things," Jamison said carefully. "When you choose to be a father—when *we* choose to be fathers—I don't think you could ever separate what Ace was to us, did to us, from that choice. Maybe it's selfish, but… We're human. You can't separate your humanness from your relationships with other people—the ones you choose, the ones you don't. Life's complicated. It isn't black and white."

Gage clapped Jamison on the back. "My God, an old dog *can* learn new tricks."

"Ha. Ha," Jamison replied with an eye roll.

Before they could say anything more to make him feel…confused all over again, Liza walked into the kitchen.

"Everyone's down for the night pretty much. You guys

are officially on lookout. But I just wanted to warn you not to play hero and not wake us up," Liza warned, and while Dev figured that warning was mostly for Jamison, she looked at all of them. "We're in this together. Always."

"I promise," Jamison replied.

Cody and Gage followed Liza out of the kitchen to their posts at the front of the house. Dev was assigned the kitchen window and door. Jamison was supposed to have the basement, but he stood there not moving for his station.

Dev shifted uncomfortably under his brother's assessing gaze. "What?" he demanded. "We had our little heart-to-heart. Now it's time to do our jobs."

But Jamison didn't stop looking at him like he understood all the horrible depths of his soul. He reached out and squeezed Dev's shoulder. "I don't think you've ever given yourself room to be human, Dev. You always wanted to be more or better, but sometimes being you is enough."

Dev didn't know how that could be true, but he also didn't know how to refute his oldest brother's words. And they hung with him as Jamison left for his post, as he spent four hours watching out. As he went to his room, where Sarah was asleep in his bed.

He didn't disturb her, rolling out a sleeping bag on the floor, but he couldn't sleep because Jamison's words haunted him. His own thoughts haunted him.

If he could be enough…what might the future hold?

Chapter Thirteen

Sarah was happy to wake up naturally, even if it was a bit late. She yawned and pawed on the nightstand for her phone. *Really* late. Almost noon. No one should have let her sleep that long.

She lumbered out of bed, winced a little at the pain in her stomach. Not like a contraction. More achy than sharp. Probably just slept on it wrong. Or just her muscles aching from all this *weight* she was hefting around.

She took care of practicalities and got dressed, wondering where Dev had slept and if she'd missed anything terrible happening. It would be nice to wake up and just… have a normal life again.

When she walked down the hall and into the kitchen, it was bustling. Almost like that normal life she'd wanted had showed up as ordered.

Of course, real life wasn't sleeping in Dev's bed or walking into Grandma Pauline's kitchen at nearly noon after having slept through chores, but it was nice nonetheless.

The two older children were at the table with a variety of dishes. Claire was in her high chair banging happily at the tray. Grandma Pauline and Rachel were hunched over the counters, mixing together what looked like cookie dough.

"What's all this?"

"We're going to decorate for Christmas," Brianna said, bouncing in her seat. "Daddy and all the uncles went to get a tree!"

"And we're going to make cookies, and have hot chocolate tonight when we decorate," Gigi said, matching Brianna's excitement.

Sarah might have smiled at their enthusiasm, but Brianna's statement had her moving over to Grandma Pauline. She couldn't think of one time in her life where she'd dared question Grandma Pauline, but the words came out of her in a hissed whisper she couldn't bite back.

"We're being threatened and you sent them to cut down a tree?" It was usually a Christmas Eve tradition anyway. While at the Knight Ranch they'd had their tree up since the beginning of December, Grandma Pauline's family had always done it on Christmas Eve, and she was a stickler for tradition.

Until, apparently, danger was in the equation.

Grandma Pauline spared her one cutting look. "Christmas will come one way or another, Sarah."

Sarah felt chagrined, even though she shouldn't. "Yes, whether we put a tree up or not."

Grandma looked at the girls, happily browsing through bottles of sprinkles. "I suppose we should let this ne'er-do-well ruin their Christmas, hide in closets until the danger has passed…if it ever does. I suppose I should have never had a Christmas for those boys when Ace was always a threat."

Sarah didn't have *anything* to say to that, and she noted Rachel kept her head down over the counter.

"Those men are out doing chores, don't know why they couldn't cut a tree down all the same. You go on and sit yourself down."

Sarah didn't know what else to do but listen. In a few short minutes, Grandma had a lunch plate in front of her. A sandwich, a clementine and a handful of pretzels. Even worried about the men out chopping down Christmas trees, the gesture made her smile and feel ten years old again.

Sadly, she wasn't ten. A ten-year-old didn't need to worry about people's lives or her baby being born. Sarah rubbed a hand over her stomach. She choked down a few bites of her lunch, though she wasn't hungry at all.

She feigned interest in the Christmas decorations, but mostly she studied her phone, where she had pictures of all three notes. She read them over and over again, still sure there was a pattern just out of reach.

The men returned, all seven of them stomping and shedding their winter layers. They left the tree in the mudroom so they could scrounge up the stand and get that set up first.

Grandma had lunch plates put together in no time. Dev took a seat next to her and peered at her phone screen.

"Looking at it won't change it."

"No. It won't. But there's a pattern. There's a…reason. I can *feel* it. I just can't work out what it is."

"Maybe you should have been a cop. Some kind of detective."

"All those rules to follow?" She wrinkled her nose. "No thanks."

He smiled at her. An actual smile. Like he enjoyed her company or liked looking at her or *something*. It had a warmth warring with an odd jittery feeling that this was *all* wrong, even though it was what she wanted. What she'd always wanted.

Now it was here and she didn't quite know what to do with it. With him.

"Whichever two of you are done first go on downstairs and get the decorations," Grandma Pauline said, still working on the cookie dough with Rachel. "They're in tubs in the crawl space."

Dev slid her phone away from her and she scowled at him. "Take a break. It's almost Christmas."

"Since when are you known for taking a break and enjoying Christmas cheer?"

"Well, I'm not, but I figure I'd start."

She felt a bit like the Grinch with a heart swelling too many sizes to possibly be healthy. With all that amazement and heart growing came this ever evolving fear that…well, a million things would go wrong.

Cody and Gage got up and headed for the basement as Grandma Pauline had instructed earlier. Sarah was distracted enough to return to her previous thoughts. Because as great as it was to have Dev here, wanting to be a father, wanting…something…it didn't matter until they were safe.

She wasn't sure she knew how to believe it was real until the danger was gone. Maybe it was all an act, or some kind of hysteria brought on by worry.

"If we could work it out, the letters, the pattern— maybe we could catch him in the act. Whether it's one of these attacks, or it's in leaving one of the letters. I know there's a connection."

"Until we know what it is, I'm not sure what we can do about it. He keeps cutting through all Cody's safety measures, and I took the dogs over to the Pullman Ranch until we know they won't get hurt in the crossfire."

"Brethren and North Star and caves," Sarah muttered, repeating the info from the letters. "Brady's standoff with the Sons was in the Badlands. So maybe—wait. Caves." She grabbed Dev's arm. "Crawl space. A crawl space is like a cave. Like Gage said. Anth could only hurt him if—"

Dev was already to the basement door. He yelled a sharp *stop* as he flew down the stairs. Sarah had to struggle to her feet. "I think there's something in the crawl space. I think—"

"It's a bomb," Dev yelled from the basement. "Get everyone out."

CODY BARKED ORDERS into his phone as they ran upstairs. Everyone who'd been in the kitchen was already filing out the door.

"Do we have everyone?" Cody asked.

"Yes. We made sure," Sarah answered. She had a handful of coats in her arms. Grandma Pauline and the girls were already long gone, and the rest of the Wyatts were trailing out behind them.

Dev took Sarah by the arm as they got to the mudroom. He didn't chastise her for still being inside, just pulled her with him as they hurried outside.

"Let's get away from the house. None of us know enough about bombs to know how much power that one could have."

"We need to get out of the elements," Liza returned. "We grabbed what boots and coats we could, but not enough for everyone to be out in the cold like this."

Liza was carrying Gigi. Brady had Brianna since she was too big for Nina to carry and Cody had been back with Dev. Felicity had Claire wrapped in someone else's coat. Duke had his arm linked with Grandma— and Grandma didn't even yell at him for treating her like an old lady.

"Head to the stables," Dev said. "That'll give us shelter." And cover if the explosion was particularly violent.

It hadn't been a large device. Dev wasn't even sure he'd have thought it was a bomb if Cody hadn't been certain and Sarah hadn't thought the crawl space was dangerous and connected to the last letter. Still, who knew what kind of damage it could do? If they were in the stables, they'd all be together and the walls should protect them.

God, he hoped.

Dev's gaze swept the area around them. No sign of anyone. No shots rang out. The move to the stables made him nervous, but there was no other choice with a bomb in the house.

Which could have been Anth's purpose.

Dev pulled open the stable door and ushered everyone inside. He double checked to make sure they had everyone, then closed the door.

The horses neighed and nickered. They weren't getting the kind of exercise they were used to, even with the cold winter months. They were restless, and it didn't settle Dev's nerves any.

"I called in North Star," Cody said once they were all in the barn. "Shay has a bomb expert on her team. He's in Washington right now, so I'll have to go back in there and—"

Pretty much everyone shouted "no" at him before he could finish that idiotic statement.

"He can video chat and instruct on—"

"No."

"You want one of the County guys going in there and getting blown up? You want to wait around for some state official?" Cody demanded, impatience bubbling.

"I want that more than I want you blown to bits," Grandma Pauline said, Nina and Brianna nodding emphatically behind her.

"We need to search the entire building. Make sure

there isn't anything here that might be a threat," Dev said in a low voice that only Jamison could hear. Obviously the children knew something was wrong, but he wanted to keep them as in the dark about the danger as he possibly could.

Jamison nodded.

"Is a bad man going to come again?" Brianna asked. "Should we hide?"

Poor Brianna had already lived through danger. Months of terror, really. One of those moments right here in this barn when she and Gigi had hidden from men after Cody.

"No, sweetheart," Nina said, kneeling so she could pull Brianna into a hug. "We're all sticking together this time."

"This could be a way to move us," Sarah whispered to Dev and Jamison, clearly also trying to keep her suspicions from the children. "To get us less protected. It could all be a farce."

Dev nodded. "Could. We're going to check to make sure nothing has been moved. We'll keep the doors closed and the girls occupied until we can get help with the bomb. Just stay put for a few."

She scowled at him, but she did in fact stay put as he moved around the stables. There was nowhere he could go where she couldn't see him, unless he went into the far reaches of one of the stalls, which he only did twice. Jamison and Brady handled the other stalls. They even went into the hayloft and rooted around up there.

But there was no sign of anything amiss. No bombs, no evidence anyone besides him and Duke had been in here.

It didn't sit right. None of this did. He was beginning to understand Sarah's line of thinking. The notes clearly meant something. The threats that—thankfully—didn't end in any harm were meant more to terrorize than to hurt.

But why?

He'd hoped action would mean something, but they could only react. The only way to act was to figure out what Anth was trying to accomplish, if it wasn't actually sentencing anyone to death.

And why hadn't he gotten a letter? Logically, Dev had kicked this all off by trying to take Ace down all those years ago when Anth had basically saved his life. Saved his life only to take it? That didn't make sense either.

Dev shrugged off his coat and put it on Sarah. How had she ended up one of the people without one?

"I'm not that cold."

"You're not that warm." He turned to the group all crowded in the center of the stables. "I can't find anything out of the ordinary or any evidence someone besides us has been in here."

"What I can't figure is how did he get inside the house? We've had lookouts. We've got everything locked up tight and I didn't notice anything amiss. How could he have been inside to plant the bomb?" Gage asked, cradling Claire to his chest. "How could he have known *I'd* be one of the ones to go get the Christmas decorations?"

"Maybe it was just…coincidence." Felicity looked at the girls and then leaned forward to whisper, "He was going to blow up the house with all of us in it."

"Felicity's right. It didn't have to be you," Dev said, scratching a hand through his hair as he tried to make sense of it. "Isn't that the point? This is all just…theatrics. We're all still alive and well. No one's been hurt—and if he can plant a bomb in the basement, surely he could catch us off guard and hurt us. Sarah was right with the last one. This is some kind of warped game."

"How much longer do we live like this?" Liza demanded.

"We know Brady's note will come next. Soon, if pattern follows. Maybe we can set some kind of trap," Sarah offered hopefully.

"Unless he sends a messenger," Cody pointed out.

"But we'd still have *someone*, if we could catch the messenger. Someone who would have some clue as to what's going on," Dev replied.

"But the notes have come in a variety of ways. How could we possibly predict when and how the next one is going to come?" Brady asked.

"It's not a bad angle. But we know one thing for sure. He's close. Really close. He got in the *house*. We need to know how," Gage insisted.

"Whatever this is, it's planned. Really planned." Dev realized maybe even more than they'd thought. "Ace has been dead for over a year. If that was the tipping point? He's had all that time to plan. And who knows—maybe it wasn't the tipping point. Maybe he's been planning this for a lot longer. I haven't had any interaction with Anth since that day over a decade ago. The ways he could have gotten into the house are legion if we go back farther than we've been on guard."

"So, why now?"

Dev shook his head. "I couldn't say. But, to Sarah's point, it's all planned. It's careful, and even if it's not logical, there's a pattern. It's not random and even if it doesn't make sense to us, there's some thread of sense. If we can access it, we can stop it."

"And if we can't?"

"There's an end game. There has to be. We just have

to keep fighting until it gets there." He looked around the stables. His entire family. Everyone he loved. Everyone he…

Sarah's hand slid into his. He looked down at her, pregnant with his child. So determined to figure out the pattern. When he wanted to act, she wanted to sit and think it through—and he figured the opposite was also true.

Balance. They had it—always had. Evened each other out, even when they were bickering. Or were they always bickering because it had been the only way to get him to engage at all for a while there?

She'd brought him back to life, whether he'd wanted to admit that for a very long time or not. It was true. She and the baby were the last missing piece and that was why he was scared of them—better to believe he didn't deserve it than reach for something that might bring him back to fully living.

But there were bigger things to be scared of—real things. Anth and losing any of these people to a madman's whims. He'd once vowed to fight everything Ace was and touched, but he'd given up on that when he'd almost died.

But there was too much at stake to ignore who and what he was. "There's too much at stake to lose, so we'll figure out a way to win."

Chapter Fourteen

Eventually between the local police department and Cody's connections to the North Star group, a bomb expert was called in. It took most of the day, but they managed to defuse and take away the bomb.

Jamison and Cody had talked about the technicalities. All the Wyatts currently employed by Valiant County helped the other officers dust for prints and try to figure out how Anth, or someone else, had gotten in to plant the bomb.

But there were no answers to be had. Everyone was on considerable edge. The house didn't feel safe. Nowhere felt safe.

Cody and Dev had set out to change all the locks in the house. Brady and Gage had gone out with the other officers to do a sweep of the property. Jamison, Duke and Tucker were keeping a watch on the outdoors with Felicity and Nina, while Rachel, Grandma and Liza were entertaining the girls by decorating the tree.

Sarah was superfluous—in actuality and size. She couldn't do anything fast. She couldn't do *anything*. She sat on the couch looking at the twinkling lights, feeling sorry for herself and thinking how pointless she was.

Which didn't do anyone any good. Maybe she couldn't

act in the ways she might like, but she could still think. She *had* to think.

When Cecilia came into the room, she looked…drawn. Sarah wasn't sure what she'd been doing upstairs, but it certainly hadn't been resting up for her night assignment of lookout.

Sarah motioned her to come sit next to her. Cecilia made her way through the Christmas debris, giving Brianna's braid a little tug on the way. Brianna grinned up at Cecilia, then went back to unwrapping ornaments.

Cecilia plopped on the couch next to Sarah and sighed. "Seems so weird to be doing normal things."

"It's almost Christmas," Sarah offered, even though she'd had the same negative reaction this morning.

"Yeah. And we're dealing with bomb threats and hanging up crystal angels."

Cecilia sounded somewhat disgusted, but Sarah had begun to accept it was comforting. Stars and angels and all the symbols of the season of peace on earth and goodwill toward men.

Too bad there was one man she didn't have much peace or goodwill for. Brady would be next, if the notes kept following the pattern. Maybe that was why Cecilia looked so worried. While they were all family and all loved each other, it was probably more stressful when your husband was the next target of unknown sentencing.

Sarah should probably let it be. Focus on Christmas and hope, but… Well, there had to be some way to figure out what was coming next. "Tell me about when you and Brady faced off with Elijah."

Cecilia sighed. "I don't really want to relive that particular moment in my life, Sarah."

"Even if it helped us figure out what's next?"

Cecilia scowled. "I don't see how it would," she grumbled, but she scooted closer to Sarah on the couch so she could speak in low tones the girls wouldn't hear over their chattering. "It all started with me hiding Mak from Elijah." Cecilia's friend had had a baby with Ace's protégé in the Sons. When the mother had been hospitalized, Cecilia had taken the baby to keep him from going to Elijah. She and Brady had worked to keep Mak safe from both Elijah and the dangerous reach of the Sons.

"You miss him."

Cecilia shrugged. "I'm happy Layla's happy. Jarrod is good for her and spending a few weeks with his family in Denver is great for all of them. But, yeah, I miss having them closer."

"So, in reality, you started it."

"Excuse me?"

"I mean, you took Mak and Brady got involved. Before that, Felicity was the one being framed for murder, and Gage got involved. In fact, Felicity was the one who shot Ace, even if he did survive."

"Well, yeah, but—"

Sarah straightened in her seat, trying to find a more comfortable position for her belly. "And Nina went on the run because Ace threatened *her*. She came back because Ace sent men after *her*. Liza came to Jamison when Gigi disappeared."

"What's your point? The only reason the Wyatt boys are ever in trouble is because of us? Sorry, that doesn't fly."

"No, but listen. Why wouldn't you guys be targets too? Why wouldn't he come after Liza, Nina or Felicity? You? Even Rachel was involved because of Duke, which had nothing to do with Ace, even if it did connect to the Sons."

"I don't know." Cecilia's eyebrows drew together. "Well, technically someone shot at Liza."

"Shot *at*, not killed. Regardless, the letter referencing that was to Jamison, not to Liza." Sarah grabbed Cecilia's arm. "What if it's not about Ace?"

"How could it not be about Ace?"

"I don't know." But it made more sense. Liza, Nina and Felicity had had specific run-ins with Ace. Cecilia had been involved with his protégé being hurt. The women should be more involved, but Anth was focused solely on the brothers.

Of course, they were the actual relations to him. Was it about blood? Brotherhood?

"The notes all say treason. I thought it had to do with leaving the Sons, but is it something more? Something… personal? Beyond Ace, I mean."

Cecilia took some time to think that over. "Well, we don't know how Anth was raised. Ace was in the Sons, but by all accounts Anth wasn't there. Nor was his mother there."

"Our mother." She'd had to explain her blood connection in the barn this afternoon, and she could feel the *pity* from all her sisters. That her parents hadn't been bad people and were now dead. That she was connected by blood to someone terrorizing them.

Cecilia smiled sadly. "I know that's…"

Sarah shrugged. "I don't know what it is. I haven't had time to work it out really." She rubbed her belly, hoping her baby never had to have complicated feelings about their parentage. "But you're right. He wasn't with his parents that we know of. Until after the Wyatts were all out of the Sons."

"It's possible he was there in the few years Liza was out, but it seems unlikely."

"Still, he was with Ace when Dev tried to arrest him. So, wherever he was, he knew Ace. He was working *with* Ace. Even if he did help Dev, he's connected to Ace."

"Maybe the betrayal is a deeper familial sense. Maybe he's not blaming them for Ace, but they didn't come for him. They didn't help him. They all got out, but he… We don't know what he did, but maybe it was terrible."

"But he made Dev promise not to tell anyone about him," Sarah pointed out, though she thought there had to be something to this line of reasoning. Something about family and connections. Not just Ace. It had to be more. Or the brothers wouldn't be singled out the way they were.

Cecilia sighed deeply. "I wish I thought all these mental circles would get us somewhere, but I think we just have to wait. Wait for him to make a mistake and hope…" Cecilia didn't finish her sentence and shook her head.

Sarah got the feeling she was worried about Brady being next to get a letter. About him being the next target. Even though no one had been hurt yet, anyone *could* have been by the bomb. Anyone *could* have been shot. It seemed a bit of blind luck that they were all still intact.

Still, it was disturbing to see Cecilia, of all people, look so…worried and helpless.

"You're a fighter," Sarah said, hoping to see some of Cecilia's usual stubborn surety.

"We're all fighters. But even fighters get tired." Her hands briefly touched her stomach and Sarah's eyes went wide. She wouldn't have thought anything of it if she hadn't spent the past nine months touching her stomach, just like that.

Cecilia's cheeks turned red.

"Are you…"

"I don't know for sure yet," Cecilia hissed, looking

around the room to see if anyone was paying attention to them. No one seemed to be. "Don't say *anything.*"

Sarah's eyes welled with tears. She couldn't help it. She'd have her son soon, Nina would follow in a few months, and then Cecilia. And they'd all be cousins and...

"Stop that right now," Cecilia said, pointing her finger in Sarah's face. "We are being *terrorized.* No crying over *potentially* happy things."

"But that's exactly *when* you should cry over such things. Bad doesn't blot out the good, Cee."

"No, no it doesn't." Cecilia took Sarah's hand and gave it a squeeze. "But I'd sure like to be done with the bad."

"We will be." They had to find a way. Not just for her baby, but for *all* their kids. For all of them. For family.

DEV COULDN'T REMEMBER a time he'd been this revved and this exhausted at the same time. Two days had passed without a letter for anyone. No more dead bodies. No more attacks. Just tension and stress and so many questions he didn't have the answer to.

Sarah had floated her theory that whatever was going on had less to do about Ace's death and more about family in general, but Dev still didn't know how to wrap his head around that.

His brothers had never had any interaction with Anth—hadn't even known about his existence. Dev had only interacted with Anth once, and under the promise he'd never let anyone know about him.

Three days of nothing didn't make the obsessing over it any easier. In fact, it made it more frustrating. He couldn't shut off his mind. He could only think. Not one of his favorite places to be—and he couldn't do what he usually did when that happened—bury himself in the ranch.

No, there were people around constantly. He didn't even get his own room to sleep in what with the crowded house. Every night he went into his own room after Sarah had fallen asleep in his bed and slept on the floor.

But Sarah wasn't asleep tonight like she should be. She was all cuddled up in his bed, but sitting up, leaning against the headboard.

Something heavy shifted in his chest. A dream realized. Except Sarah was *not* his dream. He'd never let himself dream about a future because he'd been adamant there wouldn't be one.

Wasn't that the best way to avoid pain and failure?

But she made all those walls he'd built crumble, and he felt more like he'd been at twenty and stupid than he was now. He knew what could go wrong when you reached for everything. He'd had the scars to prove it.

She smiled at him and he didn't know how he'd survive any of this, even if they caught Anth and everything went back to normal.

"You should be asleep."

She sighed. "I've tried. Brain's too jumbly tonight. I hate that nothing has happened. I keep thinking if I could just work out some missing piece, we'd be able to set a trap for the next note. But if it never comes…"

"It'll come," Dev replied. This wasn't over. That's what Anth's first note had said. Which meant nothing ended until it was *over*.

"I know. That's why I can't stop thinking."

"Yeah, I think we're all having that problem." He couldn't seem to get himself to move inside the room. Instead he just leaned against the door frame.

"We share a mother. Anth and I. There should be some… bond of connection. Like you have with your brothers."

"We grew up together. It isn't blood that bonded us. It

was everything we survived. I don't have any bond with Anth and we share a father. I've actually met him, even if it was only once."

Sarah looked down at her belly, smoothed her hands over the bump. "It's weird…isn't it? There's a connection here, and he's coming at us when I'm nine months pregnant?"

"There's no way he could know that, Sarah. Our own family didn't."

"I know. I just… It's the thinking. He's making us wait on purpose because he has to know we're sitting here driving ourselves crazy trying to understand him. And we can't, can we? We don't know him. I grew up knowing I was adopted, but loved. So loved. I didn't remember anything about my parents, and I'm not saying I never thought about them, but I was given a life I could never resent. I really doubt he had that."

"Yeah. But he wasn't with the Sons, so it was possible."

Sarah shook her head, her blond hair falling out of its messy braid. Her hair on his pillowcase made his heart ache all over again, but she kept talking about Anth and danger, and for the first time in his life he didn't want to focus on the bad.

"He wouldn't have hooked up with Ace, wouldn't have scared my mother enough to leave me with Duke and Eva, if he had some good life somewhere."

"Maybe."

She fixed him with a look—one of *those* looks that meant she had some…plan or *something*. A battle light, he would call it. He was too weary to figure out an excuse to walk away—get away from Sarah's constant battles.

Or, you kind of like them.

"What was it like to grow up in the Sons?" she asked, clasping her hands over her stomach.

That was not the battle he'd expected, and in hindsight he probably should just walk away. But the answer wasn't as traumatizing as she was probably expecting.

"I don't know." At her sharp look, he shook his head. "It sounds flippant, but it isn't. I don't… It feels like it all happened to someone else. I don't try to remember and the more I don't, the more foggy it gets."

"Did you feel alone?"

He scrubbed a hand over his face. "No. I always had Jamison, and… I think we remember our mother a little better than the younger ones. I think she loved us, but…"

"But what?"

"Her whole life was survival. Her own. We were… pawns of that survival. Which sounds harsher than I mean it. It's hard to blame her…doing what she could to stay alive."

"Couldn't she have escaped back to Grandma Pauline like you all did?"

Dev shrugged. These days he couldn't seem to feel anything for his mother except a sort of pity. What little he remembered of her was of a woman beaten down by… everything. "Maybe. I don't think she knew how. Whatever…whatever attracted her to Ace kept her a victim of his mind games. Or maybe she didn't want to leave. I was a kid. I don't know. I know she feared for her life, but hell, maybe she liked that."

Sarah grimaced, but Dev couldn't deny the possibility. There were too many awful things he'd seen and endured to think some people didn't enjoy or crave that kind of thing.

"After your mother died, what happened?"

"I don't know. We kept...living. Jamison took care of us. Kept us together. Taught us how to survive and planned our escapes. He stepped into her role, I guess. And did a better job of it."

"Anth didn't have either. Not a loving family. Not even the Sons."

"We don't know what he had."

"No. We don't. But what if he had nothing?"

Dev had the uncomfortable memory of what his father had done to them all at seven—except Cody, who they'd managed to get out before Ace's...ritual.

"There's no record of Anth Wyatt," Dev said carefully. "It's possible... Well, what if Ace kept him isolated from everyone? He expected us to be able to survive in the wild at the age of seven. Why not Anth too?"

"What do you mean survive in the wild?"

He cursed himself for forgetting himself. Forgetting that there were things he didn't want to get into. Didn't want to rehash. *Like all of it?*

But it was Sarah, nine months pregnant with his child, who was waiting for an answer. Who was trying to understand, and he didn't have it in him to change the subject. Not when she was in his bed, her hands on her stomach where his own child's heart beat.

"Ace had a ritual. When we turned seven, he'd leave us in the Badlands by ourselves. We had to survive on our own with no supplies for as many days as years we were old every year on our birthdays."

"At *seven*?" Sarah demanded, wrapping her arms protectively over the child inside of her.

That child would never know the kind of terror Dev had known, if he could help it. If he had any say. He'd lay down his own life to keep that child happy and safe.

He cleared his throat, hoping to deflect the wave of emotion. "I was twelve when Jamison got me out of there. He had to do it until he was eighteen."

"Jamison being stuck in that awful place longer than you were doesn't mean your trauma wasn't bad. Twelve days all alone in the Badlands when you were a baby."

"I was hardly a baby."

"You were. Seven or twelve or whatever. And it *is* a trauma. It's awful. No kid should have to survive it."

"But… The thing is, Sarah? We did. We survived it and here we all are. Still surviving." Which was a much more hopeful thought than he'd had in a long while. Survival… He had done that. For years on end—as a kid, then after his coma and injuries. Survival he was good at.

But his brothers hadn't just survived. Now they were all living. Building. Shouldn't he be doing the same? Wasn't it time to build?

No. Right now was still survival. "We should go to bed. Rest while we can. You especially."

She nodded, still studying him with that speculative look. Then she glanced at his sleeping bag on the floor. "You know, you don't have to sleep on the floor. You're certainly not getting much rest."

"Less to do with the floor and more to do with…you know, constant danger."

She pulled back the covers and scooted over in the bed. "There's plenty of room."

All those complicated emotions that had been crashing around inside of him stilled under that very not-innocent offer.

He cleared his throat. "I don't think—"

"Oh, don't be so…*you* about it. I'm just offering to

share your bed. It is yours, after all. You deserve a good night's sleep too."

"I'm pretty sure that bed was made for two, not for three."

She rolled her eyes. "Just come to bed."

He should ignore her. Turn off the lights and climb into his sleeping bag. Stick with sanity, reason and just taking time to...evaluate the situation. But when he turned off the light, she turned on her phone, the light a guiding beacon as if he didn't know the way to his bed by heart.

It wasn't really that big of a deal. She was just offering him part of his bed. He'd sleep next to her and nothing would happen. This didn't mean anything. Or didn't have to. It was just a better place to sleep.

Gingerly, he got into his own darn bed.

She laid the covers over him, then curled up next to him—her pregnant belly pressing against his side, her head nudging onto his shoulder until he had to put his arm around her. She laid her hand on his chest and moved in closer.

There was a physical pain in the center of his chest, right where she placed her hand. He didn't know what it was, only that it made it hard to breathe. He felt...everything.

For a man who'd spent a lot of time focusing on feeling nothing, it wasn't just overwhelming, it was paralyzing. But she didn't do anything. She just lay there, snuggled up against him, her hand resting over his raging heart.

Until, second after second, he relaxed. It wasn't going to kill him—probably. Sleeping like this was just...

"It'd be nice, wouldn't it?" she asked, her voice soft and...something else. Something he didn't associate with Sarah. That vulnerability she was trotting out all of the sudden.

"What?" he asked gruffly, wishing he didn't feel so clumsy with her.

"This."

Nice was not the word. That was too easy, and this was…all those things he'd never given himself a chance to believe in. He had his family, but it wasn't…*this*. He didn't have a choice about loving his family, caring about their well-being. He didn't have a choice about being bonded with his brothers over everything they'd been through.

He had a choice with Sarah, because he'd been making the choice to ignore and avoid for years now. There was too much at stake to change his mind, but she kept… changing it anyway.

It's what she'd always done. Pulled him out of or away from his worst impulses. She was always giving to him, and what did he ever give to her?

He'd keep her safe, come hell or high water, but didn't she deserve more than just *safe*? Didn't she deserve the things he'd told himself he didn't. A partnership and…

She cared about him. Enough to fight for him. Didn't she deserve him to care back?

He placed his hand over hers on his chest. "I guess it would."

She chuckled into his neck. "You guess. Such a sweet talker."

"I wasn't *trying* to sweet-talk you."

"No. Why would you need to when I'm throwing myself at you?"

"You're not throwing yourself at me."

Her lips grazed his jaw. "Aren't I?" she asked huskily.

That pain in his chest turned into heat—made all the hotter by how much he remembered of their night together. It had haunted him all this time, because nothing else had ever stayed with him, moved him, *changed* him quite like that.

Maybe it had taken time to come to grips with the change, but it had started then.

He still held her hand on his chest. She had small hands, but they were rough from ranch work. She was small in general, even with the baby belly, and yet she was one of the strongest, hardest ranchers he'd ever worked beside.

"Sarah…"

"Dev…" she returned, clearly mocking the gravity in his voice.

"I don't know what I have to offer you."

She shifted, her arms sliding around his neck. "It's pretty simple. All I want is you."

Which reminded him of what Jamison had said. *Sometimes being you is enough.* But Dev thought maybe Jamison had it wrong. It wasn't just being yourself—it was wanting to be more of yourself because of someone.

Because of her. Because of Sarah he wanted to be better. To live. To give. It was a terrifying realization, but there was so much terror going on around them, real, psychological terror, that his feelings for her didn't seem quite so overwhelming. Not such a disaster.

No, it seemed a bit like…those good things he'd convinced himself he couldn't have because of a decision he'd made in his early twenties while being beaten almost to death by his father.

Maybe it was time to forgive that kid, just like he would have forgiven all of his brothers—just like his brothers had forgiven him.

Forgiveness seemed too complicated a concept when she was kissing him, pressed up against him, in his bed. He could figure out forgiveness later. For tonight he could just be him. Just be what she wanted. Later he'd worry about being what she needed.

He pulled Sarah's hand from his chest and pressed a kiss to her palm. Then to her wrist. He shifted onto his side and slid her arm up and over his shoulder. Her belly was between them, a reminder that no matter what happened, they'd created life together.

She'd brought him back to life because of it. So he kissed her. He let himself pour all the different emotions inside of him into her—fear and worry and all those dark spaces he didn't think were good enough. These small little buds of life inside of him, of revival. The tiny but growing warmth of hope she'd given him, year after year.

She kissed him back with all of her strength and determination. No surrender or passive acceptance—a challenge, because she'd always been one. And he thought, she always would be one. Which seemed about right. It seemed like just the thing he needed.

But she was soft. There were vulnerable parts to her. It wasn't all strength against strength—her hard head against his. No, they'd have to explore these more tender areas too.

Which right now felt like heaven.

She sighed against his mouth, languid and perfect. "I love you," she murmured.

The words had him freezing.

She didn't stop moving against him. "You don't have to say it back. You don't have to feel it yet. I've got quite the head start."

"I don't…" It was all too much. Every time he thought he was taking this small, positive step—she flipped everything on him.

"And I know you didn't *know* I was in love with you this whole time because I didn't really admit it to myself."

She kissed the corner of his mouth, held tight around his neck. "I was talking with Cecilia the other night about everything and… Well, we shouldn't ignore Christmas or love just because someone wants to hurt us."

"No, we shouldn't. Sarah, I—"

"And you're not there yet. It's okay." She pressed her mouth to his. "Don't stop," she murmured against his lips. "Ignore everything I've said."

But how could he ignore *love*? How could he go back to the place he'd been when she'd introduced a whole new level? One he didn't understand.

One she deserved. And if she deserved it, didn't that mean he needed to find it in himself to figure it out? "I don't know where I am. I'm not even sure I know *who* I am. I don't know how to love or how to be a partner. I've been…dormant or something."

"That's ok—"

"Would you let me *talk*?"

"It's just, if you say it now, it's only because of the baby. Because of danger. It wouldn't be real if you said it now."

He understood what she meant, and yet he didn't find himself nodding in agreement. There was a denial inside of him, and that meant all he had was the truth. "I don't understand half of what I feel about you, but it's all real."

She inhaled sharply, but she didn't let him go. She didn't wriggle away. She held him tighter. "Then show me."

Chapter Fifteen

For the first time in her life, Sarah woke up next to a naked man. It was quite an interesting position to be in.

In the early morning light, she could study him. The blanket was only pulled up to his waist, so his entire upper body was bared to her. All the things she hadn't been able to see last night. The impressive lean muscle of his arms from all the work he did. The smattering of dark chest hair.

There were scars. She wanted to trace them, find some way to soothe those old hurts. Those old betrayals.

She'd told him she'd loved him and he hadn't run away. Granted, she'd been throwing herself at him in the moment, but still. He'd stayed. He'd made love to her anyway.

She knew he'd take his time, and he'd make sure that what he felt was love, and that he could give it to her. Which didn't make it hard to wait for an answer, all in all. He'd find those answers. He was just a little on the slow side when it came to emotional stuff.

He'd get there. He wouldn't have slept with her if he didn't think he could get there.

Slept with her. She couldn't help the silly grin that spread across her face. The world around them might be falling apart thanks to their shared half brother, but together she finally had everything she wanted.

And wasn't that the way? Hopes and dreams never seemed to come true conveniently, and danger never seemed to wait for the appropriate moment to make an appearance.

His eyes blinked open. He stared at her and then the room around them. "It's morning."

"Seems to be."

He got up on his elbows, frowning at the door. "No one woke me up for my turn as lookout."

"I mean, or they didn't…want to interrupt."

Dev blinked once, and then a slow horror crept over his expression. She couldn't help it. It made her laugh.

"I'm glad you find it funny," he grumbled, tossing off the covers and getting out of bed.

Sarah watched avidly and with some disappointment as he pulled on boxers, then jeans. He grabbed socks from his dresser and when he sat down to put them on, he did so on her side of the bed.

He looked down at her, still lying on his pillow. She was sure her hair was a tangled mess and she likely looked as haggard as she felt. Still, he reached out and smoothed some hair off her cheek with a gentleness that had a lump forming in her throat.

"You haven't had any contractions?"

Despite the emotion swallowing her whole, she was determined to play this off as no big deal. If she convinced him it was just normal, just *good*, maybe he wouldn't talk himself out of it. "No, your penis did not spur me on to labor."

He rubbed his hands over his face, but he ended up laughing. "You always say the damnedest things."

She grinned at him. "It's part of my charm."

He stared at her so long the grin started to die. It was too serious a look, too serious a study.

"It is," he finally said, with great gravity. "Are we really going to do this? Love each other. Raise this baby together. Be a family. Are you sure that's what you want?"

And there it was. On another man she might call it uncertainty. But she'd been there when he'd survived being beaten near to death by his own father. It was a caution ingrained in him from all the ways life hadn't been fair.

But in that tragic, unfair childhood he'd had Jamison. And Grandma Pauline. So she truly believed…he had the capacity to move past that caution. If given the right push. "I conned you into being the father of my baby, didn't I?"

"I'm serious. I know you set a goal and go after it. I know you accomplish everything you want to. It's who you are and… I admire that about you. But you have to be sure this is really what you want."

She had to take a breath at that, because as much as she loved him, she wasn't so sure he saw her for what she was. Wasn't sure anyone did. She had walls and facades of her own.

But he'd cut to the heart of her. "I imagine there will be some surprises along the way," she said slowly, trying to work through the right words. But sometimes there was no right word, no plan. There was only…honesty and heart. She didn't like those times, but she knew if she was going to get through to Dev on a permanent level, she'd need to offer that to him. "Some hard times. But…we've already done that. I don't know why it would change. Not when we love our ranches, our families. We want to raise this baby together. It's not some fairy tale I've envisioned. It's what we already have. Only together."

His hand was still on her face, still gentle. He seemed to sit and carefully absorb each word. Then he leaned down and pressed a quick kiss to her mouth. "I'm going to go make sure nothing happened last night."

She nodded, but she pulled the covers back. "I'm coming too. But it'll take me about an hour to get there so you go ahead."

He helped her out of bed first, but then he left the room while she got dressed and then headed for the bathroom. She wasn't haven't contractions, but she definitely felt weird this morning. Maybe she just needed to eat.

After pulling her hair back in a sloppy ponytail, she headed for the kitchen. She stopped short at the way a majority of her family was huddled around the table. Felicity and the girls were missing, as were Duke, Rachel and Tucker—who were probably out doing chores.

"Oh, no. What is it?"

"Brady's letter came," Dev said flatly.

"How?"

"Knives," Brady replied, his voice void of any inflection. Sarah stepped closer and there were a variety of daggers in plastic bags on the table. Along with the letter. She assumed they'd put the knives in the bags in the hope there'd be fingerprints on them—but Sarah doubted it.

"What does it say?"

"'Brady Wyatt,'" Cecilia read before her husband could, acidity dipping from every word. "'Crimes: The subject has been the perpetrator of a wide variety of crimes since childhood. Extreme stalking, harassment, kidnapping, manslaughter and treason. Sentencing: For these acts, I do hereby sentence Brady Wyatt to death. This will be meted out at the judge's discretion through the method B. Wyatt will remember from his father.'"

Sarah turned her gaze to Brady. Clearly he knew what that last line meant, but he made no effort to explain, didn't *want* to explain.

At least, until Cecilia slid her hand over his on the table. Then he let out a long sigh. "It's knives. Ace used to throw them at me. I'm pretty sure the six knives on the door were Ace's." He gestured to the blades on the table. "Like, actually his collection. Passed down to Anth, with the stories of what Ace did to me, I assume."

"Well, you don't go outside, he can't throw knives at you. Problem solved," Cecilia said fiercely.

Brady's mouth curved slightly, as if he was trying to offer Cecilia a reassuring smile and failing.

Rachel, Duke and Gage came inside, snow clinging to their hair. They were still wearing their coats and boots instead of leaving them out in the mudroom. "Another letter?" Duke said gravely.

Brady nodded.

"Take off your gear now and come eat. All of you sit down and eat," Grandma Pauline insisted. She frowned at Rachel's back. "What's on your coat, sweetheart?"

"My coat?"

Grandma Pauline reached out for the back of Rachel's coat, but she stopped short. "Duke."

"What is it?" Rachel demanded.

"Don't move," Duke said sharply. His gaze moved to Tucker, who moved around to Rachel's back too.

Tucker swore, but it wasn't an angry kind of swearing. There was a horrified note to his tone.

"What's going on?" Rachel demanded. She started to reach back, but Tucker took her hand.

"You've got a note pinned to your coat," he said, his voice rough.

"What? That's impossible."

Everyone at the table immediately got up and crowded around Rachel's back. Sure enough, there was a piece of paper safety-pinned to the back of her coat.

Tucker's letter.

Tucker Wyatt
Crimes:
  The subject has been the perpetrator of a wide
variety of crimes since childhood. Following in his
brother's footsteps, he has committed treason with
the terrorist North Star group, along with falsify-
ing evidence, and involvement in false arrest and
imprisonment.
Sentencing:
  For these acts, I do hereby sentence Tucker
Wyatt to death. This will be meted out at the judge's
discretion through the method T. Wyatt deemed ac-
ceptable through his own connection to the terror-
ist group.
—AW

"He broke the pattern," Sarah said. "He didn't try to hurt Brady first before he delivered Tucker's letter."

"Someone get some gloves and get this off her," Tucker snapped, which was rare for the usually even-keeled Tucker.

Sarah turned to Dev. "What do you think it means? He broke the pattern."

Dev's eyebrows drew together. "Tomorrow is Christmas Eve. He says we all committed treason, and the only betrayal we could have done in his mind would be against the Sons. Family? Ace? Maybe it all…culminates on Christmas?"

Jamison worked to get the safety pin and letter off of Rachel's coat without disrupting any potential fingerprints.

"So where's yours?" Tucker said.

Dev inhaled sharply. Sarah slid her hand into his. She had a terrible feeling about all this—about Dev not getting one first, or with this back-to-back set. About *everything* accelerating beyond the pattern she was still struggling to make sense of.

"I don't know," Dev said, squeezing her hand. "I really don't know."

THAT NIGHT, Dev listened as Jamison outlined all the local police were doing, and how the feds were getting involved.

"No prints on anything. The bomb was dangerous. It could have done some significant damage and they've sent it on to the feds to see if they can track down who bought the materials. But as for evidence we'll be able to use against him? Nothing."

Dev didn't feel in any way, shape or form comforted. Nor did any of his brothers.

The letter on Rachel's coat was the biggest concern. Had he been in the mudroom and put it on the coat? It seemed unlikely that hadn't been noticed until after they'd come in for chores. But how had Anth, or whomever, gotten close enough to pin it on to Rach's coat without her knowing?

"It's impossible. Both scenarios are impossible. She wasn't alone for no one to notice and someone *would* have noticed beforehand." Tucker stalked the kitchen. His normal calm demeanor even in crisis was gone— probably since the note had been pinned to his fiancée's actual person.

Sarah was the only woman in the kitchen. Cecilia had taken Rachel upstairs under the guise of wrapping presents—but what Dev was sure was an effort to take her mind off the fact that Anth had possibly been close enough to touch.

Liza and Nina were giving the girls baths, and Grandma Pauline was doing laundry while Felicity and Duke were in the living room encouraging Claire to walk.

Life went on, even as it was threatened.

"They'll run the prints on the knives, the new letters, and look for any kind of DNA on Rachel's coat, but hard to believe he'd leave anything," Jamison continued. "And we're using up a lot of the county's resources while not being able to fully work."

Tucker swore under his breath. All his brothers looked grim. Dev glanced at Sarah. She was standing there, worry lines etched across her face as she rubbed her stomach.

She'd been the one to focus on the pattern. The idea it wasn't as cut and dried about Ace as they might think. She was the one to put the idea in his head.

This was about *him*. His brothers might be getting the notes and threats—but the absence of him getting one *meant* something.

Dev had the horrible hope it meant he could do something about this. But he'd have to face Anth alone, and he knew no one in his family would go for that.

There was the option to sneak out, but Dev figured that caused more problems than it could solve. He needed his brothers on his side, and he...didn't know how on Earth he'd convince them to let him handle it.

But convincing them in smaller groups was his only chance. He looked around the table, then up at Sarah, who was standing at his shoulder. He wished he could get rid of her, but she'd never leave. She'd assume they were going to make plans without the women, and she wouldn't budge.

So he somehow had to win Sarah *and* his brothers to his way of thinking.

Good luck.

"I think I should go out and do the evening chores on my own." Because he was no orator or persuasive speaker. There was only what he thought and what should be done.

"Right," Cody said sarcastically. "Hop on out there. We'll just huddle up in here and see what happens."

"Well, why not?"

"Because it's idiotic," Sarah said, crossing her arms over her chest. "Possibly the stupidest thing I have ever, *ever* heard you say."

"I have to agree," Jamison said.

"He didn't leave me a note. That means something."

"Maybe you'll get one tomorrow. We don't know what he's doing." Gage shook his head. "Patterns or not, we don't know how to predict what a psycho is going to do. I don't think giving him an easy target is in anyone's best interest."

Dev wasn't so sure. A target was…action. It was something. It could spur action and that could spur reaction. He could tell he wasn't going to get anywhere with them, though. Too many noble souls, and Dev found he didn't want any of them to sacrifice that.

So, he'd have to figure out another way.

"All right. I'll have Duke go with me." Maybe one-on-one outside he could convince Duke to let him go off on his own. His family would be pissed, but someone would know where he was.

Dev stood and headed for the living room, but Sarah followed, stopping him in the hallway by grabbing his arm. "I know that look. That's *my* look."

"What look?"

"A goal. A plan. One you don't want anyone to know about. Grim determination to do things your way, no matter the cost."

He looked down at her and sighed. "I just said I'd get Duke. No going outside alone, so I'm getting your father—you know, the other rancher in this house."

"Aside from me."

"You're out of commission for the time being, Sarah. You know that. Now, the evening chores need to be done with what little daylight we have left."

Still she didn't let go of his arm. "Don't do anything stupid. Promise me."

He looked at her and hated how much worry was there. How valid it was. "I don't have a death wish."

"Anymore."

He smiled a little, if only because it was fair enough. "Anymore," he agreed. "It has to end, and I'm the one… I don't have a letter. I should have been first."

"He warned you. You got an 'it's not over' letter."

"I should have been first. I wasn't. We got two sentencing letters in one morning—and one wasn't for me. I'm the only one who's met Anth. Who even knew he existed. You're the one who said there's a pattern that has to mean something."

"So what if it does?"

"Sarah. At some point, this has to end."

"That doesn't mean you'll be the one to end it alone. We have to end it together." She gave his arm a shake as if to get through to him. "So, promise me."

He didn't know how to promise her something so nebulous. Especially when she didn't mean don't do something stupid, she meant don't get hurt. He couldn't promise that.

"I love you," he said instead, because there was a very

good possibility of getting hurt, and she deserved the words. "And I love our baby. I absolutely want to be around. I'm not going to run off half-cocked because I'll let my guilt force my hand."

"But?" she demanded, tears heartbreakingly filling her eyes.

"But, I'll do whatever it takes to protect my family. I *have* to." He placed his hand over her stomach. Any day now, that baby would be born. Any day now, he would have a child in his arms. His own. "I'll do everything I can to survive, but survival means nothing if we don't win."

"It's not about winning."

"Maybe *win* is the wrong word. I don't know what the right one is. I want you all safe. I want this over. I want a *life.* We all deserve one. If I'm the target or the center or the purpose, I can't wait around for *him* to decide how to end it. You're going to have this baby any day now. We need this danger taken care of. Now."

She blinked up at him, a tear falling over on her cheek. It tore him in two. Even if she'd been a little more emotional since she'd gotten pregnant, it didn't ease the pain of seeing her cry. Of knowing *he* was making her cry.

He wiped away the tear for her and she sniffled. She shook her hair back and glared up at him. "If anything happens to you, I'll kill you myself," she said, and then stalked away from him down the hall.

Dev blew out a breath. He wished he could be swayed by her emotions or her threats, but in the end he'd do what he had to do.

Chapter Sixteen

It turned out Sarah didn't have to kill Dev. Yet. He and Duke returned from the evening chores without incident—though Sarah didn't trust the look they gave each other as they came inside.

Sarah let everyone bustle her off to bed. She didn't sleep, but she lay there, eyes open. When the contractions tightened her belly, she watched the time. They were sporadic, and as long as they were, there was no way she was telling anyone about them.

Not while Dev was so determined he had to be the one to solve this horrible problem. No, she couldn't leave him.

He came in halfway through the night after his turn as lookout and slid into bed with her.

"Nothing going on," he murmured as she snuggled into him.

"Good."

"Sleep."

She didn't. It was too hard with the worry on her mind and the contractions popping up without warning. She couldn't be shipped off to the hospital. It was terrible timing. Baby would just have to stay put. Besides, he wasn't due for another day.

She'd power through. She'd read tons of stories about women who'd had long, elaborate labors. Who'd had contractions for days and days before going to the hospital. She would be fine. Especially for her first time, she was certain her actual delivery was a ways off.

It had to be.

Christmas Eve dawned, pearly and snowy. Sarah gave half a thought to how bad the roads would be to get her to the hospital. But it wasn't like a whiteout blizzard or anything. It was just a slow-falling snow that kept accumulating.

She wasn't going to be dumb. She'd tell everyone with more time than she needed. Maybe when her contractions were ten minutes apart. Or if her water broke. That would be her guide.

As the day wore on, lookouts and chores interspersed with Christmas crafts and baking with the girls, she was certain she was right. She could go an hour without having a contraction. Although then they usually sped up for a while after one of those hours before tapering off again.

But they did keep tapering. They weren't regular exactly. And no one noticed. As long as no one noticed they couldn't be *that* bad.

She was pretty sure Dev and Duke had something up their sleeve every time they went to take care of ranch chores, but they always came back. No sign of anything. Except that *look* they gave each other.

Sarah lumbered into the living room after dinner. She'd tried to go to sleep early but she was antsy and uncomfortable.

All her sisters, except Cecilia, were wrapping the girls' presents from Santa. Cecilia was stationed outside the sleeping children's room as lookout.

All the men decided to do a sweep of the property while the women prepared Santa's arrival. Which left

Sarah feeling even more antsy. "He's going to do something stupid. I can feel it."

Her sisters and Grandma Pauline looked at her with no small amount of pity.

"I assume you mean Dev," Rachel offered, expertly taping off another corner of shiny red wrapping paper.

"Yes, I mean Dev." Sarah winced as a contraction started—but the doctor had said as long as she could speak through them, she was fine. *Fine.* "One of these times he's not going to come back because..." She had to stop and take a breath—but that wasn't the same as not being able to speak through them. *Right?* "He's off doing something stupid trying to end this all by himself."

"I'm sorry, girl, but stopping a Wyatt boy from doing something stupid is like stopping the Earth from spinning," Grandma Pauline said, curling ribbon with a pair of scissors. Then she looked up at where Sarah was standing, one hand pressing on her belly, desperately trying to arrange her face in something other than a grimace of pain.

"Are you having contractions?" Grandma Pauline demanded.

"Not...really."

"Not *really*?" Liza shrieked, leaping to her feet.

"Just here and there. Very far apart."

"Lord almighty," Grandma Pauline said as all the women started to get to their feet.

"Wait. Where are you going?"

"You have to get to the hospital."

"I can't! We can't. It's not time. You're not supposed to go until the contractions are closer together. Besides, Santa has to come. You have to finish."

"Your contractions might be close together by the time

we brave the roads to get to town," Liza said, helping Grandma Pauline to her feet. "Don't be stubborn, Sarah."

"It is not time yet," Sarah repeated, ready to fight them off. She wasn't going anywhere. Not on Christmas Eve. Not with Dev out...doing whatever he was about to do that she was just certain was going to get him hurt.

"Sarah." Grandma Pauline's voice was gentle, which had tears welling in Sarah's eyes. "I know you're scared. That's all right. But we need to go."

Sarah wanted to argue more, but Grandma being gentle with her made her feel...small. Silly. Like maybe all this fixation on Dev doing something stupid was just an attempt to take her mind off the fact that she was in labor. When she didn't know how on earth she was going to push a baby out of her.

Before Sarah could say anything, acquiesce or argue more—because she really didn't know which to do—the door to the kitchen slammed open and footsteps thundered toward them.

"Fire." Tucker stumbled in, panting. "Stables are on fire. Called 911, but—"

Sarah looked around at the women in the room. She could see her sisters were reluctant to go because of her. But the stables weren't just housing the horses for the Reaves ranch right now. They had all the Knight horses too.

She couldn't stand the thought of anything but everyone working to get them safe. "Go. Please. Take care of this first. I promise you, there's time on my end."

Felicity and Nina exchanged a look, Sarah supposed because they'd both given birth. Felicity gave a little nod. But they didn't rush out of the room. "We have to think this could be a trap."

"The horses are in the stables," Sarah said desperately.

"And the hoses will be frozen. It'll take forever for the fire department to get out here. If you let the men take care of it, they'll do something extra stupid."

"That's true," Nina agreed, but she looked at Sarah's stomach with some trepidation.

"Nina, stay here and watch the girls with Cecilia," Liza ordered, already heading for the door. "Grandma Pauline, you're on Sarah duty. You'll have Cee and Nina if things get hairy on the labor front."

"I don't need—"

But Liza, Rachel and Felicity were already gone, following Tucker out into the kitchen, which would lead them back outside. There wasn't time to talk it over. Time was of the essence.

Grandma Pauline looked at Nina. "Grab a gun and go guard the girls' rooms with Cecilia. Sarah and I will get the rifles and sit tight on this level."

Rifles. Sarah pressed a hand to her tightening stomach. "He isn't after us. He's after the boys."

Grandma Pauline sighed. "That doesn't mean he won't come after us to get to them."

DEV DIDN'T THINK anyone was under the assumption the fire was just a fire. Jamison had instructed everyone to stay with a partner—one to be part of the bucket brigade, and one to stay close to watch out for any attacks.

Because no one could argue with the fact they had to get the horses out of the stables before the fire consumed them.

There was no way to get hoses working in the subzero temperatures, so they'd had to start a bucket brigade, passing buckets of water from the one spigot that wasn't frozen. They'd never be able to put out the fire in its entirety. They just needed a space to get the horses out.

He could hear their worried whinnies, but it looked like the fire had started from the outside. If that was the case, he could still save them.

Jamison was stationed closest to the blaze, determining where to throw the buckets of water.

"I've got to go in," Dev said over the sounds of the howling wind and the crackling blaze. Snow was falling but not at a rapid enough pace to extinguish the man-made fire. The smell of gasoline was almost overwhelming.

It had been set. To get them out here, but the women in the house were armed. Capable of fending off an attack. Every group of people was taking precautions. Though Dev didn't think Anth was going for the house. No, he wanted him out here. Outside where there was less protection, less cohesiveness.

They'd been drawn out to be targets. Dev was sure of that. Once he saved his horses, he'd be whatever target Anth wanted. It was time to end this.

"It's still too dangerous," Jamison said.

Dev shook his head. "Too much longer and we lose the horses. Just water down my coat. It'll only take me a few minutes to get them out."

"It'll take longer than that. You know it will. Those horses will freeze. You're going to have to pull them out. It'll take time."

"Give me three minutes. Just three."

Jamison paused. He took the bucket handed to him. "Your leg?"

"It'll hold up," Dev insisted. He had to save at least some of the horses. They were as innocent in all this as his family was.

Jamison looked down at the bucket he was holding.

"All right. This should douse you. You take more than those three minutes…" He trailed off.

"I promise. Dump it on me."

Dev braced himself for the cold, but there was no fully bracing for the icy cold seeping through his coat. Immediately his teeth began to chatter.

"Three minutes," Jamison repeated.

"Three minutes," Dev agreed. He crouched low, kept his wet sleeve over his mouth, and then moved. The flames had definitely come from the outside, so while the inside was full of smoke, there were only a few places the flames had broken through.

It would only take a few more places of breakage to have the whole place engulfed what with all the straw and hay as tinder. Dev didn't spend any time deliberating. He moved through from one side to the other, opening stall doors.

Like Jamison had predicted, the horses only bucked and neighed in fear of the smoke and flames. It would take more than the three minutes—so Dev set out to do the most he could in what time he had.

He managed to get three out by covering their eyes with rags and leading them with a heavy hand. But after the third, Jamison grabbed him before he could go back in.

"I've got four more to go," he rasped. "I'll go in on the other side. It'll be quick."

"Take Du—"

But Dev broke Jamison's grasp and ran. He couldn't wait for backup or a lookout. He had dwindling time to get his horses safe. He ran to the back of the stables, which was closer to the remainder of the horses. Fire engulfed the frame of the door, but with his wet sleeve covering his arm, he slid the bar out of the way and shoved the door far enough open that he could get the horses out. Then Dev ran inside, keeping low, keeping his mouth covered.

His eyes stung, his throat burned, but he worked to get the four horses out. The last one was the hardest, Sarah's stubborn mare of course being the most difficult.

Dev was about to admit defeat so he didn't die of smoke inhalation, but the horse finally moved forward and then ran off into the dark night.

Dev stumbled to his knees outside the stable, gulping in the fresh air. His throat felt raw, like it had been burned itself. His leg ached in all the normal places but with a piercing pain he hadn't felt in a while. But the horses were safe, even if they were now running all over creation.

Dev looked up to the the man who stood there waiting for him. It wasn't Duke or one of his brothers. Or at least, one of his full brothers.

"Merry Christmas, brother."

Dev shivered inside his wet coat as he sat back on the snow. He breathed heavily—cold and hot at the same time. Pain in his leg, in his eyes, in his throat. But this was what he'd wanted. A one-on-one. Face-to-face with the man who'd clearly made *him* a target even if he'd used his brothers too as smoke and mirror distractions. "I've been waiting for you, Anth."

Dev couldn't make out much of his features in only the light from the blaze of the fire. The orange glow made him look like some kind of demon from a children's fairy tale.

"Have you now? Seems like you've been conspiring with the brothers who've done so much wrong. Betrayed you and yours over and over again. It doesn't seem like my notes got through to you at all." He held up something in the flickering light, but Dev didn't know what it was.

But something exploded in the distance, a light flashing past the rise. The Knight house maybe, or their stables. Dev couldn't be sure. But he saw as his brothers and sisters-in-law began to run for it.

"That should keep them busy," Anth said cheerfully.

But what Dev hoped to God Anth didn't see was that while a majority of the figures had run off toward the other explosion, it wasn't all of them. Unless they were obscured by the dark, only seven ran for the explosion. That meant at least two were either still on the other side of the barn or running for the house.

Anth laughed as the stables began to moan and creak under the weight of the flames. "You think you know what I want, Dev. But you don't have a clue."

Chapter Seventeen

The contractions were no longer slowing down. Grandma Pauline held her hand while Sarah lay down on the couch and tried not to panic. She couldn't panic about labor when there was a fire and a madman out there.

"Breathe," Grandma Pauline ordered.

Sarah tried to listen, tried to focus on the Christmas lights twinkling around them, instead of her own body. But her thoughts kept whirling around. All the ways this was the worst timing *ever*, and how was she going to make it?

"I was stupid and selfish," she muttered. If she'd told Dev or anyone about her contractions she might be on her way to the hospital, with Dev at her side, rather than worried about him out there fighting fires and trying to save their horses.

"You are young and maybe a little foolish, but neither stupid nor selfish," Grandma said matter-of-factly. "My mother had me in this very house. We both lived to tell the tale. If there wasn't a fire and someone out there likely threatening us, you'd be on your way to the hospital. As it is, we've got a fire truck and an ambulance on the way."

"If they can get here." The 911 dispatchers had been apologetic, but had emphasized how long the response time might be due to weather and available emergency vehicles.

Still, help was coming. Even if she ended up having the baby here, help was on its way. For all of them.

She knew without a shadow of a doubt Anth was out there. Why would there be a fire if he wasn't? And if he was out there, he wouldn't be alone. He'd have backup. Wouldn't he? Enough to outnumber all of them?

Especially while they were busy trying to save her horses. Dev's horses.

"Breathe, Sarah," Grandma Pauline said sternly.

"He's out there. He has to be out there and they're all…"

"Smart individuals who'll do what they can to keep their loved ones safe. We have extra help on the way. You need to focus on you. Your contractions are getting closer and closer together. Let's focus on this little Christmas baby."

Sarah tried to nod. Regardless of what terror might befall them, she was in labor. Actual going-to-have-a-baby-in-a-house labor. No amount of danger, not even an act of God, was going to change or stop that.

"Did your mom have a doctor with her?" Sarah asked, trying to focus on baby-having and baby-having alone. Her son. She had to bring him into the world. Somehow.

"No, ma'am. It was February. A raging storm. Whiteout blizzard, or so she always told. She had my grandmothers with her and that was it. And look at me. Eighty years later, still kicking."

Sarah wanted to smile but another contraction washed over her. She tried to picture it. Eighty years ago. Having a baby with only a mother's guidance in the middle of a blizzard, knowing if something went wrong, that was it. For both of them.

She had help coming. An ambulance for her, fire department for the horses. But where was the police officer who was supposed to have been watching the road? She opened her mouth to say something about him, but there was a commotion in the kitchen and Brady and Liza burst into the living room.

"He blew something up over toward the Knight property," Brady said, coming to kneel next to Grandma Pauline. "Most ran over there, but Liza told me about Sarah. I thought I should be here."

"You got any of your EMT stuff?" Grandma demanded.

"I'll go get it in a second. First, I want to check her out. What are the contractions like?"

"Painful. You're not going to deliver my baby, Brady. That's weird."

He didn't even acknowledge she'd spoken. "How far apart are they?"

"Five minutes," Grandma Pauline said. "On the regular. Imagine it'll get closer and quick."

"Has your water broken?"

Sarah shook her head. "That's good, right? It's still going to take a long time if my water hasn't broken. Right? You don't have to deliver my baby. It'll be fine. Have you even delivered a baby before?"

Brady offered what she supposed was meant to be a reassuring smile. "It's definitely not a bad sign. As is the fact you're lucid. I'll go get my kit. It won't help with labor per se, but we can get a blood pressure reading and start sterilizing." Brady got to his feet.

"Wait, you didn't answer my question."

But Grandma Pauline waved him on. "Liza, you go with him. Then if the coast is clear you tell everyone fighting those fires to come home. The horses are safe— let the rest burn. Get all those boys inside. Now. If he's out there lurking about, we all need to be together. Things and even houses can be replaced. People can't." Grandma gave Brady and Liza a stern stare. "Now."

Sarah struggled to sit up. "I should help. I should—"

"Sorry. Your one and only job is labor," Brady offered. "You sit tight. Let us handle things." He and Liza rushed out the way they'd rushed in.

"He's out there. He has to be out there." Sarah sagged back onto the couch. She was going to hyperventilate if she didn't calm down. She focused on her breathing. "Anth is out there. He could pick them off. He could—"

"There's all sorts of things he could," Grandma Pauline agreed. "There's also all sorts of things your family can do to thwart him. We'll have Liza bring them all back home, and Brady will get what he can to help you have a safe delivery. We're survivors, Sarah Knight. Don't you forget that."

Sarah swallowed and tried to nod, keeping her hand in Grandma's. Survivors. Yes. All of them were. Fighters, like she'd told Cecilia the other night. Things might be scary, they might look grim, but they'd all faced those things before.

And won. Survived. Lived and continued to love.

Yes, it would be okay. It would have to be okay. Even if everything burned. Even if Brady had to be the one to deliver her baby. They would survive. All of them.

With a pop, the lights went out. Grandma Pauline's hand squeezed hers. "It's all right, girl," she whispered.

But Brady hadn't returned and Sarah knew it definitely was not all right.

Especially when she felt the warm, wet trickle of her water breaking.

"So, what is it you want?" Dev managed to ask, though his teeth were chattering so hard it was a wonder he got any words out.

"We have an opportunity. You and me. The chance to do what Ace never could." Anth spoke in much the same way Dev remembered Ace speaking. With a calm, determined fervor. If you didn't know better, it was easy to get swept away in.

Too bad Dev knew much, much better. "L-live normal, s-sane lives?"

Anth snorted. "No. That ship sailed. That's the kind of thing my mother tried to give me." He scoffed. "Who wants normal? She tried to convince me to settle for so much less than I deserve. I had to hurt her. I had to show her. I was born for so much more. So were you, Dev."

For someone who wanted to do what Ace never could, he sure sounded a lot like their father. Still, Dev couldn't make sense of being singled out. "Why me?"

"Well, for starters, you realized being beholden to law and order was beneath you."

Dev opened his mouth to argue with Anth. His law enforcement career had ended because of the physical limitations of his body, thanks to Ace. But one thing Dev had learned in dealing with Ace: don't try to reason with an insane person.

If he played along he could see what Anth might divulge. If Anth was here, he was far away from the family. If Dev could keep Anth right here, they weren't just safe, they had a chance to end this.

"I had hoped showing you what monsters your brothers were would change the tide, but you remained stubborn about it. You continued to protect them. You saw their crimes. Always protecting them, and for what?"

Dev wasn't sure how to answer. Anth was no more sane than Ace had been. It was almost exactly like talking to his father. He'd feel more sympathy for Anth if he hadn't talked about being made for more than his mother wanted to give him.

In Dev's experience, when someone tried to give you the escape hatch, you took it. You were grateful for them. Dev hadn't been grateful enough for Grandma and Jamison—dousing too much of it in self-loathing.

But he'd wanted them. Always what they could give, even when he didn't believe he deserved it.

He knew better now. That part of his life was over. He had to find a way to end this with Anth—once and for all.

"Well, y-you c-certainly b-beat us. Though we're still alive, so I'm not sure what the point of those s-sentences was."

"I couldn't kill them," Anth said, as if that was obvious. "That would have turned you against me. Eventually, they'll have to get what's coming to them, but we'll make that decision together. We'll do it together. You do see how wrong they were. How many horrible things they've done. Don't you?"

"Yeah. I mean, I didn't at first." Dev tried to think of what Anth would want to hear. "But your notes were... convincing. I was just confused since you didn't kill them."

"We can. We will. Together. That's what I have to offer you, Devin. A partnership. Building the thing Ace never could. True freedom. True power."

Dev racked his brain for something to say. Some way to agree with Anth, but this was so insane he didn't know how to even pretend to be that out of touch. He tried to think back to his childhood, those fuzzy memories he'd tried to push so far away they never surfaced.

When Ace had raged, what had Jamison done? Played the part. Puffed him up. Made the conversation about Ace, not one of his disappointments or escaped sons.

Dev wrapped his arms around himself, rubbing his hands up and down his coat sleeves, trying to create some warmth. "Y-you've certainly shown you're as s-smart as he was. Smarter," Dev quickly amended.

"It's amazing how easy it is to set traps when you plan for years. Ace taught me that, but I took it farther. I always took what he taught me farther. He could never get the cops on his side. Me? I befriend one underpaid cop, tell him what he wants to hear for *years*, then it's easy to get him to look the other way with a simple down payment."

Dev's stomach curdled. He'd certainly considered the fact Anth had had time to plan. And in that planning had been able to do things like plant the bomb and pin a note to Rachel's coat without them knowing how. Palming a key at some point when they weren't as diligent, knowing their patterns and where one could hide to be close but no one knew.

But paying off a cop—one who worked *with* his brothers—to look the other way. Dev hadn't even considered that once.

"Now things are about to start really going down. So let's cut to the chase. I'm giving you the chance, Dev. To see the error of your brothers' ways. I'm the true brother. I saved your life. And you're a true brother, because you didn't tell them about me. You passed the test. Now it's time to start over. I got rid of Ace—"

"Y-you… Ace died in prison."

"You don't think I arranged that? You don't think I arranged *all* of it. Convinced Ace to go after your brothers. Encouraged him to swim in that psychosis. Ace was flawed. Too obsessed with himself, with you all." Anth sneered. "He cared more about size and numbers and being a *god* than actually acting out his vengeance. He didn't understand that the weak had to be eradicated. The disloyal had to be cut out, root and all. I learned. He kept me isolated. Alone. And I learned the power in being small."

"There's power in family too. In working together. Isn't that what you're proposing? Us? Family?"

"It has to be the right family. Your brothers failed the tests, Devin. They care more about law and order and themselves. But you. You care about the right things. That's why we have to start over. Stay small. Just you and me. You can thank me now, Dev."

Dev tried to work through all that, but decided in the end to just push it away. To just go along with whatever Anth said until they were close enough he could knock that gun out of his hands.

"Thanks," Dev managed, though admittedly it didn't sound very sincere.

"Do you understand what I've showed you? Do you understand what we can build? Not the Sons of the Badlands. We aren't sons. We're power. And power over many corrupts. Ace should have kept us small. He should have focused on family alone. Instead he had delusions of grandeur. We won't do that. Our kingdom will be small, but it will be mighty. And it will be built on our blood alone."

"Our?"

"You're righteous, Devin. Or at least, you have the potential. To keep our bloodline pure. To keep our group strong. We have to start all over. It's taken me years to disband the Sons, to undermine their power and influence. Kind of funny how North Star helped me do that."

Dev's vision was dimming. It was too cold and he was wet. He'd inhaled a lot of smoke despite his best efforts.

But he had to stay awake. Stay alive. He couldn't let the elements take him any more than he could let Anth win.

"Now, we'll take over the power vacuum and truly succeed. If you can prove your loyalty. These past few weeks have made me wonder. You've stood by your brothers. Will you stand by me instead?"

"I kept your secret. You're right about that. But I have a quiet life here." Dev tried to think of what words would get through to Anth, but he didn't think there were any. No combination of truth or lies. He couldn't outtalk someone who thought the way Anth did.

"You were made for more, Devin. I think deep down you know that. Don't you know that? Ace was left to die. Through his miraculous—"

"Spare m-me Ace's origin s-story," Dev grumbled. He started to move, in the hopes he could stand. But the gun in Anth's hand went from pointing at the ground to pointing at Dev's heart.

"His origin story is ours. He failed. But we? We can succeed. Based on his foundation. Better. I know he tested the six of you like he tested me. We were made in his image, but better. We can be better, Dev."

"I'm going to stand up or I'm going to pass out and freeze to death right here."

Anth *tsk*ed. "No, I don't think so. Stay seated." He seemed to test the aim of the gun, holding it one way and then another, but always pointed at Dev. "How about this? A test. You pass, you can stand and move on to the next step. You fail? Well…"

Dev didn't think that'd end too well for him, but what other choice was there? If he could stand up, he could lunge for Anth. He could maybe get the gun. Sitting here in the snow he couldn't do a damn thing. "All right."

"Who's the father of Sarah's baby?"

Anth didn't shoot, but the pain that cracked through Dev felt like a shot. "What do you care about that for?" he rasped.

"It's a test, Devin. All you have to do is tell me the truth."

It was impossible to tell what Anth knew. What he didn't. Did he care about Sarah's pregnancy because he knew the baby was Dev's? Even if he'd had Ace killed, even if he viewed Ace with contempt, clearly he was Ace's son—warped in all the ways Ace had been.

The more terrifying thought was he cared because Anth knew he was related to Sarah. Dev couldn't give this imbalanced psychopath the truth. But a lie might get Dev killed.

"Pretty simple question, Dev. The truth. Or your life."

"I told everyone I was the father, yes." If Anth had been watching them, paying attention, he might know that. He clearly knew *something*, didn't he?

But he couldn't really know that Dev and Sarah had slept together nine months ago. There was no way he'd been at Cecilia and Brady's wedding and actually seen it.

"But?"

Dev took a shaky breath, hugging himself against the bitter cold. "But it isn't true. I'm not the father."

"You just decided to pretend to be?"

Dev couldn't tell if Anth sounded skeptical or interested, so he just…talked. Spewed whatever he could think of to say. "She needed a partner. Someone to help her out. I care about her, so I stepped up." God, he hoped admitting he cared about Sarah didn't make her more of a target. If he could convince Anth of this, he could get Anth away. Promise to join whatever insane group Anth had made up. Pretend to care about some cult.

Whatever it took to get Anth far away from here.

Anth sighed heavily. Then he raised his gun. "You fail the test, Dev. I know you're the father. You don't think I was at Brady and Cecilia's wedding? Watching. Waiting. Figuring. See, that's the difference between Ace and me. He was patient enough for revenge, but he wasn't smart enough to make it matter. To build something from revenge."

Dev fought a wave of nausea—whether from the fire and possible hypothermia or the fact Anth had *been* there. Watching. On what should have been Brady and Cecilia's day with nothing of Ace's to touch them.

But it had touched them all.

"It's a shame you couldn't be honest, because I can't abide liars in our new beginning. But you're not my only chance here. You're not the only one with my blood." Without warning, he pulled the trigger, the bullet hitting Dev with a blast of fire and pain in his gut.

He fell to the ground on a howl of pain. It waved over him, black and all encompassing, but he couldn't let it win. He had to keep Sarah safe.

But Anth had already begun to walk away. Toward the house. Toward Sarah. "Sarah and I will build our kingdom," he said, loud enough to echo through the dark night around them.

"She'll kill you first," Dev managed to grind out, but Anth was already too far away. Whistling as he strode for the house.

Chapter Eighteen

Sarah heard whistling and in that moment she was more terrified than she'd been this whole time. She'd face labor with *no* help if someone wasn't out there…whistling.

"Grandma—"

"Shh."

Sarah felt something being pressed into her hand. The handle of the rifle Grandma had gotten when everyone had run out to fight the fire.

"Hide it," she whispered. Then she let go of Sarah's other hand. Sarah couldn't see, but she could hear the sound of Grandma Pauline getting to her feet. "I've got a flashlight right over there in the curio cabinet. You sit tight."

Sarah didn't want to sit tight. She didn't want to let Grandma Pauline go, and she damn sure didn't want someone to be *whistling* somewhere in the house. And what about Nina and Cecilia upstairs? Would they sit tight? Protect the girls?

Please. Please, stay up there.

The whistling grew closer and closer, and the room stayed utterly dark. Sarah thought she heard the sound of a drawer being pulled open, but still no flashlight light came on.

The whistling stopped and Sarah held her breath, finger curling around the trigger of the gun even though she had it hidden under the blanket she was lying under.

Then she heard a crack, followed by the sickening thump of a body hitting the floor.

"Stupid old woman. I hope that killed her."

Terror froze her completely still for far too long. She wanted to scream, but her breath was frozen along with the rest of her. Until her body betrayed her with a violent contraction. She groaned and thrashed against the pain, tears leaking out of her eyes. Grandma Pauline.

"*Hope* that killed her" didn't mean she was dead yet, though.

She heard footsteps above.

"Just a warning," the man's voice yelled loudly enough to be heard upstairs. "If anyone comes down those steps, I'll shoot them."

A light switched on, blinding Sarah and causing her to closer her eyes and flinch away.

"What's this? The baby is coming right now? Well, that does mess with my plans. I'll have to think about that," the man's voice said.

Sarah slowly opened her eyes against the steady beam of light coming from a flashlight pointed way too close to her face. She couldn't make out the man holding it. "Where are Brady and Liza?" she managed to rasp. He hadn't killed Grandma Pauline, though he likely had a gun. Maybe he'd missed them too.

But Brady hadn't come back.

"Those two. Who cares about them?"

"I do. *I* do." Tears leaked out of her eyes, but she tried to blink them away. Tried to focus. She had to focus on surviving this.

"Well, it's none of your business, but I haven't killed anyone tonight. Yet. Well, maybe."

"I heard gunshots. I heard…" Maybe. Oh *God*.

"Morons shot at me in the pitch black. I could have been any one of their loved ones. With all that haphazard shooting it was easy enough to turn course and come up behind them. A few quick blows to the head, and some rope, and they won't be a problem for us for a while. Do you know how well I can see in the dark? It's something of a talent I developed. You see, your mother tried to secret you away. Tried to give you light. But I was given nothing but darkness. Isolation in a little shed. I learned to do what needed to be done. To do what Ace could never do."

So he knew. Knew they shared a mother. Knew…everything. "Grandma Pauline. You—"

"Just knocked her in the head too. I didn't *kill* her. If she dies it's her own fault. I need you to understand that, Sarah. I'm not the bad guy here."

She wanted to laugh, but she was too afraid. Anth was not an average bad guy bent on pain and suffering. He was quite literally insane. Just like Ace had been.

Isolation in a little shed? Had Ace tortured him too? But he hadn't had Grandma Pauline or an older brother to save him. To tell him the truth about the good the world had to offer.

"Now, is this any way to talk to your brother for the first time, Sarah? I've been waiting to meet you. I've been looking forward to it."

Sarah didn't know what to say. She had her hand around the gun under the blanket, but she'd have to raise it and point it at him. He'd be able to fight her off before she did any of those things, especially if a contraction got in her way.

"I… I just found out about you."

"Ah. So your adopted family was full of liars." He

laid the flashlight on the table next to her. It illuminated him and her heart twisted at how much he looked like a Wyatt. Dark hair, tall and broad-shouldered. But instead of the hazel eyes, he had blue eyes. Like hers. But there was no spark of life or warmth in those eyes. Only the fervor of someone who'd had a break with reality.

How was she supposed to handle that? Go along with what they had to say? "I suppose they were."

She was gratified when he nodded. He crouched down next to her, seemingly at ease with the situation. But there was a gun in his hand, and he pointed it at her head.

"I'm here to offer you an opportunity, Sarah. A chance. A test." He frowned at her stomach. "This does put a wrench in the plans, though."

"Maybe you could come back later."

He laughed. Threw his head back and laughed and laughed. Sarah tightened her grip on the gun. He was too close now for her to maneuver the gun and get a shot off, but eventually *someone* would come to save her. She'd be able to shoot him if he turned around to fend off anyone who came in.

As long as a contraction didn't roll through her.

"Did you… Did you know your parents?" Sarah asked tremulously.

"Yes. I lived with our mother for a time. But she didn't understand me. She didn't *try* to understand me. She tried to mold me into so much less."

"C-could you tell me about our mother?" Sarah didn't have to fake the shake in her voice. The emotion. It was both fear and longing. And a desire to reach past his words into something real inside of him.

"She was stupid," he spat. "And selfish. She thought she was better than what Ace could give her. I showed her."

Sarah winced as another contraction began to steal over her. "You… What does that mean?"

"She thought she was sending me away to 'fix' me. An *institution*, Sarah. What mother sends their child to an institution? But Ace knew I was better than that. Ace knew. Sadly, even he outlived his use. He had to die for me to reach my full potential. They all did."

Sarah tried to blink away the tears, but they were falling too fast. "I don't. My baby doesn't have to die. I'll help you with whatever you need, Anth."

"That's exactly what she said. Our *mother*. Exactly the way she said it. You look just like her." Anth raised the gun, his face marred with a horrible sneer.

There was no humanity there. No hope of reaching something in his heart. If he'd ever had any compassion or sense of right or wrong, it had long since been twisted into this.

"I killed her," Anth said. "I had Ace killed. Killing you would be full circle, wouldn't it?" He glanced at her stomach again. "But there is the baby to consider. I know you're having a boy, Sarah. A boy who shares his blood with me. He could be mine."

"You need me alive to get him."

"I wouldn't count on it."

Sarah knew she had seconds at best. She wouldn't be able to get a shot off, but with the right leverage she could smack him in the face with the gun. She'd have to be quick—really quick before the contraction consumed her completely.

"Did you hear that?" she whispered, looking toward the kitchen.

He didn't lower the gun, didn't look toward the kitchen, but his eyebrows drew together. "No."

"Oh. Well then. Good." Sarah tried a fake smile. The contraction was tightening, tightening.

And slowly, oh so slowly, Anth inclined his head toward the kitchen ever so slightly. On a deep breath, Sarah used all her strength to lift the gun, blanket and all, and ram it into his face.

There was a sickening crunch, a scream of pain, but her own pain was overpowering. She lost her grip on the gun and it clattered to the floor.

DEV HAD CRAWLED his way across the snow toward the house. It was pitch black, so Anth must have cut the power. He made it to the back door, knowing he didn't have the strength to fight Anth—and didn't have a gun to shoot him with. He was shaking—both from being cold and wet and likely from blood loss.

But if he could get inside, there were guns. There was help. Surely the women inside could fight off one man. Had he really only been one man?

A man who was deluded enough to think he could take them down single-handedly. He couldn't. *Couldn't*.

Dev heard something, a scuffle or breath expelled. Something…odd. Off. He climbed for the stairs of the porch leading to the mudroom, leading to Sarah.

But he felt something in the snow. A body. "God." He reached out and felt what he could in the dark.

There was a low guttural swear.

"Brady?"

"Knocked us out," Brady rasped, then swore again. "Tied us together. Sarah's in labor. You don't have time to untie us. Go."

It felt all wrong to leave Brady tied up in the snow, but Sarah was in labor and there was no way to get them out of their bonds in the dark. He felt the body next to Brady and found what he'd hoped. Liza's cell phone.

"Is she going to be okay?" he asked Brady.

"I don't know, but I am, so that's a good sign."

Dev placed the phone in Brady's hands. "If you can get some kind of SOS message—"

"I'll see what I can do. Go!"

Dev didn't hesitate. He moved for the house. Every ounce of his body hurt. He was so cold he wasn't sure he'd survive this. But he couldn't die until he knew Sarah and the baby were safe.

In labor. Labor. Too much of a distraction. Too easy for Anth to infiltrate. Dev managed to make it to the mudroom door. Based on what he could feel in the dark it had been kicked open, splintered.

Dev felt his way through the mudroom, then the door to the kitchen, which had been given the same kicked-in treatment.

He could hear the sound of voices. Sarah's and... Anth's. If she kept him talking, and Dev had enough strength, he could maybe sneak into the living room and tackle Dev. He probably wouldn't win, but maybe he'd give everyone in the house a chance to help.

There was a scream of pain—a man's scream of pain. Followed by a woman's keening moan. Dev stumbled forward into the living room. There was a beam of light barely illuminating the far corner of the living room.

Anth was holding his face, screaming, and Sarah was writhing on the couch.

Anth turned toward Dev. Blood was gushing out of his nose—which was pointed in the wrong direction. His hand shook as he aimed the gun at Dev. But as long as he was aiming it at Dev again, he wasn't focusing on Sarah.

"I survived, Anth," Dev said. His vision was blurring

and he wasn't sure his legs could hold him up much longer. But if he could talk, maybe Anth wouldn't shoot. "Isn't that a sign? Ace would have said I was meant for more to survive getting shot. To get back here."

"Ace was a fool," Anth said. He spit blood on the floor, then got to his feet. "You're a fool."

"You should have listened to Ace. You needed a lot more than just you to take us down. You can shoot me, Anth, but you won't make it out alive."

"You could have been better. You could have been—"

A gunshot exploded from behind Dev. Dev couldn't see who'd done it in the dark shadows, but Anth went down with a thud without another word.

Dev rushed forward. "Sarah."

She was crying and she grabbed on to him. "You're okay. You're okay. You're okay. The baby's coming. Is he dead?"

"I think so. We need to get you to the hospital."

"Ambulance coming. But it's snowy and…" Sarah wiped her nose with her sleeve then frowned at him. "Dev, you're bleeding."

"It's fine. I'm fine. I have to go get Brady and Liza. I have to… Who shot Anth?"

"I did." It was Grandma Pauline's voice. Frail and far-away-sounding. Dev jumped up and grabbed the flashlight. He pointed toward the voice. Grandma sat in the opposite corner of the room, small pistol in her hand, blood trickling down her head.

"Cecilia," she said, her voice weak.

It took Dev a minute to think through the shock to realize she was trying to yell at Cecilia.

Dev tried to get up, but his legs wouldn't hold him. Sarah was groaning in pain. "Cecilia. All clear," he called.

Immediately thundering footsteps sounded. Cecilia

appeared and paled. "God. Nina! Nina, get down here! The girls will be okay. Get down here."

"Check if he's dead," Dev instructed. "Then go out to the porch. Brady is tied up but he's awake. I'm not sure about Liza. I…" His brain fumbled. It felt like the world was going gray.

"Dev? Dev?"

"It's okay. I'll be okay." He had to be okay. For Sarah. "The baby is coming."

"Yes. Yes. An ambulance is coming but the roads are bad and there were accidents and—"

"He's dead," Cecilia said flatly as Nina flew down the stairs, gun still at the ready.

"Grandma's hurt," Dev said, pointing to Grandma in the corner. Nina immediately rushed to her.

Cecilia stood and stalked away from Anth's body. "Are you sure he was alone?"

Dev nodded. "Yeah. Turns out one person can do a lot of damage with too much time alone to plan."

"I'll go get Brady. And the others. Then I'm going to call that ambulance again." She disappeared.

"Dev, come help me get Grandma up," Nina said. "We'll put her in the chair."

Dev tried to get to his feet. Tried to do anything to move away from where he was sitting next to Sarah on the couch. "I…can't."

"What? Why can't you?" Sarah demanded, hysteria tingeing her words.

Dev took her hand. He tried to tell her everything was going to be okay, but his throat was too tight. He pressed his forehead to her hand.

"Devin, you tell me right now what's going on."

He could hear the tears in her voice, hated that he'd put

them there. "Anth managed to get a shot off. I'm okay. Just...a little hurt."

"Shot!" Sarah screeched.

But voices began to echo through the kitchen. Not just Cecilia and Brady. That was when Dev noticed flashing lights. The ambulance and fire department. God, thank *God*.

Weakness stole over him, but Sarah had a death grip on his hand. She was his anchor. Just like she'd always been. The thing that had kept him alive. Even when he'd been in that horrible darkness, it hadn't twisted into whatever had afflicted Anth.

Because he'd had her. And his brothers. His grandmother. Anth had been given a mother who had cared, who had tried. But it wasn't enough.

Dev would make sure it was enough for him. Always. So they all had to make it. *Had* to.

"She's in advanced labor," Brady said. He was leading a uniformed EMT over to Sarah with Cecilia's help.

"He's shot," Sarah said. "Dev's shot. Grandma's hurt. Please. Please, look at them. I'm okay." But the last word came out as if she was speaking through clenched teeth.

"We'll get to everyone," the EMT said calmly. "You don't worry about that."

The uniforms reminded Dev of what Anth had told him. "He'd befriended and paid off the deputy that was supposed to be our lookout. He's still out there."

"No, he's not," Jamison said. "I called the department for backup when I couldn't get a hold of him. He'd tried to speed away from here after the fire. He crashed. No word on his status, but it was a nasty wreck."

Dev blinked and looked around the room. An EMT was doing something to him he couldn't quite feel, which was probably bad. But his whole family was here. Bleeding. Dirty with smoke. Wet and frozen with cold.

But here. Alive. Breathing.

So he focused on being alive and breathing too. Pain sizzled through him as the paramedic dealt with his gunshot wound. The medic looked up at Dev. "Going to need to transport you, ASAP."

"Her first. Please."

The EMT looking over him glanced at the EMT checking out Sarah. She shook her head. "Afraid not. This baby is coming now."

Chapter Nineteen

Sarah wanted to scream. Dev was shot. Grandma Pauline was hurt. But they were focusing on *her*. No matter how she protested, there were people telling her to breathe, and then push.

The pain was unbearable.

"Don't let him die," she ground out, pushing with all her might.

"I'm not going to die," Dev said from somewhere behind her. They'd put him on a stretcher and were doing something to him back there, but she couldn't see.

She pushed and pushed and breathed when they told her to. She demanded Dev talk to her and she yelled at the EMTs to help Grandma Pauline, though apparently Brady was tending to her. But Brady had his own head wound, and so did Liza.

"What about the girls?" Sarah demanded after another excruciating painful push. If she focused on her fear for everyone else, she didn't think about the fact that she kept pushing and nothing was *happening*.

"You're doing great," the female EMT encouraged her. "One or two more and then the head will be out."

The head. Her baby's head. How was this happening? Cody had gotten the lights back on and the Christmas lights twinkled around her. Anth's body had been taken away. Those who hadn't been injured were taking turns taking showers and checking on the sleeping girls.

And she was having her baby. In Grandma Pauline's living room. After having survived a brush with a psychopath.

"Come on, Sarah. Push."

Nina was holding her hand, squeezing it. Someone was holding her legs, but she'd lost track of who and how. Which was probably for the best. She just pushed. Pushed and pushed and pushed.

"That's it. That's it. You're almost there. Deep breath, one more big one."

Sarah didn't know where she found the energy to push more. She would have sworn she was spent, and still she pushed. There was no choice. No way to stop this.

"That's it. That's it."

Pushed and pushed and felt the horrible, painful pressure slowly ease as she collapsed back into the couch.

"You did it. You did it. One more and he's out."

Sarah did everything they said. She heard her baby cry. The squirming mass of limbs was placed on the sterilized fabric they'd draped over her. She wasn't supposed to touch him yet, but she could feel his warmth, *him*.

"He's here," Sarah murmured, looking at her baby. Her son.

"And we need to load up and get to a hospital. We're going to wrap him up and take care of him, all right?"

Sarah nodded, because she couldn't speak. She could barely breathe. She was exhausted. Wrung out, and they'd taken her baby away. But he was here. Here and making noise. Alive. Safe.

"See him, daddy?" Sarah heard the EMT ask Dev. She managed to twist her head to see Dev get the first glimpse at their son.

Their son.

In the midst of terror and tragedy, a miracle had arrived.

PAUL KNIGHT WYATT was perfect. His smattering of hair was dark, his eyes were blue—which everyone told him would change, though Dev held out hope he had Sarah's eyes. Regardless, all eight pounds of him made up for everything that had been a part of his delivery.

Dev had not been able to hold his son, or kiss the love of his life, or anything important for the first few days. They'd been relegated to separate hospital rooms, where they could only communicate through video chats on their phones.

But they did those, regularly, even when the pain meds made him a little loopy and one of his brothers had to hold the phone for him.

Sarah and Paul had gone home first. Paul, named after the woman who had saved Dev's life too many times to count. She'd shot Anth, and ended the nightmare. Just like she'd once welcomed him into her home, promising to keep him safe. And loved.

Grandma Pauline had beaten them all home, of course. Though she'd suffered a concussion, she'd been back at the ranch the next day. Liza had needed an extra day of observation because she'd had concussions before.

Everyone else who had battled the fire had been checked out for smoke inhalation, but had invariably been able to go home that night. Though Duke had stayed with Sarah since Dev couldn't.

It was eating him up inside.

When a nurse came in to check his vitals, he harassed her about going home. She patiently told him that was up to the doctors, but surgery following a gunshot wound was pretty serious.

He'd growled at her retreating back, scowling deeper when Jamison entered the room. "I am not in the mood for visitors."

"I wouldn't be so sure about that," Jamison said cheerfully. "I've arranged a little bit of a surprise for New Year's Eve, but it's not authorized, so you're going to have to be a good boy."

Dev only grunted.

"Trust me. You're going to want this surprise."

Brady came in, pushing a wheelchair in front of him. "Gage is distracting the nurses. Let's go."

Dev frowned at them. "You're not breaking me out."

"You're not ready to be broken out," Brady replied. Still, both his brothers helped him into the wheelchair, Brady manning the chair, Jamison pushing the IV cart. They put some blankets over his lap and draped a coat over his shoulders. "Now, don't say a word. Got it?"

Dev couldn't say he *did* get it, but his head and body ached, so he did what he was told as his brothers wheeled him through the hallway, to an elevator, then all the way down to the main floor. And right out the front doors.

"I thought you said you weren't breaking me out." It was cold, but sunny. Dev squinted against the bright sunlight after days of fluorescent lighting. Brady stood behind him, manning the wheelchair, but Jamison walked to the parking lot. To a truck.

His truck.

Sarah got out of the passenger seat and Jamison pulled a baby's car seat out of the back. Every grumpy, angry, pain-fueled thought emptied out of him as she came over, smiling.

"I thought you might like a chance to hold your baby."

Dev didn't trust his voice, so he just nodded. Jamison

and Sarah fiddled with the car seat and wrapped the little bundle up in layers and layers.

After a few minutes, Sarah placed Paul in his arms. She settled a blanket around both of them. "There's your daddy," she whispered to Paul. "We've been missing him. Haven't we?"

Paul was bundled head to toe, pretty much only his eyes and mouth showing. Those eyes were wide and alert and gazed right at Dev.

"Look at you," he murmured, bowled over, body and soul. Heart and mind. Just…blank because all he could do was stare at this baby—*his son*—and feel.

He had no idea how long he simply held his son against him and looked, tried to memorize every expression, every inch. Eventually he raised his gaze to the woman he loved. Who'd given birth to this baby on his grandmother's couch. Who'd survived and was standing there *smiling*. And he was just saturated with gratitude. With love. And hope. "Thank you," he managed to say, though his voice was rough.

"For giving birth?" she asked with a laugh. One hand rested on his shoulder, and the other gently touched Paul's cheek. "I didn't have much of a choice. He was coming out one way or another."

"No. Thank you for saving me."

She looked from Paul to him, smoothed the hair on his forehead. "You're muddled. Grandma Pauline did that."

"She saved my life, probably more than once all things said and done. But I'm not talking about that. I'm talking about…me. Without you, I'd still be…missing."

"Without us," Sarah said, nodding toward their son in his arms.

"Yeah. Yeah. We have to get married."

Her smile died, turning into a confused frown. "You couldn't even phrase it like a question?"

"Why would I do that?" He grinned up at her. "You're going to marry me." There were no doubts, and Dev wouldn't waste another second of his life.

Never again.

Epilogue

One Year Later

She married him. In a small intimate ceremony on the ranch as soon as Dev got out of the hospital. Their families, their dogs, their horses had been there as they'd promised to love and cherish each other forever.

They'd moved into the Knight house, since Grandma Pauline had Brady, Cecilia and later on baby Paula living with them.

Grandma Pauline had quite the array of great-grandchildren named after her.

They put to rest the ghosts of Ace and Anth—together and with their family. As another Christmas dawned, life was good.

Dev stepped into the mudroom and wiped his boots on the mat. He hung his coat up on the peg, shaking the snow off of it. His leg ached, but his wife had snuck out early and done most of the chores before he'd noticed she'd gone.

She'd let him handle the evening chores, and so he'd gone out with his father-in-law and done the work of keeping the Reaves and Knight ranches running, even on Christmas.

When Duke had gone inside Grandma Pauline's,

where the festivities would be, Dev had begged off a few minutes. The moon shone bright above. They'd had a blizzard last week so the entire area was covered in snow. Glittering, Christmasy snow.

He and Sarah had taken Paul out to play in it this morning, and Dev didn't know when he'd ever been so happy.

Actually, he did know. Never. Never in the whole of his life had he been able to access this well of happiness. Because he'd had brothers who'd sacrificed for him, a grandmother who'd given him a foundation to build on, but it had been Sarah and Paul who'd finally brought him to *this*.

The families had grown and the living room was packed. Nina and Cecilia had given birth to healthy girls. Jamison and Liza had adopted three siblings ranging in ages from five to fifteen. It wasn't smooth sailing, but Liza and Jamison were well-equipped to deal with the unique challenges of adopted older children touched by tragedy.

While Cash and Brownie lived with his family at the Knight ranch, Brady and Cecilia had adopted two dogs, and Rachel had gotten a guide dog. All five animals were curled in various spots around the house, because Grandma Pauline had shocked them all and lifted her ban on having animals in the house.

For the great-grandchildren's sake.

Dev took a moment to watch, to enjoy. Sarah had taught him how to do that too. When Paul caught sight of him, he let out a squeal and wriggled away from Sarah.

Dev grinned and crouched down, holding out his arms. "There's my guy. You going to walk to Daddy?"

Paul gurgled an answer, his hazel eyes lighting up with mischievousness. The boy got into everything, loved horses and dogs more than anything else, and held his parents' hearts in his small pudgy hands.

He was *this* close to taking his first steps.

Sarah picked him up and placed him on his feet. The boy bent his knees, over and over again, before taking one step forward. He immediately collapsed, but chortled merrily as his butt hit the ground. Then he crawled the rest of the way to Dev, squealing when Dev picked him up and gave him a little toss.

"Da!"

"You're going to be a walking machine before we know it, aren't you?"

Sarah came over to stand next to him. "I think we've got some major baby proofing to do then."

Paul babbled happily, flinging himself over to Sarah and then wiggling back down to the ground. He crawled over to Grandma Pauline and began babbling happily to her, one small hand resting on Cash's head.

Dev would have gladly slid his arm around Sarah's waist and enjoyed the moment, but Jamison came over.

"Come on," Jamison said, nodding toward the kitchen.

Dev frowned, but got to his feet and followed his brothers back into the kitchen. Gage was getting beers out of the fridge, handing them out. Everyone except him and maybe Tucker seemed to know what was going on.

Though it dawned on Dev eventually that this is exactly what his brothers had done for him last year. Dev grinned.

"What are we doing?" Tucker asked.

"We're inducting our newest member," Jamison said with mock seriousness. "Welcome, Tuck. You've officially joined our ranks."

All eyes turned to Tucker.

"What are you guys... Wait. You know?" He frowned. "Who told?"

"Your wife isn't great at keeping secrets," Gage offered. "And neither am I, since I was the one who over-heard her telling Felicity."

"And spread the word," Tucker said disgustedly.

"Just to the club," Jamison said, raising his beer bottle. "The father's club. Welcome."

Tucker rubbed his fist over his chest. "Is it going to be this terrifying the whole time?"

"Worse," Dev offered.

"And worse and worse and worse," Cody added. "I'm going to have to survive two girls going through puberty, Tucker. Nothing is as terrifying as that."

They laughed and chatted, razzed Tucker about the coming responsibilities and sleepless nights. It was good, and it was right, but Dev couldn't help but think about last year. There had been so much terror and pain and suffering. He wanted to commemorate that somehow. How far they'd come from six scared boys in their father's gang.

"You know, it's been a year now," Dev said. "A year of peace and stability, aside from the fear of puberty and whatnot. We've…had to fight a lot to get here."

"Survived a lot to get here," Gage said.

"Yes, we have," Jamison agreed. He smiled, raising his bottle. "And now we get to live."

Dev clinked his bottle with his brothers. As toasts went, it was the best he could think of. He glanced into the other room, where their wives and grandmother, the women who'd helped save them in a variety of different ways, sat with their children.

So that they could be here.

Living.

Which was finally exactly where Dev Wyatt wanted to be.

* * * * *

INVESTIGATION
IN BLACK CANYON

CINDI MYERS

For Carol Berg

Chapter One

Sun glinted off the hood of the late-model black pickup, the glare almost blinding. Rocks and cactus ground under the tires as it rolled toward the canyon rim. The walls of the canyon glowed red with the early morning light, in shades from pink and orange and deepest vermillion. But the man behind the wheel had no appreciation for the view. His hands gripping the steering wheel until his knuckles ached, his jaw clenched in concentration, he forced himself to keep his foot on the gas pedal when everything in him screamed for him to put his foot on the brake.

The front tires skidded in loose shale at the canyon's edge and then, in the kind of slow motion he had thought only happened in movies, the truck launched forward, rear wheels momentarily hanging up before the pickup plunged downward. Somersaulting in the clear, thin air before striking the rocks with an impact that sent steel and glass exploding outward, the screech of metal and the shattering of glass reverberated against the granite cliffs.

But there was no one around to hear the crash. No one to see the truck as it careened off the rock and hurtled into the dark abyss.

CARA MEAD PULLED her Toyota Prius into the visitor's lot near the entrance to Black Canyon of Gunnison National

Park. She wiped her sweaty hands on her black slacks and breathed deeply, trying to slow her racing heart. She didn't want to be here, speaking with these people, but she owed it to Dane to try. Something was very wrong and she was determined to keep talking until she found someone who would listen.

Feeling bolstered by the thought, she shoved open the driver's door and stepped out. The intense heat of the Colorado sun was mildly tempered by a stiff breeze that swirled dust across the gravel parking lot and set the small sign at its entrance swinging. Ranger Brigade Headquarters, the sign read. Cara frowned. Was she in the right place? Should she drive to the park headquarters instead and ask to speak to a ranger?

No. She had read enough articles in the local paper to know that the Ranger Brigade was the law enforcement agency charged with investigating crimes on public land in this corner of Colorado. Land that included Black Canyon National Park.

She crossed the lot quickly and pushed open the entrance door to the plain, low-slung building.

A middle-aged woman behind a metal desk looked up. "May I help you?"

"I need to speak to an officer," Cara said. "I need to report a crime."

The woman's eyes behind her blue-framed glasses widened. "I'll see who's available."

She disappeared behind a door and emerged a few moments later with a man in a khaki uniform. Tall and clean-shaved, with short-cropped brown hair, he looked like a law enforcement recruitment poster boy. Though *boy* wasn't exactly the word she would have used, if they had met under different circumstances. "I'm Officer Beck," he said. "How can I help you?"

"I need to report a missing person," she said.

"You might be better off talking to local law enforcement," Officer Beck said. "Would you like me to put you in touch with the sheriff's office?"

"I've already spoken to them," she said. The woman who had taken her report there had showed no sense of urgency. "The person who's missing said he was headed to Black Canyon of the Gunnison. If something has happened to him here, isn't that your concern?"

"Why don't you come back here where we can talk?" He motioned for her to follow him and led her down a short hallway to an unadorned gray-painted room furnished with a table and three chairs. He sat on one side of the table and indicated a chair for her to sit across from him. He waited until she was seated before he spoke again. His eyes met hers. "I'm going to record this for our records. Start with your full name, then tell me who's missing and why you think something might have happened to him."

She had thought Officer Beck was ordinary until that moment—just another jaded man with a badge who had already made up his mind about her and her situation ten seconds after she'd walked into the building. But when Beck's eyes met hers, she felt the jolt of his concern and an almost physical connection that startled her. She glanced at the microphone between them, swallowed hard, then began with, "My name is Caroline Mead—Cara. The person I'm concerned about is Dane Trask. He's my boss at TDC Enterprises. He's been gone two days—and that's really not like him. He hasn't contacted me or anyone else at work. I haven't been able to reach him. None of his neighbors has heard from him. His daughter is out of the country and I haven't been able to reach her, either."

"Maybe he went camping or decided to take a few days to himself."

"But it's not like him to just take off without telling anyone anything."

"Why do you think he's in the national park?"

"The last time I saw him, on Wednesday, about six o'clock, he had his backpack and said he was coming here to the park to hike and try to clear his head. When he didn't show up for work the next day, I knew something was wrong."

Officer Beck plucked a clipboard from the end of the table and took a pen from his shirt pocket. "Let's start with some vital statistics."

Cara gave him the details she had memorized—Dane was forty-one, six feet two inches tall, and weighed one hundred and eighty pounds. He had brown hair and blue eyes, a tattoo of a coiled snake on his right biceps, and he drove a late-model black Ford pickup. That last time she had seen him he'd been wearing sunglasses, khaki hiking pants, hiking boots, a black cotton shirt over a black T-shirt, and was carrying a black backpack.

"Has Mr. Trask ever done anything like this before?" Beck asked. "Gone off and not told anyone?"

"Never. He's always meticulous about giving me his schedule. He's really dedicated to his work and to his volunteer activities. I don't think he's even taken a vacation in the three years I've known him."

Beck nodded. "Was hiking in the park something he did often?"

"Sometimes."

"What kind of shape was he in?" Beck asked. "Do you think he might have been injured or suffered a heart attack or something while he was hiking?"

"He was in great shape." She leaned across the table, searching for the right words to convey just how capable Dane was. "He's a former Army Ranger and he still works out like he could be called back to active duty at a moment's notice. He hikes and runs and bikes and lifts weights. He definitely doesn't look like a desk jockey."

"TDC—that's in that big new building on the edge of the park?" Beck asked.

"Right. They've had a satellite office in Montrose for years, but two years ago they decided to relocate their main headquarters here and built the new campus."

"What kind of work does Trask do there?"

"He's an environmental engineer. TDC does all kinds of infrastructure projects, from building schools and factories to hazardous materials mitigation. There are about three hundred employees at this location, but thousands worldwide."

"And you're his assistant?"

"Administrative assistant." She knew Drew Compton, one of the partners at TDC, still referred to all the admins as secretaries, but his suits still looked like they were out of the eighties, too. She stared into Beck's eyes, determined not to let the intensity of his gaze unnerve her. At least she had the impression he was really listening to her, unlike the woman who had taken her statement at the sheriff's department. "Will you try to find him?"

He sat back and his gaze shifted away. "Do you know if anything was worrying Mr. Trask? Has he seemed preoccupied? Depressed?"

"Not depressed, but he was preoccupied. Something was on his mind, I just don't know what." Dane had been spending more late nights at the office and had been a little absentminded the past couple of weeks, which definitely wasn't like him.

"If you had to guess, what would you say was bothering him?" Beck asked.

"I don't know." She had lain awake much of last night,

reviewing every conversation she and Dane had had, searching for any clue as to what might have happened to him. "I thought maybe it was something at work. He's been putting in a lot of late nights and early mornings."

"Was there a specific project he was working on?"

"Several. He did everything from analyzing concrete samples to reviewing environmental testing reports. At any point in time, he might be involved in dozens of jobs."

"What is your relationship with Mr. Trask?"

"He was my boss. And my friend."

"Were you involved with him romantically?"

"No!" She fought down a flush. "Dane and I are both professionals and we had a professional relationship." Yes, Dane was a good-looking, even charming, man. But she had never felt attracted to him romantically and she was sure he felt the same about her. They respected each other and they cared about each other—as friends. Sometimes friendship was even more important than romantic love.

"Was he involved with someone else then—someone who might know better what was bothering him?"

"He wasn't dating anyone at the moment—at least, not that I know of. He ended a long-term relationship with a woman, Eve Shea, last year, though they were still friends. She told me Dane hasn't been in touch with her. His daughter, Audra, is twenty-two. I've been trying to get hold of her, but her voice mail says she's out of town, and she hasn't returned my calls."

"Maybe Mr. Trask is with his daughter."

"He would have told me if he was going away. He had meetings scheduled for the next day and he wouldn't have simply failed to show for them."

Beck seemed to be considering all this. He studied her, not saying anything, until she began to feel uncomfortable, but Cara forced herself to remain still and wait him out. "You really should file a report with local authorities," he said.

"I did," she said. "A woman took my statement, but she didn't seem very concerned. She told me she would put the report on someone's desk, but not to expect to hear anything soon." She pressed her lips together, afraid to say more. She could have told Officer Beck that she had dealt with similar attitudes from law enforcement before. They wouldn't extend themselves to do anything they didn't see as important. The woman at the sheriff's department had sized up Cara as a lovesick admin pining for her hunky boss, who was probably off romancing another woman. She had hoped for better from the Ranger Brigade. "Are you going to look for him?" she asked again.

"We'll look," Beck said. "But you may not like what we find."

Something in his tone chilled her. "What do you mean?"

"One of the sad statistics about national park visitors is that some of them come here with no intention of ever leaving. We have to deal with a number of suicides every year. If, as you say, Mr. Trask was troubled by something…" He let his voice trail away, though his eyes remained locked to hers, watching for her reaction.

She sagged back against the chair. "Dane would never take his own life," she said, her voice shaking. "And when I said he was worried, I didn't mean he was depressed. He was…preoccupied. Like a man trying to figure out a puzzle or solve a problem. That's Dane—he's a problem solver. Suicide wouldn't be a solution to him."

"Then it's possible he met with an accident. He could have fallen and been injured. Some of the terrain in the park can be treacherous. It's one reason we discourage people from hiking alone."

"He told me once that Army Ranger training was all

about learning to survive when the odds were against you. If he was injured, he wouldn't give up. He'd try to get to help. Or, if that wasn't possible, he'd wait for help to come to him." She tried to fight back the image of Dane hurt and alone in the wilderness, waiting for more than two days now for someone to find him.

"We'll do our best to search for him," Beck said. "But we have a dozen officers covering more than a hundred and thirty thousand acres of territory, when you consider the park and the surrounding public lands. Did he say where he intended to hike?"

"No." The word was almost a whisper. One man in that vast territory would be so easy to miss.

"We'll start by searching all the trailheads and parking lots for his vehicle. If we find it, that can help narrow the search. And we might be able to borrow a Park Service plane. We can talk to campers and hikers, see if any of them spotted him or—"

A knock on the door interrupted him. "Come in," he called.

The woman who had greeted Cara when she'd entered the Ranger Brigade headquarters eased into the room. She glanced at Cara then addressed Officer Beck. "We just had a call from Mike Griffen at park headquarters. Hikers off Dragon Point spotted a vehicle wrecked in the canyon. He wants someone to go with him to check it out and, since everyone else is away right now…"

Beck stood and, heart in her throat, Cara also rose. "Tell Mike I'll meet him at the overlook," he said.

"What kind of vehicle?" Cara asked.

Beck and the woman stared at her. "He said it was a late-model Ford pickup," the woman said. "The hikers couldn't get close, but they took pictures, and they said it didn't look like it had been there long."

Cara swayed but held steady. Dane might still be all right, trapped in the truck, but alive. She closed her eyes and said a brief prayer.

When she opened them again, the woman had left and Beck was staring at her. He put a hand lightly on her shoulder. "You need to stay here," he said, his voice gentle.

"A late-model Ford truck," she said. "It could be Dane."

"All the more reason for you to stay here."

"Oh no, I'm coming with you." She slung her purse over her shoulder and clutched her car keys. "Just try and stop me."

Chapter Two

Jason Beck squeezed through a narrow opening in the dense underbrush crowding the steep side of the canyon. He and Black Canyon National Park ranger Mike Griffen had spent the last hour and a half hiking down into the canyon, scaling car-size boulders and skidding down gravel washes to the twin music of rushing water and the descending trill of a canyon wren that followed them down. The temperature was at least fifteen degrees cooler here, where the sun's rays rarely reached, with snow still piled beneath the snarled strands of scrub oak and pinyon in mid-April. The brush grew in tangles they had to fight through.

"I'd like to get hold of one of these guys before he decided to drive over the edge and read him the riot act," Mike grumbled as he pushed the branch of a gnarled pinion out of the way. "If they had any idea how much it costs taxpayers to extricate them and their vehicles out of this canyon, maybe they'd go off themselves somewhere else."

"One of the other park rangers told me y'all had to pull a car out of here last year," Jason said.

"Yeah, and one the year before that." Mike removed his hat and mopped sweat from his brow with his shirtsleeve. "I don't get the attraction. It's not like driving off a cliff is a quick or easy way to end it all." He shuddered then pulled a bottle of water from his pack and drank deeply.

Jason drank from his own water bottle and considered the task ahead. The worst thing about a suicide wasn't really finding the body, but telling the family. Cara Mead wasn't related to Dane Trask, but she was the one who had reported him missing, and she was here, so he'd have to break the news to her first. He had tried to persuade her to go home and wait for his call, pointing out that it could take hours to reach the wrecked vehicle and determine the condition of the driver. She had stubbornly refused, so he'd left her waiting in her car at the overlook. At least she had had sense enough not to want to climb down with them.

"You're pretty new on the job, aren't you?" Mike asked.

"I've been here two weeks." Jason answered the next question before it could be asked. "From Washington, DC." He was the first national parks police officer assigned to a duty other than the National Mall. With the growth of the Ranger Brigade task force within Black Canyon of Gunnison National Park and adjacent public lands, his superiors had deemed it time to have one of their own on the team. He'd been their lucky pick.

He would have liked his first case to be something other than a potential suicide.

"This must be a culture shock," Mike said, sweeping his hand to indicate the wild landscape around them.

"Not really," Jason said. "Before I transferred to parks police, I was a ranger at Glacier and Yellowstone."

"No kidding!" Mike grinned. "We'll have to compare notes sometime. I bet we know some of the same people."

"Probably." Jason stowed his water and adjusted his pack. "Ready to keep going?"

"We'd better. When it gets dark down here, you can't see your hand in front of your face." Mike started out again, picking his way along what must have been an animal track. "Hey, I've been meaning to ask," he called over his shoulder. "Who's the woman?"

"She works for the man who may be the owner of this truck," Jason said. "She reported him missing."

"Then she probably saw this coming," Mike said. "In my experience, family and friends usually know something wasn't right, even if they didn't expect suicide."

"She says he wouldn't have killed himself—that he wasn't depressed." Cara's certainty about this had struck him—that, and her insistence that she and her boss weren't romantically involved.

Mike stopped and looked back at him. "Does she think something else happened? That someone else drove him off the cliff?"

The hair on the back of Jason's neck stood up. "She never mentioned anything like that. Maybe it's an accident."

Mike looked up, toward the canyon rim. "To end up down here, someone would have to turn into the overlook and drive across some pretty rough country for several hundred yards. Not impossible, but not likely, either."

"Let's keep going and see what we find."

As they pressed on, Jason distracted himself from the grueling nature of their hike by thinking about Cara Mead. He wouldn't have minded meeting her under better circumstances. The attractive blonde's combination of tender concern and iron determination intrigued him. He'd offended her with his question about her relationship to Dane, but she hadn't let either anger or fear get the best of her. She didn't think much of local law enforcement, but she'd been willing to put her trust in him.

They rounded a bend in the canyon and Mike pointed ahead to a path of broken limbs and scarred earth. "We're getting close," he said.

A hundred yards farther on, they caught their first glimpse of the truck. It lay on its side in the creek, the cab partially crushed, both headlights and all the windows shattered. As they drew nearer, Jason could make out the license plate. "The plate matches the number registered to Dane Trask's vehicle," he said.

"I don't see anyone in the cab," Mike said.

They scrambled the last few yards to the wreck, Jason searching the creek and the surrounding terrain for any sign of a body. When they reached the pickup, Jason leaned into one broken window to look inside. "There's no one in here," he said. "No blood, either. The seat belt isn't broken."

"Maybe he wasn't wearing it," Mike said, coming up behind Jason. "He might have been thrown clear the first time the truck hit the ground."

They both stared up the steep slope at the tangle of brush and rock. Jason cupped his hands to his mouth. "Dane Trask!" he shouted.

"Dane Trask!" echoed back in a hollow imitation of Jason's voice. As the echo faded, he strained his ears, hearing nothing but the clear, descending notes of the canyon wren.

"What now?" Mike asked.

Jason checked his cell phone. No signal this deep in the canyon. His radio wouldn't work, either. "We'll hike back up and call Ranger Brigade headquarters," he said. "Time to bring in a search dog."

Mike turned to the wrecked truck. "It's going to be a bear of a job getting this truck out of the canyon. We might have to bring in a helicopter."

Jason clapped him on the shoulder. "I'll leave that to you." He pulled a camera from his pack. "I'd better take some photos, just in case this turns out to be a crime scene."

"If you do find the guy alive, let me know," Mike said. "I'll haul him in for trashing the canyon."

Jason squinted through the viewfinder at the mangled vehicle. If Dane Trask had gone over the edge in this truck, it would be a miracle if he was still alive. And Mike wouldn't be the only one standing in line to ask him questions.

CARA HAD PULLED her car into the meager shade of a pinion at the overlook and sat in the driver's seat, phone in hand, reviewing every text message she'd had from Dane over the past two weeks. Messages about schedule changes, meetings he wanted her to add to his calendar, a lunch order he'd asked her to pick up. Ordinary business-related correspondence.

Yet she couldn't shake the feeling that he had been distracted by something. His mind sometimes wandered when she was talking to him, and too many nights when she left work he was still hunched over his desk, staring at his computer monitor or at stacks of printouts. When she'd ask what he was working on, he would shrug off the question. "Just reviewing some data. Have a good evening."

She checked the time. Almost four hours had passed since she had followed Officer Beck and a park ranger to the overlook. "You should go home," Beck had said. "I promise I'll call as soon as we know something."

At home she would only pace and fret—essentially what she was doing here. But here she could see with her own eyes what was happening, and not have to rely on an officer who might not want to give her all the details. Beck might even think he was protecting her from ugly reality, but she was an adult. She didn't need protecting. She had seen ugly before, and she knew it was better to face it than to pretend.

She shoved open the car door and walked down a short trail to the edge of the overlook. The wild beauty of this place drew visitors from all over the world. They came to marvel at the deep chasm sliced into the high desert landscape, with its painted granite and sandstone cliffs and abundant wildlife. But Cara didn't see the beauty today—she only saw the danger in a canyon so remote and full of hazards. She hugged her arms across her chest and closed her eyes, focusing on the warmth of the sun beating down on her skin, the scent of pine and sage on the breeze that caressed her cheek, and the utter silence and peace of the afternoon. Dane was tough. He had skills and he was at home in wild places. If anyone could survive out here, it would be him.

Feeling calmer, she turned and walked back up the trail to her car. When she opened the driver's-side door a few minutes later, something on the seat made her catch her breath. She scooped up the object—a bright red USB flash drive, about two and a half inches long. Despite the heat of the day, a chill shuddered through her.

"Cara!"

Clutching the drive, she whirled to see Officer Beck striding toward her, his tall frame and broad shoulders silhouetted in the late-afternoon sun. He looked scarcely winded by the hard climb out of the canyon, though, as she moved closer to him, she saw the sheen of sweat at the open collar of his shirt and the torn sleeve of his uniform. "Dane?" The single syllable was all she could manage, fear clogging her throat.

Beck shook his head. "We didn't find him. The license plate on the truck is registered to him, and the description fit, but we didn't find anyone down there—dead or alive."

She swayed, her knees weak, whether with relief he hadn't found a body or fear of Dane still down there somewhere, suffering, she couldn't say. Beck put out a hand to steady her and led her back to her car. He pushed her gently into the driver's seat then pulled a bottle of water from his pack and offered it to her. "You've been waiting a long time," he said. "That's not easy."

She sipped the water, trying to pull herself together. "I was trying to prepare myself for the worst," she said.

"This doesn't mean he's alive," Beck said, his eyes intent on her. "He could have been thrown from the truck on the way down."

She handed the water bottle back to him. "What are you going to do now?"

"We're going to bring in a dog to search for him. And we'll have people looking, too." He looked toward the sun, sitting low on the horizon. "We've got less than an hour of daylight left. We may have to continue the search in the morning."

She nodded, still reeling from the news that Dane's truck was in the bottom of the canyon—without Dane.

"You need to go home now," Beck said. "There's nothing else you can do here. I can get someone to drive you."

"I can drive myself." She swung her feet into the car and reached for the button to start the engine. Only then did she remember the flash drive and let out a surprised "Oh!"

Beck stiffened. "What is it?"

She held out her hand, the flash drive lying on her palm. "I got out of the car just now and walked to the edge of the canyon to look down," she said. "When I came back, this was on the driver's seat."

He frowned at the flash drive. "Could it have fallen out of your purse or your pocket?"

She shook her head. "It's not mine. I'm sure of it."

"Then whose is it?"

She swallowed hard. He wasn't going to believe what

she had to say—she didn't believe it. "Look at it again," she said.

His gaze returned to the drive. "There's some kind of logo on it—WHW."

"Welcome Home Warriors. It's the veteran's organization Dane founded. He gave these out all the time to promote the cause."

Beck's eyes met hers—skeptical, but not completely disbelieving. "You think this flash drive belonged to Dane Trask?"

"I think he left it for me," she said. "I think he's still alive. And he was right here."

Chapter Three

The sick feeling that had filled Jason when Cara Mead had showed him the flash drive stayed with him all the way back to Ranger headquarters. He'd felt real sympathy for her up until that moment. All right, if he was being honest, he'd been pretty taken with her, had thought he'd even like to know her better. Being new in town, he didn't know many people outside of the office, and she was pretty and close to his own age. He'd been thinking he might ask her out.

When she'd come up with that wild story about the flash drive and her boss having put it in her car, he'd realized she might be just another nutcase. He'd met plenty of them in his job, attention seekers or the truly delusional. He just hadn't expected it from such a pretty young woman.

He parked his black-and-white SUV in front of the long, low building near the entrance to Black Canyon of Gunnison National Park and crossed the gravel lot to the door. A United States flag snapped in a stiff breeze on a pole at the corner of the building, and a profusion of purple lupines rippled in the wind, their candy-sweet smell drifting to him.

After five years patrolling the National Mall, the vast emptiness and stark beauty of the high desert country around the canyon still moved him. Everything was so different here. Maybe that's why he had thought the people would be, too.

He pushed open the door and stepped into an office filled with activity. Officer Carmen Redhorse looked up from the copy machine. "What have you got there?" she asked.

He looked down at the evidence bag that contained the flash drive. Cara Mead hadn't wanted to give it to him, but he'd insisted. It was evidence in this case, though evidence of what, he wasn't sure. "A woman came in to report her boss was missing in the canyon," he said. "She says this belonged to him." No need to go into the whole story now. "While she was here, a report came in from the park that they'd found a vehicle off Dragon Point. Turned out it was the missing man's vehicle, but no sign of him."

Carmen grimaced. "He could be anywhere down there if he was thrown from the car when it went over," she said.

"It was a truck, but yeah. The park rangers are still looking." He glanced at the flash drive. "I doubt this will be much help, but I figured we'd better take a look."

"Let's see what you've got." Officer Mark Hudson approached. Like Jason, he was a newer addition to the force, replacing the former tech expert who, the story went, had married an heiress he'd met while on a case and relocated to Los Angeles to start a charitable organization devoted to helping street kids. "Hud" had come to the Ranger Brigade from the DEA, and had a reputation as a tech wiz.

Jason followed Hud to a desk on the far side of the open office space. Hud settled in a chair in front of a laptop and pulled on a pair of gloves. He then carefully removed the drive from the evidence bag and inserted it in the port on the side of the computer. A few keystrokes later and a series of numbers filled the screen.

Jason leaned over Hud's shoulder and studied the numbers: 25.5, 16, .72. "Any idea what we're looking at?" he asked.

Hud hit a few keys and a spreadsheet with letters and numbers appeared on the screen: 3H, 18.O, 2H, H2SO4 and others. The columns to the left were filled with more numbers.

"I think these are chemical notations," Hud said. "Sulfuric acid is H2SO4. I think 2H is deuterium. So maybe the numbers are percentages or something. What kind of work did the missing man do?"

"He's an environmental engineer for TDC Enterprises."

Hud tapped a few keys and more letter-and-number combinations replaced the first. "That fits," he said. "This looks like some kind of report. Maybe a chemical analysis."

"But an analysis of what?" Jason asked. And was it just nonsense Cara Mead had thrown together to try to keep his attention on her, or real evidence in this case?

"I'll print this out," Hud said. A few seconds later, the printer adjacent to his desk whirred to life.

"TDC Enterprises has that big campus right on the edge of the park," Lieutenant Michael Dance said as he joined them. One of the original members of the Ranger Brigade, he'd come to the squad from Customs and Border Protection. "Is that why this woman thought he disappeared here?"

"She said the last time she saw him, he was headed into the park," Jason said. "He liked to hike here."

Hud removed the drive from the computer, returned it to the evidence bag then stripped off the gloves. "What was her reaction when you told her his truck was at the bottom of the canyon?" he asked.

"She thinks he's still alive." He nodded toward the evidence bag. "She was waiting up top while a park ranger and I hiked down to check on the truck. When we got back, she said she found that on the front seat of her car. She thinks the missing man—Dane Trask—left it for her. That it's a clue."

"Welcome Home Warriors," Carmen said. She joined the group by Mark's desk.

"That's what it says on the drive—WHW," Jason said.

"Dane Trask was involved with that group," Carmen said. "I met him when he and my husband worked an event together. WHW hosted a bunch of veterans for a week of hiking and rafting and stuff like that." She glanced at Jason. "My husband, Jake, served in Afghanistan. He'll be upset to hear Dane is missing. He'll want to help."

"Jake works for Colorado Parks and Wildlife," Dance explained to Jason and Hud. "He'll be good if we need to conduct a search."

"If the park service doesn't come up with anything, they may ask for our help," Jason said. "In the meantime, I want to talk to Dane Trask's daughter."

"If he has a daughter, why didn't she report him missing?" Hud asked.

"That's one thing I want to find out," Jason said.

"Did this woman—who was she again?—give you any other information that might be useful?" Dance asked.

"Her name is Cara Mead. She's Dane Trask's administrative assistant at TDC," Jason said. "She said he'd been preoccupied with something at work, but he wasn't the type to take his own life."

"And she said he left this flash drive in her car while you were down in the canyon?" Hud asked.

"Yeah. But that's crazy, right?" Jason said. "According to her, he sneaked up there while she was standing out at the overlook, then left without trying to talk to her or anything."

"That overlook is three hundred yards from the parking area," Dance said. "You can't see the road from the overlook because of the way the terrain slopes away. So it's not impossible."

"But why do something like that?" Jason asked.

"Maybe he's hiding from someone, or running from someone," Carmen said.

"It might be worth talking to her again," Hud noted. "Find out what that report on the flash drive means."

"Or come right out and ask her if she made the whole thing up," Dance said.

Jason nodded. They were right. He needed to talk to Cara again. But he wasn't looking forward to finding out she might really have been lying to him.

CARA HAD BEEN calling Audra Trask's cell phone for the past couple of days, getting a Mailbox Full message ever since this morning. Desperate to talk to Dane's daughter, she drove to Audra's building and climbed to the second-story apartment.

Audra Trask, a cloud of messy dark hair framing delicate features, answered the door with what looked like a half-eaten cheeseburger in one hand and a large soft drink in the other. Her eyes widened when she saw Cara. "Oh my gosh—your phone call! I swear I was going to call you back first chance I had, but things have been so crazy around here." She held the door open wider. "Come on in."

Not waiting for a reply, she turned and walked back into the living room, where unopened mail covered the coffee table and the sofa was all but obscured by mounds of clothing. "Sorry the place is such a mess, but I just got home and between jet lag and having been away ten days, I barely know which end is up."

"Where were you?" Cara asked.

Audra stuffed the last bite of cheeseburger in her mouth and chewed before she answered. "Sorry, I was starved. And I've been craving an American fast-food burger for at least the last week."

At Cara's blank look, she added, "I was in Paris and my cell phone didn't work over there. I know your message said it was urgent, but I figured I couldn't really do anything until I got home anyway, so…" She frowned. "What's wrong? You look upset."

Not wanting to panic Audra, Cara hadn't mentioned Dane, only that she needed to hear from Audra right away. "Have you heard from your father?" she asked.

"Dad? No, why?" Before Cara could answer, Audra's face paled. She clutched Cara's arm. "Is he okay? Was there an accident? Is he in the hospital?"

This was the other reason Cara hadn't been more specific on the phone: Audra was excitable and had a very active imagination. She took Audra's hand and led her to the sofa, pushed aside a pile of clothes and urged her to sit. "Two days ago, your dad left the office and said he was going hiking in Black Canyon of the Gunnison," Cara said. "As far as I can determine, he hasn't been seen or heard from since."

"Oh my gosh! Did he fall or something? I know they say you're not supposed to go hiking by yourself, but Dad did it all the time and he's…well, he's Dad."

As in Dane the former Army Ranger. Dane who could do anything. Cara squeezed Audra's hand, silencing the flow of words. "We don't know what happened." She swallowed hard but forced herself to continue. "His truck was found at the bottom of the canyon this evening. Dane wasn't in it, and there was no sign of him."

For once, Audra didn't have anything to say. She stared, mouth open, eyes wide and troubled.

"I think he's still alive," Cara hastened to add. "And probably okay. While I was out at the park, away from my car, someone left one of those Welcome Home Warriors' USB flash drives he's always giving out on the front seat of my car. I think it was your dad."

"Why would he leave a flash drive in your car?" Audra asked. "Why not a note?"

"I don't know," Cara said. Maybe Dane was in danger and the flash drive was the only way he could think to communicate. But she didn't mention this to Audra.

The doorbell rang. Audra looked toward the door but made no move. "Are you expecting someone?" Cara asked.

"Not really. But when my friends hear I'm back in town, one of them might stop by." She shoved to her feet and went to peer out the security peephole. She turned back to Cara, eyes wide. "It's two cops."

Cara stood, also. "You'd better let them in."

If Officer Beck was surprised to see Cara with Dane's daughter, he didn't let the emotion show on his face. He merely nodded to her, then stepped aside to let the other man with him move forward. Blond and blue-eyed, this new man, also dressed in the khaki uniform of the Ranger Brigade, introduced himself as Officer Mark Hudson. "Officer Beck and I would like to ask you some questions about your father, Dane Trask," he said to Audra.

Beck turned to Cara. "We won't keep you," he said.

She debated pretending not to take the hint, but she was so drained by the day's events she decided to save the argument for another time. She could call Audra later to find out what the two Rangers wanted. She'd leave quietly now, but she hoped the handsome cop didn't get the idea she would just as willingly stay away from his investigation.

AUDRA STARED AT Hud for so long that Jason wondered if she remembered there was another person in the room. He cleared his throat and she flinched, as if startled. "Cara told me my dad's truck somehow ended up in the bottom of Black Canyon and nobody has seen or heard from him for two days." She clutched her head with both hands, tousling her wild mane of dark hair even further. The hair was the only thing big about her. She was small-boned and fine-featured, only a little over five feet tall, and slender. "I've been out of the country for the past ten days—in Paris, visiting friends. To come home to this is just so disorienting."

"Why don't we sit down and talk?" Hud touched her arm and led the way to the sofa, which was buried under mounds of clothing.

"Oh gosh, I'm so sorry." Audra began gathering armfuls of clothing and tossing them onto the room's only chair, which was already covered in garments, so that most of the new ones slid in a heap to the floor.

"It's okay," Jason said. "Let's just sit and talk."

"When was the last time you saw or heard from your father?" Hud asked when they were all seated—Hud and Audra next to each other on the sofa, Jason perched on the coffee table.

"The day before I left for Paris. He took me to dinner that night, as kind of a celebration, you know?"

"What took you to Paris?" Hud asked. "Just a vacation, or business?"

"Not business." She laughed. "I run a preschool and childcare center. Friends from college live in Paris and they've been after me to come see them for ages. I had to save for, like, two years to afford the trip, so it was kind of a big deal."

"How did your father seem to you?" Jason asked. "Was he upset or did he seem preoccupied?"

"I don't think so," she said. "But then, I was so excited about the trip that I might not have noticed."

"Did you notice anything unusual?" Hud pressed.

"Not really." She wrinkled her forehead.

"What is it?" Jason leaned toward her.

"It's just…well, right before he left, he told me to be careful." She shrugged. "He always told me to be careful, so I just smiled and said, 'Sure, Dad.' Instead of telling me goodbye and leaving, he grabbed my hand and looked me in the eye and said, 'I mean it. You be careful—in Paris and after you get home.'"

Chapter Four

Intuition wasn't something that played well in court or carried much weight on paper, but Jason had learned to trust his own instincts when it came to investigations. Audra Trask's statement that her father had warned her to be careful seemed innocent enough, but Jason had a sense it could be significant. "What did he want you to be careful of?" he asked.

She shook her head. "I don't know. He's always been very protective of me. When I was a teenager, I loathed it, but now that I'm older, I think it's really sweet. But this was over the top, you know?"

"Do you think he told you that because he was afraid of something?" Jason asked.

She frowned, and didn't say anything for a long time. "That's hard for me to answer," she said after a moment. "He's my dad, and kind of my hero. A little larger than life." Her smile carried the suggestion of apology. "It's immature, I guess, but I always think of my father as someone who isn't afraid."

"Would you say you and your father are close?" Hud asked.

"Yeah." She smiled, and the effect was pretty breathtaking. Jason thought Hud's eyes might have glazed over for a bit. "It's funny, really," Audra said. "I mean, he and my mom never married and, for big chunks of my childhood, he was deployed and I didn't see him. But he's always worked hard to be part of my life." The smile melted away. "What do you think has happened to him?"

"How often do you usually see your father or talk to him?" Hud asked.

"We have lunch or dinner at least once a week when we're both in town," she said. "And we talk or text almost every day. Except not while I was in Paris. My cell phone didn't work there, and I didn't want to bug my friends to use theirs all the time. I knew I'd see him when I got home." Her expression clouded and she bit her lip.

"What's your relationship to Cara Mead?" Jason asked.

The question pulled her back from the brink of a breakdown. "Cara? Well, we're friendly, but we're not really friends. I mean, she works for my dad, so I talk to her when I stop by his office sometimes, but we don't socialize or anything."

"What about she and your dad?" he asked. "Do they socialize?"

"You mean date?" Audra shook her head, hair whipping around. "Maybe he'll take her to lunch on her birthday or something, but they aren't, like, a couple."

Jason relaxed and ignored the way Hud was staring at him.

"What happened to my dad's truck?" she asked. "How did it end up at the bottom of the canyon?"

"We think someone drove or pushed it over," Hud said.

She looked confused. "But who would do something like that? And where was my dad?"

"Your father served in the military, on active duty, I understand," Hud said.

She nodded. "Yes. He was in Iraq and Afghanistan. With the Army Rangers."

"Did he have any trouble readjusting to civilian life after he was discharged?" Hud asked.

"Not that I'm aware of. I mean, he doesn't talk about his service much, but I don't think he ever struggled with PTSD or anything like that."

"Any history of depression?" Hud asked.

"No." She leaned forward and actually grabbed his wrist. He leaned back, startled, but she held on. "You think he committed suicide? Well, he didn't. He isn't like that."

Hud looked at Jason. Audra still had a grip on him that was probably uncomfortable, though probably not dangerous. Jason took the evidence bag with the flash drive and passed it to her. "Have you ever seen this before?" he asked.

She let go of Hud to accept the package. "Dad gives these out to lots of people," she said. "I have one around here somewhere."

"Can you think of anyone else who might know where your dad is or what he's doing?" Hud asked. "Anyone he might have confided in?"

"Not really. I mean, he has lots of friends, but he isn't the type to spill his guts to other people. I mean, most guys aren't, right?"

"What about girlfriends?" Jason asked.

"He hasn't dated anyone since Eve."

"Eve?" Hud asked.

"Eve Shea. His ex-girlfriend. They were together three years before they split up. She wanted to get married and have babies, and he didn't want that. They're still friends, but I don't think he would have confided in her."

They asked a few more questions about Dane's state of mind, where he might have gone, et cetera. But Audra Trask didn't appear to know anything helpful. At last, both officers stood and Audra walked with them to the door. "If you think of anything, call us anytime, night or day," Hud said, handing her his and Jason's business cards.

"I will."

They left her studying the cards. Unlike Cara, she didn't demand to be kept up to date on any information they found. She probably trusted them to tell her what she needed to know.

Back in the parking lot, Hud said, "Anyone could have left that flash drive."

Jason nodded. "But a random stranger leaves a flash drive that once belonged to Dane Trask in the car of his administrative assistant, who has just reported Trask missing—while I'm down in the canyon checking out Trask's wrecked truck?"

"So, yeah," Hud agreed, "not a random stranger. Someone who knew Dane."

"Someone who knows something about his disappearance," Jason said. "Someone who knew who Cara was, and why she was at the park."

"Dane would know that. Who else?"

"That's what we need to find out."

SATURDAY MORNING, JASON stood at the Dragon Point overlook with Lieutenant Randall Knightbridge and his search dog, Lotte. The dog and her handler had returned only that morning from a training exercise outside Denver. Lotte, a fawn-colored Belgian Malinois with black-tipped fur and movie-star eyes, kept her gaze fixed on Knightbridge as he approached, one of Dane's worn gym socks, which Cara had retrieved from a gym bag in his office, in a plastic pouch in his hand. He unsealed the bag and held it open while she shoved her nose inside. "Seek!" he commanded.

The dog took off, nose scanning back and forth across the dry earth around the overlook. Nearby, a few early tourists looked on curiously. The faint track where the truck had driven over the cliff was still visible in a few spots, but an onlooker would have to know what had happened to realize what he or she was looking at. The bare rock around much of the area obscured the true nature of the tragedy.

Lotte circled around them, whining. "She's not picking up anything," Knightbridge said. He looked around the area. "It's been—what?—at least three days since that truck went over. Lots of traffic here, not to mention the bare rock doesn't hold scent well."

"So maybe Dane was here with the truck and maybe he wasn't." Jason rubbed the back of his neck. "And maybe he was here Friday when we found the truck—when his assistant says someone left that flash drive in her car."

"Lotte has an excellent nose, but she's not a miracle worker," Knightbridge said. He whistled to the dog and she trotted back to his side. "Let's head into the canyon. If this guy is anywhere, he's there."

The National Park had decided to stop issuing permits to hike and camp in the inner canyon at least until the truck was pulled out. In addition to the possibility that a curious hiker would compromise a crime scene or even vandalize the truck, park authorities didn't want to deal with the trauma of someone potentially finding Dane's body. Much better to leave that to the professionals.

As a National Parks Ranger, Jason had seen his share of dead bodies, mostly heart attacks and victims of falls, but there had been one suicide. It wasn't something he liked to think about. But it was important to Trask's family, and to the case, to try to find him, whether he was dead or injured, or fleeing a crime or an enemy.

"Believe it or not, I've only been down here one other time in the past three years," Knightbridge said as they navigated the steep trail into the inner canyon. They descended through thick stands of stunted pinyon and juniper trees and prickly Gambel oak, then through a grove of aspen, the leaves stirring like a crowd of whispering children in the hot breeze.

"I was here yesterday when we found the truck," Jason said. His thighs still ached from the steep climb.

"Who needs a gym, right?" Knightbridge asked, though his bulging biceps suggested he lifted weights on a regular basis.

"I said I was looking for work that was a little more physical than patrolling the National Mall," Jason said, skirting around a boulder and pushing past a tree branch.

"Most of the action is up top," Knightbridge said. "And most of it isn't in the national park. The Curecanti National Recreation Area and Gunnison Gorge are more remote, so people tend to think they can get away with crime there. Sometimes they do, but we do our best to stop them."

"I'm still trying to figure out the crime in this case," Jason said. "Is Dane Trask a suicide victim? Or a murder victim? Or did he try to fake his own death? And why? Is he running from a crime he committed, or from something else?"

"Maybe we have to find him to figure any of that out," Knightbridge said. "What does his family say?"

"His daughter's been out of the country and doesn't know much," he said. "I talked to his ex-girlfriend this morning, but they split up months ago and she says, as far as she knew, everything was fine. I haven't found anyone else he's close to, except his administrative assistant, who first reported him missing."

"Maybe Lotte will help us get some answers."

At the sound of her name the dog, who had been bounding ahead of them down the narrow trail, turned and looked toward them, mouth half open in what really wasn't a smile but looked like it. Maybe Jason should get a dog now that he was living in a place with so many trails and parks to explore. His rental was awfully empty with just him rattling around in there.

He'd like to start dating again. He'd been friends with a lot of women in DC, but nothing had ever clicked with any of them. Too bad the one woman who really interested him since he'd moved to Colorado was involved in this case. Not that anything prevented him from asking her out, but she didn't seem to have a very high opinion of law enforcement in general, so why set himself up for failure?

Approximately an hour and a half after starting out, they reached the canyon and hiked another half hour along the river to reach the site of the wreckage. Knightbridge dug the bag with Dane's sock out of his pack and commanded Lotte to "Seek!"

The dog began scanning the ground around the wreckage, tail wagging.

"If she finds him, I hope he's still alive," Knightbridge said. "She gets depressed when she finds someone dead. It's the downside to being a search and rescue dog—she likes the rescue part. So do I, for that matter."

"Have you done much of this kind of work?" Jason asked. He hadn't yet spent much time with the lieutenant, who stood out among the other Rangers with his full-sleeve tattoos. "Looking for missing people in the park?"

Knightbridge nodded. "Too much. Most of the time it's just a kid or hiker who wandered off course and we find them okay. But sometimes there's no happy ending." He glanced at Jason. "Suicides are the worst."

Jason nodded. "I guess people like all this wide-open space, where their family doesn't have to find them."

"But we do." Knightbridge nodded toward the searching dog. "We did a search like this two years ago. A guy from Sweden, of all places, rented a car in Denver, drove all the way out here and went off near Tomichi Point. He mailed a letter to his brother back in Stockholm, telling him what he intended to do. The brother got the letter five days later, called us and we went searching. We found the car quick enough—it was equipped with locater technology. But we had to get Lotte to find the body." He grimaced. "It was an awful mess."

They watched the dog continue to search. "Can she find anything after this much time?" Jason asked.

"We haven't had any rain or much foot traffic down here," Knightbridge said. "And the ground is wetter here near the river, so it holds scent better. So there's a good chance she'll pick up something."

As if to confirm his assessment, Lotte headed for the wrecked truck and began nosing around the door. Knightbridge followed and wrenched the door open for her. The dog stood with her front paws on the truck's footboard, sniffing the interior.

"We know it's Dane's truck," Jason said. "Of course his scent is going to be inside."

"Seek!" Knightbridge commanded again.

The dog retraced her steps, scanning the ground all the way around the truck. Finally, she returned to Knightbridge and sat at his feet, looking at him alertly. "She's not finding anything," he said. "Either Dane Trask was thrown from the truck before it ever got down here, or he wasn't in it when it went over the edge."

Jason looked up toward the rim of the canyon far above. "Start the engine, get the vehicle headed downhill and jump back," he said.

"Waste of a nice truck." Knightbridge fed Lotte a handful of treats from a pouch on his belt.

Jason walked around the vehicle, examining it more closely than he had the day before when he had been focused on looking for a person trapped in or beneath the wreckage. Parts of the vehicle were bashed in by collisions with rocks or trees on the way down, while other sections were relatively unharmed. The truck bed, though twisted to one side, was intact, the tailgate still latched.

Knightbridge peered into the truck bed. "What's that?" he asked.

Jason moved to stand beside the lieutenant and stared at the bright yellow bandana lying crumpled in the bed of the truck. "That wasn't there yesterday," he said. No way he and Griffen would have missed it.

Knightbridge lowered the tailgate and climbed into the bed of the truck. "There's something wrapped up in it," he said. He knelt and carefully teased apart the folds of fabric. "It's another one of those flash drives."

Jason studied the blue drive, the WHW logo in script across the plastic casing.

"That bandana has the logo for TDC all over it," Knightbridge said.

Jason shifted his attention to the yellow bandana and a shiver ran through him. "That's not the only thing on it," he said. "If I'm right, that stain on the back is someone's blood."

Chapter Five

Cara yanked another weed from the raised garden bed in the backyard of the little Victorian bungalow she was trying to transform into her home. Demolishing a wall or ripping out plumbing would have been a more satisfying way to work off her frustrations, but she had finished all of that type of work last month and was into the rebuilding phase, so she had turned her attention to this future vegetable and flower garden. With every dig and pull at a stubborn clump of weeds, she imagined yanking on a certain smug Ranger's head.

She'd actually believed Officer Jason Beck—as Audra had referred to him—might be different from most of the other lawmen she'd dealt with. He'd listened to her concerns about Dane and had seemed to really care.

Then she had showed him that flash drive and his reaction told her he'd thought she was crazy. Or worse, a liar. When she'd talked to Audra earlier that morning, her impression of him hadn't improved. Apparently, he'd spent part of Audra's interview insinuating that there must be something going on between Cara and her boss.

She wrapped her hand around a thick tuft of foxtail and gave it a savage pull, blinking back tears. Jason Beck wasn't worth crying over. She'd wanted to trust him, but he was just like the others—the cops in Houston who had brushed her off when she urged them to do more to track down her brother's murderer. Sure, Corey had been an addict who had been in and out of trouble for years. He'd probably been killed by someone who'd supplied him drugs. But that didn't mean his murderer didn't deserve to be punished.

Those cops hadn't showed much interest in finding justice for Corey. His murderer had never been found and, even after almost three years, the knowledge still hurt.

And it had hurt to see the concern in Jason's eyes turn to wariness as he had looked at the flash drive and listened to her story about it appearing on her car seat, a message from Dane. He had looked at her the way those cops in Houston had—as if she and her concerns didn't matter.

She tugged hard at a clump of dandelions and they came free, dirt flying, rocking her back on her heels. She brushed a clump from her face and winced as it smeared. Just then the thud of a car door closing made her whip her head around. A pair of long, khaki clad legs headed her way. She shoved to her feet and faced Ranger Jason Beck.

"Ms. Mead." He inclined his head, and she straightened, resisting the urge to scrub at the dirt on her cheek and brush dried grass from her jeans. She didn't need to pretty herself up for him.

She said nothing, the silence stretching awkwardly between them, his brown eyes studying her. Evaluating. Heat spread through her and her skin prickled with awareness, as if his gaze was a physical touch.

"I took a look at that flash drive," he said finally.

"Yes?"

"I'm going to need your help figuring out what it means."

She hadn't expected that—asking for her help. "Sure. Uh, I guess you'd better come inside."

She turned, aware of him following her into the house. She stopped in the entryway to toe off her sneakers then went into the kitchen, where her laptop was already set up and running. She pulled out the chair and pointed to the one adjacent. "You can sit there."

A voice in her head nagged that she should offer him a glass of water or something, but she ignored it. This wasn't a social visit. "Let me see the drive," she said.

He took the drive in its small plastic bag marked "Evidence" from his shirt pocket and laid it beside her computer. "I'm going to have to handle it to insert it into the USB port," she said.

"It's okay to touch it," he said. "We already checked for prints."

She leveled her gaze at him. "And?"

Clearly, he didn't want to tell her, but she held his gaze and didn't move. A hint of red came to his cheeks. "We didn't find any," he said.

Triumph surged through her. He was stubborn, but so was she, and she wasn't going to let him get away with withholding information that could pertain to Dane's disappearance. She pulled the drive from the bag and clicked it into the port on the side of her laptop. A message flashed on the screen: How do you want to open this file?

She highlighted the first choice, Excel, and a spreadsheet filled the screen. Jason moved his chair until he was seated right beside her, his shoulder brushing her arm as he leaned forward to study the display. "What are we looking at?" he asked. "Do you know?"

"It's a water quality analysis." She pointed to the left-hand column. "These are the elements tested for." She slid her finger to the next column. "These are the quantities found in the sample, expressed as parts per million, compared to acceptable levels in this final column."

"Most of the numbers in that last column are zeroes," he said.

"Right. Because most of this is nasty stuff you don't want to find in water."

He nodded, brow furrowed. "So what is all this nasty stuff?" he asked.

"Thorium, uranium, deuterium—the first two are radioactive to varying degrees. And then there's arsenic, mercury and lead. Those can kill you, or at least make you very sick."

He sat back and continued to stare at the screen. She turned in her chair to study him. He wasn't movie-star gorgeous, but he had strong features she found attractive— Roman nose, square chin, deep-set dark eyes with dark eyebrows and dark lashes that she, as a pale blonde, envied. He shifted his gaze and met hers, and her cheeks heated, embarrassed to be caught staring.

"Where is this report from?" he asked.

She turned her attention to the screen once more. "There's no information about that. The header is missing. I think this is just a section cut and pasted from a larger report."

"And you said this USB was lying on the front seat of your car when you returned from the overlook?"

"I said it because it's true."

His frown deepened. "Your car wasn't locked?"

"No. I only stepped away from it for a few minutes and there was no one around."

"You didn't see anyone? No one else on the path to the overlook?"

"No one. The area was deserted." How many times did she have to tell him?

"This wasn't a drive of yours you forgot about?" he asked. "Maybe it fell out of your purse?"

"No." She shoved her chair back and stood, glaring down at him. "Why won't you believe me?"

"It's my job to be skeptical." He stood, also. A head taller and uncomfortably close. "I have to draw conclusions based on evidence not gut feelings."

Did that mean that in his gut he believed her? "Dane uses this kind of flash drive," she said, forcing herself to remain calm. "And this—" she indicated the screen "—is the type of report he analyzes every day."

"His daughter told us he gave these drives out to a lot of people," he said. "Maybe someone else who works at TDC, or a competitor, left the drive for you."

"Fine, if you want to think that. But why?"

Instead of answering, he reached into his other pocket and took out another evidence bag with another flash drive, this one blue, the WHW logo stamped across one side. "Where did you get that?" she asked.

"It was found this morning in the bed of Dane's pickup, wrapped in a TDC bandana."

"In his pickup? In the bottom of the canyon?"

He nodded. "I don't believe it was there yesterday," he said. "The bright yellow bandana stood out against the black truck, and I don't think I or the park ranger who assisted me would have overlooked it."

"Then do you believe me now—that Dane left these for us?"

"I believe someone left them," he said. "But I don't know yet who that was, or why."

"Maybe it was a cry for help," Cara said. "Or a clue as to what is going on. What's on that second drive?"

"I thought you and I could look at it and see."

That he had waited for her impressed her a little—but only a little. He had already admitted that he didn't understand the information on the first drive. She accepted the new drive and inserted it in a second port on the side of her laptop.

"It looks like more of the same," he said as letters and numbers filled the screen.

"It's a little different," she said. "This one is tracking water quality over time." She pointed to a graph at the right of the columns of figures. "It shows water quality worsening over time."

Jason regarded the screen again. "So what does it mean?"

She looked at the rows of numbers and letters. "It's a bad sample," she said. "Someone is really out of compliance."

"Where is it from?" he asked.

Cara shook her head. "Without a header, there's no way of knowing. It's the same for the first report. They give us some information, but not enough."

"What type of place then? If you had to guess."

"An old mine? A toxic waste dump? I really can't say."

"I thought all the mining around here was for gold and silver." This part of Colorado was pockmarked with abandoned mines dating from the late 1800s, most abandoned a hundred years ago.

"There's uranium, too," she said. "And they used arsenic and mercury to separate the precious metals from the worthless rock. All that stuff built up over the years and rain washes it down into streams and rivers." She studied the screen again. "TDC has some government contracts to clean up contaminated sites in the area. Maybe this is an initial analysis from one of those."

"Which brings us back to the question, why leave it for us to find?

"I don't know." She hit the button to print a copy of each report. "I'll compare this to files on Dane's computer at work and see if I come up with anything." She slipped both drives back into their evidence bags and handed them to him.

"I'll need a list of people Dane knew," Jason said. "Friends, romantic interests, coworkers. Anyone who might have insight into why he left and where he went."

Her spirits lifted. "Then you don't think he killed himself?"

He held up one hand. "At this point, we're not ruling out any possibility."

"But you haven't found a body."

He didn't answer. Instead he said. "Before, you told me the last time you saw Dane, he had a backpack."

"Yes. He was putting it into his truck. Did you find it?"

He hesitated and she wanted to shake him.

Finally he said, "It wasn't in the truck, or anywhere at the scene. An animal could have dragged it away."

"Or Dane has it." She stood, too agitated to sit still any longer. "But how did his truck end up at the bottom of the canyon? Did someone kidnap him and push the truck over the edge?"

"Why would someone kidnap him?" Jason asked. "And if he was kidnapped, how did he put the flash drive in your car?"

"Maybe he got away?" Dane stayed in shape and was tough.

"Then why not ask for help instead of leaving a meaningless portion of a report in your car and taking off again?"

"He must have had a reason," she said. Maybe it didn't make sense to someone who didn't know Dane. "He's one of the smartest people I know. And he's not impulsive. When he does something, he has a reason."

"Look, I want to help you," Jason said. "But you're

not giving me much to work with. This doesn't look like a kidnapping to me. What's the motive? And where's the ransom demand?"

"Dane didn't kill himself," Cara said. "He wouldn't. If he wasn't kidnapped, then what's going on?"

"Maybe he ran away," Jason said.

"Ran away from what?"

He settled one hip on the corner of the table, a casual pose, though his expression remained guarded, focused on her. "Sometimes, people try to fake their own death in order to start over with a new identity somewhere else," he said. "Usually, it's because they want to escape debt or a bad relationship, or a crime they've committed."

"Dane wasn't in debt," she said. "He didn't have bad relationships and he's certainly not a criminal."

"Do you know that for sure?"

She hated the doubt that pinched at her. Dane was her boss, not her lover or even her best friend. She wasn't privy to his secrets. "I never saw anything to make me suspect trouble of any kind," she said.

"Get me that list of contacts," Jason said. "I'll see what I can find out."

"I'll type that up for you now." She sat in front of the laptop once more. While they had been talking, she had received two new work emails. On a Saturday? She frowned at the subject line on each—Re: Dane.

"What's wrong?" Jason moved in beside her.

She opened the first email.

From: M.Ruffino@TDCEnterprises.org
To: C.Mead@TDCEnterprises.org
Re: Dane
Cara, I you need to box up all of Dane's files and records.

I want everything from his desk and office. Someone will be by at 9 sharp Monday morning to pick them up.
Mitchell Ruffino, VP of Operations
TDC Enterprises

Heart beating hard, she opened the second email.

From: M.Ruffino@TDCEnterprises.org
To: C.Mead@TDCEnterprises.org
Re: Dane
Keep this information strictly confidential.
Remember—I want everything.
MR

Cara glanced up at Jason. "I don't understand what this means," she said.

"Maybe it's standard procedure when an employee goes missing," he said.

She pulled out her phone and dialed the number for the TDC switchboard. Even though it was Saturday, it wasn't unusual for people to be there, putting in extra hours on projects in a time-crunch. She punched in the extension for the vice president's office, expecting to get his voice mail.

Instead, Ruffino himself answered. "Ruffino."

"Mr. Ruffino, this is Cara Mead. I received your email about boxing up all of Dane's files. I don't understand. What's going on?"

"It's standard procedure when an employee is part of a criminal investigation," Ruffino said. "Everything in that office is now evidence."

She sagged back in her chair, the breath knocked out of her. It was several seconds before she could speak.

"Ms. Mead?" Ruffino asked.

She wet her lips and forced words from her throat.

"How is Dane part of a criminal investigation?" she asked. "What's going on?"

"I'm afraid your boss is in serious trouble," Ruffino said. "We believe he's been embezzling money from the company for some time."

"Embezzlement?" The word sounded foreign on her tongue.

"That's right. He's stolen a considerable sum of money and we intend to prosecute to the fullest extent of the law. Now, you get all those files together for me. I want them ready by 9:00 a.m. sharp on Monday." Not waiting for an answer, he hung up.

Cara laid her phone on the table beside the laptop, stomach churning.

Jason put a hand on her shoulder. "Are you okay?" he asked. "What did he say?"

She looked up to meet his gaze and the concern in his eyes made hers burn with tears. "He said Dane stole a lot of money from TDC. But that can't be right. I'm sure it can't be right."

Chapter Six

At the entrance to TDC Enterprises, Cara punched in the code to silence the alarm with shaking hands, acutely aware of the security camera focused on her. Did anyone actually look at the footage from that camera? If anyone asked why she was at the office at six in the morning, she'd tell them she was anxious to have all of Dane's files and equipment boxed up and ready to go when whoever Mr. Ruffino was sending to retrieve them showed up at nine.

She crossed the small lobby to the elevator, the piped-in music that apparently played twenty-four hours a day sounding overly loud in the stillness. Alone in the elevator as it rose to the fifth floor of the building, she practiced taking deep, calming breaths, though her heart continued to pound and her stomach rolled with nausea.

This must be some huge mistake. Dane hadn't really stolen money from the company. Why would he? He made a six-figure salary and, unlike some of their coworkers, didn't live an extravagant lifestyle. He didn't take exotic vacations. His truck wasn't cheap, but it wasn't a Porsche, either. He lived in a modest home that had once been part of a ranch. His hobbies of hiking, fishing and volunteering with Welcome Home Warriors didn't take much money.

The police suspected he'd run away. And sending his

truck into Black Canyon certainly looked like an attempt to fake his own death.

But that didn't explain the flash drive with the excerpt from a bad water quality report.

After the emails from Mitchell Ruffino, Jason hadn't said much. He'd listened to her protests that Dane wouldn't steal and promised to check into it, but doubt was written large in his expression. He probably saw all kinds of innocent-looking people do horrible things every day. Dane was just another criminal to him.

And she was just another woman who had trusted the wrong man.

She opened the door to the engineering department and flipped on the lights. After the subdued lighting of the elevator and hallway, the banks of bright LEDs made her wince. She hurried to her desk, right outside Dane's private corner office. As the chief environmental engineer for TDC, Dane ranked his own space. The other analysts and assistants worked in an open space crowded with desks and office machinery. Cara prayed none of them would decide to come in early this Monday morning.

She fished a key from an inside pocket of her purse and unlocked Dane's door. He'd presented her with the key last month, saying he might need her to access his office for him when he was working off-site. At the time, she'd been pleased with this gift—now she wondered if, even then, Dane was planning his escape.

She flipped on the lights and powered up the computer, then, while waiting for the machine to boot up, turned to the row of filing cabinets that filled one wall of the office.

The lateral files contained maps, architectural drawings and copies of deeds, surveys and historical documents related to the properties TDC had either developed or was thinking about developing. These included local projects such as a new elementary school not far from the park entrance, to abandoned mining sites the company was charged with cleaning up, to overseas office buildings and shopping malls. The firm of Terrell, Davis, and Compton had its fingers in pies all over the globe.

Dane's job focused primarily on environmental impact statements, soil analysis to determine the foundation type best suited for a property, and water analysis for potentially contaminated sites.

The computer screen glowed with a photo of a smiling Dane and his daughter, Audra. More than one visitor had mistaken the photo for one of Dane and his younger girlfriend or wife, an assumption that never pleased him. It didn't help that he looked younger than forty-one, with no gray in his thick brown hair, or that Audra, twenty-two, was the result of a brief relationship he'd had in college. Though he and Audra's mother had never married, Dane had developed a close relationship with his daughter over the years.

Cara fished a flash drive from her purse—not the little red one Jason still had in evidence, but a slim silver one with the capacity to copy all of the files on Jason's computer. She inserted the little device into the USB port, typed in the command to copy, then returned to the filing cabinets.

Five minutes later, she was in front of the scanner, feeding in documents and sending them directly to her own laptop. She bounced one knee in agitation as she waited for the first pages to scan. What she was doing was strictly against company policy and maybe even illegal. She didn't know if an IT expert would be able to tell that she had copied Dane's files. She planned to attempt to wipe the scanner's memory when she was done with the hard copies, but didn't know how successful she would be.

She hadn't slept much the night before, worried about Dane—what he might have done and why, and where he might be now. She probably needed caffeine. Then again, the idea of coffee on her queasy stomach made her even queasier. And she didn't need anything more to hype her up. As it was, when the water cooler in the corner gurgled, she almost dropped the entire contents of a folder full of mining surveys.

She didn't even know why she was going to all this trouble. What was she planning to do with all this stuff she was copying? Last night, as she had lain awake, unable to sleep, she'd hatched a plan to go through all of Dane's data to figure out what the information on the flash drives meant. He had left that first drive in her car for a reason. It was a clue as to why he had disappeared and, right now, at least, it seemed she was the only person who cared enough to figure it out.

Standing in Dane's empty office with the light glaring and the scanner whirring, Cara just felt foolish. But she fed the next document into the scanner, feeling she had stepped too far over the line to stop now.

As the sun rose over the peaks to the east of Black Canyon of the Gunnison on Monday morning, Jason set barricades to close off the Dragon Point overlook. A quarter mile farther up the road, park employees were closing access to this stretch of the South Rim Road. Tourists would be disappointed not to be able to admire and photograph some of the park's most iconic views, but the park service needed to get Dane's truck out of the canyon without the distraction of onlookers.

The wrecker, a 50-ton unit from Grand Junction with a specialized boom, backed toward the canyon rim, easing between boulders, warning beeper blaring, sun spotlighting the gleaming red sides. The driver stopped well back from the edge, left the truck running and he and the vehicle's two passengers climbed out.

They joined Jason at the rim. "I don't see the truck," the younger, shorter man with a bushy beard said.

"It's down there," Jason said. "It's black and in the shadows." The depth and narrowness of the canyon meant the wreck was in shadow most of the time.

"Take a portable spotlight with you," the driver told the bearded man. "And don't forget your safety gear. The last thing I want is to have to haul your carcass out of there."

The young man nodded and returned to the truck to don a bright yellow-and-orange reflective vest and hard hat. Then he shouldered a backpack, switched on a headlamp and started toward the trail leading into the canyon. Jason had no desire to make the hike down into the canyon a third time, but he felt a twinge of concern. That trail wasn't for amateurs, especially in the dark. "Has he ever made that hike before?" he asked.

"Rob's idea of a good time is free-climbing stupid sick cliffs," the third man, ruddy-faced and clean-shaven, said. "He's been looking forward to this."

"While he's headed down there, we'll get the boom ready," the driver, a paunchy man in his fifties, said.

While the two men worked extending the boom in sections, setting up outriggers to balance the rig, and hooking up cables, Jason let his mind wander. Was Dane Trask out there somewhere in the darkness? Or was he on his way to Tahiti or some other exotic locale, his new life funded by money he'd stolen from his employer?

Cara hadn't said much after she'd spoken to Ruffino, only that she couldn't believe Dane would do something like that. Jason wanted to do his own follow-up on the criminal investigation the TDC vice president had mentioned, but he was stuck at the overlook until the wrecker had done its job, without cell service or internet.

The driver came to stand beside him, watching as the other man operated the remote control for the boom. "Do you do this sort of thing much?" Jason asked.

"Similar. Usually it's a truck driver who's gone over the edge on a mountain pass. But there have been a handful of suicides."

"We haven't confirmed this is a suicide."

The driver spat a stream of tobacco juice. "You don't think someone accidentally drove off that cliff, do you?"

Jason didn't bother with a response.

An hour later, he caught the glimmer of a light signaling from the bottom of the canyon. The driver returned to his truck and a few moments later called out, "We're ready!"

The groan and squeal of cables and the scrape of metal on rock made Jason's teeth hurt. The noise grew louder and he regretted not thinking to bring earplugs. The wrecker driver and his helper, he noticed, both wore ear protection.

Inch by inch, the mangled pickup rose out of the canyon. As it hung in the air, it looked even more pathetic than it had on the rocks below, like a child's toy someone had stepped on. "What happened to the driver?" the boom operator asked over the din.

"We haven't found him yet," Jason said.

The operator shook his head. "I'll bet he didn't walk away from that one."

The mangled truck reached the rim of the canyon and the ruddy-faced operator guided it over the rocks. Then he ran forward to help the driver with the cables.

A horn tap made Jason look around in time to see a Ranger cruiser ease past the road barricades. The vehicle parked and Hud got out. "How's it going?" he asked when he joined Jason at the edge of the canyon.

"These guys did a great job," Jason said. "I'll talk to the operator in the canyon when he gets back up here, see if he spotted anything unusual, but I'm not expecting much."

"Yeah, well...we've had a new development I thought you'd want to know about."

Jason tensed. "What is it?"

"You were right that it was blood on that bandana. Human, and type A positive. Dane Trask's blood type."

BY THE TIME the first employees began filtering in at eight thirty on Monday morning, Cara was about to pack away the last of the documents and seal the last of the boxes. Her best work friend, Maisie, found her in Dane's office, stacks of cardboard banker's boxes surrounding her.

"Uh-oh." Maisie's eyes widened as she assessed the situation. She moved closer, lowering her voice. "Did Dane get fired? Is that why he hasn't been around the past few days?"

Cara shook her head. "All I know is I got an email from Mr. Ruffino on Saturday, telling me to box up all of Dane's stuff."

"Mr. Ruffino himself emailed you?"

"I know, right?" Cara said. She didn't remember the vice president of operations ever speaking to her. She was a little surprised that he even knew how to contact her, though she supposed that was the sort of thing a VP should know. Though Misters Terrell, Davis and Compton had visited during the new building's grand opening, for the employees that worked at the company's headquarters, Mitchell Ruffino was the man who ran the show.

Maisie frowned at the growing stack of boxes. "What's going on?" she asked. "Have you heard from Dane?"

Cara shook her head and added a stack of files to the box. "No, and I'm worried about him."

"If he's gone, are you going to work for the new chief engineer?" Maisie asked.

"I don't know," Cara said. She hadn't even considered what might happen to her if Dane truly was no longer employed by TDC.

Maisie gave her a sympathetic look and squeezed her arm. "Whatever happens, you'll make it through. You'll do a good job no matter where you end up."

"Thanks." She sealed the lid on the box and reached for another.

"Can I do anything to help?" Maisie asked.

"Thanks, but this is the last box."

Just then, two men in gray suits appeared in the doorway. "Caroline Mead?" one asked.

Behind Cara, Maisie made a squeaking noise then slipped by her, past the two men and out the door.

Cara didn't blame Maisie for making herself scarce. The expensive-looking gray suits were the only thing that looked corporate about these two, who had matching shaved heads and muscles. The only difference between them was that one was African American and the other was white. They looked like a matched set of bodyguards, all hard lines and muscular planes.

"I'm Caroline Mead," she said.

The white man fixed her with a cold-water stare that chilled her through. "We're here for Mr. Trask's things," he said.

She took a deep breath, fighting for calm. "This is everything," she said, indicating the boxes stacked around her. "The laptop is in that bag."

The guy opened a desk drawer. It was empty. Cara had cleared out the contents of every one. She had even boxed up the spare jacket and gym clothes from the closet in the corner.

The black guy hefted two of the heavy boxes, while the white guy took the laptop and another box. They were almost to the door when their exit was blocked by a third man.

"I'll have to ask you to put those back" said a voice that made Cara weak at the knees. She grabbed the side of the desk for support and tried to see around the broad back of the white guy.

"Officer Beck, is that you?"

Chapter Seven

The distress in Cara's voice made Jason clench his free hand into a fist. Had these two suits been bullying or intimidating her? "Officer Beck and Lieutenant Dance, Ranger Brigade." He thrust the warrant in his other hand toward the black man. "These files are evidence in an ongoing case and we'll be taking them into custody."

The man looked as if he wanted to argue. His knuckles paled where he gripped the file boxes.

Lieutenant Michael Dance stepped in closer behind Jason, his broad-shouldered form effectively blocking the doorway.

"We were told to deliver these to Mr. Ruffino." The white guy set his burden on the desk behind Cara and shifted enough that Jason thought he caught a glimpse of a shoulder holster. Since when did office workers go around armed?

"Keep your hands where I can see them and move into the outer office, please," he said. He stepped back to allow the two men to pass. Dance moved out of the way, also, one hand resting not-so-casually on the butt of his service revolver. Jason guessed these two set Dance on edge as much as they did him.

"What's the meaning of this?" the white guy blustered, turning back to Jason. "Everything in those boxes is the property of TDC Enterprises. You can't just barge in here and seize it."

"That warrant says we can," Jason said, aware that all semblance of work in the outer office had ceased and half a dozen men and women at the various desks around the room were watching the drama play out. He glanced to his right, to where Cara remained frozen in front of the desk. "We're investigating the disappearance of Dane Trask. We believe items in those boxes may help reveal his whereabouts."

The black man held up both hands. "I need to call Mr. Ruffino to let him know what's going on," he said. "I need to get my phone."

"Go ahead," Jason said.

With exaggerated slowness, the man took a cell phone from the inside pocket of his suit jacket and punched in a number. "Mr. Ruffino, this is Durrell. There are two cops here with a warrant authorizing them to take the contents of Dane Trask's office into evidence for a case they're working on."

Durrell listened for a moment, nodding, then thrust the phone toward Jason. "He wants to speak with you."

"Who are you and what organization are you with?" a man's slightly nasal voice demanded as Jason put the phone to his ear.

"Officer Jason Beck, Ranger Brigade."

"The Ranger— Oh, that outfit based in the national park."

"That's correct," Jason said. "Who are you and what organization are you with?"

"I'm Mitchell Ruffino, vice president in charge of operations for TDC. What could Dane Trask possibly have to do with Black Canyon National Park?"

"His truck was found yesterday in the bottom of the

canyon, having plummeted off one of the overlooks," Jason said. "This was after he was reported missing."

"Who reported him missing?" Ruffino demanded, sounding as if he intended to find and punish that person.

Jason glanced at Cara again. She was leaning forward, a look of intense concentration on her delicate features.

"I don't think that's relevant," Jason said. "But we're investigating Mr. Trask's disappearance and the contents of his office could contain vital evidence."

"I can tell you why Trask disappeared," Ruffino said. "He skipped out because he embezzled a hundred thousand dollars from this company and knew he was on the verge of being caught. Those files are vital to recovering our stolen money."

"As part of my investigation, I contacted other area law enforcement agencies and none of them reported charges being filed or accusations of embezzlement being levied against Mr. Trask."

Silence greeted his words and, for a moment, Jason wondered if Ruffino had hung up, perhaps to storm to this office and confront him in person. Finally, the executive said, "You must understand that organizations such as ours prefer to conduct our own internal investigation into the matter before we turn things over to the police."

"You can certainly do that," Jason said. "Meanwhile, until our investigation is complete, we're taking custody of these items. They will be returned to you when we no longer need them."

"I'll need to see that warrant," Ruffino said.

"Of course. Mr. Durrell can bring it to you now."

Ruffino did hang up on him then. Jason handed the warrant to Durrell. "Mr. Ruffino wants to see that now," he said.

Durrell took the paper, then glanced at his partner. With a last glare at the two cops, the men left the office.

Jason and Dance moved farther into the office. Dance shut the door behind them. Cara leaned against the desk, her face pale. "What's going on?" she asked.

"After I left you yesterday, I made some phone calls," Jason said. "I discovered TDC hadn't filed any charges of embezzlement or theft or anything else against Dane Trask."

"Corporations often like to hush up that sort of thing," she said.

"Your missing person's report and the discovery of Dane's truck were enough for me to get authorization to take a look at his bank accounts. If he was embezzling tens of thousands of dollars, none of it was getting anywhere near his personal accounts. And he hasn't used his credit cards or his cell phone since you saw him last. Someone trying to fake his own death would know enough to avoid those two things, but it takes a lot of money to start life over someplace new and I didn't find anything showing Trask had stashed away funds." He put his hand on the topmost box. "I need to dig deeper, and for that, we need these files."

She nodded, looking relieved.

"I'll see about getting a dolly to carry these out," Dance said, and left them.

When he was gone, Jason moved closer to Cara. "Are you okay?" he asked.

She nodded. "Yeah. It's been a tough morning."

"Who were those two?" he asked. "The guys who came to collect the boxes?"

"I've never seen them before in my life." She rubbed her arms, as if trying to warm herself. "They looked tough."

"They looked like bodyguards," Jason said. "Why would Ruffino need that kind of muscle?"

She blew out a breath. "I don't know, but I feel a lot better, knowing you'll have the files instead of them." Her eyes met his. "I know it looks bad, Dane disappearing, and then these accusations about embezzlement coming out, but I can't believe they're true. He just wasn't—he isn't—that kind of man."

"Some criminals are very good at fooling people," he said.

She lifted her chin. "I know that. I'm not as naive as I look. But Dane isn't a criminal. I don't know what's going on, but I'm going to try to find out."

"You need to leave the investigating to us," he said.

Her gaze remained steady, considering. "You've already done more than I expected," she said. "I thought you believed I was making the whole thing up."

He had believed that, at least at first. But spending time with her yesterday, he had detected no deception in her story, and her loyalty to her boss had touched him. What would it be like to have another person believe in him so fiercely?

And the memory of that pickup, smashed at the bottom of the canyon, had stayed with him. If Dane Trask had sent that vehicle over the edge himself, it was the act of a desperate man. Jason wanted to know what was behind that desperation.

The door opened and Jason took a step back, putting a little distance between himself and Cara. Dance wheeled in a dolly. "Any suggestions where we should look first?" Jason asked Cara.

"The computer," she said. "Anything Dane is working on is there." She pressed her lips together, as if tempted to say more.

"Anything else we should know?" he asked.

She shook her head, avoiding his gaze now. Disappointment clawed at him. She was being evasive, either lying or holding something back.

Some people had an instinctive distrust of the law. Other people feared anyone with a badge or shied away out of guilt.

Solving this case would be much easier if he could get Cara to trust him. But he sensed she wasn't one to let down her guard easily. She was going to make him work for any bit of trust he might get.

"WHAT WAS ALL that about?"

Maisie didn't waste any time cornering Cara after Jason and his partner had left the office, taking all of Dane's work with them. Eyes shining with curiosity, she leaned over Cara's desk, her voice just above a whisper. "Is Dane really being investigated? Did he really steal from the company? And where is he now?"

"I don't know the answer to any of those questions," Cara said. Which wasn't a lie. The whole exchange this morning had left her sad and confused. On the one hand, Jason seemed to believe that Dane was missing and possibly in trouble. On the other hand, it certainly looked like Dane could be guilty of something.

"Well, come on. Dane was your boss. You must know something."

Cara shook her head. "I don't know anything, really."

Maisie blew out a breath, stirring her long brown bangs. "Well, at least the cops were hot. And who were the two suits? Great bodies, but kind of scary-looking."

"I've never seen them before," Cara said.

"Me neither, but if they work here now, I need to find

out where." Maisie grinned. "A little scary could be exciting, you know?"

Cara would take safe and calm over scary and exciting any day, but merely gave her friend a weak smile. "I'll let you know if I find out anything else."

Maisie returned to work and Cara tried to focus on formatting a report Dane had sent to her right before he'd walked out of the office with his backpack. She paid close attention to its contents, hoping he had left her some clue as to what he was up to. But the report—a summary of the water and soil analysis at the site of a potential office complex TDC planned to build in Nevada—was routine and boring. "All preliminary tests show the site well-suited for the project as outlined," Dane had concluded.

Every time the door to the office opened or someone approached Cara's desk, she braced herself, expecting Mr. Ruffino to summon her and grill her about Dane and everything that had happened. But nothing happened.

At five o'clock, she headed home, the flash drive with Dane's files buried deep in her purse. Though Jason had said he intended to search the documents for clues about what might have happened to Dane, Cara believed she was better equipped to see the significance of the information.

At least she owed it to Dane to try.

Two blocks from her home, she pulled up to a stop sign and glanced in the rearview mirror. Two cars back, a black SUV with dark windows idled. She stared at the vehicle. Hadn't she seen it as she'd turned off the road that led from TDC headquarters? It had been parked on the side of the road. She had registered its presence, but otherwise not thought much about it.

She made a left turn and the SUV turned, also. Impulsively, she swung right onto the next street. The SUV cruised past and she breathed a sigh of relief. The morning's ordeal and her own guilt over copying Dane's files were obviously making her paranoid.

She made her way home down a series of back streets. Once she thought she saw the black SUV waiting at an intersection ahead, but the driver signaled a turn in the direction opposite the one she was traveling. She gripped the steering wheel tightly and told herself she was being silly.

Still, relief flooded her when she reached her home, the small cottage with its steeply pitched green-metal roof and delicate wooden gingerbread outlining the broad front porch a welcome sanctuary from the stresses of the day.

Inside the house, she changed into yoga pants and a T-shirt, fixed a sandwich and a glass of iced tea, and sat at the kitchen table with her laptop. She downloaded the documents she had scanned in that morning, then inserted the flash drive with all the files from Dane's computer and studied the file listing.

Dane had worked for TDC for six years and many of the files dated back to those early days. She decided to focus on the most recent data, in the hope that something Dane had written about or marked would provide a clue as to his current situation and whereabouts.

She determined that in the two weeks prior to his disappearance, Dane had been working primarily on analyzing water samples from three sites—the property in Nevada slated for the new office building, a Superfund cleanup of an old mine near Black Canyon, and the new elementary school, also nearby. She studied the columns of numbers and abbreviations. She didn't have Dane's scientific background, but she thought she was sharp enough to spot any big discrepancies.

But after an hour, her head ached and she had found nothing in the reports for the three properties that raised alarms.

She got up to stretch her legs and refill her tea glass.

The sun had set and dusk was fast turning to dark, so she moved to the front window to pull shut the drapes. The street was silent, the trees, parked cars and shrubbery in front of neighboring houses reduced to black smudges against gray shadows. Everything looked normal, yet it didn't feel that way. She couldn't shake this edginess that made her skin crawl—as if she was being watched.

She jerked the drapes shut, checked that the locks on the front and back doors were secure, and told herself to snap out of it. Then her cell phone rang, the country ballad she'd chosen as her ringtone sounding overly loud in the stillness.

She hurried to the reclaim the phone from where it danced on the kitchen table, vibrating and ringing. She didn't recognize the number on the screen, so she answered cautiously, prepared to hang up on an automated sales call. "Cara? It's Officer Beck. How are you doing?"

"Hi. Uh, I'm okay, I guess." She lowered herself into the kitchen chair. The last person she'd expected to hear from was Jason Beck. "Did you find something useful in Dane's files?"

"Not yet. I just wanted to check in because you looked pretty shaken when I left this morning."

"Yes, I was shaken. I had two thugs and then two cops in the office."

"Hey, cops aren't so bad." His tone was teasing.

"Maybe *you're* not so bad. I can't say the same about others I've met."

"Hmm. Something tells me there's a story behind that statement. Some day I want to hear it."

Cara remained silent. She could count on the fingers of one hand the number of people who knew about her brother. Nothing like bringing up a murdered sibling to put a damper on a conversation.

She gave Jason credit for being able to take a hint. "What happened after I left TDC this morning?" he asked.

"Nothing," she said. "I mean, people talked about Dane, but no one really knew anything. Then everyone went back to work."

"Ruffino didn't grill you?"

"Why would he?" she said. "I'm just another cog in the wheel to people like him."

"I spoke to the sheriff's office," Jason said. "Dane's daughter, Audra, filed a missing person's report with them a few days ago. We encouraged her to do so."

"They wouldn't listen to me when I talked to them," she said.

"Sometimes they pay more attention to family."

"So what happens now?" she asked. "Do you turn the search for Dane over to the local sheriff?"

"No, we have priority, especially since Dane's truck was found in the canyon. But Audra's report formalizes everything and maybe frees up some resources. I'm still trying to arrange for a plane or a helicopter to do an aerial search."

"I wish there was more that I could do," she said.

"When you were packing up Dane's things this morning, did you have a chance to look through much?" Jason asked. "Did you see anything that struck you as odd or different?"

"Not really." She bit her lip, resisting the impulse to confess that she had made copies of all of Dane's records. That probably qualified as theft of company property or something, and he didn't need to know. "You'll let me know if you find anything, won't you?" she asked.

"I'll keep you as informed as I can."

What does that mean exactly? She started to ask as much when a scraping sound on her front porch made her almost drop the phone. She knew that sound—it was the noise she made every time she returned home after dark and discovered she'd forgotten to leave the porch light on. Invariably, she ended up banging her shin on the cast-iron planter of petunias. The combination of the planter scraping on the wooden porch floor and muttered cursing was unmistakable.

"Cara? Are you still there?"

"I'm still here," she whispered. She tiptoed toward the front door and pressed her eye to the peephole. Was she imagining that darker shadow next to the porch post?

"What's wrong?" Jason asked. "I can hardly hear you."

She moved away from the door, all the way into the kitchen. She grabbed the largest knife from the magnetic bar by the stove. The problem with a weapon like that was that she'd have to get really close to use it.

"Cara?" Jason's voice was louder now.

She pressed the phone tight against her ear. "There's someone on my front porch," she said softly. "Someone who shouldn't be there."

"Lock yourself in your bedroom. I'm calling 9-1-1 and I'm on my way."

Chapter Eight

Jason skidded around the curves on the rough mountain road from his rented cabin to the highway into town. Headlights on bright, he scanned the roadside for deer or elk that might decide to leap into his path, and listened to the chatter on the police radio for any word that the Montrose police had apprehended Cara's intruder.

With the locals on the way, Cara didn't need him to run to her rescue. She probably didn't want him. But he was going anyway, compelled by a mixture of curiosity and protectiveness and attraction. Something about her drew him. She was a puzzle he needed to figure out, almost as much as he needed to solve the puzzle of Dane Trask's disappearance.

On the surface, the story looked straightforward. A man is stealing money from his employer. He finds out he's on the verge of getting caught, so he fakes his own death and skips town.

But something about TDC's insistence on that narrative didn't ring true to Jason. The company's haste to confiscate Dane's computer and files wasn't normal operating procedure in his experience. Throw in two beefy guys in charge of retrieving the files, and every instinct told him he needed to look a lot closer at all of this.

He reached Cara's neighborhood and turned onto her

street. Her house was dark, with no sign of the local cops or of an intruder. Jason drove past the house, parked around the corner and walked back, moving as soundlessly as possible and keeping to the shadows.

The house was a square two-story cottage, with a steeply sloped metal roof, windows flanked by wooden shutters, and a covered porch across the front. Secluded in the shadow of a massive lilac bush, he studied the scene and froze as something moved on the porch. Something large and bulky, just below a large window.

He drew his service weapon, a Glock 22, and a large flashlight and approached the porch. When he was standing directly opposite the bulky figure, he raised the gun and switched on the flashlight. "This is the police!" he shouted. "Stop and put your hands where I can see them."

The figure—a man dressed all in black, including a black ski mask pulled down to obscure his face—shielded his eyes from the glare of the light with one upraised arm. He thrust the other in front of him and barreled forward, almost knocking Jason off his feet. The gun fired, the bullet well off course, thudding harmlessly into the dirt.

Jason holstered the weapon and raced after the man, but big as he was, the guy had speed. By the time Jason reached the end of the block, the man was gone.

Jason retraced his steps to the house. Lights were on inside now, as well as in all the houses around Cara's. Nothing like a gunshot in the middle of an otherwise peaceful night to rouse people from their beds.

A Montrose Police Department black-and-white pulled to the curb as Jason approached. He held up his hands. "I'm the Ranger Brigade officer who called this in," he said.

The local cop climbed out of the patrol car and approached. He was young, fit and looking a little uncertain. "We got a report of an intruder," he said after he had examined Jason's ID and returned it to him. "Have you seen anything?"

"He was on the front porch." Jason motioned toward the house. "He was trying to force the window. You might want to take a look at it in a minute. Meanwhile, he ran that way." He pointed down the street.

The officer glanced down the street then reached for his shoulder mic. "Do you have a description of the suspect?" he asked.

"He was big, beefy and dressed all in black," Jason said. "He was wearing a ski mask and gloves." He turned to start up the walk.

"Sir, where are you going?" the young cop asked.

"I'm going to check on the woman inside the house."

The young cop didn't say anything. It wouldn't have mattered to Jason if he had. He didn't want to wait any longer to find out if Cara was okay.

He rang the bell then knocked. "Cara, it's me, Jason."

The door swung open and Cara, barefoot and wearing yoga pants and a loose T-shirt, stared at him, a large knife in her right hand. "What's going on?" she asked. "Did you catch him?"

"He ran away," Jason said. "I think it's safe to put the knife away now."

She stared at the knife, as if trying to remember why she was holding it. She set it on a small table by the door then stepped back and held the door open wider. "You'd better come in."

His first thought upon entering the house was that it smelled like her—warm and spicy with a touch of sweetness. He hadn't really noticed this when he'd stopped by with the flash drive the other night. Next, he took in the framed photographs, books and plants that filled this front room. It wasn't an unpleasant clutter, but a homey one. All these personal items pointed to someone who was making a home in this space, not just biding time until something better came along.

"This is a great house," he said.

"Thanks. It was a dump when I bought it, but it's coming along. I did most of the work myself." He didn't miss the note of pride behind the words.

"You did a great job." He ran his hand along the smooth wood of a built-in sideboard as she hugged her arms across her body. Was she cold or merely defensive?

"Are you okay?" he asked when they had passed through the living room into the kitchen.

"A little scared." She rubbed her shoulders as if to ward off a chill. "And a lot angry. How dare someone try to break into my home? Did you see him?"

"Yes. He was crouching under that window." He nodded toward the big window to the right of the front door. "He was dressed all in black, with a ski mask, so I can't tell you who he was, or even much about his appearance."

"All the windows and doors have good locks, but maybe I need an alarm system, too." She leaned back against the counter, arms crossed over her chest. "This is supposed to be a safe neighborhood. I haven't heard of anyone else having a break-in."

Jason took up position beside her—close, but not touching. His first instinct was to comfort her and to tell her not to worry. But his law enforcement training vetoed that approach. "Is it possible this attempted break-in is connected to Dane's disappearance?" he asked.

Her face paled and she hugged herself even more tightly. "Why do you say that?"

"I've never met Dane Trask. Is it possible he was trying to break in?"

"Dane wouldn't have to break into my house. All he would have to do is knock and I'd let him in."

"What does Dane look like?" Jason asked. He'd seen the ID photos of the man, but they didn't show much.

"He's about six feet tall, slender build, dark hair cut short, blue eyes."

"The guy who was trying to break in was bigger than that," Jason said. "Bulkier, and a little shorter, I think."

"Dane wouldn't break in, and he wouldn't frighten me this way."

"All right, then let's look at this from another angle. Maybe whoever was trying to get in here wants something you have or something you know."

Pink bloomed on her pale cheeks. "Why would anyone think I have or know anything?" she asked, avoiding his gaze.

He moved to stand in front of her. When she didn't raise her eyes to his, he gently nudged her chin until her eyes met his. "Did you turn over all of Dane's records this morning?" he asked. "Or did you keep something back? Maybe something you didn't think was important?"

"I turned over everything," she said, lowering her gaze. Her expression grew troubled. "But I made copies of everything before I did."

"Why did you do that? Were you afraid data might be compromised or lost?"

"I wanted to look through everything to see if I could figure out what Dane was working on before he left."

"What did you find out?"

"He had three jobs he was involved in—an office complex in Nevada, a Superfund mine cleanup in the mountains near here, and the new elementary school near the national park." She shook her head. "Nothing looked out of the ordinary."

"Did anything match the fragment of the report on the drive that was left in your car?" he asked.

"No. But if someone was trying to break into my home because they're afraid I'll find something in those files, then I'm more determined than ever to keep looking. And don't waste your breath telling me I shouldn't get involved. I'm already involved and I'm a lot more likely to spot something off about those reports than you are."

Her eyes met his and what he saw there sent a thrill through him—not fear, but fierceness, a determination to keep going over his and anyone else's objections.

Her gaze shifted from his eyes to his lips and awareness crackled between them. He put a hand on her arm and she leaned into the touch, leaned into him, her face tilted to his, her eyes half closed, her breathing quick and shallow.

He caressed her upper arms and angled his head toward hers, blood rushing, heart racing—

The doorbell jolted them apart. Cara gaped at him, dazed, then rushed from the room.

He hurried after her. She checked the security peephole then opened the door to the young officer Jason had spoken to earlier and an older, female officer with very short blond hair. "Did you catch the person who was trying to break into my house?" Cara asked.

"No, ma'am," the younger officer said. "But we're still looking for him. Are you missing any personal items?"

"No. He didn't succeed in breaking in," she said.

The female officer turned to Jason. "Would you recognize the man if you saw him again?" she asked.

"Probably not," he said. "He was wearing a ski mask and gloves."

"There are some tool marks around the window frame, but you must have scared him off before he got very far," the younger officer said.

Some of the color had leached from Cara's face again. "What if he comes back?" she asked.

"Call 9-1-1 and we'll have someone here right away," the woman said. She gave Cara her card and the two left.

Cara sat on the sofa in the darkened room. "I don't know how I'll sleep, worried whoever that was will come back."

"You could go to a hotel," he said.

"I can't live in a hotel." She sat straighter. "And it makes me angry all over again that this creep might run me out of my home." She looked toward the door. "I'll just sit up all night, and tomorrow I'll call the alarm company."

"Don't you have to work tomorrow?" he asked.

"If I still have a job." She shrugged. "Without Dane there, I'm having to work to look busy. Once someone in payroll or accounting or human resources realizes they're paying me to do nothing, I'll be out the door in no time."

Jason could have made a smart remark about executives being paid millions to do nothing, but thought better of it. "If you're going to sit up all night worrying, I'll sit with you," he said.

"You don't have to do that!"

But if he didn't, he'd probably lie awake in his own bed, worrying about her. "We can take a look at those files you copied. Maybe both of us working together will spot something."

She smiled, and the force of the look rocked him back on his heels. It wasn't the kiss he had wanted earlier, but it was something.

CARA MADE COFFEE and brought two cups to the table. The caffeine probably wouldn't improve her jitteriness, but she hoped it would sharpen her focus. If she was going to help Dane, she needed answers.

She sat and pulled her chair up closer to the table. Jason

positioned his chair beside her. She caught the scent of him—starch and soap and clean man—and a tremor raced across her nerves. Sitting there with him, the world silent and dark around them, felt so intimate. When he'd run his hand along the sideboard, a shiver had raced through her, as if he was touching her with such tenderness.

She shook off the thought. It had been a long time since she'd been this close to anyone. After Corey's death, she had felt so fragile for so long. Relationships took energy she didn't have to give.

"Tell me more about Dane," Jason said. "He must have been a pretty great boss for you to go to so much trouble to help him now."

"He is a great boss." She refused to speak of Dane in the past tense. "He's a good person." How could she explain this so that Jason would see that Dane wasn't the type of person who would steal anything, much less a hundred thousand dollars? "Dane paid the electric bill for one of the building custodians who was about to get his power cut off. He didn't make a big deal about it or say anything, he just went down to the power company and paid the bill. I only found out about it by accident. He helped people like that all the time—veterans especially, but other people, too."

"Did he help you?" Jason asked. "Is that why you're so loyal to him?"

She felt shaky again, unnerved that this man could read her so clearly. "You don't miss much, do you?" She took a sip of her coffee, not even tasting it. "When my brother died, Dane insisted on buying a ticket for me to fly back to Houston to be with my family. I had to stay longer than I was entitled to for bereavement leave, but he pulled strings somehow and made sure I got paid during the extra time off."

"That's a great boss, all right," Jason said.

"It wasn't the money that mattered most," she said. "When I got back after the funeral, he didn't try to pretend nothing had happened. He talked to me. He asked me about my brother, and he didn't get upset when I cried. Talking to him made things easier."

"I'm sorry to hear about your brother," he said. "What was his name?"

The nervousness she had been fighting melted away with that question. Most people's first reaction was "How did he die?" or "When did he die?" But Dane had asked for his name first.

"His name was Corey. He was two years younger than me, and we were pretty close." She took a deep breath. "He was murdered."

Jason stiffened but didn't recoil. "That's tough," he said. "Really tough. I'd like to hear what happened—if you want to tell me."

"Corey had a problem…" She began as she always did. "With heroin and prescription painkillers. He'd tried to kick the addiction a few times—even did a stint in rehab once. But he kept going back. When my parents called to tell me he'd died, I was sure they'd say it was an overdose. But he'd been shot." She swallowed. "Three times."

Jason's hand covered hers. He didn't speak, but the warm pressure of his hand on hers said volumes. "Did they find his killer?" he asked after a moment.

"No."

He withdrew his hand and leaned back, putting distance between them. "Is that why you don't like cops?" he asked.

"I don't dislike cops," she said. She didn't dislike him. "But I don't trust them. The ones assigned to my brother's case didn't seem to think he was worth their time." The memory still hurt and she had to look away. "Dane offered to pay for a private detective to investigate, but I couldn't let him do that."

"I'm sorry you had to go through that," he said. "And I'm glad Dane did what he could to make it easier on you."

She liked that he didn't try to defend the Houston cops. And maybe he saw Dane in a more favorable light now.

She pushed the half cup of cooling coffee away. "I can't do anything for my brother, but I can try to help Dane. I thought we could compare all the water quality reports from the three jobs he's working on with the fragment of the report on the flash drive I think he left for me to see if we can find a match."

"Is it possible his disappearance has nothing to do with his work?" Jason asked.

"Anything is possible," she said. "But he never mentioned any trouble in his personal life."

"His daughter said he didn't have a girlfriend. Not a current one, anyway."

"I know he dated women from time to time, but his last serious relationship ended six months ago. He was still friends with the woman."

"Is that Eve Shea? Audra mentioned her, too."

"Yes, Eve. They dated several years before they broke it off."

"Why did they break up? You said something about it before, but I can't remember."

"I think she wanted to get married and have children. Dane's daughter, Audra, was grown, and he always said he didn't want more children."

"And he got along well with the daughter?"

"Yes. They were close. And before you ask, she didn't have any trouble in her life, either. She's a smart young woman, financially and emotionally stable. Dane always said he never worried about her, she had such a good head on her shoulders."

"How about Audra's mother?"

"She was a brief relationship he had in college. She's married to an ophthalmologist and lives in Kansas City. She and Dane weren't close, but they got along well. She always invites Dane to anything that involves Audra—birthday parties and that sort of thing. I never sensed any animosity there."

"All right, we'll focus on the job," Jason said. "I just don't want to be shortsighted and miss any other possibilities."

She nodded and pulled up the first file. Jason was rising higher in her estimation by the moment. But talk was cheap. His actions would count more with her.

Chapter Nine

Jason tried to focus on the columns of numbers and letters on the computer screen, but his sleep-deprived brain insisted on shifting his attention to the soft curve of Cara's neck, or the floral scent of her hair. He was lost in a fantasy that involved kissing her neck and threading his fingers through her hair when the sound of his name recalled his attention.

"You're not listening, are you?" Cara asked. She had bluish smudges under each eye and looked exhausted.

"I'm sorry, no." He wiped a hand over his face, as if that would somehow wake him up. The clock in the lower right-hand corner of the computer screen read 3:11 a.m. "I'm not really a numbers guy."

She sat back. "We're not finding anything, anyway. Do you want to try to get some sleep? I can't promise my sofa is that comfortable, but you're welcome to it."

He shook his head. "Not yet." He was too wired from all the coffee he had consumed over the last few hours. "Let's just talk. Tell me how you ended up in your job."

"I have a degree in business. I don't want to be anyone's boss, but I'm good with details. TDC is a good company to work for."

It sounded boring to him, but she didn't sound unhappy with the work.

"What about you?" she asked. "How did you end up as a cop?"

"I did a year in the Peace Corps after college," he said. "Then I got a job working with teens in an Outward Bound type project. I like being outdoors, so I decided to become a park ranger. I was drawn to the law enforcement aspect of the job and eventually the National Parks police. And now I'm here."

"Wow," she said when he finished. "I bet that's not the usual career path."

"You might be surprised. All kinds of people work in law enforcement."

"Maybe you're different because you were a park ranger first," she said. "I can't imagine you've had to deal with too many seamy crimes to make you jaded."

"As a park ranger you deal with people," Jason said. "Some of them aren't so nice. Some of them believe they can get away with more in a wilderness setting." He'd had to deal with murder, rape, kidnapping and a host of lesser crimes. The fact that these wrongdoings took place in otherwise idyllic settings sometimes made them seem even more horrific.

Cara turned her attention back to the documents on the computer screen, so he did, as well, reading again the notes about turbidity and parts per million of arsenic and mercury. At the bottom of the report a section described the appearance of the water, whether or not it was cloudy or clear, silty, muddy, green with algae, et cetera. She pointed to a single word in the description box: *bloody.* "Look at that."

Jason's eyebrows lifted. "He's saying there's blood in the water?"

She shook her head. "No, I remember this. There was a lot of iron in the water, and suspended minerals, so that it was very red and thick. Like ketchup. Or blood. Dane wrote that in the original report and we joked about freaking out the engineers who explain these reports to clients. Sure enough, someone higher up kicked it back and he had to change it to something like 'red from high mineral content.'" Her fingers flew over the keys, searching for a different file. "But now I know where this fragment of a report is from."

She found the file she wanted and pulled it up in split screen alongside the information from the first flash drive. "These are reports from the Mary Lee Mine, a Superfund site TDC is helping to mitigate—that is, clean up."

"Do they do a lot of that kind of work?" Jason asked. "I thought they were primarily a construction concern."

"They've done some. This is a bigger project, but something they hope to do more of. The federal government is in charge of cleaning up a lot of these old mine sites around the country, but they're spread pretty thin and money is always tight. So someone at TDC approached them with the offer that TDC would do the cleanup in exchange for some other land the government owns, where TDC would like to build a new project. There aren't many companies that could manage something like that, but TDC persuaded the right people that they could."

"Are both these partial reports related to that project?" Jason asked. "And are we supposed to pay attention to the project or just the word *bloody*?"

"I think it's the project. I might be wrong, but this feels right. Dane devoted a lot of hours to this site, and a couple of times he mentioned how complicated and frustrating it was."

Jason watched over her shoulder as she scrolled through the original report on the property—the one that matched the fragment they had received on the first flash drive. "If all of that nasty stuff is in the water," he said, "how do you get it out?"

"There are different ways. You can divert the most poisonous stuff to holding ponds, then use a series of filters to remove the poisons before returning the clean water to the stream. That isn't always practical, so another way is to use settling ponds—divert the water, let it sit for sometimes years, the heavy metals and poisons settling out into gravel. Then that gravel has to be hauled away and disposed of. It's complicated and the process can take years. One of the things Dane did was regularly test the water to see if the levels of harmful substances were dropping."

She pulled up another document. "This is from the files I copied from Dane's computer," she said. "It was created a couple of months ago. See how much the toxin levels have dropped compared to his initial report?"

"That's what they're supposed to do, right?" he asked. "If the site is being decontaminated."

She frowned at the screen, then shook her head. "I'm getting a bad feeling about this."

"What's wrong?" Jason leaned in closer and caught the scent of her hair, subtle and floral. Feminine.

"This was only three months after TDC took over the mitigation at the Mary Lee Mine," she said. "Yet the values on some of these toxins have dropped more than half."

"They were doing a really good job."

She shook her head. "I remember Dane told me it could take a decade or more to clean up some of these sites. Even if you go in and remove all the soil in the waterway, you have to find the source of the contamination and get rid of it, too.

"In the case of mining, that could be tons of waste rock, and materials stored deep in the mine tunnels. One reason these sites take so long to clean up is that there are so many potential sources of contamination, and the materials you're dealing with are so toxic." She glanced at him. "You can't just take what you remove from the area and spread it around somewhere else. It has to be cleaned up before it can go anywhere and, again, that can take years."

"So how did TDC get such an improvement in such a short time?" he asked.

"I don't know. I'm sure Dane was wondering about that, too."

"What about the second flash drive?" Jason asked. "The one that was wrapped in the bandana in the back of Dane's truck?"

"It's another report," she said. "But not a water report. That one deals with contaminants in soil. I haven't found a link to anything on Dane's computer yet."

He put a hand on her shoulder, meaning to reassure her, maybe offer some comfort. "It's been a long day. Time to get some rest." She closed her eyes and rested her cheek against the back of his hand and he froze, fighting a fierce longing to wrap his arms around her and pull her close, to somehow ease some of the burden she carried.

The moment passed. She opened her eyes and sat straight. "I want to go to the Mary Lee Mine," she said.

"Where is it?" Jason asked.

"In the mountains near here. I want to see for myself what TDC is doing up there."

"I'll go with you," he said.

"I didn't invite you."

"I'm inviting myself. I want to see this place, too."

She looked him in the eye and he didn't look away. He was prepared to argue with her about this. If something was going on at that mine that Trask wanted them to know about, no way was he going to let her walk into possible danger alone.

Her smile surprised him, its warmth doing something to his core, making it hard to catch his breath for a few seconds. "All right," she said. "We can go tomorrow, after work. You might be useful to have around, after all."

Useful. Like a tool or a helper. Maybe she did think of him that way. The knowledge rankled, but he was nothing if not stubborn.

And he had always liked a challenge.

By SIX THIRTY on Tuesday morning, Cara had drunk entirely too much coffee, slept a few fitful hours in her bed while Jason dozed on the sofa, and learned that Jason Beck was funny, smart and distractingly sexy in a way that almost made her forget he was a cop. Warmth spread through her as she remembered that moment when she had leaned against him, his hand so comforting and steady on her shoulder. She wanted to attribute her feelings for him to a combination of lack of sleep and frayed nerves. But maybe those weren't the only reasons she felt so unsteady and almost happy around him—though happiness seemed an impossible emotion, given the seriousness of the situation. But emotions were fickle, she knew that.

And emotions wouldn't help her find Dane or solve the puzzle of what he was up to.

She showered, dressed and stumbled into the kitchen to find Jason scrambling eggs and burning toast. "I should have warned you, the bread sticks," she said, yanking the toaster plug from the wall and fishing out two slices of only slightly too dark bread. "But you didn't have to fix me breakfast."

"I needed to eat, so I figured you did, too."

Part of the night on her less-than-comfortable sofa hadn't lessened the man's appeal. The beard stubble and rumpled shirt gave him a rough-around-the-edges masculinity that made most of her tingle. Was this what being in danger did to her—got her all worked up over the cop who'd come to her rescue?

Jason set a plate of eggs and toast and a mug of coffee on the table in front of her. "I can follow you to work, then go home and clean up before my shift," he said.

The scene was so domestic and comforting, as if they were longtime lovers and he spent the night at her place all the time.

Except the closest they had come to intimacy was that almost kiss in this very kitchen before the local police showed up. And surely that had only happened because she was so shaken and dazed by finding out someone had tried to break into her home. She shivered and forced down a swallow of coffee. "I'll call the alarm company as soon as I get to work," she said. She glanced across the table, to where he was shoveling in eggs. Obviously, bad guys didn't lessen his appetite. All in a day's work.

They parted in her driveway and she tried to push down a feeling of dread as she drove to her office.

The engineering department buzzed with conversation when Cara entered, but everyone quieted as she made her way to her desk. She ignored the stares, trying to act as if this was just another day. The thought was comforting— she would get to work at her desk as usual, and any moment now Dane would walk in and she'd find out this had all been a misunderstanding.

She started to stow her purse in the bottom drawer of the desk, but froze as she caught sight of a black-bordered notice someone had laid over her computer keyboard, where she would be sure to see it.

Memorial Service for Dane Trask
Saturday, April 25
10:00 a.m. Canyon Ballroom

"That was posted on the bulletin board in our break room this morning." Maisie came to stand beside Cara, a worried expression on her elfin features.

"How can they have a memorial service for Dane?" Cara asked. "He isn't dead." Jason would have told her if Dane's body had been found—wouldn't he?

She reread the notice twice, but it still didn't make sense.

"So you didn't already know about this?" Maisie asked.

Cara shook her head. "No." She picked up the notice, folded it in two, and slid it into her purse.

"Where are you going?" Maisie asked as Cara turned to leave.

"I'm going to find out more about this," she said.

She paused outside the elevator, studying the company directory and considering her options. When the elevator car arrived, she stepped inside and pressed 7. Executive offices. She might as well go all the way to the top.

Mitchell Ruffino occupied a large suite of offices in the corner of the top floor, with a breathtaking view of Black Canyon and the snowcapped peaks of the San Juan range. But before Cara could reach him, she had to get past his administrative assistant—a very attractive blonde with a close-fitting suit and an icy expression. "You can't see Mr. Ruffino without an appointment," she said, her gaze sliding over—and past—Cara.

"I need to speak with him about this memorial service for Dane Trask." Cara unfolded the notice and showed it to the woman. "I'm Mr. Trask's admin."

The woman scanned the notice. "What about it?"

"I need to speak with Mr. Ruffino." She met the blonde's icy stare with an even chillier one of her own. After what seemed like five minutes but was probably only a few seconds, the blonde picked up her phone. "Have a seat over there," she said.

Heart pounding, Cara perched on the edge of a stylish though uncomfortable chair. Maybe she should leave and go back to her desk before she made things worse for herself and Dane. If TDC wanted to have a memorial service for someone who wasn't dead, why did she care? When Dane was found, he'd probably laugh about it.

A slightly older, dark-haired woman approached Cara. "Mr. Ruffino can give you five minutes," she said. Without waiting for an answer, she turned and walked away.

Cara hurried after her. The woman stopped before a set of double doors. "Go in," she said.

Cara took a deep breath then shoved on the door. Mitchell Ruffino sat behind a desk the size of a pool table, in an office that was easily as large as one floor of Cara's home. "Shara said you wanted to speak with me about Dane Trask's memorial service," he said.

She walked to the desk and stood, back straight and head up, determined not to look like a schoolkid called to the principal's office. She was prepared to look Ruffino in the eye, except that he never lifted his gaze to meet hers. "Dane isn't dead," she said. "How can you hold a memorial for him?"

"This isn't the same as a funeral," Ruffino said with the patient air of someone explaining a simple concept to a dim child. "This is merely a memorial to commemorate what Dane Trask meant to this company."

"But you're accusing him of stealing from you," Cara said. "Why would you even want to memorialize his time with the company?"

"I'm sure the theft was merely the result of an undiagnosed mental illness, perhaps the result of his time in the war," Ruffino said. "We can acknowledge that, and acknowledge the many contributions Dane made to this company. We want to show the public that we're not the villains here."

Nausea churned her stomach. "So this is just some kind of twisted publicity stunt?"

"The public is always watching what we do," Ruffino said. "If more companies remembered that, maybe they would strive to do more good."

She stared at him. What kind of non-answer was that? Apparently, it was the only answer she was going to get. Ruffino picked up his phone and gave her a pointed look. "You should get back to work now."

Back at her desk, Cara stared at her phone for a long moment before she picked it up and punched in Jason's number. He answered on the second ring. "Cara? Is everything all right?"

"TDC just announced that they're holding a memorial service for Dane on Saturday morning."

"A memorial service? But Dane hasn't been declared dead."

"That's what I said, but it turns out this is someone's idea of a good way to make TDC look all forgiving and understanding and righteous—or something. Dane may have stolen from them, but they're willing to honor him anyway."

"That doesn't really make sense," Jason said.

"Will you come to the service?"

"Oh yeah. I want to get a closer look at the TDC executives, if nothing else," he said. "And I think we need to wait to visit the mine."

"Why?"

"For one thing, I'd like to gather a little more background on the place. For another, we might learn something useful at this service Saturday."

"I doubt that," she said. "I think it's all for show."

"Humor me. We can check out the mine on Sunday."

"All right, it's a date."

He chuckled, and embarrassment flooded her. Why had she said that? She and Jason were not dating. They were involved in a serious investigation. "I'll see you Saturday," he said and ended the call. But he couldn't stop her from fretting over whether she was upset over Dane or over the fact that a cop had her in such turmoil.

Chapter Ten

Dane's memorial was held in a large meeting space TDC used for business seminars and public events. Cara, dressed in a black dress and low heels, had to push past a line of reporters and cameramen to reach the entrance, but they all ignored her. They were probably waiting around for a statement from Mr. Ruffino.

"Cara, over here!"

Cara whipped her head around and found Audra waving from a back corner of the room. Relieved to spot someone who shared her dismay and grief, Cara hurried toward Dane's daughter. Audra wore a bright red dress, a red scarf wound in her long hair. "Red was—is—Dad's favorite color," she said when she caught Cara staring at the dress.

"Your father loves you in anything," Cara said.

"You know Eve Shea, right?" Audra turned to introduce the slim blonde to her left. Dane's former girlfriend looked pale and weary, but she mustered a weak smile.

"Of course Cara and I know each other," Eve said. She glanced around them. "Do you have any idea what is behind this farce? How can you have a memorial service when you don't have a body or even confirmation of a death?"

"I don't know," Cara said. That was easier, and probably less upsetting, than trying to explain the publicity stunt angle.

"It's almost time to start." Audra took Cara's arm. "We need to take our seats up front."

Eve took a step back. "Those seats are for family," she said. "I don't think—"

"I'm not going to sit up there by myself," Audra said. She took hold of Eve's arm with her free hand. "You two can pretend you're my aunts or cousins or something, if it makes you feel better."

"All right," Eve said as Audra marched them toward the front of the room. "But I'm not sure Dane would want me here. I'm the one who broke things off between us, after all."

"I want you here," Audra said.

They were almost to their seats when Bert Levy, from the surveying department, stepped into the aisle. "I'm sorry you have to go through this, Audra," Bert said, his watery brown eyes downcast. He ran a big hand through his thinning blond hair. "They're not really saying Dane is dead, are they?"

"Until they show me a body, I won't believe my father is dead," Audra said. She flicked the ends of her scarf over her shoulder. "This is just a show TDC is putting on to mollify their conscience."

The lines on either side of Bert's mouth deepened. "Some of us wanted to put together teams to search for Dane," he said. "But when I took the idea to Mr. Ruffino, he shut me right down. He said it was too dangerous and we needed to leave it to the professionals."

"Well, thank you for trying, Bert." Audra patted his hand. "Thank you a lot."

The three women had just settled into their seats on the first row, just below the raised dais, on which was centered a large photograph of Dane, when a commotion behind them made them turn to look.

Jason Beck and Officer Hudson stood in the middle of the aisle. Each of them wore simple, dark suits with white shirts and understated ties. But the civilian clothes did nothing to hide the fact that they were law enforcement. Their erect posture and the wary way they continually scanned the crowd gave away their profession.

Jason's eyes met and held Cara's gaze. Something stirred in her, an emotion she didn't want to examine too closely. "Why is he always looking at me like that?" Audra whispered.

Cara blinked. Jason had been looking at her, not Audra. She started to say as much when she realized Audra was referring to Jason's partner. Officer Hudson had his eyes fixed on Dane's daughter.

"I wouldn't call that a bad look," Eve said. "I'd say the hunky cop is interested in you. And not as a suspect in any crime."

"Oh really," Audra said. Her cheeks flushed a deeper pink and she fluffed her hair before she turned to face forward once more.

Jason and Hud slid into chairs two rows behind and across the aisle from Cara and the other two women. She forced herself to face the dais as the lights dimmed and Mitchell Ruffino strode to the podium. "Thank you for coming today to honor a man who contributed a great deal to the success of TDC Enterprises in the past six years," he said. "At TDC we believe in acknowledging the contributions of our employees, and wanted to do so for Dane Trask, before any more recent events are allowed to tarnish his memory."

"This is the kookiest event I've ever been to," Eve, seated on Cara's right, muttered.

"Hush," Audra said as a screen rose from the center of the stage. Music swelled and a photograph appeared of Dane standing with a group of men in suits, each holding a shovel. Dane, in khakis and boots, the sleeves of his white dress shirt rolled up to reveal tanned forearms, stood out from the crowd of executives. Here was clearly a man who didn't spend all his time seated behind a desk.

The slide shifted to one of Dane making a presentation at a conference. Then the slides shifted abruptly to photos of a younger Dane in uniform. A murmur rose from the crowd, and Ruffino began to read a list of Dane's military accomplishments—battles he was part of, medals and commendations he had received.

"Dane Trask made a great sacrifice to serve his country," Ruffino intoned. "But as we all know, the effects of war do not end upon discharge from service. Dane Trask was not immune to the mental wounds battle can inflict."

"Dane would have hated this," Eve fumed. "This whole assumption that every soldier must have something wrong with him. That, of course, they're all too messed up to function in society. He worked hard to dispel those stereotypes."

"Dad was saner than any of us," Audra agreed. She sniffed and blotted tears.

Cara squeezed Audra's arm. Inside, she was seething. She thought she knew what Ruffino was doing here. When Dane was found, the press and public would discredit anything he said because, after all, he was struggling with mental problems brought on by his war service. She didn't believe that for one second. Whatever had been bothering Dane over the last few weeks, she was pretty sure it had nothing to do with the war.

The last photograph was a blow-up of Dane's company identification picture. He stared into the camera with a serious expression, a handsome man in his prime, who managed to appear smart and capable in what was essentially a corporate mug shot.

Ruffino droned on about Dane's accomplishments for TDC. "You will be hearing other things from TDC in the coming days about Dane Trask, some of it not very pleasant. But now is not the time for those. Today, we are remembering the good things Dane did, and the good man he was."

Audra bowed her head and began to sob. Cara slipped her arm around Audra's shoulders and glared toward the podium. The longer she sat there, the more furious she became.

Ruffino—who had been the only person to speak—concluded his remarks and dismissed the gathering. He had scarcely moved away from the podium when Jason was at her side. "I think Ruffino should be glad looks can't really kill," he said. "The way you were staring at him sure looked lethal."

"He's lying about Dane having any kind of mental or emotional problems related to the war or anything else," she said. "Dane was all for getting help for people who needed it, but he despised the way too many people saw every soldier as troubled or messed up." She looked around at the crowd of press and coworkers, along with some Welcome Home Warriors members who had come to honor Dane. "This whole event was just a twisted way for TDC to pat themselves on the back before they get on with destroying Dane's reputation."

"Let's go outside where we can talk," Jason said. He took her hand and led her out a side door, into a walled courtyard furnished with benches and a burbling fountain. The gurgle of the water helped to drown out the murmur of the crowd leaving the auditorium.

Cara turned to face him. "Bert Levy, one of the TDC surveyors, told me he and some others wanted to organize teams to look for Dane, and Ruffino told him to leave that work to the professionals."

"Ruffino gave him good advice," Jason said. "The last thing we want is someone else lost or injured in that rugged country." He patted her shoulder. "Sometimes things that seem suspicious are just big companies protecting themselves—from true liability, or many just from bad press. That's probably what was behind this show today."

"Don't patronize me!" she snapped.

He took a step back. "I would never do that."

The intensity of his gaze, and the edge of anger in his voice, made her flinch. But she couldn't look away. Maybe he wasn't patronizing her. Maybe it was only her own helplessness making her feel this way. "Doesn't it bother you?" she asked. "Trying to find answers, yet only coming up against more questions?"

"It can be frustrating," he said. "But it's part of the job. People lie, and they try to hide things. You have to admit, if Dane wants us to know something, it would be a lot easier if he'd come out and tell us, instead of leaving cryptic hints."

"Maybe he can't come out and tell us," she said. "Maybe someone is watching him. Guarding him. He has to be careful."

"Who's guarding him? Who's watching him?"

She squeezed the sides of her head. "More questions I don't have the answers to."

"Try to trust that I'm looking for the answers to those same questions," he said.

"Don't shut me out of the investigation," she said. "Let me help you. And where I can't help, don't leave me in the dark about what's going on." She moved closer and touched the back of his hand. "I don't want to interfere or to tell you how to do your job. I just want to know that you're still trying to help. Don't give up on Dane."

He took her hand and squeezed it. "I'll tell you as much as I can." When she started to protest, he continued. "If I don't tell you something, it's because legally I can't, or because doing so might compromise our case, or even put you in danger. But I won't leave you to wonder and worry. I won't give up on Dane, and I won't give up on you." He released her hand. "Maybe we'll find out more when we visit the Mary Lee Mine tomorrow. If you still want to go?"

"Of course I want to go," she said.

"Great. I'll pick you up about ten."

"Cara, we're over here!" Audra's shout and wave distracted her, and when she looked back again, Jason was gone. But his last words echoed in her mind. He wanted her to trust him, and she had never needed to trust someone more.

Sunday morning, Jason arrived at Cara's house promptly at 10:00 a.m., driving his Ranger Brigade SUV and in full uniform. "You look very official," she said as she slid into the passenger seat.

"Yeah, well, sometimes the uniform opens doors and inspires cooperation." He looked rueful. "And sometimes it doesn't."

They drove for forty-five minutes, making small talk about nothing important. Cara wondered if he was purposefully avoiding mentioning the case or what they might find at the mine. Or maybe he was just someone who didn't have a lot to say in the morning.

The Forest Service road that led to the Mary Lee Mine had recently been widened and covered with a thick layer of gravel. The stumps of trees cut to effect this transformation stuck up like broken teeth along the roadside. After two miles of them listening to the gravel ping off the underside of the SUV, the road stopped at an iron gate, eight feet tall and twelve feet wide, equipped with a keypad, a speaker and the single glaring eye of a camera.

Jason pulled up to the speaker and keypad and lowered his window. He pressed the button on the speaker and waited. Nothing happened. He pushed the button again. "Hello?" Again, there was no response.

"Care to guess the gate code?" Jason asked. "Maybe something you use at TDC?"

Cara shook her head. "We don't have a gate at TDC."

He studied the area for a long moment, then turned the SUV around and drove back down the road a quarter mile, pulled off to the side and cut the engine. "What now?" she asked.

"I thought we'd take a little hike."

Cara looked down at her shoes. They were flats, not heels, but not designed for rugged country. "I don't know how far I'll get in these shoes."

Jason opened the driver's-side door. "You're welcome to wait for me here. It would probably be safer if you did."

"You're not leaving me behind." She slid to the ground and came around to meet him.

He handed her a bottle of water from a cooler in the rear of the SUV and grinned. "I never thought you would, but it's fun to get a rise out of you."

It wasn't "you're beautiful when you're angry," but it was close enough. She debated pouring the water on him, but she was thirsty, so she settled for glaring at him. He laughed and she felt the sound somewhere below her navel. That was the confusing thing about all her dealings with Jason Beck. Her lips said one thing but her body was having an entirely different conversation.

JASON AND CARA hiked away from the SUV, through the woods roughly parallel to the gate and the tall fence on either side of it. Jason waited for Cara to ask where they were going, but she remained silent, except for the occasional curse when she stumbled on the rough ground. He would have insisted she stay behind if he had had any hope of her agreeing. As it was, he felt better having her with him. He could keep her safe—from what or who, he couldn't say—and she was more likely to recognize something out of place at the mine.

When they had been walking about ten minutes, he stopped and waited for her to catch up. "What are we looking for up here?" he asked. "At the mine site?"

"I don't know," she said. "I only visited a reclamation site once, and that was before I worked for TDC. It was just a couple of big hills with grass growing on them. A sign explained that the hills topped clay bunkers full of hazardous waste dug from the ground around the mine, and the holding ponds behind the hills were collecting more hazardous sediment that filtered out from the water. Once clean, the water was diverted back to its original channel."

"So we're looking for digging or earth-moving equipment? Things like that?"

"I think so." She looked toward where they could glimpse chain-link fencing through the trees. "But we're not going to see anything if we can't get past that fence."

"Let's keep walking," he said. "Maybe we'll find a way." It didn't seem practical to him to fence off the entire property, which was just under five acres. Especially with no near neighbors, no close-by hiking trails, and the only road being the one that led to the locked gate.

Ten minutes later, the fence abruptly ended. No other fence bisected it and no cameras surveilled the area, unless they were hidden. A single red-and-white sign proclaimed Danger! Entry Forbidden!

He took Cara's hand and led her around the fence, past the sign. They were now officially trespassing. Not the best position for a law enforcement officer to be in. His goal was to get in and get out as quickly as possible. If he spotted anything suspicious, he'd do his best to obtain a legal warrant to check things out.

He guided them back toward the gate, reasoning that any heavy equipment in use on the property had entered from that direction. They wound around thick knots of pinion, through the slender white trunks of aspen and over outcroppings of rough granite, until they stood at the edge of a clearing, mounds of rocks like crumbling pyramids all around them.

They picked their way around the rocks, piles of various-size stones in half a dozen shades of gray. Cara stooped and picked up a small chunk and slipped it into her pocket. Jason pretended not to notice. "Did all of this come out of the mine?" he asked.

"I don't know," she said. "I think at least some of this is mine waste—the stuff left over after the ore is removed. That's what makes those big yellow-and-orange spills you see down the sides of mountains. A lot of the mines themselves are flooded. When they were working mines, pumps ran all the time to keep out the water. Now the water fills up the tunnels and leaches harmful chemicals out of the rock."

"And the radioactive stuff?" he asked. "Where does that come from?"

"That comes from rock," she said. "Uranium ore. But I'm not sure if they mine that in this area. I thought that was farther south and west of here."

"Dane's report mentioned a couple of radioactive isotopes."

"That's true. Maybe they did mine uranium here. I'll have to do more research."

He put a hand on her arm. "Let's get a little closer to the gate and see what we can see."

The area around the gate looked deserted, save for a small, locked shed. Cara turned in a full circle, surveying the area. "I really don't see anything that looks suspicious," she said.

Then the first gunshot exploded in the rocks to her left.

Chapter Eleven

Cara heard the loud report and looked up to see Jason launch himself at her. They hit the ground together, hard, as more bullets thudded into the dirt around them.

Someone was shooting at them? Why?

Jason rolled with her to the cover of a depression in the trees then rose up on one elbow, weapon in his other hand. "Stay down!" he barked.

"I think I'm smart enough to figure that out on my own," she muttered as she pressed herself as far into the dirt as possible. Her heart beat painfully. Was it possible to die of fear before a bullet found her?

The reports sounded even louder now, then she realized Jason was returning fire. She pressed her hands tightly to her ears, closed her eyes and mashed her cheek into the dirt.

She didn't know how long she lay there before she felt a gentle tug on her arm. She opened her eyes, prepared to lash out at anyone who tried to drag her away, and met Jason's concerned gaze. "I think they're gone," he said. "We need to get out of here."

He helped her to her feet. "Are you okay?" he asked.

She nodded. "Are you?"

"Yeah. Come on." He paused at the edge of their cover to collect several of the spent bullets and drop them into his pocket. Then they retreated the way they had come, jogging over the rough ground, arriving at the SUV, panting hard.

She slid into the passenger seat and buckled the seat belt with shaking hands as he started the engine. "That's a pretty extreme reaction to trespassers," she said when her breathing had slowed to almost normal.

"I don't think they were serious about killing us," he said.

"Those bullets seemed pretty serious to me."

"They had us cornered," he said. "They could have moved in and finished us off. Instead, they left. I think they just wanted to frighten us."

"They succeeded." She pressed a hand to her chest, as if that could calm her still wildly beating heart. "Did you ever see anyone? All I got a good look at was the ground underneath those trees."

"No. They were firing from behind the shed, I think."

"I never saw another vehicle," she said.

"I didn't, either. But it could have been parked out of sight somewhere nearby."

"Are you going to report this?" she asked.

He glanced at her. "I probably should."

"But you'd have to admit you were trespassing. And that you didn't find anything."

"I would."

"Or you could say you were there at the request of a TDC employee," she said.

"Are you authorized to visit TDC work sites?"

"No, but it would take some digging to find that out. I work for the company and I don't even know where you'd get that information. And it's not a lie. I work for TDC. I asked you to come with me."

"I insisted on going with you."

"If I hadn't wanted you along, I could have figured out how to give you the slip."

"You sound pretty sure of yourself."

"I can be devious when I have to be."

He must have heard the laughter behind her words because the dimple on the right side of his mouth deepened with his smile. When was the last time she had flirted with a man like this—and enjoyed it so much?

"Want to go somewhere and grab a bite to eat?" he asked. "I don't feel like going home just yet."

Was he asking her out? On a date?

No. A date required planning. Washing her hair and shaving her legs. This was just two people who happened to be together at dinnertime. "All right. Anything but sushi."

He shook his head. "And here I was going to suggest sushi." When he winked, she couldn't help but laugh, even as a sinking feeling settled in the pit of her stomach. If she didn't watch herself, she'd fall fast for Jason. And everybody knew speeding was bound to get you in trouble.

Jason asked Cara to choose a restaurant and she suggested an Italian bistro housed in a former Victorian home. Diners sat at white-clothed tables, two to three per room, classical music playing softly on hidden speakers. It was a lot more romantic than he had anticipated, but the diners were casually dressed and the prices modest, so he began to relax a little and enjoy the calming atmosphere and the pleasant company.

Cara had persuaded him to stop by her house so that she could wash the streaks of dirt from her face and hands and change into jeans and a flowing blouse that brought out the green of her eyes. She'd put on pink lipstick and dusted on some face powder, hiding the freckles he found so appealing. He'd taken the opportunity to clean up, also, and to change into the jeans and button-down shirt he kept in a bag in the back of the SUV.

"Tell me how you ended up in Montrose," he said after they had given their order for dinner.

"I came for the job," she said. "I was living in Texas at the time and wanted to move to Colorado. I started looking for work, applied online, and was hired after a phone interview. I'd never even heard of Montrose before, but after I got here, I fell in love with this area—the river, the canyons, the mountains. There's a little of everything here. What about you?"

"I came for work, too."

"Right. So where's your family?"

"My mom and dad are in New Hampshire. I have one sister in Upstate New York. What about your family?"

"My parents are in Houston. My brother was my only sibling." She looked away, her expression more guarded. "After Corey died, my parents sort of fell apart. He was their baby and, I guess, kind of the glue that held us all together."

"I imagine a loss like that is hard to get past."

"It is. But I don't want to talk about Corey tonight. Or about Dane."

"What do you want to talk about?"

"Books, movies. The kinds of things people talk about when they're getting to know each other."

She didn't say "when they're on a first date" but that's what this felt like. So, over homemade pasta and a bottle of red wine, they discussed books—she admitted to being a fan of suspense novels—sports—she loved baseball and hated football—and music—singer-songwriters and older rock and roll were at the top of her list.

By the time they had finished the last of the bottle of

wine and eaten the last piece of bread, the candle at their table had guttered out and the street outside the restaurant was dark.

As they walked to his SUV, he slipped an arm around her waist and she didn't object. He didn't want the evening to end. Should he suggest going somewhere for coffee?

She stopped suddenly, so that he stumbled on the uneven sidewalk. Before he could speak, she gripped his hand, hard. "That car parked at the curb across the street..." she said. "Look, but don't let the driver see you looking."

He knelt and pretended to tie the laces of his hiking boot, and looked past Cara's legs to the dark sedan parked in front of a house that was being remodeled, the front yard filled with a Dumpster and heavy equipment. He made note of what he could see then rose, took Cara's arm and led her along. "Do you recognize him?" he asked.

"I think it's one of the two men who came to Dane's office to collect all his things," she said. "The big black guy."

"Durrell." Jason remembered the name. "I think you're right. Maybe he lives around here."

"Then what is he doing parked across from the restaurant where we just happen to be eating?"

"Maybe he's waiting for someone."

"Or maybe he's watching me."

They reached the SUV and he unlocked it and opened the passenger door for her.

As she swung into the seat, she looked back over her shoulder at him. "You think I'm being paranoid," she said.

"No. I think it's a theory worth testing out."

"How are we going to do that?" she asked.

"Let's see if he follows us."

He drove, not in the direction of Cara's house, but away, toward the reservoir and open road and barren landscape that offered few hiding places. As they left town, he checked his rearview mirror. "I think that's the same car back there," he said.

Cara studied the side mirror. "I think you're right."

Jason slowed but the car behind him slowed, as well, not drawing any closer.

"What do we do now?" Cara asked.

"Maybe we have some fun with him." He gave the SUV gas, shooting forward until they were doing almost ninety miles an hour.

Cara, white-faced, clutched the armrest. "Do you know what you're doing?" she asked.

"Of course. I'm a trained professional." He slowed abruptly as they crested a hill. The sedan roared up behind him, giving him a clear view of the driver.

"I'm sure that's the man from the restaurant," Cara said.

"The car doesn't have a front plate," Jason said. "But I think it's the same person, too."

The driver dropped back out of sight. "Did he leave?" Cara asked.

"I doubt it," Jason said. He turned left onto a side road, drove to a clump of dense trees on the shoulder and parked beneath them, facing the highway. About a minute later, the sedan passed them.

"Why is he following us?" Cara asked, agitation straining her voice.

"My guess is he thinks you'll lead him to Dane Trask." He put the SUV into gear and pulled onto the highway once more.

Cara turned to watch out the back window. "I think you lost him," she said after a few minutes. She swiveled around and settled into the seat.

"Where do you want to go?" Jason asked.

"Take me home," she said.

He tightened his grip on the steering wheel. "I don't

want to frighten you," he said. "But it's possible that's who was trying to break into your place Monday night."

She didn't make a sound but he felt the change in her, like a drop in the temperature. "I have new locks and an alarm system," she said. "I won't let these people drive me out of my home."

"You're welcome to stay with me tonight. Or I can stay at your place." He tried to make the invitation sound casual. "No strings attached."

"Thank you." She touched his arm, the gentlest brush of her fingers that nevertheless had every nerve standing at attention. "But I think I'll be okay. If he only wants to find out where Dane is, he's wasting his time with me."

What if that's not all he wants? Jason thought but didn't say. "If you see any sign of him or his vehicle, or you see or hear anything suspicious, call 9-1-1," he said. "Then call me."

"I will. I promise."

He drove past her house before stopping, scanning the neighboring driveways for any sign of the dark sedan with no front plate. Cara said nothing. When he came around a second time, he pulled to the curb in front of her house. "Thank you for a lovely evening," she said. "Even if the rest of the day was a little more eventful than I would have liked."

"Thank you for the good company," he said. "If I have to be shot at or tailed, I'd rather do it with you than with anyone else."

She laughed, though he thought it sounded a little forced. "We'll talk more tomorrow," she said.

"Let me walk you to the door."

He took her arm as they proceeded up the walk then took her key, opened the door and walked through the house, checking that everything was in order. She didn't protest, but she didn't invite him to stay, either.

Back at the door, she turned to him. "I'll be okay," she said. "Really."

She looked a lot calmer than he felt. "If you need anything…" he began.

"I'll call you." She pressed a finger to his lips then kissed him gently, a closed-mouth peck that nevertheless had him breaking out in a sweat.

Cara closed the front door behind him and he waited to hear the locks snick into place. He then walked to the SUV, drove around the block and sat parked under a tree. He'd wait here awhile, keeping watch. Just in case.

THE NEXT MORNING, a bleary-eyed Jason, having stayed parked near Cara's house until almost four in the morning, stepped into the office of commander Grant Sanderlin. FBI Special Agent Sanderlin had joined the Ranger Brigade exactly two months prior to Jason's arrival, but had settled into the leadership role quickly. Tall, slender, his sandy-brown hair shot through with silver, he had icy blue eyes, the clipped speech of a New Englander, and a reputation as a strict but fair supervisor.

"I agreed to accompany Cara Mead to the Mary Lee Mine yesterday afternoon," Jason said. "She was uncomfortable going there on her own, given the circumstances surrounding her boss, Dane Trask's, disappearance."

"What circumstances made her fear for her safety?" the commander asked. "Is she fearful Trask might try to harm her? Does she believe he's hiding at the mine?"

"No, sir." Jason had to tread carefully here. He had to justify his actions with facts not supposition. "The flash drive left on the front seat of Ms. Mead's car the day we discovered Trask's truck in the canyon contains a fragment of a water quality report Ms. Mead believes is from the Mary Lee Mine," he said. "TDC has a federal contract to remediate contaminants at the mine site. The fragment of the report on the flash drive is similar to, but different from, the most recent water quality results for that mine, as reported by Trask. A copy of that report was on his work computer, and Ms. Mead reviewed it before she handed all of Trask's files over to us. She wanted to visit the mine to see if she could find anything to account for the differences between the reports."

"What did she expect to find?" Sanderlin asked.

"I'm not sure," Jason said. "In any case, we weren't there long before someone fired on us. A semiautomatic rifle, I think." He laid the spent bullets he had collected from the ground around their hiding place on the desk. "I believe the shooter was deliberately aiming wide," he said. "Not intending to kill us, but to scare us off."

"One shooter?" Sanderlin asked.

"I believe so. I never saw anyone, or any other vehicle, in the area."

Sanderlin studied the bullets. "What does Ms. Mead say? Does TDC have an overzealous security guard? Or a trigger-happy squatter?"

"She hasn't found out anything yet," Jason said. If she had, she would have called him.

"Sit down." Sanderlin gestured to the chair across from his desk. Jason sat and the commander regarded him with a measuring gaze. "Last night I saw the news report about Dane Trask," he said. "The coverage portrayed him as a troubled veteran with financial difficulties."

"My investigation so far hasn't borne that out," Jason said. "Dane Trask is a former Army Ranger who served in Afghanistan and Iraq. Since his discharge, he founded an organization—Welcome Home Warriors—that provides services for veterans. The organization, and Trask himself, have a good reputation."

"What does Ms. Mead say about her boss?"

"She believes he's innocent of any wrongdoing and may be in trouble," Jason said.

"Were she and Mr. Trask romantically involved?"

Jason was beginning to understand Cara's annoyance with everyone asking that question. "No, sir," he said. "They had a professional relationship only."

"Emotions can color how the individual interprets facts," Sanderlin said. "That's why it's worth knowing about any connections between the principals."

"Yes, sir."

"TDC seems very certain about their assessment of the situation," Sanderlin said. "If Trask is still alive and operating in our territory, we need to respect that he may be exactly what TDC says he is—desperate and potentially dangerous."

"Yes, sir." Even if Cara was right about Dane's innocence, the man's military background made him capable of violence, especially if he felt cornered. "I'm focused on finding Trask," he said. "Any other criminal charges will be the sheriff's concern."

"It's possible Trask is the person who fired on you yesterday," Sanderlin said. "He may have had another vehicle stashed somewhere, or he may have an accomplice."

"I'm looking into that," Jason said.

"If you find evidence that points to Trask hiding out at the mine, I'll authorize seeking a search warrant," Sanderlin said.

"Thank you, sir. That's not the only suspicious incident yesterday, unfortunately," Jason said.

"What else?"

"When I was driving Ms. Mead home, we noticed a car

following us. She recognized the driver as an employee of TDC. He was one of the men assigned to collected Trask's files and computer, before we took them into custody as evidence. I recognized him, also. He followed for quite a while until I evaded him. I stayed parked near Ms. Mead's home for several hours after that, but didn't see him again."

"You're certain he was following you."

"Yes, sir."

Sanderlin considered the new information. "Do you think this was the same person who fired on you and Ms. Mead at the Mary Lee Mine?"

"I don't know."

"I don't think there's any action we can take right now, but keep me updated."

When Jason returned to his desk, Hud was leaning against it, arms crossed. "How did things go with Ms. Mead yesterday?" he asked.

"Fine." Certainly their dinner had been pleasant, and though her kiss good-night had been brief, he'd felt real emotion behind it.

"I had an interesting call while you were out joy-riding with the lovely Ms. Mead," Hud said.

"Oh? What was it?" Hud had the look of a man with an interesting story to tell.

"The Smokeys have a campground thief that has them stumped."

Jason didn't even wince at the slang for park rangers. He'd heard much worse. "What is it? A clever chipmunk or maybe a bold bear?"

"No, they're pretty sure this one is human," Hud said. "Because it doesn't just take things—it leaves other things in exchange."

Jason leaned forward, suddenly more interested. "What kind of things does he steal?" he asked.

"Food, mostly. A water bottle. Soap. Nothing really valuable, but it freaks people out, you know?"

"And what does this thief leave in exchange?" Jason asked.

"A few times the guy left money, but most of the time it's other stuff. A penlight. A fishing lure. A stick carved into a squirrel." Hud shook his head. "But I was thinking you might be interested."

"Maybe it's Dane Trask," Jason said. "Sneaking into the campground to get things he needs and leaving items in trade."

"That's my guess, too," Hud said. "The park rangers haven't hit on that suspicion yet, so I didn't mention it, though you can, if you want. For now, they're playing things close to the vest. They don't want to panic the tourists, but they're planning to set a trap for the thief."

"What kind of trap?"

"They're setting up a fake campsite, complete with a cooler full of goodies and a picnic table set for a party. They're going to have two rangers in a blind nearby, ready to pounce." He rapped his knuckles on the desk. "With luck, Trask could be in custody by tomorrow."

Would Cara be cheered by this news or even more distressed at the thought of Dane in jail?

Chapter Twelve

Chaos greeted Cara at TDC headquarters Monday morning. No one was at their desk, and the din of conversation drowned out the piped-in music. "What's going on?" she asked Maisie, who was passing her desk with a large potted palm hugged to her chest.

"The big bosses are here and there's going to be a press conference. Come on, help me with these plants." She shoved the palm into Cara's arms and retrieved a four-foot-tall ficus tree from its normal resting place behind Cara's desk.

Cara followed her friend through the crowd to the elevator, finally emerging on the second floor and making their way to a large conference room.

"Put the palm at that end of the dais," Maisie directed. "Behind the ferns."

Cara did as instructed, while Maisie arranged the ficus at the opposite end of the dais, which had been set up with a skirted conference table and four chairs.

As she was wondering who the chairs were for, VP Mitchell Ruffino entered, followed by Charles Terrell, Gary Davis and Drew Compton.

Maisie grabbed Cara's arm and dragged her out the door on the opposite side of the room. "The last thing you want is for one of them to notice you for the wrong reason," Maisie said.

Cara shook free of her friend's grip. "What is going on?" she asked. "What's the press conference about?"

"I have no idea," Maisie said. "But it must be big, if all three of the bigwigs are here."

A crowd of what was clearly media, complete with shoulder-held cameras, large microphones and on-air makeup, hurried past. "Come on," Maisie said. "We can stand at the back of the room and watch."

Charles Terrell, silver glinting in his brown hair and close-cropped goatee, looked more like a movie star than a CEO. The other partners in the firm, portly, balding Gary Davis and rail-thin, curly haired Drew Compton, looked even homelier next to Terrell, but all three conveyed an air of grave seriousness as they filed onto the dais and took their seats before the press and assorted onlookers.

Mr. Ruffino, in a funeral-worthy black suit, stood at the microphone and scowled like a disapproving priest. "On behalf of TDC Enterprises, I am going to read a statement," he said. "Then we will entertain brief questions."

He studied the paper in his hand for a long moment as flashbulbs flared and cameras hummed. Then he cleared his throat and began to read.

"'It is with great regret that I must inform you that an engineer formerly employed with TDC Enterprises, Dane Trask, is now a fugitive from justice. Mr. Trask, whom we believe has embezzled a large sum from our company, disappeared shortly after the decision was made to file charges against him. He is still at large and is considered armed and dangerous.'"

Cara gasped as a larger-than-life-size image of Dane appeared on a screen behind Ruffino's shoulder. In the photo, he was dressed for a hike and smiling, the dramatic painted cliffs of Black Canyon of Gunnison National Park rising behind him. Ironically, TDC had used the same image at Dane's memorial service on Saturday.

"'If you encounter this individual, do not attempt to confront him yourself,'" Ruffino continued reading. "'We ask that you call the hotline number we have established. TDC is offering a $25,000 reward for information leading to the apprehension of Trask.'"

Ruffino looked up from the paper. More flashbulbs flared and a chorus of voices rose.

"How much money did Dane Trask steal?"

"Why such a large reward?"

"What was Trask's job with TDC?"

"How did you uncover the embezzlement?"

"Where was Trask last seen?"

"Are you saying now the memorial service you held for Trask on Saturday was premature?"

The questions rose from all sides, many repeated more than once. Instead of answering them, Terrell took Ruffino's place at the microphone and spoke about how this unfortunate episode didn't erode his faith in the many loyal employees of TDC. "One bad apple will not spoil the whole crop," he declared. "TDC will continue its commitment to quality work and community involvement in the future."

"So Dane really did steal from the company!" Maisie spoke softly, but there was no missing her excitement. "And now he's on the run. It's like a movie or something."

Cara wanted to protest that Dane hadn't stolen anything, and that he wasn't dangerous, but how did she know that for sure?

Ruffino announced that the press conference was over. Terrell, Davis and Compton filed out of the room and a couple of uniformed security guards began ushering everyone into the hallway. Cara slipped away from Maisie to the stairs, using the climb to the fifth floor to try to organize her thoughts.

A few days ago, Ruffino had said Dane had stolen a hundred thousand dollars but the company wanted to hold a memorial service and heap praises on him anyway. It was a lot of money, but a huge enterprise like TDC could deduct such a loss from taxes, and maybe the powers-that-be thought singing Dane's praises would score them a lot of good publicity.

What had happened to change their minds? Why offer one-quarter of the amount Dane had supposedly stolen as a reward? Why alert the public when local law enforcement was already searching for Dane?

She slipped into her office and made her way to her desk. Sinking into the chair, she swiveled toward her computer, hoping to distract herself by reading through old files and reports. But the computer wasn't there. She blinked, then noticed other things missing. Her in-and out-boxes were both empty and the desk calendar with a bad pun for each day was gone.

Heart racing, she pulled open the center drawer. A few paperclips and stray pens lingered in space that had previously held her spare change, a pack of gum, bandages, aspirin and a nail file.

The other drawers of the desk were completely empty, except for her purse. Everything else that was hers, or was related to her work, was gone.

CARA LEFT THE OFFICE. She didn't say anything to anyone, she simply walked out. After the shock of the press conference, she was in no mood to track down her few belongings from that desk. She could deal with that tomorrow.

She got in the car, intending to drive until she had come to some conclusion about the next step she should take.

Jason would probably tell her to trust him and his colleagues to find Dane, but the cops assigned to her brother's case had said much the same and had ended up doing nothing. She hadn't been able to help her brother, but she might be able to help Dane. That thought made it impossible to sit at home and do nothing.

She ended up at Black Canyon of Gunnison National Park, maybe out of some subconscious desire to retrace Dane's steps, to figure out what had gotten into his head that day. As she parked at the Dragon Point overlook, she was startled to find two Ranger Brigade SUVs, and Jason with Officer Hudson.

"Cara, what are you doing here?" Jason asked as she approached.

"Have you found any sign of Dane?" she asked. "I'm worried he might be out there alone and hurt."

"We don't know for sure the blood we found was his," Hud said. "Only his type."

"Blood?" She staggered, suddenly dizzy. "What blood? Dane's blood? Where?"

Jason grabbed her arms, steadying her. "The bandana the second flash drive was wrapped in had some bloodstains. Not a lot of blood." He glared at Hud. "It matches Dane's blood type, but it wasn't necessarily a recent stain. It could have been from a long time ago. And it might have been from someone besides Dane."

She pulled out of his grasp. "Why didn't you tell me?"

"I didn't tell you because I didn't want to upset you."

"I'm already upset. Or hadn't you realized?"

Hud's shoulder-mounted radio crackled and he turned away. Jason looked back to Cara, his arms outstretched, as if he wanted to touch her again. But he kept his distance. "We haven't found any more blood," he said. "It may not even be significant."

"You've spent how many hours at my house the past few days and you didn't think to mention this? I thought you weren't going to shut me out. But that's exactly what you're doing."

"I need to go," Hud said, taking a few steps toward them.

"Do you need help?" Jason asked. Did she imagine the desperation in his eyes?

"No." Hud glanced at Cara. "You'd better stay here and take care of this."

Cara glared at him. She was not a "this."

After Hudson left, Jason moved to her side. "What are you doing here?" he asked. "Why aren't you at work?"

"You're telling me the truth about the blood? There wasn't much of it, and you haven't found any more?"

"Yes. We've been searching for several days and we haven't found anything." He took her arm. "I know you want to stay informed about this case, but it would be irresponsible of me to tell you about something—like that bloodstain—before we knew for sure it even pertained to the case. And though you don't want to hear it, I'm going to say this anyway. You're Dane's friend. You're not another investigator. I can't share everything with you."

She stared at the ground, the truth of his words grating. "Just don't keep anything really important from me, okay?"

He squeezed gently. "Okay. Now, what are you doing here? You're obviously upset."

"TDC held a press conference this morning," she said. "Mitch Ruffino, Charles Terrell, Gary Davis and Drew Compton—TDC—were all there. I've never seen all of them together in one place like that. Terrell lives in Hawaii, I think, and Davis and Compton are in Denver. But this was important enough to get all of them together in one place."

Jason waited, eyes fixed on her, but not pressuring her. She wondered if he was naturally so patient or if it was something he had learned on the job. "They announced that Dane had stolen a lot of money from the company, that he was a fugitive who was armed and dangerous, and that they were offering a $25,000 reward for information leading to his apprehension."

Jason's neutral expression dissolved. "Twenty-five grand is a lot of money," he said. "They'll have people swarming all over here, playing amateur detective."

"Does this mean they've filed charges against Dane?" she asked.

"I don't know," Jason said. "We'll have to check. Is that why you're here? Because you were upset by the press conference?"

"I'm here because when I returned to my desk after the press conference, I discovered someone had cleaned it out. All my files, my office supplies and all my personal items were missing."

Jason frowned. "Did someone say something to you? Explain why that was done?"

"I didn't give them a chance. I just left. I wasn't in the mood to deal with them right now." The last thing she wanted was someone to placate—or worse—lie to her.

"Come with me to Ranger headquarters," he said. "I'll see what I can find out. And I'll let you know right away."

"All right."

It was better than sitting at home doing nothing and she wanted to believe Jason was sincere about giving her information about the case when he could. She drove behind him to the headquarters building, parked her car in a visitor's space and followed him inside just as two officers—a man and a woman—were headed out. "We've got a suspected trafficking victim over on the lake," the man, whom she recognized as Lieutenant Dance, said.

"The marina owner called it in," added the woman, Officer Redhorse, according to her name badge. "He saw one of the flyers we put up around the area."

"Good luck," Jason said, holding the door open wider to allow Cara to precede him into the office.

"Human trafficking?" she whispered as she followed him to his desk. "Here?"

"Remote areas are ideal for traffickers," Jason said. "There aren't as many people to ask questions. But it's a real concern." He nodded to a chair at one side of his desk. "You can sit while I make a few phone calls."

She sat, and he telephoned the Montrose County Sheriff's department, identified himself, and asked for any wants or warrants for Dane Trask. He put the phone on speaker so Cara could hear the response. "Trask is wanted on suspicion of fraud and embezzlement," the woman on the other end of the line said. "He's considered armed and dangerous."

Jason glanced at Cara, his gaze full of concern. She forced herself to remain steady and not give in to fear.

"Mr. Ruffino said that about Dane being dangerous at the press conference this morning," she said after Jason had ended the call.

"Does he own guns?" Jason asked.

"I don't know. I never saw him with one, but he was an Army veteran. Army Rangers. He certainly knows how to use a gun."

"He would know how to hide and how to survive in the wilderness, too," Jason said.

"I just remembered something else I thought was odd about that press conference," she said. "After saying all that about how dangerous Dane is, they didn't tell people to call the police if they saw him. They said to call a special hotline number they'd set up."

"That is a little unusual. Maybe it's something new the sheriff's department is doing. What was the number?"

She dug in the pocket of her pants and pulled out a business card. "They gave everyone who attended the press conference one of these," she said.

He took the card. Black block letters on the plain white card proclaimed:

WANTED: DANE TRASK.
6'2", 180 lbs., dark brown hair, blue eyes, 41.
$25,000 Reward for Apprehension of this Dangerous Fugitive.
If you see him, DO NOT APPROACH.

There was a phone number. Jason took out his cell phone and punched it in. A woman's pleasant voice answered. "Do you have information about Dane Trask?" she asked.

"Who am I speaking with?" Jason asked.

"This is the hotline for information about Dane Trask. Do you have information?"

"Is this the police?" Jason asked.

"No. This is a private hotline related to the $25,000 reward we're offering for information about Dane Trask's whereabouts. Do you have information?"

"Who is running the hotline?" Jason asked.

"Do you have information about Mr. Trask?" she persisted.

He ended the call.

"A number like that is going to be inundated with false sightings, isn't it?" Cara asked. "If TDC is paying for even one person at a time to answer the phone around the clock, they're investing a lot for the slight chance that they'll be able to sift out one good piece of information from all the crackpots."

"They obviously are very interested in finding him." He tucked the card in his pocket and switched off his computer. "Did they say if he stole anything besides money?"

"No," she said. "What would he steal?"

"Valuable materials. Secrets?"

She stared at her lap, troubled by the idea. "What if he did find a secret?" she asked. "Something the company didn't want anyone else to find out about? What if they threatened him and that's why he decided to disappear?" It sounded like the plot of a detective novel, but things like that could happen, couldn't they?

"I'm not saying that couldn't happen," Jason said slowly, as if picking his words carefully. "Only that we don't have any proof that it did."

"You don't have any proof that he stole from TDC," she said. "Only their accusations."

"My job isn't to prove Dane's guilt or innocence," he said. "My job is to find him and bring him back safely."

"You may have to do the first to have any hope of the second," she said. "One thing I know about Dane—he doesn't give up. On people or ideas. It isn't in his nature. It's one of the things that makes him such a good friend."

And it would make him a formidable enemy.

Chapter Thirteen

Cara fortified herself to face whatever awaited her at TDC headquarters on Tuesday with a double cappuccino and a large blueberry muffin. She wore her sharpest suit and most comfortable dressy flats. If she ended up being escorted from the building, she didn't want to risk tripping in heels and falling on her face.

Maisie intercepted her as soon as she exited the elevator on the fifth floor. She pounced from just outside the door and seized Cara's arm. "What is going on?" Maisie demanded.

"What do you mean?" Cara eased from her friend's gasp. Had Ruffino made another announcement about Dane? Had news reporters recovered some sensationalized bit of gossip?

"Your desk is gone, that's what I mean," Maisie said. "And you weren't here yesterday afternoon. I tried calling your cell and didn't get an answer."

Cara winced. "I didn't get home until after nine and by then it was too late to call," she said, not entirely lying.

"Where were you?" Maisie asked. "I thought you were in jail or something."

"In jail?"

Maisie looked sheepish. "Well, not really. But I

never thought Dane would steal a bunch of money from TDC, either."

Cara opened her mouth to protest that Dane hadn't stolen anything, but the elevator doors parted behind them and the imposing white man who had tried to take all of Dane's files emerged. "Ms. Mead," he said. "Mr. Ruffino will see you now."

Maisie gaped as the man took Cara by the arm and pulled her into the elevator. Cara thought about resisting, but how far would she get fighting off this man who outweighed her by a hundred pounds and appeared to be solid muscle? Instead, she moved as far away from him as possible in the elevator. "What does Mr. Ruffino want with me?" she asked.

"To talk." He didn't even look at her and, when the elevator opened on the top floor of the building, he stepped off without a glance back.

She could have run, but where to? And she wanted to talk to Ruffino, to demand to know what he had done with her personal belongings, and her desk. To question him about his charges against Dane.

The bodyguard—she couldn't think of him in any other way—disappeared behind a closed door and Ruffino's administrative assistant, Shara, took his place. "This way, Ms. Mead. Can I get you some coffee?"

"No, thank you." Any more caffeine and she might jitter across the floor like a wind-up toy.

Ruffino looked up as Cara stepped into his main sanctum. "Good morning, Ms. Mead. Please, sit down."

She thought about insisting on standing, then told herself she was being ridiculous and sat. She wasn't going to find out anything if she annoyed the man from the start. "Where are my things and where is my desk?" she asked.

"Your personal items have been moved to your new

office," he said. "The desk is being refurbished. You'll have a new one."

Relief stole her breath and she was grateful she was sitting, her entire body felt so wobbly. Despite the cavalier attitude she had assumed, she'd been really worried about losing her job. The prospect of unemployment with a mortgage to pay had a way of doing that to a person. She cleared her throat. "What will I be doing?"

"You'll be in our data division."

She ran through her mental list of company departments. As Dane's administrative assistant, she had been part of engineering. She couldn't remember a data division. "Do you mean data processing?"

"Yes, that's it. They had an opening, and since you're no longer needed to assist Mr. Trask, we thought it would be a good fit for you."

She swallowed hard. Data processing was an entry-level position, a tedious one that involved inputting long columns of data into endless spreadsheets. It was honest, necessary work, but a job for which she was vastly overqualified. "My training is as an administrative assistant, not a data processor," she said.

"I'm sure you'll have no trouble with the new position," Ruffino said. "And in these difficult times, it's always a good idea to be flexible." His eyes met hers and she got the message he was sending: you're lucky to have a job at all, so you'd better take this one.

Gripped by the fear of failing to find another job and ending up in foreclosure, she nodded and managed to choke out, "Thank you."

"I've reviewed your employment records," Ruffino said. "You're a smart young woman. You've worked for Dane Trask for several years now."

"Yes, sir. Three years." Though if he'd reviewed her records, he already knew this.

Ruffino met and held her gaze once more. "I'm going to ask you an important question, and I want you to answer honestly. Will you do that for me?"

She nodded.

"Did you notice anything unusual about Trask's behavior in the last few weeks or months?"

"Nothing unusual."

"Nothing?"

"He worked a lot of long hours," she said. "And he seemed…preoccupied."

"Did he mention what was claiming so much of his attention? Any particular job or project that concerned him?"

"No. We…we didn't have that kind of relationship. I mean, he was my boss. He didn't confide in me."

Ruffino looked disappointed. "And you didn't observe anything particularly erratic or unstable in his behavior?"

"No." She sat straighter. Was he implying he thought Dane was mentally ill? "Dane was the same smart, thoughtful, generous man he'd always been."

Ruffino sat back, looking pensive. "I understand."

What did he understand? She cleared her throat. "I find it hard to believe Dane would have stolen from TDC," she said. "It seems so unlike him."

"It's very natural, I believe, for a single, perhaps lonely, young woman to become enamored of a forceful, handsome man like Dane Trask," Ruffino said. "I imagine he could be very persuasive, preventing you from seeing his true nature. All the more reason to move you to a different position. One where you can make a fresh start." He stood. "I'm glad we could have this little talk."

Is that how he saw her? A pathetic, love-starved spinster, crushing on her boss? Of all the sexist clichés. She stood, trying to find words that would express her outrage but not get her fired. Before she could form a coherent sentence, the door opened behind her and the bodyguard came to stand beside her chair. "Mr. George, escort Ms. Mead to Data Processing," Ruffino said.

"I know where it is," she said and strode past George.

Unfortunately, she had to wait for the elevator and George easily caught up with her. He didn't say anything, or try to touch her, but his looming presence irritated her. As soon as the elevator door opened, she stalked off and all but ran down the hall to the data processing department. "I'm Cara Mead," she told the large woman at the first desk she saw. "I've been assigned to this department."

The woman looked Cara up and down, taking in the purple suit and Italian leather flats. Cara was seriously overdressed for data processing. "Your desk is in the back corner," she said. "You can get started right away. Enter all the reports you find in your in-box into a single spreadsheet. If you have questions, Amy, who works next to you, will help."

Cara nodded and stalked to her desk, ignoring her co-workers. The encounter in Ruffino's office had left her hurt, insulted and afraid. Vice presidents like Mitchell Ruffino didn't single out administrative assistants like her. They didn't make a point of demoting them to data processing. Those kinds of decisions were made in human resources, or because a department head requested a particular employee.

If Ruffino had a hand in putting Cara here, was it because he deliberately wanted to insult her? Or because he wanted to keep an eye on her?

Did he think she could lead him to Dane?

"THESE ARE SOME of the things our campground thief has left behind. Quite a variety." National Park ranger Mike Griffen indicated the half dozen items arranged on one corner of his desk. Jason picked up a small carving of a squirrel and examined it. It was crude, but had a folk art appeal.

"The thief didn't fall for your trap, I guess," Jason said.

"Nope. He hit up a campsite right next to the blind where we were hiding. I don't see how he did it."

A former Army Ranger probably wouldn't have much trouble outwitting most people, Jason thought. "What did he steal?"

"He took some leftover fried chicken out of a cooler in the back of a minivan and left this." Mike held up a Mont Blanc pen with a barrel that looked like polished marble.

"Nice," Jason said.

"Yeah. It's worth a lot more than the chicken he took."

"Can I borrow this to show to someone?" Jason asked.

"Do you think you know who it belongs to?" Mike asked.

"Remember the pickup we pulled out of the canyon? I think it might be the guy who owned it."

"What, he plunged into the canyon and just walked away?" Mike shook his head.

"I don't think he was in the truck when it went over," Jason said.

Mike's skeptical expression didn't fade. "And he's just hanging around the park now, living off stolen fried chicken? Why?"

"Have you heard the news reports about Dane Trask?" Prime time had been full of reports about the TDC engineer turned thief.

"The guy who stole all that money from TDC?" Mike scratched his head. "I remember now that the truck's plate was registered to him, but I didn't make the connection.

That's the guy you think is stealing chicken? We've got a dangerous felon running loose near the campground and you're just now getting around to telling us?"

"I don't think he's a threat to your campers and I'm not even sure your thief is him," Jason said. "Has he approached or threatened anyone?"

"No. As far as I know, no one has even seen him. He doesn't damage anything, and he always leaves something in exchange." Mike made a face. "They're calling him the Black Canyon Bandit, like he's some folk hero or something. I heard some people are even leaving stuff out for him—cookies, beer. One guy left a grilled steak, hoping to get a souvenir, I guess. I had to threaten him with a ticket. He's lucky a bear didn't tear up his camp."

"I'll let you know if I find out anything else," Jason said. He slipped the pen into his pocket then took some photos of the other items Mike had collected from the Black Canyon Bandit's victims.

Back at Ranger headquarters, Carmen Redhorse flagged him down. "We just got a call for an agency assist over on the north rim. Want to ride along?"

"Sure." He hadn't had occasion to visit the north side of the national park since his initial orientation tour.

Jason slid into Carmen's SUV after she shifted a pile of paperwork and gear from the passenger seat. "Any progress on tracking down Dane Trask?" she asked as they headed toward the north side of the canyon along the steep rim road.

"I think he might be the person who's been stealing food from campers in the south rim campground," Jason said.

"I wondered if he was still around." Carmen ran her palms along the steering wheel. "The person I'm taking you to meet is my husband, Jake. He's a wildlife officer and he really does have a case he needs help with. But mainly, he wants to talk to you about Dane."

"You mentioned they worked together as part of the veteran's group Trask founded."

"Welcome Home Warriors. Yeah, Jake really enjoyed that. He'd like to do more, as his schedule allows. He said he had some things to tell you about Dane that might help with the investigation. But I'll let him fill you in."

"How did the two of you meet?" he asked. "Were you working a case together?"

"Not exactly." She grimaced. "I actually thought he was up to no good and tried to arrest him. Turns out he was working undercover, trying to help his family. Just goes to show first impressions aren't always correct, I guess."

For the next hour, as they made the long drive to the north side of the park, they talked about Jason's background as a park ranger and her work as one of the original Ranger Brigade members.

By the time they pulled into an overlook on the north rim, Jason was anxious to meet the man who had managed to impress this obviously not-easy-to-impress woman.

Jake Lohmiller was a lean, muscular man with close-cropped brown hair and startling blue eyes. He climbed out of his Colorado Parks and Wildlife SUV and came to meet them, grinning at his wife before turning to offer a firm handshake to Jason. "Carmen's told me a lot about you," he said. "And more about this case you're working on."

"Your wife says you know Dane Trask."

Jake nodded. "He and I worked together a couple of times on a veterans' benefit, taking disabled vets into the wilderness to fish and hike, and stuff. The work he's doing with Welcome Home Warriors is great."

"What was your impression of Trask?" Jason asked.

Jake shook his head. "When I heard he'd supposedly

stolen a bunch of money from his employer, I was blown away. He just never struck me as someone who cared about money. He never talked about money, and he didn't have a flashy lifestyle. He didn't talk about traveling or expensive hobbies, and he wasn't into drugs or drinking. I can spot that kind of lifestyle a mile away."

"His admin, Cara Mead, says the same thing," Jason said. "But we both know some criminals are very, very good at hiding their crimes."

"Yeah," Jake said. "But something about this just doesn't ring true. I mean, why dump his truck into the canyon and then go on the run?"

"Because he found out TDC had learned about the embezzlement and he could be facing jail," Jason said.

"Then why continue to hang out in the area?" Jake asked. "Why not take all that money and run away to Brazil or something?"

"So what do you think is going on?" Jason asked.

"If he was the one who sent that truck into the canyon, he did it for a reason," Jake said. "Dane wasn't an impulsive guy. And he had training to survive for a long time in the wilderness."

"Jake, he's stealing tourist's fried chicken," Carmen said. "That's not exactly living on the edge."

"He's taking advantage of easy pickings," Jake said. "But I'm telling you, those Army Rangers know how to live off the land if they have to. My guess is he has snares and other supplies to allow him to stay out for a long time."

"But again, why?" Jason asked. "Why, when he has family and friends in town, and money for a lawyer to defend himself against TDC's charges? He's not going to be denied bail on an embezzlement or fraud charge. Why fake his own death and go on the run if he really is innocent?"

"If he ran, it's because he felt he didn't have any other

choice," Jake said. "And he's still here because he has something to prove. He's trying to stay alive until he can stop whoever is after him."

"Why would TDC lie?" Carmen asked. "What do they have to gain by discrediting one of their own employees?"

"Maybe he found out something about one of the executives," Jake said. "Something they don't want known?"

"It's an interesting conspiracy theory," Carmen said. "But I'm not sure I'm buying it."

"You didn't know Dane," her husband said. "I do, and I'm telling you, whatever he's up to, he's got a good reason." He turned back to Jason. "I don't know if that helps you any. I just wanted you to know."

"Thanks. It gives me a little better picture of him, anyway." He took the pen from his pocket. "Do you recognize this?"

Jake studied the pen, then shook his head. "No. Is it Dane's?"

"I don't know." Jason tucked the pen away once more. "Now, what's this about a case you need help on?"

For the next fifteen minutes, they discussed the poacher Jake was trying to track, a bow hunter known for firing arrows into animals and leaving them to die. "This guy has killed six deer out of season over the past two years," Jake said. "We know it's the same guy because the arrows are all the same. And they're not cheap arrows, so he's stupid as well as wasteful. But we aren't having any luck catching him, so I'm trying to spread the word."

"We'll be on the lookout for him," Jason said.

"And I'll be looking for Trask," Jake said.

"What do you think?" Carmen asked when they were in her SUV once more, headed back to headquarters.

"I think I trust the word of a law enforcement officer more than I trust some executive I've never met," he said.

"And I'm frustrated that if Dane Trask really is in trouble, he didn't turn to the police for help instead of running."

"Some people don't trust cops," she said.

People like Cara, he thought. But she needed to trust him—so that he could help Dane and so that he could be there for her.

Chapter Fourteen

Dane Trask was topic number one at TDC Enterprises these days. Around the desks in the data processing department, conversation buzzed about the reward the company had offered for Dane's apprehension, about what Dane had done with the money he'd stolen, and about what would happen to him when police finally caught him.

No one included Cara in these conversations, though she couldn't help overhearing, and she couldn't ignore the curious glances cast her way. She wanted to glare at all of them and shout that Dane was innocent, but she knew that response would only fuel more gossip.

When Maisie stopped by her desk at lunchtime on Thursday, two days after Cara had transferred to data processing, Cara wanted to leap up and hug her. As they headed together for the cafeteria, she felt like a prisoner momentarily released from her cell. "How's it going in DP?" Maisie asked, as they made their way to a back corner table.

"I'm bored out of my skull," Cara admitted.

"Are you looking for another job?" Maisie asked.

Cara knew her answer should be that she was polishing her résumé and searching for a position that made better use of her skills. But she couldn't bring herself to do that just yet. "I'm hoping Dane will come back to work and I'll get my old job back," she admitted.

Maisie's eyes widened and she leaned toward her friend and spoke in a low whisper. "Cara, honey, Dane isn't coming back. His truck crashed in Black Canyon. And if he is still alive, when they find him, he'll be in jail for a long time."

He didn't do anything wrong, Cara thought, but only pressed her lips together and shook her head. "It's surreal," she said after a moment of awkward silence. She looked down at her turkey sandwich, unable to eat another bite. "I don't believe Dane is guilty of embezzlement, and I don't believe he's dead."

"You don't believe, or you don't want to believe?" Maisie looked more concerned than sympathetic. "I'm worried about you," she added. "It's one thing to be loyal to your boss, but what you're doing goes beyond that. I mean, you're ruining your life for the guy."

"I'm not ruining my life," Cara said. "I didn't ask to be transferred to data processing. I didn't ask for people to spread nasty rumors about me and Dane."

"I was hoping you hadn't heard those," Maisie said.

"How could I not hear them? It's not like anyone is trying to keep their suspicions a secret." She shoved the uneaten sandwich aside. "So far I've heard that I'm having an affair with Dane, I'm having his baby, or I'm going to be running away to Tahiti with him." She blew out a breath in disgust. "The truth is, I haven't heard from Dane, I don't know where he is, I never dated him, and I never wanted to date him. Why can't people accept that a man and a woman who work together can be friends without being lovers?"

"Because the lovers angle makes a better story?" Maisie patted her hand. "I believe you," she said. "And I've set the gossipers straight when I get the chance, though most of them know better than to say anything to me in the first place."

"Thanks," Cara said. "That means a lot."

"Not that I'd blame you if you were into Dane," Maisie said. "I always thought he was kind of hot."

She winked, and both women burst out laughing, though there was no joy behind Cara's mirth. She just wanted this whole ordeal to be over and her life to go back to normal.

"Speaking of hot," Maisie said, looking over Cara's shoulder.

Cara turned and her breath caught when she spotted the familiar, khaki-clad figure working his way across the cafeteria. "Now there's a man you shouldn't mind spending more time with," Maisie whispered.

Jason didn't smile in greeting, but his eyes did meet Cara's with a flash of warmth. "Your supervisor said I'd find you here," he said. "Sorry to interrupt your lunch."

"I need to go for my walk now." Maisie slid out of her chair and offered it to Jason. She patted Cara's shoulder as she passed.

"I didn't mean to run your friend off," Jason said.

"It's okay." Cara tried to mean the words but she was aware of heads turned in their direction. She liked Jason, and was even glad to see him, but word of him coming to see her would spread like a virus in a petri dish and the next thing she knew, people would be saying that she was suspected of some crime, too. "Have you found out something about Dane?" she asked.

"Is that the only reason you think I'd want to see you? To talk about the case?"

She flushed. "It's the middle of the day and we're both working. Hardly the time for a social visit."

"Fair enough." He withdrew something from his pocket and held it out to her. "Do you recognize this?"

Her breath caught as the overhead lights glinted on the barrel of the expensive pen. She knew it was expensive because she had charged the purchase to her credit card last December. "That's Dane's pen," she said. "I gave it to him for Christmas last year." She met Jason's steady gaze. "Where did you find it?"

"Someone stole some fried chicken from a camper's ice chest at the park," he said. "They left this pen in exchange."

She put a hand to her chest, her heart beating rapidly beneath her fingers. "Dane's alive. And in the park."

"It looks that way." He pocketed the pen once more.

"You need to tell Mr. Ruffino," she said. "Finding that pen means he isn't dead. You should let people know."

"And risk hordes of people descending on the park in the hope of collecting that $25,000 reward?" He shook his head.

She sagged back in her seat. She'd been so thrilled to have confirmation that Dane was alive that she hadn't considered the repercussions. He wasn't dead, but he was also a wanted man with a price on his head.

"I talked to Jake Lohmiller this morning," Jason said.

She forced herself to focus on Jason once more, and not her worries for Dane. "Who's Jake Lohmiller?"

"He's a wildlife cop, married to one of our team. He's also a friend of Dane's. They worked together with Welcome Home Warriors. He agrees with you that Dane wasn't the type to embezzle."

"It's good to know someone else is on Dane's side." She gave him a sharp look.

"I'm on the side of trying to find Dane—alive," he said. "It's up to the courts to determine guilt or innocence."

"You don't have any proof he's guilty and you have my word and the word of another cop that he's innocent. That ought to count for something."

He looked pained. "It does. But arguing Dane's guilt or innocence doesn't really help us find him."

"That pen tells you he's still in the park."

"Yes, but it's a big park. There are a lot of places for a man to hide. Especially with Dane's skills."

She straightened her shoulders. "Take me there," she said.

"Take you where? The park?"

"Yes. Take me to some of the places Dane might hide. Maybe he'll come out and talk to me."

Jason looked doubtful. "I know you don't want to believe it, but Dane might be dangerous."

"I won't believe he's dangerous to me." She gave him a pleading look. "It's worth a try, isn't it?"

"All right. When do you want to go?"

"Saturday?"

"That will work."

She stood. "I have to get back to work now."

"I'll pick you up at your house Saturday morning," he said. "We should make an early start, before it gets too hot. We should leave your place by seven."

"All right. I'll see you then."

He leaned forward and, for a moment, she thought he might kiss her—right there in front of all her coworkers. Instead, he moved back. "See you," he said, and turned and hurried away.

Back at her desk, Cara stared at the stack of statistics that needed inputting. She had never felt less motivated to do her job. Instead, she picked up the phone and punched in Audra's number.

Audra answered on the fifth ring, sounding out of breath. "Did I catch you at a bad time?" Cara asked.

"No, I was just finishing up playground duty. Now I have a couple of hours when I'm supposed to be doing paperwork." A chair squeaked and she let out a big sigh. "What's up?" she asked.

"Have you heard from the Rangers recently? Or the police?"

"A female police officer came to my office yesterday and asked me a bunch of questions about Dad—if he suddenly had a lot more money, if he was acting secretive, et cetera. I told her I hadn't noticed anything and Dad isn't one to throw money around. If anything, I think he's a little cheap. Though he'd probably say he's just not materialistic." She laughed.

"I just talked to Officer Beck, with the Rangers."

"Hud's friend. I remember."

Since when was Officer Hudson "Hud"? Cara pushed the question aside. "The Rangers don't think your father is dead," Cara said. At least, Jason didn't. "They think he's still in the park, stealing food from campers and leaving things behind in payment. He left a pen I gave him for Christmas last year."

"No one told me that! No one tells me anything."

"Cops are good about keeping families in the dark," Cara said. "I don't know if it's on purpose, or they're too busy, or they just don't think, but I've learned you have to keep after them. If you want to know anything, you have to call and ask for an update." Though even when she had done that with her brother's case, she hadn't always been able to get straight answers to her questions. At least Jason tried to be helpful.

"I don't have time for those kinds of games," Audra moaned. "I have a business to run and we're breaking ground on the new facility soon and there's just so much to deal with."

"You have a new facility? Where?"

"It's actually part of the new elementary school near the national park," Audra said.

"The one TDC is building? Dane worked on that project."

"Yes, but Dad had nothing to do with us ending up in there. The district is trying to attract and retain teachers, so they decided to offer on-site childcare and preschool. I bid for the contract and won, so as part of the new construction, they're designing a space just for us. In addition to caring for the children of teachers, parents will be able to drop their younger kids at preschool when they deliver their older children to school. And we'll offer after-school care, as well. It's a really big deal and so exciting, and now all this with Dad—I swear, when he comes home, I'm going to give him a big hug and then I'm going to wring his neck."

"Call and talk to Officer Hudson about this," Cara urged. "I'm sure he'll fill you in."

"I will. Thanks for the heads-up. Now, I really do have to get to this paperwork."

Cara ended the call and debated dialing Eve Shea, Dane's ex-girlfriend. But she scarcely knew the woman, and she might not want to hear about Dane.

"Cara? Have you finished processing those reports?" Nina, Cara's new supervisor, loomed over the desk. Long-legged and large-chested, with a rather small head, Nina reminded Cara of a stork. Her penchant for feathered earrings didn't lessen the impression.

"Yes, ma'am." Cara would race through the stack in her in-box without bothering to try to comprehend it.

"Then if you have time for personal phone calls, you have time for another batch of reports," Nina said.

"Of course." Cara flashed a smile she hoped Nina would

read as fake, but the supervisor wasn't even looking at her anymore. She was scanning Cara's desktop.

Her gaze landed on an agate paperweight and she reached over and picked it up. "This thing could be used as a weapon," she said. "Where did you get it?"

"Mr. Trask gave it to me for Christmas," she said. He had remembered purple was her favorite color, and that she was interested in geology. In that way, he'd managed to add a personal touch to a gift that was appropriate for a supervisor to give an employee.

"I'm sure you know there are some very serious charges being leveled against your former boss," Nina said.

I haven't exactly been living under a rock, Cara thought, but merely nodded.

"Some people are wondering if you had anything to do with his crimes."

This wasn't news to Cara, but having Nina come right out and say it still hurt. "If Dane did anything wrong, it was without my knowledge," she said.

"So you don't believe he's guilty?"

"I don't know what to believe, Nina." She turned toward her computer. "I just want to keep my head down and do my job."

She felt Nina's gaze on her for a long moment before the supervisor moved away. Cara looked at the paperwork and thought of Dane. Where was he right now? Did he realize how much trouble he was causing her and everyone else in his life?

"If Dane Trask is behind the petty thefts at the camp-ground, why is he wasting our time with these games?" Commander Sanderlin addressed the team Friday morning from the head of the long conference table. "This is something the park rangers can handle. They don't need us."

"Except that Trask is a missing person who may have been the victim of foul play," Jason said. "We can't assume he's behind the campground thefts."

"His admin identified the pen the thief left behind as belonging to Trask," Dance pointed out.

"Someone could have found that pen, and Trask's other belongings," Hud said. "They might have found Trask's body, too. We can't be sure he didn't die when his truck went into the canyon. His body might have been thrown clear."

"Knightbridge, what were the results of your campground search with Lotte yesterday afternoon?" the commander asked.

Lotte, resting on the floor next to Randall Knightbridge's chair, thumped her tail at the sound of her name. "Lotte picked up Trask's scent in the campground," the lieutenant said. "But she lost it at the creek." He shrugged. "This confirms he was there, but not where he is now. Given his military background and training, he's going to be difficult to track unless he makes a mistake."

"You're to proceed as if Trask is armed and dangerous," Sanderlin said. "We don't know why he's chosen to hide out in the park, but it speaks to a level of desperation that might lead a man to do anything."

"Tomorrow morning, I'm taking Cara Mead with me to hike near the campground and in the backcountry near there," Jason said. "She's hoping to draw Trask from hiding, since she's likely to see her as an ally."

"I'm not keen on involving a civilian in an investigation," Sanderlin said.

"That's why I wouldn't let her go on her own," Jason said. "She could have, as someone just taking a walk in the park, and I couldn't have stopped her. I thought it was better to have someone from law enforcement with her."

"You make a good point." Sanderlin consulted his notes. "Keep me posted on your progress with the case. In the meantime, we have other business to attend to. Does anyone have any developments to report?"

"Park Service reports they stopped a man armed with a .38-caliber revolver on the Deadhorse Trail yesterday," Michael Dance reported. "He claimed not to have seen the notifications that firearms aren't allowed in the national park. Then he admitted he was searching for Trask, hoping to cash in on the reward money."

"TDC has been publicizing that reward in a big way," Carmen said. "We're probably going to see a lot more of that kind of thing as word spreads that Dane has been active in the park."

"Be extra vigilant," Sanderlin said. "We want to get to Trask before some cowboy with a gun decides to be a hero."

"I always wanted to be a hero," Hud quipped. He turned to Jason. "Isn't that why you signed up for this gig?"

"Sure," Jason said. "That and the cool uniform."

"Don't forget the chance to work outdoors in all kinds of weather and have people call you names and even shoot at you on occasion," Hud said.

"You two are a riot," Carmen said. "You ought to take your act on the road."

"Right now, you need to take it to work." Sanderlin closed his notebook and stood. "Let's get after it, people."

Hud slapped Jason on the back as they exited the room. "Come on, I want to show you something," he said.

"What is it?"

"You'll see."

They climbed into Hud's vehicle and he headed down the road to the campground and past the river crossing and the camps. After they passed the last campsite, he stopped to unlock a gate and bump down a dirt track, past a machinery shed. "Taking the scenic route, I see," Jason said.

"I think you'll find this interesting." He parked the truck when the road dead-ended and led the way down a barely discernable trail through the brush.

"Do you think Dane Trask has been down here?" Jason asked.

"I came here yesterday when I had some free time," Hud said. "I asked myself, if I'm an Army Ranger, a trained survivalist, if you will, where would I set up camp that would be convenient to the campground, yet tough for anyone to find me?"

"And your answer was here?" Jason swatted a drooping willow branch out of his way.

"It makes sense, don't you think?" Hud asked.

"I hope you're leading me down here to show me something," Jason said. "Though Trask doesn't strike me as the type to leave anything behind he doesn't want us to see."

"I agree," Hud said. "And I figure he probably knows we're looking for him."

"So?"

"So check this out." He parted a thick growth of Gambel oak to reveal a small clearing. A clearing populated with at least a dozen rock cairns. The stacks of rock had long been used as trail markers in treeless or rocky areas. More recently, however, a fad had begun of tourists leaving the rock towers on beaches, in campgrounds, and along trails, to the point where part of Jason's last jobs as a ranger in Glacier national park had been to remove the cairns that were in violation of Leave No Trace principles.

"You think Dane Trask built these?" Jason asked as he and Hud walked among the stacks of rocks, some carefully balanced creations, others more haphazardly arranged.

"I doubt random hikers ended up here," Hud said. "That

trail we took in is just a faint game track. I think Trask put these here, knowing someone looking for him would eventually come across them."

"I think you're right," Jason said. He didn't have anything but intuition to back up that claim, but as a cop, he'd learned to rely on intuition more than he would ever admit out loud. "But if Trask left these for us to find, why?"

Hud shrugged. "It could be just to mess with us. Have us waste time trying to see some message where there isn't any."

"TDC is a construction company with projects all over the world," Jason said. "Maybe these rock towers are a reference to them."

"But why?"

"I don't know." Jason squatted to take a closer look at the nearest cairn. Nine rocks of descending size, stacked one atop the other. Plain gray quartz. He picked up the top rock and held it, and thought of the piles of rocks at the Mary Lee Mine reclamation site. Were these cairns some oblique reference to that?

"We could stake out the place and hope he comes back," Hud said. "But I'm betting he won't. I wouldn't be surprised if he stopped visiting the campground. It's getting too dangerous, and I think he's smarter than that."

Jason stood. "I think you're right." He plucked the top rock from the cairn he had just examined and stuffed it in his pocket.

"What are you going to do with that?" Hud asked. "Examine it for fingerprints?"

"Just an idea I have," Jason said. He had remembered the rock Cara had collected at the Mary Lee Mine. Maybe she could help him interpret Dane's latest message.

Chapter Fifteen

Jason picked up Cara at her house at seven o'clock Saturday morning. Instead of his Ranger Brigade SUV, he drove a white Chevy pickup with an Only You Can Prevent Forest Fires bumper sticker. "You could almost pass for a Ranger," he said, surveying her khaki hiking pants and long-sleeved white shirt.

"The hat spoils it," she said, putting on a wide-brimmed straw sun hat trimmed in pink ribbon.

"I don't know," he said. "You might start a new trend. Do you think straw would suit me?"

He made a goofy face and she laughed and shook her head. "No, the Stetson suits you," she said, referring to the dun felt hat that was part of his Ranger Brigade uniform.

"If you think that's good, you should have seen me rock the Smoky Bear model," he said.

"Is that what it's called, really?" she asked.

"That's what some people call it. It's also known as a campaign hat, or the flat hat, because it has a flat brim. I still have a couple in my closet." His grin turned to a parody of a leer. "I'll have to model them for you some time."

The image of him wearing nothing but the hat warmed her through, and she quickly looked away. "Where are you taking me this morning?" she asked after a moment.

"I thought we'd hit the back country near the camp-grounds, since we know Dane has been there."

"Has he taken anything else?" she asked.

"No. I think maybe it got too risky for him. That means he may have moved on to another area of the park, or even out of the park."

"I know this is a long shot," she said. "But if he is out there, I want him to see me, and to know that I'm still on his side."

"There's something else I want to show you," he said. "And see what you think."

"Something to do with Dane?"

"I'll let you be the judge of that."

He stopped for iced coffee and cinnamon buns at a drive-thru on the edge of town. "I've got some protein bars in my pack, if we get hungry later," he said, handing her one of the drinks.

"Thanks, but I've got my own emergency rations." She patted the day pack between her feet.

"Oh? What's that?"

"Snickers candy bars. I figure they're about as healthy as most energy bars, and they taste a heck of a lot better."

He laughed. "You may be on to something." They headed for the park, through cornfields and farm coun-try, past barren ground white with alkali, then onto rolling fields of sagebrush and scatterings of cattle, their black bodies gleaming in the early morning sun. "I always imag-ine what it must have been like for the first peoples to see the canyon," Jason said. "Imagine riding or walking across this relatively barren landscape and coming to this mas-sive chasm of brilliantly colored rock."

"Living so close to the canyon, I guess I take it for granted," Cara said. She stared out the window at the pass-ing scenery. "Dane loved it there, though. He said hiking or fishing in the canyon was the one way he could truly get away from it all."

"If he spent a lot of time there, he probably knows it well," Jason said.

"He took backpacking trips into the canyon," she said. "He spent a week there once, by himself. He and Eve were still together at the time and he said she worried about him the whole time, and hated that there was no way for her to get in touch with him."

"Everything you're telling me proves it's going to be tough to locate him if he doesn't want to be found," Jason said.

He waved to the attendant at the entrance gate and turned right onto the road to the campground, a steep, curving ribbon of pavement that descended to the level of the Gunnison River and Morrow Dam. Fly fishermen waded in the sparkling water, sending graceful casts into the shadowy undergrowth or into midstream pools formed by fallen branches or boulders.

"TDC has distributed posters of Dane all over town," Cara said, reliving her shock at coming upon one of these flyers at the local grocery store. It featured a photo of Dane taken at the company picnic last year, and another from his official work badge. In the first, he was smiling, carefree. In the second, he wore no smile and his dark suit made him look severe, even threatening. "Soon everyone is going to know what he looks like."

"All the more reason for him to stay out of sight," Jason said.

"But why is he staying hidden?" she asked. "Why not come out and fight to prove his innocence?"

"I guess that's the big question in all of this," he said. "What's really going on?"

He parked at a locked gate past the campground and led

the way along a narrow path choked in places with brush. When he stopped abruptly, Cara almost plowed into his back. "Hud showed me this yesterday afternoon," he said. "I want to know what you think."

"What am I supposed to be looking at— Oh!" Jason had stepped aside to reveal a grouping of rock towers. She had seen similar groupings before. Once when hiking Utah's canyon country and again beside high alpine lakes. Some people constructed them as works of art or as a form of meditation. Others built them to guide hikers on trails that weren't well marked. She recalled the photo in Dane's office of a grouping of such rock structures beneath a stone arch in Utah.

"Dane built these," she said. "I'm sure of it."

"Why are you sure?" he asked.

She touched the top of one structure. "They fascinated him. He took photographs of rock groupings whenever he came upon them."

"Then why did he build these?" Jason asked. "Why would a man on the run take the time to build all these cairns?"

"Because he knew someone would see them," she said. "He's trying to tell us something."

"Why be so cryptic? Why not come right out and tell us what we need to know?"

"Because he's afraid we won't believe him? Because he wants the police to discover something for themselves?" She lightly touched the top of the next cairn she passed. It didn't wobble.

"What do you think he's saying?" Jason asked.

She wished she had a quick answer for him, a solution to this whole puzzle. But her mind was blank. Did the clue lie in that photograph of the Utah cairns, now packed away in some evidence locker? "There was a photograph of cairns like these in the things from Dane's office," she said. "You should look at that."

Jason nodded. "All right. Anything else?"

She stared at the piles of rocks. Nothing about them seemed unusual or significant.

"There were piles of rocks at the Mary Lee Mine," Jason said. "Not cairns like these, but do you think he's telling us to look there?"

"Maybe?" The idea seemed far-fetched. "I tried looking at those reports again, but other than the fact that the reports show a lot of contamination, they don't tell us anything significant. The whole reason TDC is working the property is to get rid of the contamination."

"What about that rock you took from the site?" he asked.

"What rock?"

"The one you picked up just before the shooting started. I saw you put it in your pocket."

Her face burned. "It was just something to remember Dane."

"Do you still have it?"

"Of course." It was on the table in her living room. Just a yellow-gray lump of rock that didn't mean anything to anyone else.

"Do me a favor and take another look at it when you get home. Tell me if you see anything unusual about it."

"Okay." She pulled out her phone, took a few photographs of the cairns and then they walked back the way they had come. "What now?" she asked.

"We can look around more," he said. "See if you spot anything else."

She shook her head. "I don't think he's here. I don't think anyone is here."

"Then what do you want to do?"

She studied him from beneath the broad brim of her hat. "This," she said and stepped forward and kissed him.

She could tell she had caught him by surprise, but he had good reflexes and he kissed her back, arms encircling her waist as she reached up to caress his shoulders. When their hat brims collided, she tore hers from her head and let it flutter to the ground. His mouth was firm and warm against hers, his fingers kneading her hips in way that sent tension spiraling through her core. She arched against him and felt his erection, hard and insistent.

When he finally broke the kiss, they were both breathless. He looked as dazed as she felt. "That was pretty nice," he said.

"Only *pretty*?"

"It was very nice, but I like to leave room for improvement. You know they say things get better with practice."

"*Things*? Are you always so eloquent?"

He snugged her against him once more. "All right, then. Kissing gets better with practice. And sex." He nipped at the side of her neck.

"Well, why didn't you say so?" She traced her tongue along his jaw. This felt so good. So right. Why had she waited so long to open herself up to these feelings again?

"Maybe I like to let my actions speak for themselves." He kissed her again and her body hummed with pleasure. Oh yeah, she'd been wanting this.

"This is nice, but maybe we should go somewhere more comfortable," he said.

"Mmm." She rested her head on his shoulder. "Aren't you supposed to be working?"

"Right now I'm interviewing a witness and collecting evidence."

"Is that what you're doing? Do you think you're going to find any evidence under my shirt?"

He withdrew his hand and straightened. "We probably should continue this particular investigation when I'm off-duty," he said. "And much as I hate to see you go, I should probably take you home now."

She smoothed the collar of his uniform shirt. "All right. But why don't you come over tonight for dinner? We can discuss the case—and other things."

"I'll come prepared for an in-depth investigation." His exaggerated leer made her laugh. She couldn't remember when she'd laughed with a man this way. Not since before Corey died, surely.

That fog of happiness lasted all the way back to her house and halfway up the front walk. Then Jason stopped and pulled her back. He swore and she followed his gaze to the front door. The screen hung by one hinge and the door itself was a splintered mess. A sick feeling washed over her. "What—?" It was the only word she got out before her throat closed.

"Stay here," he said. He released his hold on her and strode toward the beat-up door. Keeping to one side, he surveyed the damage then stepped past the debris and into the house.

Less than a minute later, he joined her on the walk. "I'm going to call the local cops to handle this," he said. "We'll wait until they arrive, then you can go in and look to see what is missing."

"They took my things?" Anger pushed out some of her fear. She was almost as upset about the destroyed door as she was her belongings. She had spent a solid week stripping, sanding and repainting that door. "Was it the same scumbag who tried to break in the other night?"

"Maybe." Jason pulled out his phone. "Let's see what the local cops have to say."

A Montrose police officer arrived twenty minutes later,

took a look at the splintered door and called for backup. He took their statements, including the information about the attempted break-in almost two weeks before. Then he escorted them into the house. After the destruction of the door, Cara had expected the worst, but the interior seemed undisturbed. "Tell me what's missing," the Montrose officer said.

"My laptop," she said, stomach sinking as she stared at the end of the kitchen table where the computer usually sat. She scanned the rest of the downstairs rooms. The television was still in its place, along with some other small electronics. Upstairs, all her jewelry was still there. Even the bit of cash she kept tucked in her underwear drawer was still in its envelope.

She followed the city cop and Jason back down the stairs. "Is anything else missing besides the computer?" the officer asked.

She looked around the room again, her gaze resting on the coffee table. "The rock is gone," she said.

"A rock?" The cop looked puzzled.

Cara ignored him and turned to Jason. "The rock I took from the Mary Lee Mine. It was right here on the coffee table and now it's gone."

"Was it some kind of valuable mineral specimen or something?" the officer asked.

"No, it was just a yellowish-gray lump of rock, about the size of my fist." She made a fist to demonstrate.

"It had a lot of sentimental value," Jason offered.

The cop shrugged and wrote it down. "Anything else?"

"No." Cara turned back to Jason. "Who would want my computer and that rock?"

"Come on." He put an arm around her. "Pack an overnight bag and let's go to my place. You can't stay here with the door like that."

"I can go to a hotel," she said, not enthusiastic about the prospect.

"You don't want to be alone right now."

The fact that he understood that made her feel even closer to him. While he and the Montrose officer chatted, she went upstairs and shoved some clothing and toiletries into a bag. Once downstairs again, she grabbed her phone charger from the kitchen then rejoined them in the living room. "I saw some scrap wood out back," Jason said. "If you've got a hammer and some nails, I'll seal off the doorway before we leave."

She'd been so dazed she hadn't thought of that, and was grateful he had. The Montrose officer gave her his card and a case number and told her he'd let her know if anything turned up. "You might keep an eye out online and at local pawnshops," he said. "Sometimes crime victims have better luck in tracking down their own belongings than we do."

It only took Jason about fifteen minutes to hammer a piece of plywood over the opening to the door. "The Montrose police will do extra drive-bys today and tomorrow to keep an eye on the place," he said.

"I don't think whoever did this will be back," she said. "I think he got what he wanted."

"You might be right."

Neither of them said much on the drive out toward the park. Jason turned his pickup onto a side road and wound up a hill to a log cabin in a grove of cottonwoods. "How in the world did you find this place?" she marveled as they climbed out of the vehicle.

"A ranch worker used to live in this place, but there's more gas wells than cattle on the ranch today, so the owners decided to rent it out." He took her overnight bag and led the way to the front door.

"It's certainly remote enough," she said.

"I like remote," he said. "And it's closer to Ranger headquarters and the park than I would be in town."

"There is that. It's close to TDC, too." She indicated the office complex, barely visible in the distance.

"That, too." He pushed open the door and led her into a simply furnished square room dominated by a large plate-glass window that offered a watercolor-worthy view of wildflower-covered rolling plains and distant mountains.

"Wow," she said, drawn to the window as if by suction.

"Yeah." Jason moved in behind her. "This view pretty much sold me on the place."

He wrapped his arms around her and she leaned back into him, comfortable and comforted. "I'm glad you were with me this morning," she said. "I'm glad I didn't have to deal with that by myself."

"I wish we had showed up just a little earlier and caught whoever it was in the act," he said.

She swiveled around to face him. "No one's going to convince me this doesn't have something to do with Dane," she said. "My laptop has the files I copied from his computer on it. And that rock was from the Mary Lee Mine. It's where he's been trying to point us from the very first, I'm certain. It's one of the jobs Dane was working on before he disappeared. He must have discovered something at that mine or about it that someone else doesn't want made public. It could be the reason he felt he had to leave."

"I'm not saying you're wrong about all of that," Jason said. "But we don't have any proof."

"We need to go back up to the mine," she said. "We need to get another rock."

"And then what?" he asked.

"I don't know. We can have it tested or something."

"We could do that. And maybe this time the person who shot at us won't aim wide."

The terror of those moments under fire was still with her, so she couldn't argue with him. "Then what are we going to do?" she asked.

"I agree that Dane may be pointing us to the Mary Lee Mine. So let's take another look at that report he left on the first flash drive, and on his other files related to the Mary."

"But my computer with the files was stolen."

"But the Ranger Brigade has Dane's computer with the originals. We can go there after we have some lunch and take another look. I'll ask Hud to help us. He's our resident computer nerd."

"You don't have a resident environmental engineer, do you?" she asked. "One who can think like Dane?"

"Sorry, can't help you there." He squeezed her shoulders and stepped back. "Now, how about some lunch? I can offer you a turkey sandwich or peanut butter."

She opted for the turkey, which wasn't bad, and studied the rest of the cabin while she ate. The living room was furnished with a recliner, a sofa, a television and gaming system, and a couple of tables. The basics. A single bookshelf was crammed with paperbacks and hardbacks, everything from government reports and textbooks to bestsellers. Jason seemed to favor history and science, with a smattering of off-the-wall humor and some classics.

A dining nook sported a wooden table and chairs that looked antique, possibly original to the cabin. The kitchen was all yellow-laminate countertops and pine cabinetry, functional but not attractive enough to be dubbed retro or vintage. When she went to the bathroom to freshen up before they ate, she checked out the two bedrooms. One, obviously Jason's, held a king-size bed, a large dresser and a gun safe. The bed wasn't made but the room was otherwise neat. The second bedroom held a single bed, a chair and a lamp. The spare room of a person who didn't have company often.

"The well water here isn't that great," he said when she rejoined him in the kitchen. "So I hope you like Coke. I'm out of bottled water, so it's either that or coffee."

"Coke is fine," she said. "How long have you lived here?" she asked.

"Five weeks. I'm pretty much the newest member of the Ranger Brigade, which is why I was by myself at headquarters the afternoon you showed up to report Dane missing."

"Guess it was my lucky day," she said, flirting again, but also serious. She held her breath, waiting for his response.

"Mine, too," he said.

Happiness filled her, making her feel stupid. She was supposed to be worried about Dane, and her job, and the fact that someone had broken into her house. She needed to buy a new door, and she should really update her résumé and start looking for a new job. Yet she was helpless to do anything but sit across the table from Jason and bask in the warmth that filled her.

"When you go in to work Monday, see what you can find out about Anthony Durrell and Walter George," Jason said.

Some of the warmth faded. Apparently, he hadn't been basking in a romantic glow but had been thinking about the case. "The two men who came to my office to get Dane's computer?" she asked. "You think they're behind this break-in? Durrell is the man who was following us last Sunday night, right?"

He nodded. "I ran the names through our database, and

didn't come up with anything. Which makes me suspect the names might be aliases."

"TDC requires a criminal background check on all new hires," she said.

"Maybe someone got careless. Or figured out a way around the check. All I want you to find out is how long they've worked for TDC and what their job titles are."

"You're law enforcement," she said. "Can't you call the personnel office and they have to tell you?"

"They don't have to tell me anything without a subpoena," he said.

"I'll see what I can find out," she said. "I know I never saw or heard of either one of them before they came into the office that day. TDC has hundreds of employees around the world, maybe thousands, but our office only has about a hundred, and I thought I knew, or had at least heard of, all of them. Which makes me think they were hired recently, and maybe for a very specific job."

Was the job going after Dane?

Was their job now to go after her?

Chapter Sixteen

After lunch, Jason drove Cara to Ranger Brigade headquarters. When they entered, Hud had a rapt group of fel-
low Rangers gathered around him near the notice board.
"When I stopped the guy and asked him what he was doing
with a naked mannequin tied to the top of his car, he said
it was for an art project. He couldn't transport it inside the
car because he was afraid his dog would eat it."

"What kind of dog?" Knightbridge asked.

"Big. One of those big white ones you see with sheep
sometimes."

"A Great Pyrenees," Carmen said.

"That's it. Anyway, I asked the guy if he could show
me his project. He said sure, so I followed him to this big
open field up in the high country, full of Alpine sunflow-
ers. Just a beautiful setting." He made a face. "Except not
so beautiful because this guy has, I kid you not, at least
a dozen naked mannequins set up out there, posed like
they're having sex. Pretty kinky sex, judging from some
of the positions. I told him he couldn't do that on public
land. What if some kids came along? He told me that's why
he'd chosen such a remote location, and that he was very
careful to clean up after himself and leave no trace. He'd
been doing this for months and hadn't had any trouble."

"So he was taking pictures of the lewd mannequins?" Dance asked.

Hud nodded. "He had a whole camera full of shots—in fields of wildflowers, posed on top of rocks, in the middle of a stream—maybe fifty or a hundred different shots. He said he was going to compile them in a book."

"Did you charge him with anything?" Carmen asked.

"What was I going to charge him with?"

"Public indecency," Knightbridge said.

"These were mannequins, not real people. And it's not like they were…you know, anatomically correct."

"Littering?" Dance asked.

"It's not really littering if he takes everything with him when he leaves."

"So what did you end up doing?" Carmen asked.

"I asked him if he had considered using dolls for his project. They'd be easier to pose, cheaper to acquire, and he wouldn't freak out passing motorists if he decided to strap them to the top of his car."

"What did he think of the idea?" Knightbridge asked.

"He liked it. He said it could offer a whole new dimension to his work."

Hud was the first to notice their arrival as the group broke up. "Hey, Cara," he said. "How's it going?"

"Cara needs to take another look at Dane Trask's computer files," Jason said. "Everything to do with the Mary Lee Mine. Start with the most recent files and move back through time."

"We can do that." Hud led them to his desk. "What are you looking for?"

"Anything in the reports that shouldn't be there," Cara said, settling into a chair beside the desk. "Or anything that should be there that isn't."

Hud settled behind the desk while Jason dragged a chair

alongside Cara's. As Hud's fingers flew over the keyboard, Jason watched Cara. The break-in at her home had shaken her, but she was holding steady, thinking clearly and pushing forward. Later, the impact of her home invasion and the loss of her computer, at least, might hit harder. He hoped he could be there for her when they did.

"Okay, here are all the files having to do with the Mary Lee Mine," Hud said. "There are seventeen of them, but some appear to be memos and stuff other people sent to Trask. Do you want to look at those?"

"Yes, let's start there." Cara scooted closer. "They should be easy to scan quickly."

She dismissed the first three files. They contained emails related to the government contract and asked Dane to do a routine environmental assessment on the property showing "before" values to use as a baseline by which to judge TDC's progress with mitigation. One file contained a copy of the government's testing at the site. "Save that one to compare to Dane's initial report," Cara said, pointing to the screen.

"This looks interesting," Hud said. "Here's a file labeled 'Concerns.'" He tapped a few keys then frowned. "It's blank."

"Can you tell if it once contained something and has been erased?"

"I can try." He made a series of keystrokes, but the screen remained empty. He shook his head. "I'm not getting anything. Maybe he created the file, intending to make a list or write a memo or something, and never got around to it."

"See if you can find his initial assessment and let's compare it to the government's EPA report," Cara said.

Hud found the assessment report, opened it and displayed it next to the one from the Environmental Protection Agency. "It looks very similar," he said.

Jason scanned the list of letters and numbers, trying to remember what each one meant. "It's like the one on the flash drive," he said after a moment. "I mean, full of a lot of nasty stuff."

Cara nodded. "It is, but…" She leaned closer, scrutinizing the information. "It's what *isn't* on either of these reports that I find interesting."

Jason studied the screen again. "There's nothing on here about radioactive elements." He looked at her. "Maybe they didn't measure that initially. You said it's not common in this area. Maybe Dane uncovered it later."

"Maybe he uncovered it later because it wasn't there initially," she said.

Hud swiveled his chair to face them. "With mines, aren't we talking about naturally occurring radioactivity from uranium and other ores?"

Cara nodded. "That's my understanding. So, if it isn't there initially, how could it just show up?"

"Maybe as they started mitigating, digging out contaminated soil and rock, they uncovered some that couldn't be detected initially," Jason said.

"Maybe." She didn't sound convinced. "I've never heard of it happening. Do you have the flash drive Dane left on my car seat?"

"I have a copy of the file that was on it," Hud said. He shrank the information on the screen and brought up the fragment of the report.

"There." Cara stabbed at the screen. "There's the thorium and the uranium—radioactive elements found in soil and water."

"This report doesn't have a header, so we don't know

it's from the Mary Lee Mine," Hud pointed out. "It could be from another property."

"A property that is contaminated with lead, arsenic and mercury, all by-products of gold and silver mining?" she asked.

"I would assume it's possible," Hud said. "We should find an expert to consult."

"You do that," Cara said. "In the meantime, I want to visit the Mary Lee Mine again." She turned to Jason. "Can you borrow a Geiger counter? To measure radiation?"

"It might take a little while to locate one," he said.

"Find one. Please." She rubbed her hands up and down her arms, as if chilly. "I've got a feeling we're on the right track here. Maybe the reason Dane ran was because he found the source of that radiation, and whoever was responsible threatened to kill him if he told what he knew."

"Would someone kill for that?" Hud asked.

"This remediation contract is worth a lot of money to TDC," Cara said. "The land they're trading for is potentially worth millions once it's developed. And then there's the company's reputation to consider. Bad publicity can sink stock shares, reduce executive compensation and stockholder dividends and, if it's bad enough, destroy the company."

"Some people will go to great lengths to protect their money and their reputations," Jason said.

Cara nodded. "But who? Charles Terrell, Gary Davis and Drew Compton? Mitchell Ruffino? Or someone else?"

After putting in a few calls to try to obtain a Geiger counter or some other instrument to measure radiation, Jason took Cara back to his place. He took a mental inventory of the contents of his refrigerator and pantry and realized the cupboard was all but bare. "I'm going to run to town for some groceries," he told her. "Why don't you relax? Make yourself at home."

He headed to the nearest grocery store and hurried through, filling his cart with ingredients for salad, fruit, fresh bread, half-and-half, butter, cheese, a bottle of wine—another bottle of wine in case Cara didn't like the first one—bagels, bacon, steak, potatoes, trail mix, bottled water, cereal, milk and a big chocolate bar. Surely he could come up with a couple of decent meals from all this, enough to take them through tonight and tomorrow morning.

When he stepped through the door, the first thing he noticed was that Cara's overnight bag was no longer where he had left it—and she wasn't anywhere to be seen.

He'd left her bag by the front door, leaving it to her to decide which room she wanted to sleep in. He knew what he wanted, but she was calling the shots.

"Cara?" he called as he carried the groceries to the kitchen.

"I'm back here!"

He shoved the bags full of cold items onto the top shelf of the refrigerator and went in search of her. "Back where?"

"Back here!"

He thought the voice was coming from his bedroom. As he pushed open the door, his heartbeat sped up a little then did gymnastics as he stared at Cara, wearing a little—very little—nightie, sitting in the middle of his bed. "I didn't really feel like resting," she said. "And I thought maybe dinner could wait."

Between the door and the bed, he managed to lose his shoes, duty belt and pager, and was fumbling with the buttons on his shirt when she leaned back, smiling. "Don't be in a hurry on my account," she said.

"Then I'll be in a hurry on my account." Aware of her

gaze on him like a caress, teasing every nerve ending and heating his skin, he managed to strip off the rest of his clothes efficiently if not gracefully. When he was naked, he turned to face her.

She stretched out her arms. "Welcome home."

The words had never sounded more inviting.

PART OF CARA had died right along with her brother—the carefree part of her. The part of her willing to trust and take life as it came. It wasn't that she couldn't have fun after Corey's death, but she did so with a hyperawareness of how good things could turn bad in an instant.

Jason helped her forget that. In his arms, she felt guilt and regret and fear falling away as easily as the silk nightgown slid from her shoulders to the floor. He loved her with a focus and intensity that compelled her to put everything else to the side. As his hands and lips moved over her, she surrendered to pleasure, so intense it made her cry out, not with pain, but with delight.

Though he devoted himself to her pleasure, he asked the same of her, guiding her hands to touch him in ways that made him groan with need, coaxing her to move with him until they balanced on the edge of completion.

Then he cradled her to him and took her over the edge, her climax shuddering through them both. He followed and they continued to move together until they were utterly spent and sated.

They didn't talk much afterward. She didn't have words to express what she was feeling. Maybe he felt the same way. But he continued to hold and caress her—as if she was something precious he didn't want to let go of—until she fell into a deep sleep. She didn't dream. Maybe because their lovemaking had been so dreamlike in itself.

SHE WOKE TO the smell of sizzling steak and her mouth began to water even before she pulled on his shirt as a makeshift robe and made her way, barefoot, to the kitchen. Jason, in a blue-velour bathrobe, his hair sticking up on one side, stood at the stove, frying steaks in a cast-iron skillet. "That smells like heaven," she said.

Before Cara could protest that she hadn't brushed her teeth or combed her hair, he pulled her to him and kissed her, still holding a spatula in his free hand. "I was starved," he said. He nodded to the sink. "If you want to help, there's stuff for a salad over there."

She washed her hands and went to work tearing lettuce and chopping vegetables. He pulled a loaf of bread from the oven, filling the room with the scent of garlic and butter, then filled two glasses from a bottle of wine that sat open in the center of the table.

"Dinner is served," he announced.

She checked the clock on the stove—only a little after eight. She hadn't slept all that long, after all, but she felt revived. "I could get used to this," she said. "You're a pretty good cook."

"No I'm not." Jason cut into his steak. "I know how to do steak, pork chops, hamburgers and eggs. I can make a sandwich and open a can of soup. I don't starve, but don't go thinking I'm a real chef."

"I do a mean macaroni and cheese and spaghetti Bolognese," she said. "Oh, and meat loaf. I can do meat loaf. And I can read and follow most recipes. It's just that, when you're only cooking for yourself, there's not much incentive to get creative. Most days when I get home from work, I just need food, fast."

"Exactly." He stabbed at the salad with a fork. "It's kind of fun to cook for someone else."

"How old are you?" she asked, feeling emboldened—

by the sex or the wine or maybe the fact that she was sitting across from him, naked under his shirt and not even shy about it.

"I'm twenty-nine," he said. "Why? How old are you?"

"I'm thirty," she said. "And why? Because you sound like you've managed to reach twenty-nine without ever being married. Is that true?"

"That's not really so unusual these days, is it?" he said. "I've never even lived with anyone, either. What about you?"

She shook her head. As long as they were confessing their pasts, she might as well lay it all out on the table. "I was engaged to a guy when Corey died. We weren't living together. I mean, we were lovers, but I wanted to save something for after the wedding. But I kind of fell apart after Corey's death and my fiancé wasn't the most patient guy." She shrugged. "I gave back his ring, sold the dress online and told myself I was lucky to find out what he was really like before I vowed 'till death do us part.'"

"What a jerk."

She laughed, covering her mouth with her hand to avoid spraying salad across the table. "When you put it that way, he really was," she said. She sipped the wine, then pointed her fork at him. "Your turn. What's your bad relationship story?"

He made a face. "She was a congressional staffer for a freshman representative. We met at a press conference on the steps of the House of Representatives. I was working crowd control and I didn't want to let her onto the dais. She didn't have her ID badge with her and pitched a fit. She read me the riot act and I asked her out."

"You didn't!"

He shrugged. "What can I say? I like strong women.

Anyway, things were great for a while, but, as the saying goes, we grew apart."

"Oh?"

"She was ambitious. And she was really into politics. I'm not either of those things. I aim to do a good job, but I don't see myself as commander one day, and I'd rather have a root canal than talk politics, much less wade into the nitty-gritty. When I refused to attend yet another fundraising dinner for her boss, we agreed to go our separate ways."

"That was very mature of you."

"Oh sure. Very mature. I didn't date anyone else for over a year."

"She broke your heart."

He shook his head. "I just felt stupid for getting involved with someone I knew was wrong for me from the start. I got a lot pickier after that. For a while, I was thinking I was too picky."

Cara pretended to focus on finding the tomatoes in her salad. "What happened to change your mind?"

"I met you."

Her heart skipped a beat and a knot formed in her throat. It wasn't exactly a dramatic declaration of love, but the words weren't idle flirtation, either. "Do you think we have more in common than this case?" she asked.

"I think we both value the same things—family, loyalty, fairness."

"Truth, justice and the American way."

She regretted the quip as soon as it was out of her mouth, but he had the grace to let it pass. "I think it's worth finding out how much we have in common," he said. "And what we can gain from our differences. For instance, do you prefer to wash or dry?"

"Dry," she said.

"That's interesting," he said. "I prefer to wash."

"Then we are a perfect pair."

Cara never would have believed washing dishes could be romantic, but with her standing barefoot in his kitchen—the sleeves on his uniform shirt rolled up to her elbows, the scent of him clinging to the fabric—and him in his bathrobe—strong legs distracting her every time he stepped away to take another dirty dish from the table—the mundane chore was both sensual and intimate.

When the last dish was done, Jason turned to her, pressing her against the counter and kissing her, his hands deftly unbuttoning the shirt and pushing it back to expose her body. She parted his robe and they came together, the need sharp and demanding, until he lifted her onto the counter and bent his head to kiss and tease between her legs until she came with a loud cry.

Then he carried her over his shoulder to the bedroom, her laughter trailing them down the hall, a joyful sound. One she hadn't been sure she would ever make again.

"What did you do last night?" Hud asked when Jason reported for work on Monday morning. "You look hung over."

Jason shook his head. "I had an early night," he said. Though, if it were possible to suffer from overindulging in sex, then maybe that was his problem, since most of the weekend had been spent in bed.

He'd say one thing for Cara—when she finally decided to do something, she gave it one hundred percent. He shouldn't have been surprised. She'd been dogged in her determination to save Dane. She had probably been the same after her brother died, wanting justice for him so desperately.

Jason didn't know if the Houston cops had really blown

her off, as she'd said, or if it only seemed that way. Like
so many law enforcement agencies, the department was
likely understaffed, underbudgeted, overworked and over-
whelmed by all the ways people found to break laws and
hurt each other.

He would do his best not to hurt her. To find Dane and
either bring him to justice or help him find it. The deeper
he delved into the case, the more he tended to believe
Cara—the man was running from something. Something
to do with his job. Whether that was because he had stolen money, or because he harbored a secret someone didn't
want exposed, Jason couldn't say.

"The Department of the Interior says they have a Geiger counter you can borrow," Dance called from across the
room. "Somebody left a message in our voice-mail box."

"What do you need a Geiger counter for?" Knightbridge
asked.

"I'm looking for radioactive material that shouldn't really be at a mine TDC Enterprises is supposed to be cleaning up," Jason said. "It showed up on an environmental
impact report and I'm trying to find the source."

"I thought you were working on the missing Dane Trask
case," Dance said.

"I am," Jason said. "This is related."

"If you say so." Dance turned his attention back to his
computer screen.

"Black Canyon staff say no more reports of thefts
from the campground," Carmen said. "Maybe the thief
has moved on."

"Or maybe he's dead."

Every head in the room turned to the speaker, Special
Agent Ethan Reynolds, another Ranger Brigade veteran.
"It's rough country out there," Reynolds said. "One wrong
move and you've fallen and cracked your head. Or worse,

you're hurt, no one knows, and you lie there until you succumb to your injuries. It's ugly but it happens."

"Trask was a former Army Ranger," Jason said. "He had a lot more training than your average tourist. And he was familiar with the area. He'd spent a lot of time hiking and camping in the canyon and the wilderness areas over the years."

"Then maybe he's still alive and headed for Mexico," Reynolds said. "Or Santo Domingo or Alaska. There are a lot of places for a resourceful person to disappear."

"Missing person cases are the worst," Knightbridge said. "Even if you do find the person alive, someone is going to be hurt because they left."

They filed into the conference room for morning roll call. Commander Sanderlin greeted them by name as he moved toward the front of the room. "We've got orders from Washington to make the Dane Trask search a priority," he said without further preamble. "Because this was his last-known location, we're going to divide the park into quadrants and search in teams. If we don't locate him there, we'll expand to the surrounding public lands. The Montrose County Sheriff's Office will also be conducting searches in their jurisdiction."

"Why the priority?" Jason asked. *And why orders from Washington?* he wondered silently.

"It turns out Trask is accused not only of embezzling from his employer, he may be in possession of material that could endanger national security," Sanderlin said.

"What material?" Knightbridge asked.

The commander frowned. "I pressed for the same information. My supervisors were reluctant to elaborate, but they implied Trask has nuclear material that could be used to construct a bomb."

"Maybe that explains the radiation in those reports," Hud said.

As far as Jason was concerned, it didn't explain anything. "So he's just carrying this stuff around in his backpack?" he asked.

"I don't know the answer to that, but he's considered armed and extremely dangerous," Sanderlin said.

Clearly, they weren't getting the whole picture here. Nothing new where the Washington bureaucracy was concerned. Jason forced himself to sit back in his chair and remain calm. More people searching for Trask was a good thing. They were more likely to find him this way. More likely to hear his side of the story when they did.

"You should also know that the sheriff's department expects to make another arrest in the case today." Sanderlin's eyes met Jason's, steady and serious. "Cara Mead is suspected of assisting Trask with the theft of the material. Federal authorities will be picking her up ASAP and holding her for questioning."

Chapter Seventeen

Cara dreaded walking into work Monday morning. She used to be proud of working for TDC, a company known for treating its employees well. She believed the work she and Dane did helped to protect the environment. TDC had won architectural awards for some of its buildings, and developed new techniques for building greener structures.

Yet she was convinced that something had happened here that had driven Dane to escape to the wilderness. And that same something had led to her being demoted and her house burgled.

She wasn't going to sit around and let them run her off the way they had Dane. She had a plan. Today, she was going to find Durrell and George. And she wasn't just going to give the information to Jason. She was going to confront Durrell about seeing him following her. He'd probably tell her some lie, but at least she would have alerted him that she was on to him, and that she wasn't going to let him get away with that kind of harassment.

She had spent the drive to work coming up with a plausible story to ferret the information she needed out of human resources. As soon as she had stowed her purse in her desk, she gathered up a stack of printouts, stuffed them in a file folder and headed for the HR department.

Donna Lapinski, six foot two in towering heels, with

shoulders so broad she probably had to have her suit jackets custom tailored, greeted Cara with a warm smile. "Cara! I haven't seen you in ages," she declared. "How are you doing?"

"I'm fine," Cara lied. "I guess you know I'm in data processing now. I'm looking for an Anthony Durrell. A new employee, I guess. I've never heard of him."

Donna's brow furrowed beneath her fluff of bangs. "I don't remember anyone by that name, but let me check." She turned to her computer and began typing. After several minutes, her frown deepening, she shook her head. "I'm not finding anyone by that name. Are you sure that's right?"

The hair at the back of Cara's neck stood up. "How about Walter George?" she asked.

A new search didn't turn up George, either. "I'm sorry," Donna said, looking truly regretful. "Maybe double-check that you have the right names."

"I'll do that. Thanks."

Cara turned to make her way back to her desk, unnerved by the encounter. When they had come to Dane's office, Durrell and George had definitely worn TDC ID badges. Had the badges been fakes?

She had just stepped onto the elevator when her cell phone buzzed. She didn't recognize the number but she smiled when she saw the text was from Jason. But her smile changed to dismay when she read his message.

Get out of the building now! he had typed. Run!!

JASON HIT SEND on the throwaway phone someone—he suspected Hud, but couldn't be sure—had left on his desk after the commander had made his announcement regarding Cara. He had stared at the phone for approximately fifteen seconds before sliding it into his pocket, grabbing his day pack and heading out the door.

He didn't want to think about the laws and regulations he had just broken by trying to warn Cara of her imminent arrest. Maybe the sheriff's office, or Homeland Security, or whomever was involved in this case had come up with evidence to indicate Cara was implicit in a plot to steal radioactive material and sell it to terrorist groups or foreign agents or something like that. But he didn't believe it. And nothing he had seen of Dane Trask and his background pointed to his guilt, either.

But Cara was the only person Jason cared about. And he was starting to care very deeply. After so many years of guarding his heart, he'd opened up wide to her. If she ended up in prison, he would feel like he was there, too.

He headed for TDC headquarters. To do what, he didn't know. Maybe only to be there when federal agents hauled her away, to let her know he was there for her. He circled the employee parking lot in his Brigade SUV, searching for her car. He didn't see it on the first pass, but as he turned back into the lot for another look, two Montrose County Sheriff's Office vehicles and two plain black SUVs drove in from the front of the building.

Just then, Jason spotted Cara exiting the building. She walked rapidly toward a back corner of the lot. He sped toward her, putting his vehicle between her and the law enforcement SUVs, which were still on the far side of the lot. At his approach, she whipped her head around, her expression rigid with fear.

Relief, coupled with confusion, relaxed her features as she recognized him. She jogged to the passenger's-side door and yanked it open. "Get in the back," he said. "And get down, so no one can see you. I'll explain later."

She hesitated only a moment, then climbed into the

back and got down on the floor. He reached back, pulled a blanket from a side pocket and draped it over her, then proceeded out of the lot. As he passed the first sheriff's department vehicle, he lifted one finger in salute. The officer at the wheel returned the greeting, and Jason proceeded past the others in the party, back onto the highway, where he pushed the Cruiser up to eighty, headed toward the lake.

"Where are we going?" Cara asked, her voice muffled by the blanket.

"I'm going to drive out to the Curecanti wilderness area. Once we're on the backroads, it should be safe for you to sit up."

"What's going on?" she asked. "Am I in some kind of danger?"

"Maybe. I'll tell you what I know when we're stopped." He wanted to look into her eyes when he told her the news, to see for himself that she was innocent.

He drove for another fifteen minutes before he turned off on a side road that led through a state wildlife area and into the national forest, all part of the Curecanti National Recreation Area, and part of the Ranger Brigade's jurisdiction. "You can sit up now," he told Cara. "I'll stop and we'll talk when we get to some trees."

She sat up and he glanced in the rearview mirror to watch her. Hair mussed and face flushed, she snapped in her seat belt and stared out the side window, her expression troubled. But she didn't ask any more questions. Maybe that was a sign that she trusted him to tell her the truth when the time came.

After bumping over the narrow, rutted road for another ten minutes, Jason turned onto a barely discernable dirt track, even rougher and rockier than the forest road on which they'd been traveling. "This looks like the kind of place where serial killers dispose of bodies," Cara said.

"Though, if that's what you have planned for me, you certainly have a unique abduction method. I didn't know what to think when I got your text."

"But you paid attention and left," he said. "Thank you for that."

"I figured you wouldn't have sounded so urgent if you hadn't had a good reason. It confused me that the message wasn't from your phone, though."

"I had to use a phone no one could trace."

She leaned forward, grasping the back of the seat. "What's going on? You're starting to scare me."

He pulled over in the shade of a lone oak, rolled down the windows and shut off the engine. The only sounds were the wind's rustling of the leaves of the tree and the ping of the cooling engine. "Come up here," he said.

She got out of the back and transferred to the front passenger seat. "Did you see the sheriff's department vehicles drive into the parking lot, just when you came out of the building?" he asked.

She shook her head. "I was focused on getting to my car. Your message really scared me. Why did I need to leave?"

"They were coming to arrest you."

All color left her face. "Arrest me? For what?"

"For conspiring with Dane Trask to steal nuclear material—and other potential terrorist activities."

"Terrorist activities?" She pressed a hand to her stomach. "I feel sick."

He retrieved a bottle of water from a small cooler on the floorboard of the back seat and handed it to her. "I don't know much," he said. "My commander announced that you were going to be arrested at the end of our morning meeting. We've had orders from Washington to beef up the manhunt for Trask. I'll have to get back soon to help with that."

"I'm not a terrorist," she said. "And neither is Dane. What proof could they possibly have of anything like that?"

"I don't know," Jason said. "But it may have something to do with the radioactivity on those reports for the Mary Lee Mine."

Cara sank back in the seat and closed her eyes. He reached over and took her hand and, for a moment, neither said anything, soaking in the quiet and calm. After a long while, she opened her eyes. "Thank you for texting me," she said. "I know you didn't have to do that. You could probably lose your job if anyone finds out you helped me."

"Probably," he agreed.

"So why did you?"

He opened his mouth to say something flippant and flirtatious—he hadn't had a chance yet to taste her famous meat loaf or he'd decided to take more chances in his life. But what came out was the truth. "Because I think I'm falling in love with you. And because I believe you're innocent."

Tears glistened in her eyes—not the reaction he had expected or particularly wanted. "What's wrong?" he asked. "Did I say the wrong thing?"

"No." She shook her head and dabbed at her eyes. "You said exactly the right thing. But what are we going to do?" She looked around. "I left work so fast, I didn't even grab my purse. Do you have a tissue?"

He had a box in the console and handed it to her. She wiped her eyes and blew her nose. "When I got your message, I'd just left the human resources department," she said. "I asked about Anthony Durrell and Walter George. The HR director had never heard of them, and she couldn't find them on her computer."

"At this point, I'm not surprised," he said. "Nothing about this case adds up."

"What are we going to do? When the sheriff doesn't find me at TDC, he'll go to my house. He may even go to your house."

"I agree. For whatever reason, TDC, or someone else, is very serious about stopping you and Trask. We need to find that reason."

"We need to go back to the Mary Lee Mine," she said.

"I don't have a Geiger counter," he said. "I've found someplace that will loan me one, but I have to go pick it up, and I doubt I can get to that today."

"I still think we need to go to the mine," she said. "I can take water and soil samples and send them off for testing. I used to mail off samples like that for Dane. I can make up a fake name."

"That takes time," Jason said. "I don't know how long I can keep you hidden."

"I feel terrible involving you in all of this," Cara said.

"I'm in now," he said. "And I'm not going to make you go through this by yourself."

She dabbed at her eyes again. "You have to stop that. I'm ruining my makeup."

"Stop what?"

"Saying such sweet things."

He leaned forward and kissed her—a gentle caress, meant to be reassuring. She clung to him a moment before letting go. His arms felt empty without her in them. He used to laugh when people—his family, usually—said one day he'd want to settle down. He liked living different places, making friends all over the world. Everywhere he'd lived—Ghana, Glacier, Washington, DC—he'd had women in his life. They'd all been special to him, but he had never had a problem moving on. Cara felt different.

She felt like someone he couldn't move on from. Someone he couldn't afford to lose.

"You need to get back to work," she said. "I don't want them to arrest you, too."

He started the SUV's engine. "I'm going to drop you off at a place where I think you'll be safe," he said. "At least for a few hours. I don't know how long I'll be on search duty, but when I get a break, we'll go up to the Mary Lee Mine. Promise you'll wait for me and won't try to go alone."

"I won't," she said. "Maybe a week ago, I would have. But you have a gun and I don't, and we may need one."

"So you just love me for my weapons."

"Oh yeah," she said. "I love a man who's armed and dangerous." She squeezed his arm, adding meaning to the teasing words. "If you're not careful, I'm going to start to rely on you."

"I think I can handle that if you can."

"You've got me thinking differently about a lot of things."

He hoped the future—their future—was one of the things she was thinking about. But maybe it was too soon for that. They wouldn't have any kind of future if they didn't deal with the danger in the present.

THE HIDEOUT JASON had in mind proved to be a rustic log cabin nestled in a hollow of land overlooking the Blue Mesa Reservoir. Constructed of weatherworn chinked logs, the cabin consisted of only one room and an outhouse. "Who owns this place?" Cara asked, as he reached up under the eaves and took down a brass key to unlock the door.

"It belongs to a friend I worked with at Glacier National Park. When he found out I was transferred here, he told me I could use the place anytime I wanted. It's been in his family for years, but they don't make it out here much."

The furnishings inside were stark: a double bed in one corner, an antique gas stove in the other, a metal sink, a table and a few chairs, and bare shelves that held a few ancient-looking canned goods. "I'll stop on my way back for some groceries and things," Jason said, setting half a case of bottled water, a can of roasted peanuts and some protein bars he'd taken from his vehicle on the table.

She walked to the window and looked out over the turquoise waters of Blue Mesa Reservoir. Sunlight sparkled on the choppy surface and boats darted about like water bugs. "No one will think to look for me here," she said.

Jason moved in behind her and squeezed her shoulders. "I'll leave the throwaway phone with you. If you need to call me, use it."

She leaned back against him, still not quite believing he was taking such a big risk to help her. In his position, she wasn't sure she would have had the courage to do the same. "Thank you," she said.

"You don't have to thank me," he said.

"I do." She turned to him. "I say it to remind myself how lucky I am." She pulled his mouth down to hers and kissed him as if it was the last chance she'd ever get to do so. She didn't want to believe that might be true, but a panicked voice inside her whispered it might.

He broke the kiss, reluctantly, she thought. "I don't know how long I'll be gone," he said. "We're supposed to start the search in the national park. If they move it outside the park, you'll have to move. This cabin won't be safe anymore."

"Maybe I won't need to hide by then." Maybe they'd find something to help prove she was innocent. That Dane was innocent.

After Jason left, Cara stood for a long time at the window, the sun hot on her face. She could make out people on some of the boats, probably having the time of their lives racing across the water. If someone came for her here, should she run for the water or for the hills? She wasn't Dane. She didn't know anything about surviving in the wilderness.

So should she surrender and take her chances at proving her innocence? Jason apparently didn't see that as an option. He hadn't even suggested it. Maybe because he sensed, as did she, that evidence didn't have much to do with the accusations being made against her.

She sat on the bed, which squeaked loudly in protest, and picked up the little pay-as-you-go phone Jason had left for her. She punched in Maisie's number and listened to it ring.

Her friend answered on the third ring. "Hello?" She sounded doubtful.

"Don't hang up," Cara said. "It's me."

"Cara!" Maisie lowered her voice to a strained whisper. "Where are you? There were cops here, looking for you. What is going on?"

"I haven't done anything wrong," Cara said. "But listen, I need you to do something for me."

"What is it?"

At least she hadn't outright refused. "I need you to scan me copies of the forms to submit environmental samples to our lab," Cara said. "You can send them to this number."

"Lab forms? What for?"

"I need to send in some soil and water samples."

"You're still concerned about your job when you have the cops after you? Cara, I don't even know if you have a job anymore. Your supervisor almost fainted when six big guys in uniform—six!—walked into her office and asked to see you. I had come down to ask if you wanted to have lunch later and saw them. It's like they thought you were dangerous or something."

"What am I supposed to have done?" Cara asked.

"They said it related to national security. Do they mean, like, terrorism?"

"I'm not a terrorist," Cara said.

"Of course you're not. But what's going on?"

"When I figure that out, I'll let you know."

"Some of the girls are saying you must be guilty because you ran," Maisie said.

"I'm not guilty," Cara said. "But I am afraid."

"Oh, honey! I'm so sorry. I wish there was something I could do to help."

The sympathy in Maisie's voice made Cara's chest feel tight. "Just send those forms, okay? Now I'd better get off the phone."

"Wait, where—?"

Cara ended the call. She hoped she hadn't already talked too long, that the Feds or whomever was after her hadn't tapped Maisie's phone, or whatever they did with cell phones. Just in case, she shut off the phone and returned to looking out the window.

Dane, where are you? she thought. *If I could talk to you, would you tell me what's really going on?*

Had Dane run because, like her, he was suddenly afraid for his life?

Chapter Eighteen

Jason and Hud were assigned to search terrain north and east of the North Vista Trail, at the far reaches of North Rim Road. The area was less than a mile, traveling down the canyon, from the place where Dane's wrecked truck had been found. The two positioned themselves thirty feet apart and began walking forward, planning to cover the entire area in a grid pattern, bushwhacking through thick undergrowth, alert for footprints or clothing fibers, or any sign their fugitive might have passed this way.

It took four hours to all but crawl across the entire search area. By the time they were done, they were hot, thirsty, bruised and scratched, and thoroughly annoyed. "This is nuts," Hud said as they regrouped beneath the shade of the overhanging canyon walls. "If this guy stole a hundred thousand dollars or whatever it was, he's not sweating down here in this canyon. He's taking it easy on a beach somewhere."

"He's supposed to be on the run with 'nuclear material.'" Jason put verbal quotation marks around the words.

"Right—he's hiking around with a few pounds of yellowcake in his backpack? Can't that stuff give you cancer or make your hair fall out or something?" Hud stowed his water bottle back in his pack. "I've spent a lot of time going through Trask's files and he strikes me as a lot smarter than that. He's a scientist, not some ignorant yahoo with an urge to overthrow the government."

Jason took off his hat and mopped his brow with the sleeve of his uniform shirt. "Then why are we out here hunting him?"

"Because somebody has evidence we don't know about?" Hud sounded doubtful. "The commander doesn't like it, either, I don't think. I could tell by the way his lip curled when he said the order came down from Washington." He kicked at a rock. "We've got better things to do than try to search every inch of the park. It can't be done, even if we had five times the staff."

"Then why are we out here?" Jason asked again.

"I think we're making a show to satisfy the higher-ups. After a day or two with no result, they'll leave us alone to go back to our real jobs."

"Maybe," Jason said. He didn't believe it. Someone was putting a lot of pressure on someone else to find Dane Trask.

"I was pretty shocked to hear that about Cara Mead," Hud said. "About her being wanted as Trask's accomplice. She seems like a really nice woman."

"Yeah," Jason agreed, wary of showing too much enthusiasm. For Cara's safety, he needed to keep quiet about their relationship.

"I guess by now they have her in custody. I hope she's got a good lawyer."

"Uh-huh."

"What's with you?" Hud asked. "You're not much of a conversationalist this afternoon."

"I'm just tired." Jason replaced his hat and straightened. "Come on. Let's search our next coordinates."

Hud took out the map and indicated a section outlined

in yellow highlighter. "This one here. There're some caves in the sides of the cliff we should check out."

"Did you bring any bear spray?" Jason asked.

Hud made a face. "Have you ever seen a bear down here?"

"No, but the park rangers say they're down here."

"If we run into any, I'll fire my sidearm to frighten them away."

"I'm not worried about black bears," Jason said.

"Why not?"

"Because I'm pretty sure I can run faster than you."

Hud laughed, breaking some of the tension, and they continued their search. Jason scanned the ground, a mix of dry, sandy earth and crumbled shale, pockmarked from past rainstorms. It was good soil for tracking because it held every imprint in the brittle surface. Everywhere he stepped, he left a clear outline of his boot, right down to the logo, on the soil.

Trask wouldn't have walked here. He'd have stuck to the rocks along the canyon wall, the rough, granite surface leaving no trace of his passage.

Determined not to waste any more time with busywork, Jason moved over toward the canyon walls. He wasn't a trained tracker, but he'd spent enough time hunting that he'd learned to read signs. Trask wasn't going to be careless enough to leave anything obvious, but it was tough for a big man like him to move through dense brush without leaving some kind of evidence behind.

His first indication that someone had been this way was a bit of lichen torn from the surface of a boulder. The bright orange growth had been smeared across the granite, just a faint smudge, possibly made by a boot slipping on the surface of the rock.

Farther on, he noted the broken tip of a stunted juni-

per, the end dangling where something—or someone—
had brushed past.

Jason almost stumbled into the rock cairns. Three of
them, one facing the other two, as if in a standoff. A chill
swept over him as he surveyed the image and goose bumps
rose on his arm. "Dane Trask!" he shouted.

Dane Trask! The words echoed back to him, the sound
hollow and distorted.

Jason turned in a slow circle, until his eyes ached from
staring, unblinking. Trask was somewhere nearby. The
message of the cairns had been clear as spring water: I
see you.

CARA FILLED OUT the forms Maisie had forwarded, with
the location of where the sample was taken and the person
the information was to be sent to. She used the name of a
woman who used to work in the environmental engineering department, one who would be familiar to anyone at
the lab who had worked with TDC samples before. She left
the time and date the sample was taken blank, along with
the address the results should be sent to. Later on, she'd
print out the forms and fill in the blanks, then mail them
off with the samples from the Mary Lee Mine.

Now all she had to do was wait for Jason to return so
they could go to the mine. She still couldn't believe she
and a cop were working together. If they weren't actually
breaking the law, they were bending it pretty significantly.
But what choice did they have? She'd never been a fan of
conspiracy theories, yet right now it felt as if she was in
the middle of a big one.

Paperwork done, she had nothing to occupy her. She
toured the cabin, which took less than five minutes, including opening every kitchen drawer and checking under

the bed. She had already viewed the outhouse, a dark, dry space inhabited by spiders and dust.

She lay down on the bed, too nervous to sleep, and studied the board-and-batten ceiling. The sound of tires on gravel made her bolt upright, heart pounding so hard it hurt. When she recognized Jason's pickup outside, she almost collapsed in relief.

A few seconds later, he came in, carrying plastic grocery bags and a paper sack from a local hamburger place. He set them on the table. "I got a cooler and some ice, too," he said. "I realized this place doesn't have a refrigerator."

"How long do you think I'll have to stay here?" Cara asked, surveying all the food she was too nervous to eat.

"I don't know."

"I want to head up to the mine while we still have light," she said.

"All right. Let's pack food to take with us."

She started to protest, but he silenced her with a look. "You may not want to eat, but you have to."

"Yes, sir."

He smirked and went out to retrieve the ice.

The sight of the Snickers bar among the groceries brought a lump to her throat. It was such a stupid little thing, but she was beyond touched that he had remembered.

"What happened today?" she asked as they put the burgers and fries in the backpack.

"Hud and I spent the afternoon bushwhacking through oak brush and cactus. We didn't see anything but one skinny coyote and a bunch of rocks." He glanced at her. "I think Dane was out there, though. I think he knew we were looking for him."

"What makes you think that?"

"I found three more of those rock cairns. Like, one for

him and one for each of us. They were arranged in a kind of standoff. I think he was saying he wasn't afraid. That he wouldn't let us catch him."

"This isn't a game," she said, frustration making her words sharper than she had intended.

"I know that," he said, his voice gentle.

"I'm not upset with you—I'm upset with Dane. If he knew you were there, why didn't he just speak to you? Why all these cryptic clues and hide-and-seek?"

"Maybe he doesn't trust cops. There are people like that, you know."

"Ouch! I know. But you're not just any cop."

"Dane doesn't know that."

"No," she agreed. "But I wish I could help him see."

"Maybe we'll find something at the mine that will make it safe for him to come home and clear his name."

She nodded. "I'm ready." She held up a couple of plastic water bottles she had drained earlier. "I'll use these for our samples. We can stop on the way home at an office supply place, print the forms from the phone and pop the samples in the mail."

"Where will you have the results sent?"

"My friend Maisie can receive them. She's sort of helping me. She sent me the correct forms to send off."

"How did she get in touch with you?" he asked.

"I called her on the phone you gave me. But I didn't tell her where I was or mention you at all. And I kept the call short and shut off the phone as soon as I hung up."

He frowned, but all he said was "Let's get going."

They were largely silent on the drive to the mine, weary from the stress of the day, or simply lost in their own thoughts. At one point, Jason reached over and took her hand. He continued to hold it until they turned off the highway, a silent reassurance that lifted some of the fatigue dragging at her.

The road up to the mine was as rough as she remembered, forcing Cara to steady herself with one hand on the dash as the truck rocked through ruts and shuddered across washboarded gravel. Jason swung through the last turn onto the mine road and had to hit the brakes hard to keep from colliding with a large steel gate.

"That wasn't here before," Cara said.

"No. It's new." He indicated the posts supporting the gate. "That concrete looks fresh."

She looked past the gate, to where the road vanished into trees at the top of the hill. "How far from here to the mine?" she asked.

"From what I remember, about a mile." He backed up until he could return the way they had come. "I saw a place I can hide the truck," he said. "About a quarter mile from here. We'll hike in from there."

Wary of being spotted by whomever had shot at them the last time, they left the truck and kept to the thick growth of pinion and cedar to the side of the road. It made for slow going, and Cara was grateful for the lengthening days. Even so, by the time the first waste piles of rock loomed within sight, dusk was descending, washing everything of color and deepening the shadows.

"I'll take one of these," Jason said, hefting a grapefruit-size rock from the top of one pile and stowing it in his pack. Cara knelt at the base of the pile, unscrewed the lid on one of the plastic bottles and trickled in a handful of soil. She wrote "Soil from surface of Mary Lee Mine site" and the date and time of collection on a label she had affixed to the bottle.

"We just need a sample from that creek back there," she said, standing. She turned and was surprised to see that

Jason had drawn his weapon. "What is it?" she asked, fear rising in her throat.

"I'm just being cautious." He touched her shoulder. "Stay close. We'll walk together."

Cara strained her ears for the sound of anyone or anything out of the ordinary, but could only hear her own pounding pulse and the occasional scrape of their footsteps on the rough ground. When they reached the creek, she hurriedly knelt and collected her sample, her hands shaking as she labeled the bottle. She stood and stowed it in the pack. "Let's get out of here," she said.

Then an explosion of tree bark six inches from her right ear stung her face and filled the air with shrieking. Only when Jason grabbed her and tugged her away did she realize she was the one screaming.

JASON RAN, DRAGGING Cara after him. Gunshots pursued them, too close to be intentional misses. Their erratic movements and the growing darkness were probably the only things keeping them alive right now.

But the darkness handicapped them, too. More than once he tripped over tree roots or fallen branches. When Cara went sprawling, he hauled her to her feet and kept running. He'd holstered his weapon, unwilling to stop to try to pinpoint the location of the shooter, knowing it was unlikely he would be able to see whoever it was in the darkness, anyway.

No longer as concerned about concealment now that they had been discovered, when they reached the dirt road that led to the gate, Jason took it, running down one side. The shots that pursued them had stopped, but he knew that didn't mean they had escaped. Sure enough, a few minutes later, the roar of a revving engine tore through the darkness and headlights hit them like a spotlight.

He shoved Cara into the cover of the trees and dove after her. They ran, then fell, then tumbled down the slope, landing in a heap against the fence. "Are you hurt?" he asked, scrambling to her on his hands and knees.

"No." She shoved herself upright and he did likewise.

"Can you make it over the fence?" he asked. The ground sloped away sharply on this side, making for a longer climb. "The truck isn't far now."

"I can do it if you give me a boost."

He squatted down. "Climb on my back," he said. "I'll lift you up."

She did as he asked. He winced only a little at the feel of her hard boot heel in the small of his back. Then she was up and clambering over the fence. He turned and followed, every nerve on edge, anticipating a bullet striking him in the back.

But no bullet came, though they had to flatten themselves in the shallow roadside ditch as headlights swept over them and a black SUV roared past. They lay in the ditch for many long moments afterward, breathing hard, their only communication through their tightly clasped hands, holding on to each other as if to a lifeline.

Just when he was about to stand, more gunfire exploded—but this time much farther away. "What's happened?" Cara asked, panic edging her words.

"I don't know." Were there pursuers shooting at someone else? Or merely firing at anything that moved?

The shots died away and silence descended. He waited another ten minutes, counting his breaths, then shoved onto his knees. "Come on," he said. "My truck isn't far."

The truck wasn't far, but as the beam of the flashlight he had pulled from his belt played over it, he took in a windshield shattered by bullets, the two front tires shredded by gunfire. Behind him, Cara gasped. "What are we going to do now?"

He took her hand in his and stepped into the road. "The only thing we can do. We walk."

CARA FOLLOWED JASON, though her tired, aching legs protested with every step. Full darkness had descended, making walking away from the road difficult and dangerous. "We'll stay on the side of the road unless we hear a car coming," Jason said. "Then we'll hide in the underbrush. Sound carries out here, so we should have plenty of warning."

"Fine." All the tension of the past few days was catching up to Cara. Dragging her leaden legs along took all her effort.

"When we get a cell signal, I'll call for help," Jason said.

"You can't call the Ranger Brigade," she said. "They'll have to turn me over to the sheriff."

"We'll think of something," he said.

"Who is doing this?" she asked. "What could there possibly be at that old mine site that's worth killing someone?"

Before he could answer her, the low growl of an approaching car drifted up the hill. Jason took her hand once more and they plunged into the underbrush. They crouched in a prickly mass of Gambel oak and stared as the black SUV rumbled past. It moved slowly, the driver scanning the roadside with a hand-held spotlight.

"Down!" Jason ordered, and Cara pressed her face to the dirt beneath the oak brush, eyes tightly closed, so tense with fear, she ached.

The rumble of the engine grew fainter then died altogether. She raised her head and looked toward the darker shadow she knew was Jason. "Whoever that is, he knows we're out here and he's not going to stop looking," she said.

"He's not going to find us," Jason said. "It's a really dark night. A lot of clouds."

She hadn't paid any attention to the weather on the way here. Now she looked up and realized she couldn't see any stars. No wonder they'd had such a hard time finding sure footing. "You say that like all this darkness is a good thing," she said. "We're liable to fall and break an ankle or stumble over a cliff."

"If we stick to the road, we'll be okay," he said. "And searchers aren't likely to venture out on foot in this blackness. If they do, we'll hear them stumbling around in the dark a long time before they find us."

He stood and took her hand, pulling her up alongside him. "I'm scared," she said, leaning against him for a moment. "Those bullets were way too close this time."

"I know," he said. "It scares me, too."

"But you're a cop. You're trained for this kind of thing."

"That doesn't mean I don't get frightened. I've just learned to push past the fear." He kissed her, possibly aiming in the darkness for her cheek, but landing instead on her nose. Still, the contact—and his admission that he was only human—comforted her. They were a team and together they would face whatever was out there.

They set off along the road again. At least they were moving downhill. At least they knew they would reach cell service eventually. Jason wasn't going to turn her over to the sheriff. She had the water and soil samples from the mine, which should tell her if TDC was actually cleaning up the place or only pretending to. She'd find a way to prove her own innocence, and Dane's.

A crack of thunder so loud she felt the rumble beneath her feet made her cry out, followed closely by lightning that lit the sky like a strobe. She turned to Jason, who had his head tilted back, looking up at the sky.

Then the heavens opened and the rain began to pour.

Chapter Nineteen

Jason was beyond wet. Water squelched in his boots and dripped in his hair. It sloshed against his skin, weighing down his clothing and pooling in his ears. Mud dragged at his feet and running water turned the road into a river. Sheets of cold rain made it impossible to see, even when lightning exploded nearby in fiery light.

Cara clutched at his hand and shuffled beside him, bent over, her free arm hugging her body, water sluicing around her like sea spray from a rising mermaid. Each time a flash of lightning illuminated Cara, she looked wetter and more miserable—exactly the way he felt.

"We've got to find shelter," he said, shouting to be heard over the drum of rain.

"Where?" she shouted back.

He thought back to those long-ago Outward Bound expeditions that taught students how to build temporary structures from tree branches and vines. He'd been pretty good at the task back then, but he'd never tried to craft a shelter in the pouring rain, in inky darkness, on the side of a mountain.

"We're already so wet, what difference does it make?" Cara asked.

They could build a fire—provided they could find enough dry wood to do so. He had a tin of matches and a lighter and fire-starters in his pack. But it would take a bonfire to dry out their clothes, and that risked letting their pursuers know exactly where to find them.

He pulled out his phone, switched it on and checked the display. No bars. He switched it off to conserve the battery and slogged forward once more.

"Why is it taking so long to get to the highway?" Cara asked when they had been walking another half hour. "It didn't seem like that far in the car."

"We're traveling a lot slower on foot," he said. "We should be able to see the lights from the highway before long." But another hour passed with no lights and the road got much rougher. They had to navigate around deep ruts running with water and over sections that seemed more jagged rock than road.

"I don't remember any of this," Cara said.

Jason stopped, switched on a flashlight he took from his backpack and shone it around them. The remnants of an old barbwire fence lined one side of the road, while the other side was open fields. Cara touched his arm. "Did we take a wrong turn somewhere?" she asked. "Are we lost?"

"We must have," he said. He'd driven to the mine twice now in daylight, and definitely didn't remember that fence or this road, which was more trail that road. He switched off the light. "We need to find somewhere to stay put until morning," he said. "Then we'll have a better chance of getting our bearings."

"Sure," she said. "I can sit in the pouring rain as well as I can walk in it. You can't really drown in a rainstorm, can you?" Her voice was strained, on the edge of hysteria. Jason didn't blame her. He felt a little out of control himself.

"Let's walk up the road just a little farther, see if we can spot a bunch of trees," he said. "Maybe we can make a shelter." Those skills from his younger years might come in handy, after all.

CARA WAS SURE she was hallucinating when the sheepherder's trailer appeared in a flash of lightning. It hunched at the side of the road, boxy and white, with a curved roof like that on a Gypsy caravan, a silver stovepipe thrusting from the center. She grabbed Jason's arm. "Did you see that?"

"See what?"

She shook her head. "I don't know. I was probably imagining it, but I thought…" Lightning flashed again. "There!" She pointed toward the trailer.

"I see it." He grabbed her hand. "Come on. Let's see if anybody is home."

Up close, the trailer looked deserted—no smoke from the chimney, no lights showing at the windows. Jason knocked and called out, but no one answered. Finally, he took out his pocketknife and pried at the door. "This is an emergency," he said to Cara, and pulled the door open.

The scents of wood smoke and old mothballs greeted them, but the interior was clean and dry—blessedly dry. A lantern stood on the dinette and Jason lit it, while Cara shook out the blankets from the bed. Two coats hung from pegs on the wall, worn and much-patched, but she didn't care. The blankets and coats were dry and therefore warmer than her own soaked clothing. She was already shivering so violently she could scarcely speak. "Can you…start a fire?" she asked.

He opened the woodstove and peered inside. "Let me see if I can find some dry wood." He shed his pack and went back outside. She checked the cabinets over the small sink and two-burner gas stove and almost wept when she found a can of ground coffee, canned milk and cans of soup. By the time Jason had returned, she had unearthed a can opener and was dumping food into pots. "The stove won't light, so I'm guessing there's no propane," she said. "But we can heat this on the fire once you've got it going."

"I found a bunch of firewood piled around a tree and was able to pull some relatively dry pieces from the middle of the stack," he said, as he dropped the wood on the floor in front of the stove and set to work. "You should get out of those wet clothes," he added, arranging kindling in the stove. "Wrap up in one of those blankets."

He didn't have to tell her twice. By the time he had the fire going, she was curled up at the foot of the bed, a blanket wrapped around her. Her skin was still icy, and her teeth wouldn't stop chattering, but the hope of warmth didn't seem like a faraway dream anymore.

Jason adjusted the stove damper and stood. "That should start to warm us in a minute." He moved the teakettle she had filled to one side of the stovepipe and set the pot of soup on the other. He arranged her clothes to dry on a kitchen chair off to the side of the stove.

"You need to get out of your wet clothing, too," she said.

"You just want to get me naked and take advantage of me," he said.

"Oh, that's right. I planned all of this—including the weather and the guys with guns—so I could get you to take off your clothes. Because it's so impossible otherwise."

"Well, you know how shy I am." With that, he stripped off his trousers and began wrestling out of his wet shirt. Seconds later, wrapped in the second blanket, he joined Cara on the bed.

"Your skin is like ice," she said, reaching under the blanket to squeeze his thigh.

"So is yours." He moved over, tugged at her blanket and then shifted the coverings so that they were snuggled together, both blankets around them. The contact was almost painful at first, both of them so damp and cold, but the warmth of connection and the heat from the crackling fire in the stove began to seep in, turning pain into pleasure.

"It feels heavenly just to be warm," she said, leaning back against him and admiring the play of flames behind the glass door of the stove.

"Mmm" was his only answer, though his arms around her tightened.

"Are you falling asleep?" she asked.

"No."

She turned toward him and they kissed. Kissing progressed to touching and stroking. They made love leisurely, with no acrobatics or attempts to impress, just a gentle enjoyment of each other's bodies. Men with guns and officers who wanted to arrest her seemed a world away from this peace.

She was almost asleep when he nudged her much later. "The soup and the tea water are boiling," he said.

The words cut through her fatigue and her stomach pinched with hunger. She sat. "I'm starved."

They ate at the little dinette, wrapped in the blankets and inhaling the food—soup, followed by a can of peaches. They took turns slurping the peach juice and grinning at each other. She knew her hair was as messy as his, her face as wind-burned, eyes as bloodshot. But it didn't matter. If she had to be trapped in a sheepherder's trailer with anyone in the world, he was the only one she would choose.

They returned to the bed after they ate. She thought she would sleep but instead she found herself thinking about the day's events, as if now that she was warm, dry and fed, her mind could take in the enormity of what had happened.

"If TDC thought Dane was a terrorist, why not say so at their press conference?" she asked out loud. "Why the sudden flurry of action?"

"Terrorism is a pretty serious charge," Jason said. "Maybe Homeland Security was building their case."

"There is no case. Dane isn't a terrorist. Neither am I."

"All right," Jason said. "What evidence could TDC have given Homeland Security to persuade them to pursue the case?"

Cara started to argue that TDC didn't have any evidence, but that wasn't what he was asking, was it? She considered the question a moment. "They could have presented federal agents with the reports that showed radioactive material at the Mary Lee Mine, and pointed out that the EPA tests didn't show the same results. Dane was working at that site, so maybe they argued *he* was hiding the radioactive stuff at the mine."

She propped herself up on her elbows. "The problem is, I don't know enough about the science behind all of this to figure out everything those reports say. Dane had a master's degree and years of study in chemistry and biology and other sciences. I can build a database and I know the correct grammar and spelling for reports, and how to arrange a conference call and deal with accounting software, but I can't tell you if just storing yellowcake uranium or whatever it is terrorists use to eventually build a bomb, would result in the kinds of reports we saw."

"I don't think those details matter so much," Jason said. "All I want is to find out who is after us and stop them. Knowing why would be an added bonus, and finding Dane would be the cherry on top of the sundae. But most of all, I want you to be safe."

She laced her fingers with his. "I feel safer with you. But it's hard when I don't know who my enemy is or why they're after me."

"Try to get some sleep. Tomorrow we'll hike back to cell service and get to the bottom of all this."

She knew he meant the words to be reassuring, but returning to town wasn't a comforting idea to her. All that awaited her there were people who wanted to arrest her and put her in jail.

JASON KNEW THEY were in trouble when he woke to the sound of an engine revving and the crunch of tires on gravel. He sat up in bed and reached for his gun before he even put on his clothes. Cara still slept, curled on her side, a lock of hair falling across one cheek.

Their wet clothing had dried, so he quickly dressed and, carrying his boots, slipped to the window and peered out. The black SUV was almost to the trailer, the first rays of the sun glinting off the windshield, making it impossible to see whoever was inside.

"What is it?" Cara spoke from the bed. "Who's out there?"

"You'd better get dressed," he said, keeping his voice low. "We've got company."

"Who is it?"

"It's a black SUV. I can't see who's driving it.".

Cara moved to the now cold woodstove and dressed. "I need to pee," she said.

"You'll have to do it in here," he said. "You can't risk going outside."

She glanced out the small back window over the sink. "They can't see the outhouse from the front of the trailer," she said. "I could slip out there and be back before they knew."

"No. It's too risky."

She didn't argue, though he could tell she wanted to. "What's going on out there?" she asked instead.

"They just parked outside."

She came to stand behind him, her chin resting on his

shoulder, her breasts pressed to his back. Two men—Durrell and George—got out of the SUV. "I knew it," she whispered. "So TDC is behind this."

Jason said nothing, merely watched as the two men, dressed in black tactical gear instead of suits, studied the ground around the trailer. He cursed himself for not even making an effort to erase his and Cara's tracks after they'd arrived last night. He had been sure they were too far off any obvious path to be found.

He'd been foolish and careless, and if anything happened to Cara now, it would be his fault.

Durrell looked at George and said something Jason couldn't make out. Then each man drew a handgun and they started toward the trailer, moving at oblique angles. Jason might now have had a chance to take them out, but he couldn't kill two men in cold blood.

"Get under the bed," he told Cara.

She stared at him. "What do you mean? Why?"

"Get under the bed. If they fire on us, you're less likely to be hit there."

"And then I'll be trapped under there. I think if they try to come in this door, we need to go out the back window." She indicated the window over the dinette.

"Does that even open?" he asked.

"I'll find out."

Before he could stop her, she went to the dinette, crawled up on the padded seat and shoved at the window. It flew open, damp, cool air rushing in. "We can fit through it," she said.

He was ready for this to be over. He wanted to stand and face off with these guys. But there were two of them and he only had one gun. "Let's see what they do first," he whispered.

She nodded but remained by the window.

Jason glanced out the front window again and noticed that Durrell was moving around the side of the trailer. He was heading toward the back. They were going to be trapped. "Get out, now!" he said, and rushed toward the rear window.

He shoved Cara out ahead of him and then hit the ground hard beside her. Not stopping to catch his breath, he pulled her up and they began running. Durrell shouted, and fired. Jason searched for cover, but there was none. These open sheep pastures had long been cleared of all but the scrawniest of shrubs.

One moment, Cara was running beside him. The next, she fell. He looked back to see her sprawled on the ground, but before he could retrace his steps, Durrell was on her. He grabbed her up and hauled her roughly to her feet.

George, who had quickly caught up with Durrell, stopped and aimed his weapon at Jason. "Stop, or you're a dead man," he shouted.

"Jason, stop!" Cara called.

He didn't stop. Not because he wanted to leave Cara alone with those two, but because he had seen something she hadn't. Durrell had gripped Cara to him and fumbled in his back pocket to take out a rope. Not flexi-cuffs or even old-fashioned handcuffs, but a rope. That wasn't the tool a law enforcement officer would use, not even one under cover. A chill had swept over him at the sight and, with it, the certainty that these men weren't making an arrest or intending to take Cara into to custody.

They were killers, and if Jason let them get hold of him, he would have no way of saving Cara.

INSTEAD OF PURSUING Jason, Durrell turned back to Cara. "We'll take care of him later," he said. "He isn't going to go far out here."

Durrell pulled her wrists together behind her and wrapped them with the rope, the coarse fiber digging into her skin. "Let's go," he said, and tugged her back toward the trailer.

Inside the trailer, Durrell threw Cara onto the bed. She landed on her side, and lay staring up at them, her wrists bound behind her. "Who are you?" she asked. "What do you want with me?"

Both men ignored the question. Durrell looked around the small trailer, then dragged one of the two chairs into the center of the room. George went outside and returned a few moments later with a longer coil of rope. He studied the ceiling, then shook his head. "We'll have to do it over the door," he said.

"That's even better," Durrell said. "No fancy knots." He dragged the chair over in front of the door.

George moved over to the bed and pulled Cara to her feet. "Come over here," he said, and dragged her toward the chair.

"What are you doing?" she asked, fear rising to almost choke her.

"Climb up on the chair," Durrell ordered.

She stared at him. He hit her, hard. Her head snapped back and her vision blurred.

"What did you do that for?" George asked.

"When I give an order, I expect to be obeyed," he said.

"You shouldn't leave marks. The local cops might be smarter than we think."

"Get on the chair," Durrell said again.

Cara sat on the chair. Her face hurt where he had hit her, but the pain helped her push back some of her fear. She had worked so hard after Corey died to build a new life, with a new job, a new home. A life that didn't require her to care too much or risk getting hurt. Jason, and even Dane, had changed that. They had made her care, and now these two, and whoever they worked for, were trying to shut her down. Rage welled at the thought. She wasn't going to let that happen. She couldn't let them win.

"Don't sit!" Durrell ordered. "Stand on it."

Moving awkwardly with her bound hands, she climbed onto the chair. Behind her, George did something with the long rope, then he looped one end around her neck and fumbled behind her. "What are you doing?" she asked.

"You're distraught that the Feds have found out about your collusion with Dane Trask to sell nuclear material to foreign terrorists," Durrell said. "So you came to this deserted place and hanged yourself."

"No! I didn't collude with Dane. He didn't do anything wrong. And I would never kill myself."

"Then we'll do the job for you, but the authorities won't know any different," Durrell said. He looked at his partner. "Is everything ready?"

"I think so," George said.

"Wait," she cried. "At least tell me why you're doing this."

"Short answer—because you got nosy," Durrell said. "You got curious about things you never should have worried about. Now we need you out of the way." He looked to George. "You want to pull the chair out from under her or should I do it?"

"You do it. She's probably going to kick and I want to be out of the way."

"Wuss," Durrell said, but took a step toward Cara.

She decided when he jerked the chair away, she would kick him as hard as she could, aiming for the teeth. It might not save her, but at least he'd walk around for a while with some evidence of what he had done.

Where are you, Jason? she thought. *I hope you're far away by now, and safe. And I hope you know how much I love you, even if I never got a chance to say it.*

JASON SLOWED, fighting for breath, pain stabbing his side. He strained his ears, listening for sounds of pursuit. After the first few shots, George hadn't bothered wasting his ammunition. But why hadn't he come after Jason?

Because he was in a hurry to get back to the trailer, and Cara. The thought sent a chill through him and he began retracing his steps toward the trailer.

He approached the site at an angle, keeping to the cover of rocks and out of view of the trailer's windows. When he was very close, he used Durrell and George's SUV as a shield. Scuffling noises came from inside the trailer. Thoughts of what they might be doing to Cara made his hands shake with rage, and he forced himself to push the emotion aside. He had to put on his cop face now, focus on the job, save emotion for later. He reviewed the layout of the trailer in his mind. No back door. The window he and Cara had exited through was too far off the ground to make climbing back in practical. He'd have to enter by the front door, and hope he could catch Durrell and George by surprise, taking them out before they had a chance to hurt Cara.

A lot of ifs. What he needed was some kind of distraction—something that would make Durrell and George leave the trailer in a hurry. He moved along the side of the SUV until he reached the driver's door and tried the handle. To his surprise, the door was unlocked. He eased it open and peered inside. No keys in the ignition, so there went the idea of starting up the vehicle to get them to run out to see who was stealing their ride.

Two water bottles rested in the center console. A phone charger. A spare ammunition clip on the passenger's-side floorboard. A lighter and a package of cigarettes on the dashboard.

He grabbed the lighter, the smokes, and the ammo clip and hurried behind the trailer, to a spot in a depression about a hundred yards away. Hastily, he scraped together dried grass and twigs and touched them with the lighter flame. They flared, and he fed in larger twigs, until he had a small but healthy blaze going. Then he emptied the contents of the ammunition clip into the fire and raced back around to the front of the trailer.

Ammunition in a campfire didn't usually shoot out like fireworks, but when those bullets gassed off and exploded, they would sound like a barrage of gunfire directly behind the trailer. As Jason had hoped, when the explosions sounded, it only took about fifteen seconds for Durrell and George to exit the trailer and run for their SUV. They dove into the vehicle and George started it.

Jason's first shot punctured the left front tire. "Don't move!" he ordered, rising up alongside the driver's side. He held his Glock in both hands, aimed directly at George's face. No way could he miss from here. When Durrell raised his gun, Jason fired, shattering the front windshield and sending shards raining over both men. Still keeping the gun trained on them, he yanked open the driver's door and dragged George out of the vehicle. "Down on the ground, now!" he shouted. "Both of you."

George lay with his face in the dirt, but Durrell made a run for the trailer. Jason fired, catching him in the shoulder. He went down, screaming.

Within minutes, Jason had them both bound hand and foot, had frisked them and removed their weapons before racing for the trailer.

Cara was standing on a chair, a loop of rope around her neck, her expression resolute. He had to climb onto the chair with her to free her. She sagged against him. "What took you so long?" she choked out as he worked on loosening the rope from around her neck.

"I had to deal with a couple of guys," he said, and pulled the rope from around her neck, then went to work cutting loose her hands.

When she was free, she wrapped her arms around him and they held each other tightly, standing on a chair in that isolated sheepherder's trailer.

Durrell began bellowing. "Come on." Jason jumped to the floor and reached up to help Cara down. "We've got to deal with those two."

She shrank back. "What are you going to do?"

"Durrell is injured. He was headed for the trailer and you, so I shot him. I'd better get out there and tend to him before he bleeds out."

She didn't question the irony that he had shot a man to stop him—and would have killed him if necessary—but would now do all he could to save his life. She merely went to the corner shelves, retrieved a stack of towels and followed him outside.

Durrell had almost stopped bleeding by the time they got to him, but he shouted curses and thrashed around until Jason took out his handkerchief and gagged him. He fished a wallet from the guy's pocket and found IDs for Anthony Durrell, Tony Green and David Turner. "Which one is your real name?" he asked. But Durrell only glared at him.

George lay quietly on his side. Jason examined his wallet, which had identification for Walter George and George Walters. But he, too, refused to answer when Jason questioned him. So Jason and Cara dragged first George, and then Durrell, over to the black SUV and loaded them inside, Durrell in the rear of the vehicle and George strapped into the back seat. It was like maneuvering two big sacks of cement, and both he and Cara were sweating by the time they were done.

"I'll be so glad to get out of here," Cara said.

"Me, too." Jason handed her the Glock.

She took it gingerly. "What do you want me to do with this?"

"Keep an eye on those two." He nodded toward the rear of the SUV. "If they try anything, just pull the trigger." He didn't think that would be necessary, but he wanted Durrell and George to hear the words and believe he meant them.

Cara nodded. "What are you going to do?"

"I have to change a tire." Then he was going to drive them all to safety and, he hoped, a lot of long-overdue answers.

THEY DIDN'T GET to Montrose until midafternoon. Jason pulled in behind the sheriff's office building and called in to let them know he was outside with two criminals. By the time four deputies emerged, he and Cara were standing outside the vehicle. One of the deputies approached Cara, restraints in hand.

She forced herself to remain still, not cowering behind Jason. "Not her," Jason said before she could speak. "The two men in the car. They tried to kill us twice, and were preparing to fake Ms. Mead's suicide."

She rubbed at the faint rope burn around her neck and continued to glare at the deputy.

"Ms. Mead is the one we have a warrant for," the deputy said.

"She's in my custody at the moment, so if you want a chance at her, you'll have to wait in line," Jason said.

Cara bit her lip to keep from crying out. Could Jason,

a federal officer, really claim priority over the local cops? This whole situation was absurd, so why not?

"Who are these two?" asked a second deputy who was standing beside the black SUV, surveying its remaining occupants.

Jason took out the two wallets and handed them to the first officer. "They both have multiple IDs. My guess is their real names are something else entirely. But most recently, they've been masquerading as Anthony Durrell and Walter George, employees of TDC Enterprises."

"But they aren't really TDC employees?" the first man asked.

"You'll have to take that up with TDC," Jason said.

Cara was still nervous about walking into the sheriff's department, but she had no intention of leaving Jason's side, so she went with him when they followed the cops inside.

It took several hours to tell their story, starting with Dane Trask's disappearance, through the harassment and vandalism of Cara's home, the shots fired on them during their first visit to the Mary Lee Mine, and the mad chase through the darkness on their second visit. Cara couldn't tell how much the detectives interviewing them believed, but they recorded every word, asked a lot of questions, and didn't try to take her into custody when it came time for them to leave.

"We may have more questions for you later," her chief questioner said. "But for now, we're releasing you into Officer Beck's custody."

"I promise to keep a close eye on her," Jason said solemnly.

She waited until they were in the pickup before she punched him—lightly—on the shoulder.

"Hey! What was that for?" He rubbed his shoulder.

"That crack about keeping a close eye on me. Honestly!"

"I was only stating the truth." He grinned. "Ready to go back to my place?"

"Let's get these samples in the mail," she said, holding up the backpack she'd retrieved before they'd left the trailer. "I still want to know what they show."

They stopped by an office supply store to print the forms, mailed the samples, then headed for Jason's cabin.

WHILE CARA HAD showered, Jason had grilled steaks and opened a bottle of Pinot Noir.

Cara gratefully took a glass. "Let's not talk about the case tonight," he said.

She clinked her glass to his. "Deal." She sipped the wine and sighed. "So what should we talk about?"

"How about the future?"

She made a face. "I'll have to find a new job. I want to go back to my house, but I'm not sure how long it will be before I feel safe there again. And Dane is still missing, and I'm worried about him."

Jason pulled her into his arms and kissed her. "You'll find a new job because you're good at what you do," he said. "You don't have to go back to your house until you're ready. You can stay here as long as you like. And we're going to keep looking for Dane. So far, he's been doing a good job of staying safe and looking after himself. Remember that."

She studied him, eyes searching. "You're the man with all the answers, aren't you?"

"Right now, I have a question?"

"Oh?" A tremor went through her—excitement. Anticipation. Fear?

"I love you. You know that, don't you?"

She nodded. Then added, "Yes. I love you, too." She

gave a nervous laugh. "That was the last thing I expected, I tell you."

"What would you think about us getting married?"

Cara's heart stopped beating for a moment. She stared at him. "Married?"

"When you're ready. Sooner rather than later, I hope." He took her wineglass and his and set them aside, and held both her hands in his. "I want to spend the rest of my life with you."

"Yes," she whispered. Then, with more force, "Yes!" Happiness swelled in her like a balloon, as if she might float into the air without his hands to tether her.

TWO DAYS LATER, lab results showed traces of tritium and uranium in the soil samples recovered from the Mary Lee Mine—very different from the test results TDC had released to the public earlier.

The real identities of Anthony Durrell and Walter George turned out to be David Alexander and Kerry Waters, respectively—hired killers. TDC Enterprises issued an official statement that they had no knowledge of any of this, that the two men had presented themselves as private security.

TDC also denied any knowledge of how radioactive materials got into the Superfund Mary Lee Mine's soil and water samples. The company continued to attest that Dane Trask put the material there, though they had no explanation as to how the material would have gotten there in the quantities found. They would certainly launch an immediate investigation.

Homeland Security and the Montrose County Sheriff's Office withdrew any charges against Cara. Rather than wait to be fired from TDC, she quit and took a job with an environmental group that was threatening a lawsuit against

TDC. Though the position paid less than her old job, once she sold her house and moved in permanently with Jason, her finances would be in better shape than ever.

Dane was still missing, but Durrell and George—or rather, Alexander and Waters—were behind bars, and TDC was pledging to clean up the Mary Lee Mine site. And, as Jason had said, Dane had the skills to look after himself and would no doubt come forward when he felt safe again.

Meanwhile, Cara had a wedding to plan, and a future that included putting a lot more trust in law enforcement than she had ever thought possible.

* * * * *

COMING SOON!

We really hope you enjoyed reading this book.
If you're looking for more romance, be sure to
head to the shops when new books are
available on

Thursday 12th November

To see which titles are coming soon, please visit
millsandboon.co.uk/nextmonth

MILLS & BOON

LET'S TALK
Romance

For exclusive extracts, competitions and special offers, find us online:

 facebook.com/millsandboon

@MillsandBoon

@MillsandBoonUK

Get in touch on 01413 063232

For all the latest titles coming soon, visit
millsandboon.co.uk/nextmonth

MILLS & BOON

THE HEART OF ROMANCE

A ROMANCE FOR EVERY KIND OF READER

MODERN

Prepare to be swept off your feet by sophisticated, sexy and seductive heroes, in some of the world's most glamourous and romantic locations, where power and passion collide.
8 stories per month.

HISTORICAL

Escape with historical heroes from time gone by. Whether your passion is for wicked Regency Rakes, muscled Vikings or rugged Highlanders, awaken the romance of the past.
6 stories per month.

MEDICAL

Set your pulse racing with dedicated, delectable doctors in the high-pressure world of medicine, where emotions run high and passion, comfort and love are the best medicine.
6 stories per month.

Celebrate true love with tender stories of heartfelt romance, from the rush of falling in love to the joy a new baby can bring, and a focus on the emotional heart of a relationship.
8 stories per month.

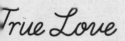

Indulge in secrets and scandal, intense drama and plenty of sizzling hot action with powerful and passionate heroes who have it all: wealth, status, good looks…everything but the right woman.
6 stories per month.

HEROES

Experience all the excitement of a gripping thriller, with an intense romance at its heart. Resourceful, true-to-life women and strong, fearless men face danger and desire - a killer combination!
8 stories per month.

DARE

Sensual love stories featuring smart, sassy heroines you'd want as a best friend, and compelling intense heroes who are worthy of them.
4 stories per month.

To see which titles are coming soon, please visit

millsandboon.co.uk/nextmonth

MILLS & BOON
MEDICAL
Pulse-Racing Passion

Set your pulse racing with dedicated, delectable doctors in the high-pressure world of medicine, where emotions run high and passion, comfort and love are the best medicine.